MAUREEN LEE LENKER

Copyright © 2025 by Maureen Lee Lenker
Cover and internal design © 2025 by Sourcebooks
Cover design by Stephanie Gafron/Sourcebooks
Cover art by Craig White/Lott Reps

Sourcebooks and the colophon are registered trademarks of Sourcebooks.

All rights reserved. No part of this book may be reproduced in any form or by any electronic or mechanical means including information storage and retrieval systems—except in the case of brief quotations embodied in critical articles or reviews—without permission in writing from its publisher, Sourcebooks.

No part of this book may be used or reproduced in any manner for the purpose of training artificial intelligence technologies or systems.

The characters and events portrayed in this book are fictitious or are used fictitiously. Any similarity to real persons, living or dead, is purely coincidental and not intended by the author.

All brand names and product names used in this book are trademarks, registered trademarks, or trade names of their respective holders. Sourcebooks is not associated with any product or vendor in this book.

Published by Sourcebooks Casablanca, an imprint of Sourcebooks
1935 Brookdale RD, Naperville, IL 60563-2773
(630) 961-3900
sourcebooks.com

Cataloging-in-Publication Data is on file with the Library of Congress.

Printed and bound in Canada.
MBP 10 9 8 7 6 5 4 3 2 1

For Margaret.
A wonderful sister, incredible
cheerleader, and the inspiration for
the sibling bond in these pages.

This book contains explicit details of
a sexual assault. Please read with care.

CHAPTER 1

SEPTEMBER 1938

FLYNN BANKS WAS BORED.

It was not an affliction to which he was accustomed. He had what his supporters called "a lust for life" and what his detractors referred to as "an unseemly fondness for booze and women." But never once had either of those things failed to hold his attention. Until now.

He sipped at the Treasure Trove Scotch in his glass. It was one of his favorites. Because if he was going to play a pirate and a scallywag on screen, he might as well drink something befitting his reputation. So, the Café Trocadero kept it on reserve for him. Usually, it came with a velvety tang that coated his mouth and slid down his throat, the liquid equivalent of a mother pulling a soft blanket over her child to tuck them in at night. But tonight, it tasted bitter. He choked down his sip and cast the glass aside in frustration. He needed to get his head on straight. He would start a new picture tomorrow, his first time with a new costar—some French ingenue whom Harry Evets was convinced was destined for greatness. But Flynn didn't like unknowns on a set. At this point, each of his pictures was a well-oiled machine, and introducing a new cog was bound to complicate things.

The turtle amontillado soup he'd ordered had gone cold

without his noticing, and he shoved the dainty china bowl away. He didn't remember the last time he'd felt this level of ennui, and it was vexing. He'd built his life around two core principles: joy and pleasure. So far, that had never steered him wrong. So why did everything feel so...rudderless lately? He could blame it on the new picture, but this was more than first-day jitters.

He thought of the letter he'd crumpled and left in his study at home. A missive from his brother. At the sight of his brother's handwriting on the outside of the envelope, he'd nearly cast the letter aside without bothering to open it. But something had possessed Flynn to read it. Mostly, he was intrigued because, until now, Edgar hadn't deigned to write him in at least a half decade. The letter's contents had been more disturbing than the usual scolding Flynn had expected. It seemed their father, the miserable bastard, was dying.

Not only that, but his "greatest wish," as Edgar put it, was to see and speak with Flynn before he died to "clear the air and unclasp a secret that lay heavy on his heart." Flynn's stomach had turned at the notion. There was only one thing he was interested in unclasping. Besides, he didn't need to bother making the long journey to Lord Banks's deathbed. He already knew his father's worst secret. It was all there in the incriminating letter he'd had tucked away in a drawer at home as insurance for years. Perhaps it was the thought of that putting Flynn off his liquor.

He'd barely scanned the rest of the letter. More of Edgar's usual complaints about the estate's finances, a request that Flynn share his "Hollywood fortune." And his personal favorite—an insistence that Flynn think of the family name and become less of a rogue.

That was rich, considering their father was the one who'd stained the Banks legacy so completely that no amount of bleach would soak it clean. But no one knew that. To the world, Viscount Banks was a magnanimous philanthropist, a man who helped orphans and war widows. It was only behind closed doors that their father unleashed the monster he truly was. Flynn winced, remembering the blows he'd taken at his father's hands. The hypocrisy was disgusting.

Flynn needed to find a dame. Particularly one Edgar would deem utterly unsuitable. That would make him feel better. His favorite coat-check girl, Cherry, was working the desk tonight. He'd given her a roguish smile and a wink; she'd harrumphed and turned her back on him. Just what he'd done, he didn't know. It could have been any number of things—forgetting to call her, leaving the club with another woman on his arm, or instigating some drunken antics he'd already forgotten. But Cherry was hardly the only girl at the Troc with a good pair of gams and eyes the size of saucers. There was nothing like a set of shapely legs to improve his mood.

He surveyed the smoke-filled dance floor of the Trocadero. A dozen couples swayed to the dulcet tones of Xavier Cugat and his band. At quick glance, Flynn had slept with at least half of the dames here. Ah well, best to leave them to their current dance partners.

He reached inside his breast pocket and pulled out a well-worn, small black book. He wet the tip of his finger and began to page through it, trying to find a single woman who didn't currently hate his guts and who didn't bore him to tears. *Dorothy Spots,* he read. He racked his brain and a vision of an absolutely stunning dame flooded his memories.

But then he remembered the squeak of her voice. She'd talked about her collection of china dolls at a pitch he thought was likely to break glass for ten minutes straight.

He fished out a pencil to draw a stark black line through her name and sighed heavily, flipping to the next page. He had a detailed notation system of stars, hearts, and strike-throughs to help him decode his muddled love life. The gals with stars next to their names were social climbers, ones looking to break into Hollywood via the stepping stone of his four-poster bed. He didn't like to see them too often, lest they get their hopes up.

Those with hearts were the ones he actually had a fondness for. Girls who were sensible and not interested in marriage or any of that starry-eyed, romantic fiddle-faddle. The strike-throughs... Well, they were best forgotten for one reason or another. Lately, he'd found more and more reasons to ink girls out of his book.

He pinched his nose between his thumb and forefinger as he paged through a series of nothing but dark lines. Then, he found one. Lily Jones. She had a heart next to her name—a cigarette girl at the Cocoanut Grove who was as unsentimental as they came. He waved over the maître d', Alain, and asked him to bring a phone to the table.

When it arrived, Flynn asked the operator to connect him to the number she'd left him. It rang twice before she picked up. "Hello."

"Lily, it's Flynn."

There was a pause on the other end of the line. He hated pauses. They usually came with regrets and recriminations. "Flynn, you've been a stranger lately."

Maybe she needed her ego stroked a bit. He understood that. "Lily, doll, you know how it is—"

"No, I just mean a lot has happened." She stopped and he heard a deep voice in the background. Lily must've put her hand over the receiver because her voice was muffled as she told whoever it was, "It's just an old friend. I'll only be a minute."

"Flynn, are you still there?" she hissed into the phone. He confirmed he was. "Listen, I can't talk long. But the long and short of it is: I'm engaged."

"I thought you didn't believe in that nonsense," he replied, laughing to cover his surprise.

"I didn't, but then I met Glenn and... I don't know, I changed my mind, I guess."

"Well, that's great, love, congratulations," he told her with unreserved enthusiasm. Marriage was for the birds, but if other people wanted to entrap themselves, he wouldn't dampen their happiness.

"Thank you," she trilled. "But listen, you should probably lose my number."

"I understand." He paused, never quite knowing how to say goodbye to a dame. "But hey, kid, we had fun, didn't we?"

Another pause. "Sure we did. But Flynn?"

"Yeah?"

"Take care of yourself, okay?" With that, he heard the phone snick as she returned the receiver to its cradle.

She'd sounded sad. Like she pitied him. Well, to hell with that. He loved his life. Sure, he'd been out of sorts lately, but it would pass. He returned to his book, drawing a line through Lily's name, but not one so dark that he couldn't erase it if she ever got divorced. He was nothing if not practical. His eyes wandered the room again and stopped on a set of legs and a pert little butt in a pair of ill-fitting trousers. Even through the ungainly cut of the pants, he could see this woman had a comely shape. A boyish athleticism. But the figure was decidedly out of place here, standing at the bar in a set of work pants, where the waiters wore black tie. Frankly, he was a bit shocked they'd let someone in dressed like that. But the doorman was a sucker for a well-timed bat of the lashes. It made Flynn all the more eager for the dame to turn around so he could see her face.

One thing was certain—the unsuitable attire meant that whoever she was, she was new here. That was exactly what Flynn needed to puncture this black cloud hanging over him.

But then the figure turned, and Flynn deflated. The khaki pants were matched with an equally dull button-down top. Now that he had his eyes above the figure's waist, he noticed they had cropped black hair and a newsboy cap on their head. As the interloper sipped at what appeared to be a glass of soda with a twist of lemon, Flynn realized he'd been ogling a man. A man with an unfairly tight butt and shapely legs.

If his taste didn't run exclusively female, he would've been intrigued enough to approach. Hollywood had a bit of something for everyone, so long as you were discreet. But as it was, Flynn needed to go back to the drawing board. He huffed, his lips spluttering like a horse, and flipped to a new page in his book. Another list of dead ends. He nursed a rankle of disappointment as a new wave of listlessness swept over him. He needed to snap himself out of this. He reached again for his Scotch and knocked it back in one gulp, wincing as it went down.

It was unseemly, really, for a man of his position to feel so disaffected. What was the point of all his money and devastatingly good looks, if not to make the most of them? But there was no shaking the sense that something had fallen out of place. A chip in the ornate pleasure dome he'd built for himself to avoid things like boredom and responsibility. Maybe he just needed a day out on the water. It was a good thing that the Catalina Regatta was coming up. There was no cure for any ailment quite like sea air. It was why he lived on the ocean and why he loved to sail. A whiff of salt water and brine was his instant pick-me-up when girls and liquor would not suffice. It had never failed him yet.

He squared his shoulders and sat up straighter. "Pull yourself together, Banks," he muttered, returning to his book with new vigor. At last, he found a name. Rhonda Powers. An up-and-comer he'd chatted up at Joan and Dash's latest house party. He'd helped her workshop new surnames because Powers was too close to his buddy Tyrone's last name. She'd flirted with him. A little, then a lot. By the time she was tucking a napkin with her address and phone number on it behind his pocket square, he'd figured his plans were sorted for the night.

They'd taken a lap around Joan and Dash's pool, kissing under the fronds of a jacaranda tree. But when Dash had caught Flynn in the kitchen refreshing his drink, he'd warned Flynn that Rhonda Powers was looking for something Flynn wasn't selling. Namely, a picket fence and a passel of towheaded kiddies.

Flynn had cursed himself for his propensity to find the clingiest dame at a party. Then, he'd turned to the peroxide blond who had walked into the kitchen moments before and extended her glass for him to refill. He'd given her a look, and she'd kissed him full on the mouth and led him out the front door by his tie.

The next morning, he'd returned to his Malibu cottage thoroughly satisfied, never knowing the blond's name. He'd had no complaints about the turn of events. But that had been a few weeks ago. Maybe Rhonda had blinked away some of the stars in her eyes that were an occupational hazard for every fresh-faced kid in Hollywood. It was worth a shot, wasn't it? At least it'd be something new. Something to break through this pall of insufferable malcontent.

He reached for the phone and said her name aloud to the operator, and then suddenly, it was as if he'd conjured her. She was there. In the Troc. Striding toward him with a fiery look of determination on her face. He smiled at her, the crooked one that had served as a skeleton key to an indeterminate number of bedrooms over the years. "Rhonda, darling."

She snarled, "You louse." Shit. It appeared she wasn't the forgive-and-forget type. Despite the intervening weeks, she was clearly still in a tizzy about the fact he'd kissed her and then disappeared into the night.

She was approaching his booth with frightening rapidity, and he wasn't particularly eager to find out what she'd do when she got there. His eyes darted around the room, desperate for an escape. But it was an open floor plan, and she was blocking his quickest route to the exit.

Flynn gulped and slid down the booth, his suit gliding along the vinyl until he was crouched under the table.

He wished he could say this was the first time he'd hidden under a table in the Trocadero, but being a rakish movie star meant he spent a surprising amount of time on his hands and knees—for better or worse. He peeked out from the edge of the booth to see if she was still headed toward him, and he sighed in relief when he noticed she had been stalled by a waiter.

He reached inside his coat for his wallet and pulled out a ten-dollar bill, sticking his hand out and slapping it on top of the table. A preemptive tip for the server currently saving him from having a black eye on his first day of production. Not that it would have been surprising to his makeup artist.

His debts paid, Flynn seized the opportunity for escape and crawled out from under the table, creeping his way to the bandstand. Still on his hands and knees, he snuck behind the upright bass player, a heavy-set Black man named Chuck. Not batting an eye, Chuck kept playing and edged forward so Flynn could crawl behind him.

"Thanks," Flynn whispered before he scurried behind the piano.

"Dave," Flynn hissed at the pianist, the cousin of the bandleader, Xavier. The Spaniard kept playing "Let's Face the Music and Dance" and looked down at Flynn without missing a beat.

"Yeah?"

"See the dame over by my usual booth? The redhead?"

"The one that looks steamed?"

Flynn's eye twitched. How did he get himself into these situations? "Yeah, that's the one. What's she doing?"

"Talking to Alain, who is trying to get her to sit down in a booth. It's a heated argument from the looks of it." All the while, Dave kept playing the song, talking out of the side of his mouth.

"Heated enough for me to make a run for it?"

Flynn watched as Dave cricked his neck to get a better look at Rhonda. "If you stay low, I'd say so. But make it quick. I'm not sure how much longer Alain can hold her."

Flynn cursed. "Thanks, Dave. I owe you one."

Dave nodded as if to say, "Think nothing of it," and Flynn crawled out from behind the piano, scurrying to hide himself amidst tables and chairs on the opposite side of the dining room.

If he stood up, Rhonda would see him and it would be all over. So he remained on his hands and knees, gritting his teeth as the diners at the tables looked down at him and gasped.

"Doing research for a role," he quipped as he crawled through the crowded dining room awash with stars and rich tourists dressed to the nines.

After what seemed an eternity, he reached the front door of the establishment. He didn't have time to get his coat. The club would send it to his beachside bungalow in the morning anyway.

The glow of the late evening September light flooded the hall as Flynn crawled through the open door. Frank, the doorman, had opened it for him without so much as a raised eyebrow. Flynn wasn't sure if that was a sign of the man's discretion or the regularity with which Flynn ended up in scrapes like this.

He stood and dusted off his suit, the knees of his trousers looking a bit threadbare. The valet had already ordered his car, but Flynn turned at the sound of a commotion behind him and caught the telltale red hair and angry growl of Rhonda Powers, now engaged in an argument with Frank.

"I know he came this way," she groused.

"Lady, I'm telling you, he's still in the restaurant," Frank argued. Thank God Flynn tipped everyone in this establishment well. Still, he didn't have much time before Rhonda broke through that door and got ahold of him.

A car, an old jalopy, pulled up to the valet stand, and he didn't even blink before putting his hand on the door and leaping over it into the front seat.

The driver shrieked, their hat falling off as they threw their head back in surprise. Flynn didn't even clock what the driver looked like, he was so busy looking behind him—just in time to see Rhonda barreling out the front door. He ducked down in the car, pressing himself against the floor and clinging to the door handle for dear life. He begged, "Drive, please!"

To his amazement, the driver did as he asked.

CHAPTER 2

LIVVY PRESSED HER FOOT TO THE GAS AND SPED AWAY from the Troc, noticing the angry woman marching out the front door. Pulling away with a stranger in the passenger seat was preferable to whatever the alternative was.

Once they cleared the driveway and she peeled onto Sunset Boulevard, Livvy took a second to process the identity of her hitchhiker. She darted her eyes to the side and was astonished to see a familiar crop of dirty-blond hair, a chiseled silhouette, and the lightly upturned corners of a mouth that seemed to hold a perpetual smirk. She hadn't picked up any old straggler who had over imbibed at the club; she'd driven off with the subject of her teenage fantasies and her soon-to-be costar—the one and only Flynn Banks.

"You're—" she started.

"The man at the bar!" he proclaimed, finishing her sentence with a non sequitur.

"Huh?" She threw him a puzzled look as they pulled up to a red light on La Cienega. She'd been so flustered by the sight of a strange man leaping into her car that she hadn't paid attention to where she was going, merely knowing she should drive east to get back to her dumpy little apartment at the Garden of Allah Hotel.

But then she remembered. She grabbed at her head, hunting

for the newsboy cap that had flown into the back seat in her alarm, and realized the dark curls that she'd tucked beneath her cap were now blowing in the evening breeze.

He grinned at her, a lascivious, devilish smile that made her feel as if she was driving naked. "You're not a man."

"Well, no," she stated, not knowing what else to say.

"I thought you were a woman, but then I realized you were a man. But you're not."

Lord, was this the man she'd spent many a teenage afternoon in a movie palace mooning over? He was a simpleton! "Of course, I'm not a man. Why would I be?"

"You're dressed like one."

"Yes."

"Why?"

"I wanted to see the Café Trocadero, so I decided a disguise was the best way. I just wanted to see it, to get a sense of it, without anyone bothering me. And no one looks twice at a man."

"You don't know the right men." Flynn grinned, and she could swear that his teeth twinkled in the streetlight. He looked like the wolf that ate Little Red Riding Hood. "Besides, honey, I looked twice at you—and I can promise you I wasn't the only one."

Livvy's mouth went dry at the pronouncement, but she swallowed and tried to ignore it. Her heart was beating a mile a minute. Flynn Banks, swashbuckler and silver screen rogue, was flirting. With her. Her sister would never believe this.

"I've never been so thrilled to be wrong in my life," he purred. She got the feeling Flynn Banks was the type that never admitted they were wrong. She supposed she should be flattered.

When they got to Sweetzer Avenue, she started to cruise ahead, but he stopped her. "Hey, turn around. Malibu's west on Sunset."

She raised her eyebrow at him. "And what precisely is in Malibu?"

"My cottage," he replied matter-of-factly. She started to protest. She may have been gaga for Flynn Banks once, but she wasn't about to go home with him five minutes after meeting him.

"I can't possibly go back for my driver," he added. "That woman back there will skin me alive. Please take me home. I'll be your humble servant forever." He made a little mock bow, as much as he could manage while seated in the car.

"That's really not necessary," she added, debating whether she should do as he asked. She couldn't very well take him back to whatever that was at the Trocadero. Was he even safe to drive after his frenzied escape? Or would he be distracted like her father, miss a stop sign, and get run down by a semitruck? She couldn't exactly dump a movie star at the side of the road. Her only course of action was to drive him home. Even if it wasn't exactly how she'd planned to end her evening.

Livvy whipped the car around in a U-turn, prompting a Pontiac going west to honk their horn as she swerved in front of them. The near-miss sent her heart pounding, but she tried to quiet it by focusing on Flynn. "I'll drive you home."

"You know, some women would consider themselves lucky to be in this predicament."

That smile again. Livvy shuddered to think what it would do to her if she looked at it full on. As it was, catching it in her peripheral vision with her eyes on the road still made her insides turn to jelly. She'd had a photograph of that smile pinned over her bed for three years. But she couldn't let him know that.

"Lucky?" she scoffed, filling her voice with a skeptical hauteur she didn't feel. "Lucky to have a strange man jump in their car and force them to drive to an unfamiliar location?"

"But, darling, I'm not a stranger." He laid his hand on her thigh, clearly trying to see what he could get away with. She tried not to flinch at the sudden blaze of desire his touch ignited in her.

She didn't know much about men. At twenty-two, she'd been kissed exactly twice, by a high school sweetheart who'd been mostly content to hold her hand. She'd never even called Albert her boyfriend.

Not that she could imagine calling Flynn Banks her boyfriend either. Because he wasn't a boy. He was pure, unadulterated man. Everything about him screamed that she should be very, very careful. Her throat was suddenly as dry as the Mojave Desert. Jesus, was it normal to want a man you'd just met this much? Because she did. More than she'd wanted anything.

"Sure, you are," she retorted. "I don't know you from Adam." She jostled her thigh, shaking his hand away. She was grateful now that he'd interrupted her when they'd first pulled away from the Trocadero. Grateful he hadn't witnessed her starry-eyed pronouncement that he was Flynn Banks. She'd only known him for a few minutes, and she could already tell that she needed to establish a more balanced power dynamic between them before they shot so much as a reel of film. Otherwise, he'd walk all over her. Or worse. Perhaps if she kept pretending not to know who he was, that would puncture his ego.

"Oh, come now, you know who I am." He grinned.

She continued to follow Sunset, now driving up into the hills on a winding canyon road. It was striking. How wild and unfettered Los Angeles was, only a few miles away from the heart of Hollywood. It felt like a different planet. Not at all like the busy metropolis in her rearview mirror, nor like the quiet woods behind the house where she'd grown up. But something alien and stark and beautiful.

She kept her eyes on the road, her need to focus in the dimming light helping her sell the lie. "No, I really don't. Should I?"

He leaned back on the bench seat and rested his arm against it, right behind her back—probably so that if they hit a bump in the road, he could wrap it around her. "Ever see *The Captain of Madrid*?"

She shook her head. Never mind that she'd seen it about fifteen times, once three times in a single day.

He grabbed at his collar and loosened his tie. He was trying to be nonchalant, but she could see that her feigned ignorance was getting to him. "Okay, how about *The Black Mask*? *The Falcon of the Sea*? *Lancelot and Arthur*?"

His voice rose in pique as she shook her head at each title. All of which she'd seen dozens of times and could practically recite from memory. She bit her lip, suppressing a laugh. It was hilarious, really, how easy it was to get a rise out of him. When she'd fantasized about being romanced by Flynn Banks, like one of the damsels in his pictures, she never imagined he'd have quite such a high opinion of himself.

"You know, I don't really go to the pictures," she told him. She was lying through her teeth now. "I'm more of a reader myself. You know, a literary type." It wasn't a lie. She had once wanted to be a novelist. Before her life had exploded. Before everything had gone wrong. Because of the man sitting next to her.

"A bluestocking," he muttered. "Just my luck." He added, "But if you're so bookish, why were you so eager to visit the Café Trocadero?"

Nuts. He had her there. It was a Hollywood hot spot, and there was no earthly reason to be interested in visiting if it wasn't to gawk at movie stars.

She took a hairpin turn, focusing on the road while trying

to devise an answer. "Um, well..." He drummed his fingers on the dashboard, and the sound made it hard for her to think. "The band! I heard the music was some of the best in town."

"I see." He didn't seem satisfied with the answer, but she hoped that he wasn't going to push any further on the subject. "So, you've never heard of Flynn Banks then?"

"Is that a beach cove around here or something?" She opened her eyes wide, trying to really sell the precocious innocent act. A memory of her school composition book, with *Mrs. Flynn Banks* scrawled across the cover, flashed through her mind. She'd written so many stories in there. Adventures and romances that featured heroes not unlike the men Flynn portrayed on screen. He had been her greatest muse once.

He buried his face in his hands. "A beach cove." He raised his head just enough to give her a sternly raised eyebrow. "No, doll, Flynn Banks is not a beach cove. It—*he* is, in fact, me."

She came to the first stop sign in what felt like miles. They'd crested the hill of the Pacific Palisades by now, and the last of the day's light had turned the horizon a magnificent orange. With the sky putting on a show before them, they started their descent back toward the water, the magical crossroads where Sunset Boulevard met the Roosevelt Highway.

Livvy gave him a look, smoothing her face to look as unimpressed as possible. "Oh."

"Oh?" he sputtered. "I tell you that I'm Flynn Banks, and all you have to say is 'oh.' Do you know how many women would kill to be in this car with me right now?"

She snorted. This time it wasn't a manufactured response. What a pompous ass he was. "From what I could tell, it seemed like the woman back at the club would kill, all right. But it was you she was interested in murdering."

His mouth hung open, slack-jawed at her response. Livvy took a measure of delight in leaving Flynn Banks speechless. But he found his tongue again quickly enough, leaning back in the seat and assuming a pose of casual indifference. "Yes, well, some of my, er, former companions don't appreciate what a challenge it is to be so in demand."

She raised her brow and rolled her eyes. "A challenge?"

He cast his hand to his forehead in mock distress. "Oh yes, dreadfully difficult being so sought after. But someone's got to do it." He winked at her.

Flynn Banks wasn't anything like what she'd imagined. He was a rapscallion and an utter cad. Yet, she still liked him in spite of herself. "Ah well, we women thank you for your service, Mr. Banks," she proclaimed in a phony transatlantic tone. "We're ever so grateful for your sacrifice."

"'Tis a nobler thing that I do now," he started, before breaking out in laughter. The sound, rich and deep, was infectious, and she joined him almost instantly.

He might have a jaw that looked like it had been sculpted by Michelangelo, tourmaline-blue eyes that sparkled with mischief, and a luscious head of dirty-blond curls, but Livvy decided in that moment that his laugh was her favorite thing about him. It wasn't like anything she'd ever heard from him in a picture, though she supposed he didn't often have a reason to laugh while swashbuckling his way through an adventure. But it was full-throated, seeming to rise from the depths of his stomach, and it reminded her of cozy nights by a fire or the soft plushness of velvet.

They were nearing the end of Sunset now, the ocean dark in the twilight. The moon had yet to rise, and as the light faded, the waves crashed ominously in the distance. "So, if you're not here because you like the pictures, what brings you to Los Angeles?" he asked.

She was taken aback. Maybe he wasn't entirely self-involved. But she didn't know how to answer. Because the truth was that she *was* there to be an actress. Even if that was never the life that she'd envisioned for herself.

"Erm, I came for a job," she replied. There. That was a version of the truth.

She'd already been to Los Angeles once before, with Judy. Last year, when Judy convinced her to audition with her for a production of *Macbeth* at the Hollywood Bowl. Livvy ended up being cast as an understudy but then found herself playing Lady M when the original star backed out to shoot a film.

Now, Livvy was back. For her sister's sake. Judy was the one who wanted to be in pictures, as a hoofer. But it was Livvy who'd signed a one-picture deal with Evets's Studios. They'd needed the money and a way to get to Los Angeles on a more permanent basis, so she'd taken the job and brought her sister with her. Because it got Judy to Hollywood.

The studio was looking to pair Livvy off with someone that could help sell her as a fresh new star—and the man they'd chosen was Flynn Banks. It was ironic, really. She'd never intended to be an actress. And now here she was, about to make a movie with her teenage dream.

"Ah, an enterprising young woman," Flynn drawled. "My favorite kind." Livvy blushed a little at the pronouncement and hoped he couldn't see the rosy flush on her cheeks in the dark. "When do you start?"

"Tomorrow, actually," she replied. That was also true.

"Excellent. A good day for it. I start a new picture tomorrow." She giggled and then clamped her lips together, trying to hold in her laughter. She could come clean right now. Tell him that she was his new leading lady. But she was enjoying this sense of anonymity too much. This opportunity to take him down a peg and be something other than yet another woman fawning over him. Never mind that once, before the accident, that was exactly what she'd been.

She didn't begrudge those women. She was certain, no matter how high his opinion of himself was, that he showed them a good time. She was having a delightful evening in his company, and he wasn't even trying to romance her anymore. Though he was charming, debonair, and ruggedly handsome, the antics she'd witnessed tonight were a healthy reminder that she would have to avoid swooning at the sight of him throughout their time on set. Flynn Banks was just a girlhood crush, and he needed to stay that way.

Besides, she'd come to Hollywood to work and help Judy chase her dreams of becoming a dancer. She didn't need to be distracted by a rogue, even if he was Flynn Banks.

They hit the Roosevelt Highway, and he directed her to turn right, driving further into Malibu. "I'm about a mile down the road," he told her. She nodded. It was fully dark, and she could only see as far as her headlights illuminated.

A prickle of fear ran down Livvy's neck as she realized how vulnerable she was in this moment. Alone. In a car. In a remote location in the dark with a stranger. Her mother would have fainted at the very idea of it. A rush of excitement trilled in her at the thought. She'd been a very obedient, straitlaced girl. But the idea of doing something that would have scandalized her mother was tantalizing.

She looked at him, and he grinned. It was a crooked smile that promised trouble, and she was sorely tempted to take that pledge.

"What—" they said in unison, both beginning to ask the other a question.

"Ladies first," Flynn replied, and she silently exhaled, assuming that his next question was going to be about what she did for work.

"What's your new picture about?" she asked. As if she didn't know.

"Oh, the usual stuff, swashbuckling and skullduggery." He smiled. She didn't need the moon; that smile could light the road alone. "I play a doctor who is arrested for treason and sold into captivity. But once I escape from my captors, I embark on a life of piracy."

"I see. And is there a lady in the picture?"

"Isn't there always?" He winked at her. It was a look she'd seen him give on the big screen a thousand times. But somehow it was both startlingly intimate and larger than life right here in front of her.

The car slowed as her knees went weak, and her foot lifted off the gas pedal ever so slowly. He cast his eyes at her legs, still covered by the man's trousers she'd worn to the Trocadero.

He gave her a knowing glance, but then continued. "She is the niece of the Caribbean colony's governor, and I kidnap her for ransom. But she's a fierce creature with a rebellious spirit. She secures me a pardon, and we take to the seas as pirate king and queen."

Livvy knew the script by heart already. But hearing Flynn describe the plot, it was as if she was being told the story for the first time. "That's so romantic." Livvy sighed, forgetting for a moment that she was supposed to be unimpressed by the movies.

"I thought you would say it was ridiculous," he drawled, seeming to know he'd caught her in a lie. "That something so silly would never happen in one of your precious books."

"I like stories with adventure and romance," she retorted. "One of my favorite books is *Treasure Island* by Robert Louis Stevenson."

"That was my favorite as a boy."

"You've read it?" she asked, a bit astonished. Flynn Banks didn't exactly seem like the bookish, intellectual type.

He pressed his hands to his heart. "You wound me. Yes, I've read it. Upward of a dozen times I'd say. I learned to sail because of that book. Begged my father for lessons. Finally, one of our groundsmen, a retired sailor in His Majesty's Navy, taught me how. Been obsessed with the sea ever since."

"Sorry. I didn't think—"

"That a movie star knows how to read."

"That's not what I meant," she replied, a look of horror on her face. But he chuckled, and she realized he was teasing.

"It's all right. It's a fair assumption. To be quite honest, it's been a while since I've read anything other than a script." Something unexpectedly wistful gleamed in his eyes. "Hollywood is... How shall I put it? A distracting place."

She nodded. "Oh, I've read about it in the papers. It's a den of vice and inequity."

He chortled. "That it is. And you're looking at one of the city's worst offenders."

He seemed proud of that fact. As if he relished being a drunkard and a cad. But there was something that charmed her about it too. He was so unabashedly, unapologetically himself. Livvy liked people who were honest about who they were. Even if *she* had been hiding the truth of her identity all evening.

"Pull off here. That's me on the left," he said. She looked where he pointed, and she could make out the outline of a home on the shore. He'd called it a cottage, and she'd expected something small and charming, like the clapboard homes they'd passed on their drive here.

But this was no mere cottage. It was a looming piece of property, a mass of white stucco and colorful tile built in the Spanish style. It was, in short, the home of a movie star.

She pulled into the driveway, which was a collection of stone and grass, artfully designed to look natural. Flynn reached over and gently placed his hand beneath her chin, lightly pressing her mouth shut.

"Stop gaping," he teased.

"I wasn't," she retorted, but he gave her a look.

"You were, but don't worry, all the ladies are impressed by the size of my...house."

He paused long enough to make her blush and then gave her a devilish wink. The man was incorrigible. Worse, she found it infernally attractive. She wondered if he might make a move, try to kiss her. Or even invite her inside.

But he didn't. He simply leapt over the side of the door of her jalopy without even opening it. "Best to go out the way I came in," he quipped. "Thank you for the lift, Miss…?"

She realized then she'd never told him her name. Liv de Lesseps was the name she'd been given by the studio. A shortening of her full first name paired with whatever the Evets publicity department had decided was suitably intriguing. She could tell him that name now. He'd know the truth of who she was in an instant. But some small piece of her wanted to cling to this unknowing. This interplay of two strangers who'd taken a drive together and whose paths were not meant to meet again. So she gave him her real name. "Blount," she smiled. "Olivia Blount."

"Thank you, Miss Blount." He tipped his hat, and then surprised her by reaching for her hand and pressing a brief kiss to her knuckles. It was polite, the kiss of a knight to his lady fair. But the sensation of his lips against her skin seared her hand, and she pulled it back, massaging her knuckles as they tingled with the ghost of his kiss.

He walked to the front door, and she began to reverse out of the absurdly long driveway. But as she neared the end of it, he ran back out and called after her. "Miss Blount, I'd very much like to see you again."

She called back, "You will, Mr. Banks." And she drove off without another word.

CHAPTER 3

FLYNN WOKE WITH A JOLT. HE TURNED HIS NECK AND A ripple of pain shot down his arm. He clapped his palm to his neck and rubbed at a knot that had formed—a result of his odd, cramped sleeping position. He blinked his eyes, trying to clear the morning bleariness and figure out where the hell he was.

He leaned his head into his armchair, and suddenly, a wave of familiar perfume crashed into him. The worn, burnt-orange velvet of the upholstery still held the ghost of his mother's scent. He steadied himself, inhaling and relaxing with each breath as the memories of the previous night returned to him. He hadn't been able to sleep, and after tossing and turning in bed for several hours, he'd gone downstairs, fixed himself a hot toddy, and wandered into the library.

It had been ages since he'd come in here. But the moment he'd entered the dark room last night, a sense of calm he hadn't felt in years washed over him. His heart rate had slowed as he observed the quiet solemnity of the library, his custom cherrywood shelves standing staunchly in rows like sentinels.

His eyes had gone straight to his favorite chair, a cozy, high-backed piece with a deep seat. The fabric color reminded him of the view of the sunset from his back deck. It was the only piece of furniture he'd brought with him from England when he'd moved to Hollywood eight years ago. He'd half forgotten it was in here. What else had he forgotten these last few years?

A book slipped from his lap to the floor, and the muffled thud shook him from his reflections. He reached down and picked it up. *Treasure Island* by Robert Louis Stevenson. He gently stroked the cover, remembering the sound of his mother's voice as she'd read the story to him when he was only a boy. It had once been the only way his mother, Violet, could get him to go to sleep. Some sleep-starved part of his brain must've remembered that old trick and brought him here last night. He opened the cover and caressed the inscription in the frontispiece, his fingers tracing the rise and fall of the ink that had been etched there long ago.

To my dearest boy, remember, always choose joy.

For so long, those words had been imprinted on his heart. They'd been all he had of his mother in the twenty-five years since she had left him. The words had sent him to Hollywood, a young man determined to suck the marrow out of life. Olivia Blount's mention of his once-treasured story had reminded him of this inscription. He hadn't thought of it in so long. Touching the words now, he could feel his mother's presence through the handwriting, and it renewed his belief that he was living his life as she hoped he would. Well, maybe with less boozing and hanky-panky, but what a mother didn't know wouldn't hurt her. All she cared about was whether he was happy. And he was. He was just going through a fallow period. So, why did he still feel so restless?

It was that damn girl. Olivia Blount was most decidedly not Flynn Banks's type. A bluestocking who'd turned up dressed like a boy at one of the most glamorous nightclubs in the world. That hadn't stopped him from dreaming about her—the perfect pout of her rose-colored lips, the curve of her pert little bottom, and her startling eyes. They had looked gray when he'd first ambushed her in her car, but as the sun had set, they darkened and took on a violet hue.

Yet, it wasn't her beauty that kept him tossing and turning all night. It was the fact that she had no idea who he was. That she wasn't the least bit intrigued by him. He thought he was a good actor, exciting and interesting on-screen. But Miss Blount had never even heard of him. That irked him. Was he so unremarkable then? There were only so many ways to grin, say "Avast," and sword fight. There were thousands of women who did know his name, who would give their eyeteeth to spend one night in his arms. Wasn't that good enough? What was one raven-haired slip of a girl, who, by her own admission, never went to the pictures?

His fingers were still absentmindedly tracing his mother's handwriting when his valet, Hugh, opened the library door, making Flynn jump out of his skin.

"I'm sorry, sir. I didn't expect to find you here."

"Bloody hell, does the entire world think I'm some uncouth ignoramus?" Flynn roared.

Hugh blinked at him, refusing to let any flicker of emotion cross his face. "No, sir. It's just that you're usually not awake at this hour."

"I went to Oxford, Hugh. I read English. I got a first!"

"Yes, sir, I was there. I recall."

"Just because I'm a scoundrel doesn't mean I'm dumb," he muttered.

"Quite right, sir."

Flynn thought again of Olivia Blount. She'd got him all mixed up. Now he was yelling at Hugh, who'd been with him since Eton. People assumed movie stars were dumb, but that was far from the truth. He'd acted opposite mathematicians and Proust scholars. Smart actors were better actors. They thought more carefully about their work, and their performances were more nuanced. He had always hoped he was one of those actors. But Miss Blount made him wonder if he'd gotten a little too comfortable. Maybe his first day with a new costar would be good for him, prevent him from resting on his laurels (and his extremely good looks).

Hugh cleared his throat, interrupting his thoughts. "Sir, shall I bring your grapefruit and coffee now?"

"What? Oh. No, Hugh, that's all right. I'll eat it in the kitchen as usual. Be up in a moment."

"Very good, sir." Hugh politely clicked his heels together and backed out of the room. Flynn stared down at his timeworn copy of *Treasure Island*, which had fallen to the floor again when Hugh startled him. He picked it up, careful not to let the pages that had come unstuck from the binding fall to the floor. It was silly, but holding it brought his blood pressure down immediately. He wanted to keep it with him to carry around his mother's reminder. Maybe he'd bring it to the studio and leave it in his dressing room. He felt as if he'd reconnected with an old friend and rediscovered some part of himself he hadn't even realized was missing.

Flynn had just set the book on the coffee table in his dressing room when Connie, one of the girls from wardrobe, knocked on his door. He had never slept with her. It was a pity, because she had great legs and cascades of golden-blond hair, but his one rule was to never sleep with the people whose job was to make you look good. Inevitably, they would be upset with him—and then his costumes might start feeling a little too tight or he'd be forced into a color that didn't suit his complexion. He knew that made him vain, but he didn't care. Everyone in Hollywood was in the business of looking good, and anyone that pretended otherwise was either a pug-nosed executive or a fool.

"Mr. Banks, wardrobe is ready for you."

"Thanks, Connie. I'll come with you." He gave one last look at the book on his dressing table and followed Connie to make the short walk across the lot.

"Miss De Lesseps is here already," Connie told him. "She's in her wig that she wears in the scene where you first meet her. Oh, Mr. Banks, it is truly absurd. Like a wedding cake on her head."

He chuckled at that. One thing he loved about working for Evets's Studios was the fact that they never skimped on costumes or sets. Harry could be cheap about some things, but not about how good a picture should look. "What's she like? Is she stuck-up like other French girls?"

He was curious. It was rare to meet your costar the first day on a project together. Usually, he'd know them, either from working together before or from bumping into them around town. But Harry had said this girl was arriving in Hollywood only a few days before the start of production.

"Well, she's not French. Turns out the studio made up that name. But she's a darling. She's so excited about everything. She squealed when we brought out the wig and her undergarments. Asked if she could bring her sister with her tomorrow to see them. She's like a kid in a candy store."

"Hmm, with a name like Liv de Lesseps, I was sure Harry had found her on a trip to Paris. But all the better. Sounds like a doll. I like her already." Flynn Banks knew one thing with absolute certainty—getting to make movies was the best job in the whole world, and he was a lucky son of a gun.

If this Liv de Lesseps felt the same, they'd get on like a house on fire. Not that he had any trouble setting the hearts of women of his acquaintance aflame. His mood was already improving, the unsettling notions of the previous night quieted by the assurance that his costar sounded like a lot of fun.

"Well, let's stop by her fitting room, and you can meet her. She's a natural. Evelyn says she could make a sack look good." Flynn's thoughts turned again to Miss Blount and how delectable her bottom looked in a pair of men's trousers. They arrived at wardrobe and Connie pushed open the door. "Her eyes! Gray in some lights, violet in others. They'll look brilliant in Technicolor with the gowns Evelyn has designed for her."

Connie's words dropped like a stone in his gut. He'd spent all night dreaming about a pair of fine eyes that matched Connie's description—and what were the odds that two different women he met in less than twenty-four hours would have such a unique set of eyes?

He didn't have to wait long for an answer, because there she was. Miss Olivia Blount. Or, he supposed he should call her Liv de Lesseps.

"You little liar," he muttered, suppressing a grin that he felt turning up the edges of his mouth. He didn't know whether he was more irritated or amused. Her eyes met his in the dressing room mirror. He pitched his voice up several octaves in imitation and gave it a ridiculous breathiness that he was well aware sounded nothing like her. "'Oh, I don't go to the pictures very often. I'm more of the literary type.' Literary type, my arse. That was some act you put on last night."

Liv, Olivia—whatever the hell her name was—had the decency to blush and look down at her feet, causing her wig, which had to be at least a foot and a half high, to tilt dangerously forward on her head. Connie, confused by Flynn's sudden outburst, had frozen in the doorway while Evelyn, the best costume designer on the Evets lot, scrambled to catch the wig and right it on top of Olivia's head. Evelyn's mouth was full of pins, and Flynn winced, hoping she didn't accidentally swallow one of them. But Evelyn was an old pro when it came to mishaps during fittings, and the wig was quickly back where it belonged with no harm done.

Evelyn faced him and put her hands on her hips. "Flynn Banks, Miss De Lesseps has been in Los Angeles for less than forty-eight hours. Yet somehow, you've already slept with her?"

"Absolutely not," Olivia scoffed, while Flynn simultaneously rolled his eyes and said, "She should be so lucky."

He and Olivia met each other's eyes once more in the mirror, and they broke out laughing together, dispelling the tension in the room.

"Miss Blount...er, De Lesseps, helped me out of a sticky situation last night, that's all," Flynn explained. "Though she needn't be so disdainful at the idea of having spent the night in my bed."

He winked at her. He expected her to blush again, but instead she held his gaze and lifted one eyebrow at him, as if she was assessing him with her intoxicating violet eyes and finding him wanting.

"Don't worry, Mr. Banks, it wasn't disdain. It was repulsion."

Connie and Evelyn broke out in peals of laughter as Flynn's jaw dropped in shock.

"You should see your face," Connie choked out in between laughs.

He glared at her. "Haven't you got my costume to fetch or something?"

Connie rolled her eyes and swept into a mocking bow,

backing out of the room still giggling. He could hear her all the way down the hall.

Flynn was used to two reactions from dames. Either they swooned at the sight of him, or having once swooned at the sight of him, they hollered at him until they were red in the face. But disdain? Indifference? Outright disgust? Never. Who was this woman, and where had Harry Evets found her? And why was he suddenly possessed with the urge to know every detail of her life—from the name of her first pet to her greatest heartbreak to the story of how she skinned her knee climbing a tree as a kid? Because he was certain Olivia Blount was the type of girl who skinned her knees climbing trees. He could tell these things.

Instead, he asked a more pertinent query. "Why didn't you tell me who you were last night?"

She shrugged, careful to move only her right shoulder as to not disturb her wig. "You flustered me, jumping in my car like that."

"Yes, but you pretended you'd never heard of me."

"Mr. Banks, you practically hijacked my vehicle to escape an angry former paramour. You are rumored to be the biggest lothario in Hollywood—"

"That isn't a rumor," he growled, but he was dismayed to discover that his wolfish tactics didn't disturb her glacial sense of calm indifference.

"That may well be." She winced as Evelyn tightened the laces on the corset they were fitting. "But I'm new here. I didn't want to spend the night before my first day on a picture dodging your unwanted advances."

"Honey, I never make unwanted advances. That's not my style." The nerve of this woman. Making him out to be a mustache-twirling villain. He was a cad, not a creep.

"A girl can never be too careful." Olivia pronounced this with the guilelessness of an innocent maid. But something more dangerous sparked in her eyes. He liked it. Probably a little too much.

"You're one of those refrigerator dames, huh?"

"Yes," she replied tersely. "And you're not the guy to defrost me. I came to Hollywood to do a job, not to be romanced."

Flynn didn't know whether to gape or laugh at her biting comeback. She was a sharp one. It was damnably attractive.

Evelyn took a step back and admired her handiwork. Olivia was in period undergarments, a corset tightened over a frilly slip and pantaloons that fell just above her knee. Women regularly wore less to go to the beach, but something about the costume was absolutely lascivious on Olivia Blount.

"There now, that's the underthings," Evelyn muttered, while tightening and marking a few places on Olivia's person with stickpins. "I'll get the gown." She followed the path of still-absent Connie out the door of the fitting room.

Flynn used the opportunity of Evelyn's exit to prowl toward Olivia. If she wanted to make him out to be some kind of predator, fine. He'd give her full jungle cat.

Olivia didn't break his gaze, instead lifting her chin an infinitesimal amount and staring him down, daring him to try it.

"You said you don't go to the pictures," he growled as he stalked in her direction. "Is that true?"

"No. I've seen a few. Here and there." Her lip quivered as she answered, and he had to hold back a laugh. She was a good actress, but he'd wager this girl had seen more than a few pictures.

"'Here and there,'" he mockingly imitated her. "And tell me, have you ever seen a Flynn Banks picture?" He leaned his head over her shoulder, whispering into her ear.

"I honestly don't remember. If I have, they weren't among my more memorable outings to the cinema." She held his gaze as she looked forward into the mirror. But her voice wavered, not with the feigned breathy trills of women pretending to be fools for his supposed benefit, but with a nervousness that belied her haughty demeanor and hinted at naughty things. Flynn knew with absolute certainty that she was lying.

"Mm-hmm. I see." He was nearly pressed against her now, but she had neither moved nor put any space between them. In fact, he could've sworn she'd just edged closer to him. "Why, pray tell, would you want to be in a Flynn Banks picture then? It hardly seems like an interesting endeavor for a girl of your... intelligence." He hissed the last word into her ear and reveled in the flush of red that crept up her neck.

He watched Olivia shiver, following the involuntary reaction as it made its way down her body and sent her knees quivering in her frilly, lace-edged pantaloons. She locked her knees and snapped her gaze back to his in the mirror. He raised his eyebrows, silently asking her a question, and she stuck her tongue out at him.

It was unexpected and elicited a short bark of laughter from him. The move made her wrinkle her nose in a way that he found ridiculously adorable. He was generally drawn to women whom he found sexy, inviting, seductive. Adorable was for kid sisters and bunny rabbits. But suddenly, Olivia's flavor of adorable seemed quite tantalizing.

"Needs must." She croaked out the words before clearing her throat and continuing. "A Flynn Banks swashbuckler would hardly have been my first choice. But the studio decides the picture, not me. Even Joan Davis had to make some stinkers before she won her Oscar."

Flynn choked back a laugh. He'd have to tell Joan that later. Of course, this woman admired Joan. He recognized the same fire and curiosity in her that his best friend Dash's wife had in spades. But Olivia's was softer, more genteel, more…innocent. "Ah, so you do know the pictures then. If you know Joan Davis."

He leaned his chin on her shoulder, and she shrugged him off in a move he could only describe as a harrumph. "Of course I know Joan Davis. She's a great actress."

He slid in front of her and sat on the ledge of the vanity in front of the mirror, his knees practically touching the tops of her thighs. "But I'm not a great actor… Is that it?"

She bit her lip and studied him, mulling something over, but then she squinted and shook her head. "Now, Mr. Banks, how would I know, considering I don't remember whether I've ever seen one of your pictures? But my guess is that you could be a good actor if you didn't let your ego get in the way."

"My ego is not as big as you think it is."

She gave a pointed look at his crotch, and he realized a moment too late that he'd opened himself up for further ridicule.

He jumped up off the dressing room counter and spluttered, "That's not what I meant."

She laughed—a warm, resonant sound that made his heart beat a little faster. "Mr. Banks, last night you were incredulous at the thought that I'd never seen one of your pictures."

"I was surprised, that's all. I've been the number one box-office star three years running."

She closed her eyes and inhaled, as if he was trying her patience. "Your box-office success aside, you're telling me this little exchange we've just had isn't about soothing your wounded ego? When I suggested your advances might be unwanted, you tried to seduce me. Or have I misunderstood your intentions?

Was this he-man act of yours about something other than proving that you're irresistible?"

He tried to think of a witty retort, but their exchange was cut off when Evelyn came back with an enormous mass of taffeta and ribbons in tow. She was followed by two more wardrobe assistants. Only Evelyn's eyes were visible over the mounds of the dress. Awkwardly trying to fit through the narrow doorway, she told Flynn, "Connie is ready for you down the hall."

"Good," he snarled, and cursed himself for sounding like an absolute prig. He stomped his way out of wardrobe, shoving his hands in his pockets. He was nearly out the door when he turned back to face his costar. "Miss De Lesseps, you may have a point about my ego. But if I ever try to seduce you, I can assure you, there will be no question as to my intentions."

CHAPTER 4

LIVVY SWORE SHE'D TRIED ON EVERY COSTUME ON THE Evets lot by the time they let her go for the day. They were beautiful pieces, swaths of satin and silk lining bodices and skirts, some decorated with fake gemstones. She had never dreamed of dressing so grandly. Back in her threadbare sweater, tweed skirt, and scuffed loafers, she felt almost bereft without the beautiful clothes. But being trussed and primped and pulled and pinned within an inch of one's life was exhausting. At least tonight, she didn't have to drive Flynn Banks all the way to Malibu.

As she barreled down Sunset, her jalopy catching every bump and groove in the road, she counted the seconds until she was home. She soon saw the small green sign that read GARDEN OF ALLAH and made a left past the hotel toward the bungalows in the back. Or, as they advertised them, *villas*. Run-down shacks was more like it.

She and her sister shared the teeny one-bedroom they could barely afford. It had taken every cent they had to move down here, so they weren't in any position to be choosy about their living conditions. Hopefully Judy would find a job soon. Then, when Livvy's weekly studio salary started coming in, they could pool their earnings and find someplace better.

Livvy parked in front of their residence and quickly locked the car. All she wanted to do was toe off her shoes and collapse face-first onto the sofa. It was moth-eaten and needed to be restuffed, but she was so tired that she didn't care a lick. She stuck her key in the front door, but her sister opened it before she'd even turned the key in the lock.

"Livvy!" Judy squealed and threw her arms around Livvy. Judy was eighteen years old, only four years younger than Livvy. But they'd lost their parents four years ago, and they were all each other had.

Livvy smiled and returned a quick hug before kicking her shoes off and making good on her desire to throw herself on the bottle-green couch.

"How was it?" Judy fluttered around the room, setting a glass of water on the coffee table for Livvy. "I want to hear everything."

She groaned, not bothering to lift her head from the couch. "It was good…mostly. Just…long and exhausting. It's going to take me awhile to get used to people calling me Miss De Lesseps. I keep thinking they're talking to someone else."

Judy stuck her nose in the air, pulling the tip of it up with her index finger and assuming an exaggerated French accent. "But Liv de Lesseps is soooo Frennchhh. It is chic, it is the essence of je ne sais quoi."

Livvy shook her head, chuckling. "That may be. But it's not my name, and it never will be. Not really. But tell me about your day. Did you find a job?"

"I think so? I won't know until tomorrow." Judy wanted to be an actress and star in musical pictures like Ginger Rogers or Eleanor Powell. But Livvy was the one who had caught the eye of Harry Evets. She'd trade places with Judy in a heartbeat if she could. Though maybe she'd ask to keep one of those gorgeous dresses she'd tried on today.

Judy sat down in the armchair covered in faded and stained floral upholstery. They had, for peace of mind, determined that the rust-colored blob on the seat cushion was a coffee stain.

"Promising?" Livvy turned her head from the throw pillow she'd face-planted into so she could see Judy more clearly. The kid was hopping up and down in her chair with excitement, her ponytail bobbing with her fizzy energy. But now that Livvy had a moment to take a good look at Judy, she noticed a brace on her sister's wrist.

"Very! It was an audition to be a waitress and a dancer at the Sphinx Club."

Livvy popped up and grabbed for Judy's arm. "Judy, what happened? You're hurt."

Judy pulled her arm back, tugging out of Livvy's grasp. "It's fine." She refused to meet Livvy's gaze. "I slipped during my audition and twisted it a little when I caught myself. It'll be right as rain in a few days."

Livvy lay back down on the couch, fighting the urge to run to the bathroom and find something to make it better. She propped her head on her hand. "You have to be more careful, kid. Don't want you breaking your wrist before your big break." Livvy winked at Judy, but her heart wasn't in it.

Judy flattened her lips into a thin line. "You mean we don't need a hospital bill to deal with before either of us are making money."

Livvy's face fell. "That's not what I meant. But I can't say you're wrong. Anyway, tell me more about the Sphinx Club. I've never heard of the place."

"It's only been around a couple of years. It's on Hollywood Boulevard."

A prickle of worry poked at Livvy. "Oh, Judy, I'm not sure

about that. Isn't Hollywood Boulevard kinda seedy? Can't you at least try for a job at the Trocadero?"

Judy twisted her face into a moue. "No. They don't have any vacancies right now. Besides, I don't have enough experience yet to dance at the Troc. This could be a real opportunity, Livvy. The manager of the club, Billy Wilkes, doesn't just employ girls at the club. He's sorta an agent too. He helps select dancers for Hollywood parties and movie extras and things like that. Besides, you know we need the money."

Livvy sat up and patted the couch cushion next to her. Judy plopped down on it and Livvy wrapped her arm around her sister, pulling her close until Judy laid her head on Livvy's shoulder. "Okay, Judy, I trust you. And you're right, we do need the money. I only want to know you won't find yourself in a situation over your head. It's my job to keep you safe. We already lost Mother and Father. I can't lose you too." Judy nestled into the crook of Livvy's arm more tightly at the mention of their parents. "I'll be at the studio all the time, and I don't want to worry about you."

"You will anyway." Judy sighed. "But Livvy, I'm not a kid anymore. I can take care of myself."

"You'll always be a kid to me."

Judy giggled and snuggled her head against Livvy's shoulder. "Oh, Livvy, I love you."

"I love you too, kid."

Judy shoved Livvy lovingly. "Now, tell me about your day. Did you meet Flynn Banks? What's he like? Everything you ever dreamed?" Judy batted her eyelashes and put her hands under her chin.

Livvy drew the pillow out from behind her and swatted her sister with it. "He's my costar now, Judy!"

"So? Joan Davis and Dash Howard were costars for years. They're married."

Livvy rolled her eyes. She felt a million years older tonight than she had last night. She hadn't told Judy about meeting Flynn at the Troc. She had told Judy she was going out for a drive to clear her head, and when she'd gotten home, Judy had already fallen asleep. Livvy wasn't even sure Judy would believe the story. It still felt like some strange dream. Surely, she had not rescued Flynn Banks from a nightclub and then proceeded to put on airs while driving him all the way to his house.

"Well, for your information, yes, I did meet him. And he's... not at all what I thought he'd be like." Judy frowned. "Oh, he's handsome and charming and all of those things. But he's a horrid flirt and has an ego the size of the Empire State Building. He's trouble, and the last thing I need is to get mixed up with a man like him."

Judy chuckled. "You honestly expected otherwise?"

Livvy lifted her shoulders and curled her arms around her legs as she drew them up on the couch. "I don't know. Maybe? I thought he'd be more like the characters he plays on-screen, a real dashing type, you know? But in reality, he's a...a...a...scoundrel."

"Oh brother. And you thought I would be the one getting in over my head?"

"What can I say? I've always been a hopeless romantic." Livvy threw herself backwards and kicked out her legs toward her sister's lap.

"But I thought you liked it in the movies when Flynn was a bit of a rogue," Judy teased, tickling the arch of Livvy's foot and making her squirm.

Livvy pulled her feet away and stuck her tongue out. "Pest!"

Judy giggled but kept her hands to herself.

"I did." Livvy sighed. "I do. But he wasn't like that. He was...a bit ridiculous actually. I pretended I didn't know who he was. That I'd never seen one of his pictures."

Judy's mouth rounded into a big O and her eyebrows shot up to her hairline. "Livvy! That's a bald-faced lie!"

Livvy laughed. "It is. But I didn't want him to see me as this starstruck kid who used to moon over him. Besides, I can't let my head be turned by a British accent and a winning smile." She paused, collecting herself. "We know what happened the last time I did that." Judy squeezed her sister's foot, reassuring her.

"He and I have to work together. So I acted like I didn't know him from Adam."

"My God, you're a better actress than I thought if you convinced him of that."

"It wasn't hard. I just pretended to be one of the ladies of the court from *Lancelot and Arthur* like we used to do. You remember?" Livvy lifted her chin, pursed her lips, and sucked in her cheeks and her nostrils, overexaggerating the look of a snooty woman.

Judy shrieked with laughter and imitated her sister. "Your Grace, I would not deign to let you kiss my foot."

Livvy responded, "No, my liege, I will not allow you to sully my pure and noble heart." The sisters broke into peals of giggles and soon they were laid out on the sofa, catching their breath.

"Oh, I needed a good laugh."

"I'm sorry Flynn Banks turned out to be a disappointment," Judy murmured.

"S'okay, he's still handsome." Judy grinned at that, and Livvy chuckled. "But I liked him better when I was inventing versions of him for the heroes in my books."

"Well, maybe he'll surprise you and give you inspiration to finish writing one of them."

Livvy's heart sank. She hadn't written a word since her parents' accident. She wasn't sure she ever would again. Certainly not while she was making a picture. The studio had scarcely given her time to breathe. And she didn't want to think about the dream she'd lost. She had a new dream now—making sure that Judy could have everything she'd ever wanted. Livvy forced herself to perk up. "Anyway, I have really gorgeous costumes! And a monstrous wig! Though I think I managed to convince them that I'd only need to wear it in the first scene. Shall we make dinner and I'll tell you all about it?"

Judy nodded enthusiastically. "I brought home half a roast chicken from the audition. I made nice with the line cooks while I was waiting my turn at the club. It's in the icebox."

Livvy stood on the couch and wrapped a plaid blanket around her like a cape. "Tonight, we eat like kings!" she proclaimed. "Or at least, like Flynn Banks." She gave Judy a wink, humming the theme to *Lancelot and Arthur* as she marched into the kitchenette. Flynn Banks might be a disappointment, but her sister never was.

CHAPTER 5

THE OCEAN FROTHED AROUND FLYNN AS HE LIFTED HIS head and gulped for air. Though the days remained warm in the Southern California sun, the Pacific was starting to cool for the season. It was bracing. The best cure for a hangover, or whatever was ailing you. Which, this morning, was a telegram from his brother that had been waiting when he got home last night.

> FATHER FADING FAST. STOP. PLEASE COME. STOP. HIS DYING WISH. STOP.

For the second night in a row, Flynn hadn't been able to sleep. His hatred for his father gnawed at him. He couldn't go to England now. Not even if he wanted to. But if he didn't, would he regret it one day? For a moment, he wondered if the memory of his father and whatever had been left unsaid would haunt him. But it wasn't possible. His father was a monster. Flynn had proof of what an unforgivable deviant Lord Banks was. Proof even beyond the pain in his left wrist that flared when it rained, the memento of the time his father broke his arm for cheating at chess. He had been eight years old. He plunged his arm into the water with gusto, trying to banish his disturbing thoughts. If he swam hard enough, if he exhausted himself enough, he could master this.

Instead, Flynn called upon a memory of a bewigged, violet-eyed actress whose knees quivered when he touched her and who looked at him as if he were a rather curious insect. Olivia Blount was a difficult maths problem, but one he was eager to solve—which was, frankly, the first time he'd ever been eager to do maths. He plunged his head beneath the foam of a wave and dolphin kicked himself forward, trying to shake it off. Olivia was a beautiful distraction, but he didn't like this churning feeling that arose in his gut every time she came to mind.

He desperately wanted to call Dash Howard. In the old days, he and Dash would have gone out to one of their favorite Hollywood watering holes and drunk enough between them to drown a small army. But Dash was domesticated now and in bed with his wife by 11:00 p.m. every night. Bloody boring.

For the millionth time, Flynn thanked his lucky stars that he was not so foolish as to chase love or romance. Look at his parents. They'd certainly proved that lesson. "Choose joy," his mother had written. And that's what he'd done, avoiding commitment like it was a life sentence. There were the joys of naked lust, and the rest was poppycock. So why did Miss Blount have him feeling so topsy-turvy?

If anything would get his head on straight, it was a bracing hour of swimming laps back and forth in front of his cottage's private beach. Only he'd been out here for nearly three-quarters of an hour, and he still felt like he'd been turned inside out. Thank God the regatta was this weekend. He wouldn't have time to get down to the marina before then, and if anything could set him to rights, it was a day on his sailboat. He lifted his head above water and noticed Hugh, standing on the deck waving at him.

Flynn swam toward the shore, standing and walking once he'd reached the shallows as the waves crashed against his knees, then his ankles. He let the morning sun hit his torso and reveled in the feeling of its warmth licking its way up and down his body.

"Hugh, what is it?" he called out.

"Harry Evets is on the phone for you. He's been trying to reach you for the last half hour."

Flynn swore loudly. Hugh didn't blink; he was quite used to it. While Joan and Dash had a familial relationship with the head of the studio and regarded him as a doting father figure, Flynn and Harry had a much more strained history. Generally, if Harry wanted to talk to Flynn, it was because he wanted to reprimand him: "Don't drag race down Hollywood Boulevard in the middle of the night! Don't borrow a horse from the Hollywood Turf Club and ride it through the canyons! Don't sleep with the wife of a rival studio head! Don't keep a pet goat in your trailer. It ate your costume! Don't replace the prop rum with real rum. The extras got drunk and threw up on the gaffer!"

The list went on and on; Flynn had heard it all. But he had been rather good lately, if he did say so himself. It had been at least a month since his last spot of trouble—when he'd found his face plastered on some rag that purported to know Hollywood's secrets. He had no idea what Harry might need to talk to him about.

He sprinted up the sand, the coarse, golden grit coating his feet as he went. He took the creaky, wooden stairs that stretched from the beach to his deck two at a time, narrowly avoiding the hole in the third step from the top that was rife with splinters.

Hugh was waiting for him with a towel, which Flynn hastily grabbed and wiped over his arms, torso, and legs. "Hugh, can you go find my little black book? It's in the breast pocket of the coat I wore yesterday." Hugh nodded in acknowledgment. The swim hadn't managed to clear Flynn's head, so he was going to have to revert to finding a dame to help him do it.

He reached for the forest-green terry-cloth dressing gown Hugh was holding open for him. Flynn tied it loosely around his waist, sat on his deck chair, and picked up the phone Hugh had helpfully placed on the round glass table.

"Hello?"

"Flynn. Finally," Harry growled.

Flynn hugged the phone to his ear, pressing it between his head and shoulder while he used the towel to dry his other ear. "Sorry, old sport, was in the water."

"That's a word I've never heard for hungover and still in bed."

Flynn bristled. Harry always expected the worst of him. Admittedly, that was usually with good reason. "It's not a euphemism. I was taking a dip in the Pacific."

"*Brrrr*," Harry exaggerated on the other end of the line. "A bit late in the year for a morning swim, isn't it?"

"It helps me clear my head. Look, Harry, I'm sure you didn't call to discuss my swimming habits. What have I done now?"

"Nothing. Well, nothing new anyway. But you and I both know you're not exactly a Boy Scout."

"Would never pretend to be. What's your point?"

Harry sighed heavily on the other end of the line, and Flynn could tell he was not going to like the answer. "Well, Flynn, we have a problem. The Legion of Decency and the Hays Code office are breathing down my neck."

Flynn chuckled. "Those old ninnies. They've got their legs crossed so tight that not even sunlight can get through. Tell them you'll say a couple Hail Marys and be done with them."

Harry barked out a hoarse laugh and cleared his throat. "Old ninnies they may be, but our pictures live and die by their seal of approval. And it seems they've got a laundry list of your exploits that they object to."

"You know, I don't think I've ever seen them all written in one place before. Could you send me a copy?" Hugh came back out from the house with a cup of steaming hot coffee and Flynn's black book and that morning's papers tucked under his arm. Flynn nodded at the table, gesturing for Hugh to set them all down. He sipped at his coffee and let the caffeinated elixir warm him from the inside. He started to leaf through the pages of his book, only half listening to Harry.

"It seems," Harry continued, ignoring Flynn's interjection, "that they've decided you are not a good role model for impressionable Americans."

"Who ever said there was any fun in being a role model?"

"Would you let me finish?" Harry spluttered. "I'm not enjoying this any more than you are."

"On the contrary, I'm enjoying it immensely." Flynn looked through the double-paned glass window shaped like an arch and saw Hugh standing in the kitchen. He was holding up eggs, as if to ask how many Flynn wanted. "Two," Flynn shouted out.

"Two what?" Harry growled.

"Not you, I'm talking to Hugh."

"I know life is a grand joke to you, but I assure you this is no laughing matter." There was a gravity in Harry's voice, a sternness that Flynn had never heard before. Not even when he had received his worst tongue-lashing, for scuttling an old-fashioned pirate ship they'd filmed on when he'd decided to take it out for a drunken evening sail. Harry's tone made him sit up straighter in his chair, the suffusion of comfort and warmth the coffee had supplied gone in an instant.

"Harry, you're acting like someone's died," he said.

"Your career will be in significant rigor mortis by next week if you don't listen to me and do exactly as I say."

"Okay, fine, fine, what do they want?"

"As I was saying, the Legion of Decency and, by extension, the Production Code Administration are concerned about your effect on the youth of this country. The PCA office has informed me that they will refuse to give a seal of approval to any of your films unless you prove you've turned over a new leaf."

"Ah, come off it, Harry. Don't let them threaten you. Joan confessed to a room full of people and to anyone listening on the radio that she'd made a stag film. I don't see you calling her up to read her the riot act for violating the Hays Code."

"Joan has also not made a picture since that night," Harry replied coldly. "We mutually agreed it was best that she take a year or two off and give people time to forget. She's enjoying her new life as a married woman. I have no doubt that when we do find her next project, it'll take a lot of favors with Will Hays and his cronies to get them to even review it before condemning it outright."

Flynn swallowed. Harry was right. He knew Joan hadn't been working. But the truth was she hadn't seemed to mind. She'd made a choice and she stood by it. Meanwhile, Flynn was being forced into whatever this was against his will. "I haven't had my name in the police blotter or the front of the gossip pages for at least a month. Isn't that a sign that I've sprouted some fresh greenery?"

"I take it you haven't seen the morning papers."

"No, I haven't." Flynn didn't make a habit of reading the papers. They usually only contained bad news. But he did subscribe to them, and Hugh had laid the *Examiner* on the table next to Flynn's coffee. The headline on the front page was about the election of a new mayor. "I hardly see what that has to do—"

"Does the name Rhonda Powers mean anything to you?"

Flynn's heart sank. What had the dizzy dame done? Flynn slept around. That was no secret. But he'd never gone to bed with a girl who hadn't made it quite explicit that she wanted him. And he always took safety precautions—getting a girl pregnant would not exactly do wonders for his reputation.

"I take it your silence means her name is familiar to you."

"Sure. I know the girl. I met her once. I kissed her in the garden at one of Joan and Dash's house parties. I know plenty of dames a lot better than her, if you take my meaning." Flynn thought he could hear Harry roll his eyes through the phone.

"That may be, but she's claiming otherwise. Quite loudly, in fact." Flynn pulled the copy of the paper toward him and unfolded it, catching a small bold-font headline above his picture, just below the centerfold. *Flynn Banks Jilts Aspiring Starlet*, it read. The story detailed Rhonda's account of her and Flynn's fly-by-night romance—a tale of love at first sight at a Hollywood party, their rushed secret engagement, and him jilting her at the altar.

Flynn snorted. "Harry, this is poppycock. Leda Price is losing her edge."

"You know very well that no one in Hollywood has seen hide nor hair of Leda Price since the night Joan and Dash won their Oscars. I told Harold at the *Examiner* if I ever so much as caught a glimpse of one of her feathered hats sniffing around the studio again, I would buy the paper with the express intention of sending it into bankruptcy. He apparently values his job, because she's been 'on leave' ever since. And since Joan and Dash robbed her of blackmail fodder, she has no leverage to crawl out of some other hole."

"Well then, what is this rubbish?"

"Flynn, you know better than anyone that there's no shortage of gossip-hungry reporters in this town."

"Well, can't you call the editor again? Ask him to print a retraction. Say it's not true. I barely know the woman!"

"That may be. But a retraction won't do any good. Do you know who Rhonda Powers is?"

"No. But I'm guessing you're about to tell me."

"She's the daughter of the founder of Shasta Peak Pictures."

"The one who died of cancer last year?"

"The very one. If you recall, he made a very large donation to the Catholic Church in his will, so that they might continue to act as a 'moral compass' for Hollywood. For the Legion of Decency, jilting their white knight's daughter is the last straw. They are convinced you are a despoiler of innocent women. Joseph Breen of the PCA office personally called me this morning to inform me that at least six cardinals from dioceses around the country are ready to denounce you as an agent of Satan."

"Couldn't we just try using that as new billing on the next picture? 'Flynn Banks, agent of Satan, to the rescue!'" There was dismayed silence on the other end of the line. "Okay, I'll take that as a no."

"They want proof that you've reformed your ways."

"I have an idea. Instead of drinking straight liquor when the press is around, I'll inject it into some oranges. They'll think I'm eating fruit and getting my vitamins! Voila, problem solved!"

Harry let out a long-suffering sigh on the other end. "That's not exactly what I had in mind."

Flynn wanted to tell Harry the truth. That it didn't matter what his plan was. That Flynn would never, could never reform. He was a rogue and a reprobate and at least three other words that started with an *r*. He wasn't going to change to satisfy some cabal of moralists. Not for Harry, not for the Legion of Decency, certainly not for a dame. No matter how much they all begged him to.

"Knowing you," Harry went on, "I am aware that any proof of reform is a tall order. But I think I have a solution."

Flynn was fairly certain he wasn't going to like whatever this solution was, but at that moment, Hugh deposited a plate full of fried eggs, bacon, and a stack of toast in front of him. He grabbed for a piece of toast and bit into it, hoping the sustenance would soften the blow. "And what is that, Harry?"

"They don't want to see you out with a different dame every night. All right? So we pair you off with a nice girl, someone squeaky clean. We make them think you've changed your ways and fallen head over heels for some ingenue."

"Those types of girls are not exactly banging down my door." Flynn looked longingly at his little black book. His plans to use a dame to forget about his father and this strange fascination with Olivia Blount were slipping through his fingers.

"Well, the good news is that we have an excellent candidate already. If, for at least the duration of making this picture, you pretend to be courting Miss Liv de Lesseps, maybe we can change their minds."

"Her?" Flynn retorted. "Miss Olivia Blount, whose nose is so high in the air I don't think she's seen her own feet in years? No. For starters, she'd never go for it."

"Oh yes she will, if she wants to keep her job. She'll do anything I tell her to."

Harry had him there. "Well, then, what if *I* say no? I don't want to spend the next three months pretending to simper over someone with no sense of humor. Besides, who would believe it?" Flynn wanted to heave. Which would be a shame considering the beautiful breakfast Hugh had placed before him.

"May I remind you that there's a morality clause in your contract?"

Flynn took a bite of toast and struggled to choke it down. He and Harry both knew that he'd violated that clause in about thirty different ways since he became the property of Evets's Studios. But Flynn didn't think he would ever be fired over it. As he'd pointed out, Joan Davis had made a stag film. Hell, that was how Harry had discovered Joan. Then she'd won an Oscar for an Evets picture and announced her secret to the world. Harry generally was a forgiving man, or at least a man who looked the other way when necessary. "Harry, that's not fair. I didn't even do anything. This time."

"'This time.' Do you hear yourself? You're one wrong step away from torching your career."

"But Joan—"

"No, I don't want to hear about Joan Davis. This world is full of pearl-clutching hypocrites, and she's laying low in an effort to wait them out. She's also on half salary. Not that that matters, because we are talking about you. You're about to make a new movie. If your pictures are condemned by the Legion of Decency, I can't sell them. If I can't sell your pictures, I can't very well keep you on contract. I don't employ stars that cost me money instead of making it."

That stopped Flynn cold. He didn't know what his life would be if he wasn't Flynn Banks, incurable rogue and movie star. He loved acting, yes, but he loved all the things it afforded him too: his Malibu beach house, his sailboat, the best liquor in the world, and the sultriest dames—and most of all, the ability to tell his family to go to hell. Without his career, he'd have to go crawling back to them if he didn't want to lose everything.

And by the sounds of things from Edgar's letter, the Banks family coffers weren't overflowing either. Sheer panic bubbled up in Flynn's chest. There had to be an easier way out of this than pretending to date Liv de Lesseps for three months. "Look, couldn't I go volunteer at a soup kitchen or take pictures with some babies?"

"No. It's too late for half measures. You are going to court

Liv de Lesseps and pretend to be hopelessly falling for her while you're making this picture, all the way through its release. You will be the perfect gentlemen and be photographed with her on your arm. You will not have any drunken exploits. The papers won't connect your name to a single showgirl or cocktail waitress. I don't care what you and Liv do behind closed doors. But if you don't give an Oscar-worthy performance to convince every starry-eyed schoolgirl and teetotaling battle-ax from here to Maine that Liv de Lesseps has made you a changed man, I'll fire you."

"But—" It was too late. Harry had hung up.

Flynn Banks was now officially dating his costar. Whether he liked it or not.

CHAPTER 6

LIVVY WAS RUNNING LATE TO REHEARSAL. IT WASN'T HER fault. Harry Evets had insisted she stop by his office to discuss the terms of her contract. She'd been ten minutes early to the lot and even beaten Harry's secretary there. Her nerves had her sweating through her blouse. She'd heard plenty of stories about what studio bosses tried to do with young, naive actresses after summoning them to their offices. She'd tucked a particularly long hatpin in her pocket that morning just in case.

But Harry hadn't called her to his office to make unwanted sexual advances. No, what he wanted was something else entirely—for her to pretend to be dating Flynn Banks. The moment he'd told her what was expected of her, she'd lost all sense of time and place.

She hadn't protested. Hadn't even asked a question. The pronouncement had left her in shock. She'd nodded and said, "Yes, Mr. Evets. Thank you, Mr. Evets." Harry would send further instructions for their first date and told her to lie low until then, and dismissed her. She had immediately run to the nearest dark, quiet, empty space she could find, which was the janitor's closet. There were a broom and a mop and the lingering smell of bleach. The overpowering scent made her lightheaded. Or was that a result of Harry's new dictate?

Ha! If Harry Evets only knew she'd dreamed of dating Flynn Banks for years. Now that she'd actually met the man, well, performing with a tiger sounded like a safer option. But what could she do? It wasn't like she had a choice. If she wanted to keep her job and pay the rent on the bungalow, she had to obey Harry's orders. She hadn't even wanted to be an actress. But now she was here, making a picture. It allowed her to keep her sister safe, well fed, and in spitting distance of the studios until Judy got her own big break. So Livvy was going to have to pretend to date Flynn Banks. That was all there was to it.

Resigned to her fate, she squared her shoulders and left the broom closet, making a beeline for the soundstage where they had scheduled rehearsal today. It was then that she noticed she was ten minutes late. She sprinted the rest of the way, arriving at Soundstage 6 completely disheveled and sweaty. Between her nerves and her mad dash, she worried she was beginning to smell. The cramp in her side made her feel like she'd accidentally stuck herself with the hatpin in her pocket. At least she was wearing black-checked shorts with a cherry-red gingham blouse, having been told to come to set prepared for athletic activity.

After wandering her way through a mishmash of wooden backdrops and discarded furniture, she finally located Flynn Banks, who was standing near a capuchin monkey in a pirate hat—a miniature version of the hat she'd seen the wardrobe department preparing for Flynn yesterday. The monkey was perched on a stand and watching intently as Flynn chatted with a man she didn't recognize. She didn't want to get too close, lest she startle the monkey.

"Banks," Livvy called out. She surprised even herself with her snappish tone and wished she was half as confident as she projected.

Flynn Banks snapped his head toward her, a congenial look on his face sharpening into something more wolfish when he realized it was her. "Well, if it isn't the woman who's going to sweep me off my feet." So, at least he knew already. She could not imagine being the one to tell the man about Harry's cockeyed scheme.

She ignored Flynn's retort, deciding it was safest to avoid the subject for now. "Who's your friend?" She gestured at the monkey and approached gingerly.

"This is Rallo!" Flynn made a face. The monkey made a face back at him, putting its fingers in its mouth, drawing its lips wide, and sticking out its tongue. Olivia couldn't suppress a giggle. "He's my sidekick. This over here is his trainer, Lionel Berry. Rallo has made three pictures with me now. This will be our fourth together."

"You better hope they don't start dating rumors about you two," she joked. Flynn laughed, deep and resonant. It reminded her of a crackling fire on a cold night. Cozy and warm and deeply masculine. It was a reminder of why she'd found him absurdly attractive when he was merely a man on a screen.

She was pleased that her joke made him laugh. She'd spent their previous two encounters annoying him to protect herself, but this charade would be easier if they got along.

"I don't know." Flynn twisted his nose up and the monkey copied him. "I think he's rather handsome, don't you?"

Livvy bit her lip and pretended to think about it.

Flynn feigned a pout. "Rallo, the lady doesn't think you're handsome!"

The monkey frowned in dismay.

"Oh now, I didn't say that!" Livvy protested. "I was just trying to find a nice way to tell you that Rallo is much better looking than you are."

Flynn laughed uproariously, which made the monkey jump up and down on his perch in excitement. "I set myself up for that one."

"He is awfully cute though."

"Thank you." Flynn batted his full, gorgeous eyelashes at her. Why was it always men who had the most wonderful eyelashes? They were completely wasted on them.

Livvy rolled her eyes at Flynn's cheesy attempt to flirt. "I meant the monkey, not you." She took another step toward them, and Flynn raised his hand in warning.

"Careful, he doesn't like strangers. It took him a whole picture to warm up to me. But now we're the best of friends. Right, Rallo?" Flynn looked at the monkey and the monkey nodded a demonstrative yes, showing all of its teeth.

"Here, Miss De Lesseps, try giving him a treat." The tall South Asian man that Flynn had introduced as Lionel put a slice of a fresh banana in her hand. She extended it toward the monkey, waiting for Rallo to make his move.

The monkey sniffed gingerly at her before meeting her gaze. He seemed both impish and impossibly wise, and she immediately liked him. He reached out and plucked the banana slice from her hand, clapping it to his mouth and eating it in one bite.

She laughed again, and Flynn did too. The sound made something warm flare in her stomach.

The monkey made a grasping gesture with its fingers, and Livvy looked toward Lionel. "What does he want?"

"Rallo, the lady does not have more bananas," the man told the monkey. But the monkey didn't seem to care. Without warning, he jumped from his perch and onto Livvy's shoulder. The sudden movement surprised her and she yelped.

"Rallo, no!" Flynn cried and leapt to remove the monkey. "Now, my friend, let's leave the lady alone."

But Livvy fended Flynn off. After the initial shock of Rallo jumping on her, she was fine. Content, actually. "No, it's all right. Let him be. If we're going to make a picture together, I should get used to him jumping on top of me."

"I wish you'd told *me* that," Flynn retorted. Out of anyone else's mouth, it would've seemed leering. But somehow, he made it ludicrously charming. He smirked at her and her heart started racing.

This was bad. This was why she'd pretended not to know who he was, and she was still determined to show him how little he impressed her. Damn Harry Evets and his stupid plan to improve Flynn Banks's image.

The monkey played with the small golden hoop earrings she was wearing, clearly entranced by the way the lights in the rafters of the soundstage made them sparkle. He attempted to nibble on the hoop, and Livvy giggled at the soft huff of the monkey's breath behind her ear. Satisfied that her earrings were not edible, Rallo scampered down her shoulder to her hand, which she made into a fist so that the creature would not fall. He perched on it and looked at her, cocking his head from one side to the other, appearing to weigh her trustworthiness. Seemingly content with what he found, Rallo wrapped his hands around her arm and squeezed, leaning his little head against her bicep. It tickled and was astonishingly gentle.

"What's he doing, Lionel?" Flynn asked in concern, edging closer, clearly ready to intervene if necessary.

"I think...he's hugging her." Lionel met Livvy's gaze. "He likes you."

Livvy smiled. She patted the monkey on the head to thank him for the hug.

Flynn scowled. "That's not possible. He threw his own shit at me for six whole weeks when we made our first picture together. I still have a scar on my finger from the time he bit me nearly down to the bone!" Flynn held up his pointer finger on his left hand as proof, and sure enough, Livvy could see a series of short, thin white lines that looked like dashes in Morse code and matched the exact width of Rallo's teeny teeth. Livvy swallowed an urge to laugh.

Rallo turned his head and looked at Flynn's finger, baring his teeth. Flynn grimaced back and Rallo twisted his head to look up at Livvy, as if to say, "Are you seeing this?"

Lionel ignored them both. "Try this." The trainer gestured, cradling his arms as if he were holding a child. Livvy did as instructed, and Rallo instantly climbed into her arms and snuggled against her.

"Oh, he's a dear," she cooed.

"A dear who nearly bit my finger off," grumbled Flynn. "He's a little tyrant is what he is."

"Oh ho ho, five minutes ago, he was your best friend that only you knew how to handle."

Flynn glared at her. "I worked like hell to win him over. And this is the thanks I get. Feeble-minded beast."

Livvy gasped in mock outrage. "Flynn's a meanie, isn't he?" she mumbled to the monkey curled in her arms. "You're not a tyrant or a beast. You just don't like loud, boorish men, do you?" As if in answer, Rallo curled more tightly against her and raised his little hand over his ear.

"I am not loud and boorish!" Flynn stomped his foot. "I treated that monkey with nothing but respect. I practically had to buy a banana farm to get in his good graces! I let the publicity department put him on the movie posters. What more does the little creature want from me?"

Lionel burst into uproarious laughter. Flynn crossed his arms and sat down in the chair next to the monkey's perch. He quietly seethed while Livvy swayed the monkey in her arms.

"Five little monkeys jumping on the bed," she sang.

"Are you singing him a lullaby?" Flynn growled.

"He looks tired." Her heart swelled at the sight of the monkey wrapping his hand around her thumb, clinging to her.

"He can't be tired. He has fencing practice with us." Flynn stood up abruptly, crossed to Livvy, and practically touched his forehead to hers to look down at Rallo, who seemed utterly content.

"Traitor," he muttered at the monkey. Rallo yawned and rolled over so his tail was pointed up at Flynn. "I see how it is. A pretty face turns your head, and you abandon all loyalty."

"You think I have a pretty face?" Livvy inquired. Flynn had not been quick to compliment her in their brief interactions the days prior. She wasn't certain that Flynn Banks had time for anyone's good looks but his own.

"Miss De Lesseps, don't flatter yourself. Anyone can see you have a pretty face. I'm merely stating a fact."

Livvy lifted her shoulder, gently shrugging. "Beauty is in the eye of the beholder, Banks."

"Not in Hollywood," he retorted. Livvy raised her eyebrows at him. "Sorry, I... Sorry, that was rude."

"If I didn't know better, I'd say you were jealous," Livvy quipped.

"He was my monkey first," Flynn replied with the petulance of a small child.

"Here, if it bothers you so much, take him." Olivia held out the monkey in Flynn's direction, willing him to pick Rallo up. But Rallo refused to let go of her thumb, and with his other hand, he immediately grabbed her shirt, not wanting to be handed over.

"He doesn't want to come," Flynn grumbled.

Olivia lifted the monkey to her face, meeting its eyes. "Now, Rallo, don't you want to go visit your nice friend, Mr. Banks?" The monkey grinned and he looked almost ghoulish, like he was taunting Flynn. But he still did not let go of her thumb. "Lionel, can't you tell Rallo to go to Flynn?"

Before Lionel answered, Flynn replied. "I don't want him to come to me because he's forced to. I want him to come to me because he wants to."

"Honestly, Flynn, he's a monkey." Olivia sighed. "It's not a personal affront." But on the inside, it tickled her that it bothered Flynn so deeply. She'd thought nothing could annoy him more than pretending to have never seen one of his pictures. But Rallo's ease with her—that really got Flynn's goat. For some reason, she found it charming. He did, it seemed, have the capacity to care about something other than himself. It was evident that his jealousy came from a genuine affection for Rallo. That he and the monkey had formed a bond over several pictures together.

But it also made something else clear: She had the upper hand in this scheme. She already knew some of his vulnerable spots and how easily she could get a rise out of him. Maybe pretending to date Flynn Banks wouldn't be so bad after all. Maybe it wouldn't be risky to her heart and her sanity.

All she had to do, literally and metaphorically, was make sure the monkey liked her more.

CHAPTER 7

FLYNN WAS STILL SULKING AND OLIVIA WAS COOING OVER Rallo when fencing master and top swordsman Fred Cavens walked onto set. Flynn quickly forgot the monkey's easy betrayal, energized by the idea of getting a blade back in his hand.

"Freddie!" he bellowed, leaping to his feet in excitement.

Fred laughed, clearly delighted to see his old friend. He ran toward him, slapping Flynn on the back. "Banks, you old bastard, how's it going?"

"Careful, Freddie, there are delicate ladies here today," Flynn hissed in an exaggerated stage whisper, making sure Olivia overheard. She looked flustered and Flynn couldn't help but grin. Finally she was the one on the back foot.

Rallo lifted his hands to his mouth and covered it, seemingly understanding something naughty had been said, which made Olivia laugh. Damn this monkey. He really was an easy mark for a pretty girl.

Cheered by Rallo's antics, Olivia smiled in Fred's direction. "That's all right. You couldn't possibly shock me more than Mr. Banks already has. Mister…?"

"Cavens. Fred Cavens. Pleased to make your acquaintance, Miss De Lesseps. I'm the fencing master and choreographer for Evets's Studios. I'm here to get a feel for how well you handle a blade and to start teaching the moves for your and Banks's big fight."

"Fred taught me everything I know. About fencing, that is." Flynn winked at Olivia, who seemed distinctly unimpressed by him.

"Nonsense, Flynn's a natural," added Fred good-naturedly.

Fred was being kind. Flynn had taken fencing as a boy in London. One could hardly be the second son of a viscount and not learn the finer points of swordsmanship. Having been born into the British aristocracy, there were certain things that were expected of him: learning horsemanship before he could walk, attending Oxford or Cambridge, and becoming an at least passable swordsman. But Flynn had never been terribly interested in fencing, and all of his instructors had been old and boring. His rotating cycle of governesses had been far more interesting...and instructive. When Harry Evets had asked if he could fence before casting Flynn in his first picture, Flynn had said yes. Because technically he could. Just not very well. Until he met Fred Cavens.

Cavens had been a fencing master in the Belgian Army before he emigrated to America. He could've opened a fencing school, but instead, he used his talents to teach Hollywood's biggest stars how to believably duel on camera. He made Flynn a far better swordsman and enabled him to do his own stunts.

"Have you ever taken up a sword, Miss De Lesseps?" Cavens asked.

Olivia gave him a close-mouthed smile. "A few times." Rallo had moved from his place in her arms back to her shoulder.

Flynn was surprised. He couldn't imagine her setting aside her books to do something quite so athletic. She was lean and lithe, but from what he could tell, Olivia Blount was an insufferable know-it-all and a bluestocking. Not exactly who he'd peg as a swordswoman. "Come, now, don't lie to Fred. He's here to help you get up to speed."

Olivia pointedly ignored Flynn's comments and turned to face Fred. "Mr. Cavens, I'm eager to learn. As I said, I have *some* experience, but I'm certain you can teach me a lot."

"Good, then, that's what's most important." Cavens had come in with an armful of weaponry, including a small sword and two flat-tipped épées, as well as an extremely tiny saber that didn't even look big enough for a child. He handed one of the épées to Flynn and gave the other to Olivia. She fumbled, not wanting to displace Rallo.

Lionel stepped in, extending his arm. "Rallo, come." Lionel made a series of clicking sounds that seemed to be some sort of command, and the monkey promptly hopped from Liv's shoulder to Lionel's forearm.

Cavens looked at the monkey. "Rallo, I didn't forget you." The monkey clapped his hands together excitedly as Cavens held out the tiny sword, with the hilt facing the monkey. Rallo looked back and forth between Lionel and the miniature saber, as if seeking approval. Lionel nodded and Rallo grabbed the sword, wrapping his little hands around the hilt.

Flynn smiled. No matter how many times he'd seen it, watching Rallo with a sword was always a delight.

Olivia giggled, the sound he'd imagine bubbles in champagne would make if you could hear them. Something unfurled in his chest. Her laugh was charming and girlish, disarming in a way he had yet to see any part of this woman be. Everything about her was on high alert, her walls built as high as Big Ben. But just now, a glimpse of the real Olivia had peeked through, a crack in her brick facade. He wanted it back.

Then Fred Cavens called his attention away from wondering how to make her laugh again.

"All right," said the fencing master. "Now that everyone has their weapon, we'll go through some basic positions—a thrust, a parry, a classical lunge. Then, if I'm satisfied with your form, we'll work on some of the fight choreography."

Flynn quickly stripped off the thick jumper he'd been wearing over his crisp, white polo shirt. He saw Olivia's gaze dart to him as a small strip of his stomach was exposed, but then she merely rolled her eyes.

That crack in the wall was gone and had been hastily spackled up. Flynn held back a sigh. He didn't take his sweater off for her benefit. He'd been chilly after his morning swim, but he always worked up a sweat fencing. He wanted the easiest range of motion with his épée.

He wafted the blade through the air, feeling it tug and follow the flick of his wrist as he gained a feel for its weight. Then he assumed a position with his legs in a lunge and his sword extended in front of him.

Rallo mimicked him, standing up on his long legs, curling his tail beneath him, and extending his miniature sword until it touched Flynn's. "It seems he wishes to duel me for your attentions, Miss De Lesseps."

"He needn't fight you for them. He's already won them heartily."

"Ohhhh"—Flynn grabbed at his chest in mock pain—"you wound me."

Olivia smirked as Rallo's small head darted between them.

"Be that as it may, I request a fair fight." Flynn held his blade to the monkey's sword, and Rallo bared his teeth in response.

"En garde then, you little beast," Flynn joked. He and the monkey matched blades, and then Flynn backed Rallo into a corner. The monkey scampered up the post he'd been sitting on and used his higher ground to fight Flynn off.

But it wasn't enough. Flynn advanced on him, practicing a scene they'd cut from one of his earlier films. Rallo remembered it too, parrying in defense before surrendering by dropping his blade and covering his eyes with his hands.

"Oh, Flynn, don't hurt him!" yelped Olivia.

The sudden outburst distracted him, and he looked back at her. Rallo used the pause to diverge from their choreography—jumping to the ground, retrieving his sword, and crawling up Flynn's pant leg and across his chest until he held his tiny sword at Flynn's throat.

"Get him, Rallo. Make him beg for mercy!"

"This is not what we practiced," Flynn hissed at Rallo. The monkey shrugged, which made Flynn laugh and drop his blade, raising his hands in surrender. "All right, fine, you win. But don't think I'll forget this."

Lionel whistled and the monkey returned to him, passing off his tiny sword to Fred Cavens on the way.

The fencing master resumed control of the proceedings. "Now that we know that Rallo hasn't forgotten how to fence, Miss De Lesseps, can you assume a starting position? Do you need me to show you?"

"I can help if you need." Flynn laughed. "I'm very good at every position." He wanted to make her blush, to push through that wall again. Instead, she ignored him and assumed a classical lunge, looking absurdly cute in her gingham blouse and high-waisted shorts.

"Is that right?" She turned only her head to Cavens.

"Very good, very good. Your form is excellent. Now, we have two fights to teach you. The first is when Flynn's character kidnaps you and you attempt to fight him off with a decorative blade hanging on your wall. The other is when you team up alongside

Flynn's crew to fend off the attacking Spaniards at the film's conclusion. Flynn, if you'll take your position, we'll walk through some basics."

He did, raising his blade again and seductively running it down the edge of Olivia's saber. She didn't even flinch as the metal shrieked against metal. She held her ground, waiting for instruction from Fred. "What now, Mr. Cavens?"

"Yes, what now, Fred?" Flynn asked. "Does she need to adjust her footing? Maybe her posture?"

"No, she's perfect. It's you who seems off-kilter, Banks. Why are your shoulders so far back? And your feet are too close together. Good God, man, have I taught you nothing?"

Olivia simpered at him. "I'll wait for Mr. Banks to adjust his position." She held still and Flynn scowled at her as Fred nudged his instep with the tip of his foot, adjusting his legs slightly.

Flynn shifted his weight, trying to sink into the easy starting position Fred had taught him ages ago. The pose should be instinctual by now, but damn, this woman threw him off-balance. And thanks to Harry, he was supposed to pretend to be going steady with her? The thought made him squirm. Thank God they didn't have to begin this months-long publicity stunt until Harry worked out the details.

Cavens frowned and stood behind Flynn, placing his hand between his shoulder blades to get him to relax. "C'mon, Banks, you know better than this."

He did, he really did.

At last, Fred seemed satisfied and took a step back. "All right, let's exchange a few easy hits so I can get a sense for how you move on your feet."

Olivia straightened her spine, and Flynn braced himself as she placed more weight on her front leg to begin her attack. She went for a straight thrust, which he easily parried. They repeated the movement three times, the portrait of civility and gentlemanly fencing. He was bored. Why did he have to be present for her fencing lessons? He yawned as he parried each of her thrusts, barely even moving.

Something flashed in her eyes and she bit her lip. "C'mon, Banks, don't go easy on me."

He raised his eyebrow at her. She wanted to fight? Fine. "En garde." He lifted his blade, smirking and giving her a wink.

She tilted her head, perhaps in confusion, and he took up the offensive, lunging and then thrusting as he drove her back toward the corner of the soundstage, where Rallo was observing from his perch. The monkey placed its hands to the side of its face in worry. Flynn thrust again and again, forcing her to retreat.

"Okay, Banks, that's enough," Cavens called out. "It's supposed to be a lesson, not a duel."

But they both ignored him, caught up in this dance of steel and skill. He sliced and parried, edging her across the room until her back hit the wall. But she refused to drop her sword, and he kept advancing until their wrists slammed together with their blades locked in a cross above her head.

She glared at him, gritting her teeth. Every inch of her seemed to be pressed against him. He could feel the rise and fall of her chest under her twee little blouse, the flutters of her heart racing from their exertions. He dipped his eyes ever so slightly down and noticed a pink color creeping up her neck and onto her cheeks.

He waggled his eyebrows. "It seems we've found ourselves in an interesting position after all."

"I thought you said you were good at all of them," she retorted.

"Indeed. Have I not left you breathless?"

"Hardly," she scoffed, but the wheeze that accompanied the word gave her away.

He leaned closer, his lips brushing the side of her face as he whispered into her ear. "Do you surrender, Miss De Lesseps?"

"Never." Without warning, she dropped her blade. The sound of it clattering to the ground startled him into releasing her wrist. Now free, she ducked and tumbled to the side.

Without her body beneath him to hold him up, he slammed into the wall, his face colliding with the soft fabric the studio used to muffle outside noise. "Oomph."

Flynn caught himself with both hands, pushing his palms against the wall and turning around in time to see her grabbing her blade from the floor. She sat in a squat and spun easily on her heel, whirling the épée in a circle toward his ankles. It was a move straight out of *The Pirate's Mask*, and his body reacted instinctually, remembering the choreography. He leapt into the air and somersaulted over her head, landing in a crouching, defensive position with his blade.

Flynn tossed his blade between his hands. "Come on, lass, give me all you've got."

She blew a stray curl out of her eyes, and one corner of her mouth rose in a smug smile. "Are you sure you want that?"

"I want the best you can give me."

She screamed in reply, as if she were an Amazon on the warpath, and ran straight toward him with her blade over her head, something wild in her eyes as she brought it down upon his head. He raised his sword horizontally, catching the blade above him. Flynn pressed up hard, holding his sword by the handle and the narrow end of the blade, careful not to slice his hand. Using his knees and his arms, he managed to push her off, sending her stumbling backwards, her butt colliding with the floor and her sword clattering to her side.

This was it. He could deliver his final blow and end this, remind her once and for all who the swashbuckler was between them. She scrambled backwards like a crab, dragging her sword with her. But just as he raised his blade to end things, she cried out.

"Rallo, now!"

From out of nowhere, the monkey leapt into the fray, throwing his tiny sword into Liv's outstretched hand. She raised the tiny foil as if it were a dagger and caught the thrust of Flynn's attack, pushing him back.

He looked at Rallo, his mouth agape. "You would help her over me?"

The monkey shrugged and scampered back to his perch. Olivia took advantage of Flynn's distraction and caught the thread of his sleeve with the tip of her full-size blade and tugged hard, upward. A loud ripping sound accompanied the move, and he looked down to see the sleeve of his shirt unraveling.

She grinned, a feline hunger in her gaze. He had never in his life been so equally furious and turned on. He pawed at his sleeve with his free hand, ripping it all the way off and throwing it to the side. "This is Brooks Brothers," he yelped. The audacity.

"I'm sure you have ten more just like it in your closet." On each word, she attacked, a mix of cutovers and straight thrusts, using both her blade and Rallo's tiny dagger. He hardly noticed when she tore at his other sleeve until she giggled.

"There, now you won't get an uneven tan."

He growled in response and ripped that sleeve off too. Their blades met and they pressed against each other again, turning in a circle as if they were dancing a tango. He felt her fumble with something against his chest. "Can't resist me, can you?" He smirked.

"No, I just don't want you to get the impression I'm too buttoned-up." He looked down and realized the double meaning of her words, as Rallo's sword cut through the threads of his shirt buttons.

She smiled and took a step back, breaking their hold. But while he was looking down, she made quick work of the front of his shirt with her sword, zigging and zagging like she was Zorro leaving her mark. As he tried to back away, helpless now, he felt himself trip over the edge of one of the practice mats Fred had set out for them.

Olivia didn't stop though, continuing to tear his shirt to shreds and coming to stand above him, triumphant. The tip of her blade met his throat, while she clenched Rallo's tiny sword between her teeth. And her hair, so neatly coiffed when she'd arrived, was now an unholy mess of black curls.

Flynn looked up at her, careful not to move his chin too low, lest he nick himself on her sword. "If I didn't know better, I'd say you were dying to get me undressed, Miss De Lesseps."

Her eyes flashed, but she stood her ground, grabbing Rallo's sword from her mouth and dropping it. The monkey scampered over to reclaim his weapon. "No, Banks, only cutting you down to size."

"Ah, exposing me?"

She blushed but didn't falter. "I rather think you're the one who's exposed yourself. As an inferior swordsman."

Moments ago, the remark would have annoyed him. It would have egged him on to prove her wrong. But she had bested him. He was impressed.

So instead of replying with bravado or machismo, he smiled and raised his hands to his chest—a tanned, broad chest lightly dusted with blond hair that he noticed her eyeing with interest.

She could tell him she had never seen his films until her face turned blue, but she could not deny that the living, breathing Flynn Banks intrigued her.

He resisted the urge to preen. Mostly because her blade was still at his throat.

"I admit defeat. You undersold it when you said you had *some* experience with a blade."

"I was the fencing champion of my county five years running."

He didn't know what he'd expected, but it wasn't that. He burst out laughing. The little minx.

To his surprise, she started laughing too, that tinkly, champagne-bubble laugh he was already starting to consider one of his favorite sounds. She moved her blade to the side and gently laid it down, offering him her hand. But he wanted to stay here one more moment—on the floor, his shirt flayed to pieces, Liv de Lesseps astride him with her sword at his throat, standing over him like a pirate queen. It was...intoxicating.

Maybe pretending to date this woman wouldn't be so bad.

CHAPTER 8

LIVVY WAS EXHAUSTED. JUDY HAD WANTED THEM TO GO out tonight to celebrate their first week in Hollywood, but it had been a very long week, full of fencing lessons, corset fittings, and only the slightest bit of acting. So, Judy had decided to try to pick up a shift at the Sphinx Club. God knew they needed the money. As for Livvy, she was going to soak in the tub with the lights off and then get into bed early to read the new book she'd picked up from the Hollywood Boulevard library. Livvy let herself in to the tiny apartment and was surprised to find Judy sitting on the couch, clutching a copy of *Reel Stories* to her chest and grinning like a fiend.

"I thought you had to work at the club tonight."

Judy waved her off. "Nah, they want me to get more dance rehearsals in before I take a shift on the floor."

"What's that?" Livvy gestured to the magazine her sister was holding.

Her sister turned it around, holding it open to a giant spread with a large script-font headline that read, *Does Flynn Banks have a new lady love?* It was plastered over images of Livvy and Flynn leaving the lot, hand in hand. Harry had arranged the "candid" photo shoot Tuesday afternoon, tipping off reporters that Flynn and Livvy were going to be taking a late lunch together, having immediately sparked to each other.

Judy squealed. "You're already in the fan magazines, and you've only been in Hollywood for a week!"

Livvy smiled wanly, and Judy shook her head. "Fame is wasted on you," her sister said, sighing. Livvy walked behind the couch and pressed a kiss to the top of her sister's head.

"It certainly is. If I could just act, that'd be one thing. I am enjoying that part of the job. But the rest of it—endless costume fittings, posing for photographers, fame? You can have it. And you will. Soon, it'll be you in those fan magazines."

Judy shook her off. "I was just teasing, Livvy. You deserve it just as much as I do. If not more."

"Deserving's got nothing to do with it. You're the one who wanted it. Who has always wanted it." Livvy looked at her sister and fought back tears. How had they ended up here? Their parents dead. Livvy doing a job that should have been Judy's. And Judy dancing in some seedy joint that didn't seem to care about protecting their employees from harm. It wasn't the life either of them had dreamed of.

God, it had been such a long week. She had considered quitting at least ten times. But then she would remember why they were here, why she'd said yes to the one-picture contract. To get them to Hollywood. To give Judy a crack at her dream. But she had made that goal before a publicity stunt with Flynn Banks was added to the equation, before she had to endure staged photo ops like the one in *Reel Stories* magazine. The whole thing was exhausting.

Judy leaned her head back against the couch and looked up at Livvy. "What's wrong?"

"Nothing," Livvy lied. "I'm just tired."

Judy patted the top of Livvy's hand gently. "I made you supper. Let me get it for you." Judy stood and Livvy collapsed on their couch. When Judy returned, she was carrying a plate and limping her way across the room.

"What happened?" Livvy leapt up, taking the plate from Judy's hands and ushering her sister back to the couch.

Judy rolled her eyes. "Are you going to fuss over me like this every time I take a spill? Dancing is hard on the body, you know that."

Livvy ignored her, crouching on the floor and picking up Judy's foot to examine her ankle more closely. She could see now that it was swollen. Not badly, but enough to tell Judy had sprained it. "First, you hurt your wrist dancing, now your ankle? What kind of safety measures does this place have?"

Judy yanked her foot out of Livvy's grasp, wincing at the sudden movement. "Livvy, you can't go to pieces every time I get a little bump or bruise. It's a normal part of the job."

Livvy eyed her sister skeptically. Judy's story didn't add up. The kid had been dancing most of her life, and she'd never sustained injuries like this in such quick succession. "It seems a bit too frequent for my taste."

"Well, that's why I need more rehearsals. This choreography is harder than anything I've done before."

Livvy wanted to argue and ask more questions. Because something was not right. Judy wasn't telling the whole truth. But Livvy was too tired, and she had to trust her at some point, didn't she? Short of quitting her job to accompany Judy to rehearsals, there wasn't much she could do besides take her sister at her word. So, she bit her tongue and reached for the plate Judy had prepared for her. "Just promise me you'll be more careful, okay?"

"If I promise, will you read this story with me?" Judy held up the glossy magazine, her eyes turning to dreamy moons.

Livvy laughed. "Sure. But let me eat and take a shower first?" Judy hugged her in response.

A half hour later, Livvy emerged from the bathroom, clad in a fluffy pink robe that had seen better days, her damp hair wrapped in a matching towel. Judy was in her pajamas, a matching set in red-and-white stripes, sitting on the couch with the magazine and a bottle of nail polish.

"Paint my toes?" she asked hopefully. Livvy could never say no to Judy, so she nodded and took a seat. She carefully unscrewed the top from the pale-pink polish and applied it to Judy's outstretched toenails.

Judy read aloud from the fan magazine. "'The swashbuckling Flynn Banks was spotted leaving the Evets's Studios lot hand in hand with his new leading lady, the raven-haired beauty Liv de Lesseps.' Oooo, Livvy, they called you a 'raven-haired beauty.'"

Livvy chuckled and moved from Judy's left foot to her right. "They're just being kind." But secretly she was a little pleased at the description.

Judy rolled her eyes and kept reading. "'Miss De Lesseps is new to the pictures, hailing from the stage. She impressed critics last summer as Lady Macbeth at the Hollywood Bowl, taking over as a mere understudy. It earned her a job with Harry Evets, and she is making her screen debut opposite Hollywood's favorite scoundrel. The two were seen headed to a small sidewalk café near the studio, where our sources tell us they were preparing to enjoy a cozy lunch.'"

Livvy snorted. "We didn't even speak. We smiled for the cameras and ordered our food separately. He didn't even pick up the tab." She started blowing on her sister's toes, wanting the polish to get a little tacky before she applied a second coat.

The second she had arrived home the other evening, she had

told Judy about the studio's PR scheme. Livvy had considered not telling her, letting Judy believe they were dating. The fewer people who knew they were faking things, the more likely they would pull this off. But Livvy couldn't lie to her sister, especially not about dating Flynn Banks.

So Livvy had told her the truth. Judy had squealed, insisted it was "just like a movie," and hugged her. But so far, the scheme felt less like a movie and more like a pantomime, with broad tableaus like this "cozy lunch" to signify the hallmarks of a relationship with nothing substantive to back them up.

"I guess a corn dog and a roast beef sandwich that we took back to our respective dressing rooms is their idea of a romantic outing."

Judy shushed her. "Let me finish! 'Flynn Banks has never been spotted out with the same woman twice, but could the lovely Miss De Lesseps finally change his roguish ways?'"

"The answer is no," quipped Livvy.

"You never know," answered Judy, a dreamy, wistful turn in her voice.

"Judy, I told you, this is all a studio setup. It's only for publicity." She was attracted to Flynn, yes, but this could never be anything more than a charade. She would only open herself up for heartbreak if she started wanting otherwise. Flynn Banks was not the kind of man anyone should fall in love with. Besides, Judy was already starry-eyed enough. The last thing Livvy needed to do was encourage her girlish fantasies.

To remind herself, Livvy looked at the old newspaper still lying on the coffee table. Evelyn had given it to her during another costume fitting. Tuesday's copy of the *Los Angeles Examiner* with another headline all about Flynn, a story from one aspiring actress Rhonda Powers, who claimed Flynn had jilted her at the altar.

She suspected Evelyn had given it to her as a warning to keep her distance from Flynn.

But for Livvy, it was a crucial puzzle piece. As soon as she'd seen the story, Livvy knew that Rhonda Powers was the reason that she had been ordered to date Flynn. Harry was trying to kill the story by inventing another romance to distract the public. It was a pretty smart idea, she had to admit.

"This"—she tapped the photo of Flynn in the *Examiner*, a staged portrait that showcased his wolfish grin and the wave in his dark-blond hair—"this is who Flynn Banks is and always will be."

Judy shrugged and wriggled her toes as Livvy screwed the top back on the polish. "There's no reason you can't have some fun though. When's he taking you on a real date?"

"None of them are real dates, Judy."

"Oh, hush, can't you just play along? You need to practice so you don't slip up in front of the press."

Her sister had a point. "Tomorrow. We're going sailing. Some race to Catalina Island. I have to meet him at the marina. I'd rather spend the day with you."

"You couldn't, even if you didn't have a date. I have dance rehearsal all day; we're learning a new floor show."

"Don't get too tired, and don't put too much strain on that ankle. You don't want to make it worse. And make sure you drink plenty of water and bring snacks."

Judy shook her head in exasperation. "Yes, Mother." But she gave Livvy a wink. Judy sighed deeply and leaned back against the pillows. "A sailing trip to Catalina sounds divine."

Livvy wrestled the other cushion and whacked her sister with it. "Cut it out!"

Judy started tickling her until Livvy was breathless with laughter.

"Okay, okay, stop, stop."

Judy barely lifted her hands. "You promise to at least try to have fun? Dating Flynn Banks used to be your dream."

Livvy rolled her eyes. "Don't remind me. I didn't know what he—"

But Judy interrupted her, tickling her with abandon and causing her to shriek with laughter once more.

"Okay, fine, I promise to try to have fun!" She gasped each word in between helpless giggles. She didn't admit that having fun with Flynn Banks was exactly what she was afraid of.

Livvy checked the piece of paper in her hand yet again and breathed a sigh of relief as she turned into the parking lot of the California Yacht Club. Flynn had hastily scrawled directions to the marina on the back of a script page yesterday, but navigating the roads of Los Angeles, she'd gotten lost multiple times. She'd found herself on the edge of an oil field before having to redecipher his messy handwriting and backtrack to where she'd made a wrong turn.

She checked her watch, the plain black-leather strap loose around her wrist. Thank God she'd left early. Despite her multiple detours, she was still on time. She put the car in park and looked grimly at the reporters lining the edge of the docks. They were no doubt here for her and Flynn. She paused and rolled her shoulders, trying to relax. The lunch setup had been child's play compared to this. Now, she really had to sell it.

This was her first official "date" with Flynn. In addition to their posed lunch, they had taken some photos during fencing rehearsal, staging some flirtatious shots with a bare-chested

Flynn. But this was something else entirely. She would be on Flynn's turf—his sailboat—and would face a crowd of reporters who knew him already. She was fresh meat for their hungry camera lenses. At least they would only be on the dock at the start and on a skiff at the finish line. There was no room for them on Flynn's boat. But that meant she would be alone with him all day. Well, not entirely alone—she imagined there would be some kind of crew. But away from the controlling hand of the studio, at any rate.

After she parked, she made her way to the marina and the crowd of reporters, her stomach twisting in knots.

"Miss De Lesseps, give us a smile," one of them crowed, and she did as they asked, hoping they couldn't see her naked terror.

"Here to sail with the pirate himself, are you?"

"Er…" What was she supposed to say to that? Some part of her brain remembered she was supposed to be helping Flynn polish his image. "Oh, well, he only plays a pirate in the movies."

The crowd of photographers laughed. "Try telling that to him," replied a tall man in a gray fedora, pointing in the direction of the dock. She followed the direction of his hand and peered through the metal gate that separated the sidewalk from the gangway to the dock. There was a flurry of activity occurring at each boat slip, with people tying knots and heaving things on and off the decks. Which one was Flynn's?

Her eyes caught on a boat with a black sail, before she noticed the boat's name. *Sea Monkey*. Painted beside it was a cartoon drawing of a small capuchin monkey in a pirate hat, brandishing a sword. It was the spitting image of Rallo.

Livvy giggled. It was adorable how much he loved that monkey. But the press pool had a point. Flynn hadn't exactly made his sailboat an incognito vessel where he could escape the prying eyes of the press and the public. The entire thing screamed, "A silver-screen swashbuckler owns this beauty!"

"So, Miss De Lesseps, is Flynn finally going to win the Catalina Regatta this year?"

Oh God. She had no idea. She didn't have the faintest notion how good of a sailor Flynn was or what his chances were in this race. But Flynn was nothing if not confident, so she plastered the best self-assured grin to her face and replied, "Flynn's going to win. Easily. This race is honestly beneath him."

"Oh ho ho," one of the reporters cried while they all scribbled what she'd said in their notebooks.

"You know he's come in second the last three years?" another reporter asked, staring at her with a deep skepticism.

Rats. She needed to ask Harry to be sure to have the PR department send over informational sheets for her to study before these dates. "Sure I do," she lied. "But this year he'll have his lucky charm by his side." She winked at the reporters, feeling like a complete fool. But for some reason, they seemed to buy it.

"Well," the man who'd mentioned Flynn's race record said. "Then we look forward to photographing your moment of victory in the Avalon harbor when you cross the finish line."

"See you there, boys!" She saluted them like a sailor and struck a pose for the camera, hoping that she could make a run for it. She needed Flynn to keep her from sticking her foot in her mouth.

One of the photographers crept up behind her and mock whispered in her ear, "Be sure he doesn't make you walk the plank." She felt his hand gently graze her backside. She hated men like this. Ones who pretended they were looking out for your welfare, when really they just wanted to take advantage of you. At least Flynn was honest about who he was. She put all of her weight into her right heel as she stepped back and trod on his foot.

He grunted in pain, and she pressed harder before springing forward. "So sorry, I thought you were a piece of rope." She batted her eyelashes at him, playing dumb. Crooking her finger into a hook, she struck a pose for the other reporters. "Arrrrr, mateys." The cameras flashed and she smiled before gripping the handle of the gate behind her and sprinting down the gangway.

She wore cloth moccasins, grateful for the closed-toe shoes as she picked her way through coils of rope and worked to avoid any particularly splintery bits of the dock. She had tried to dress for the occasion, wearing jeans and a cap-sleeve red sweater, a dark-blue silk scarf tied around her neck. Her father was a navy man, though the closest she had ever come to a sailboat was a miniature one she'd played with as a girl. But she'd always believed dressing for the job was the best way to project an air of confidence. She'd passed her first test anyway, mugging for the cameras.

"Liv?" a voice asked. Flynn's tan face popped up from behind the mast. He wolf-whistled as he took her in, and she couldn't help but blush.

"Don't do that!" she hissed, trying to make sure no one could hear her.

"What? Admire the girl who's captured my heart?" Flynn teased. He said it loudly for the benefit of the men on the dock. She looked back and watched them all scribble furiously in their notepads. She smiled in spite of herself. "Come aboard." He waved his arm, urging her to step onto the ship. "We shove off in around fifteen minutes."

He turned to the thick rope he was winding around a piece of metal as she nervously eyed the back of the boat, wondering what the best approach would be.

He looked back at her. "Don't tell me you've never been on a sailboat before!"

She grimaced and nodded.

"This isn't like when you told me you had 'some' experience with fencing, is it?"

At that, she outright laughed. Flynn had a wicked sense of humor, but she liked it. Probably a little too much. "No, no, I really have no idea what I'm doing."

"Perfect, no time like the present to learn." He stepped onto the lip of the boat, looking more like a stevedore than a movie star in a pair of dark slacks, a tight white T-shirt that accentuated his generous biceps, and a matching white captain's hat. It worked for him though. He looked roguish and windblown and absurdly handsome.

He extended his hand and Livvy took it, feeling the calluses of his palm close around her fingers as he helped her step up. She placed one foot on the edge of the boat and paused as it swayed underneath her. The noisy click of the cameras whirred in the distance.

He chuckled. "Come on, I've got you. I promise."

She gingerly lifted her other foot from the dock and stepped aboard, losing her balance and tumbling straight into the solid wall of his chest. She let out a muffled *oof* before he placed his hands on her waist, lifted her up, and deposited her on the deck. Someone, she was certain it was Mr. Gray Fedora, crowed suggestively.

But Flynn didn't react. Nor did he remove his hands immediately, instead letting them linger, making sure she had steady footing. He was looking at her earnestly, one of his eyebrows raised. "You all right?" Livvy could tell that he wasn't asking so that he could elongate this picture-worthy moment. He genuinely wanted to know.

She met his gaze and something passed between them, an electric current of want that was gone as quickly as it came. It was just that he looked so very much like the hero of one of his films right now—the sun hitting his face, turning his hair to burnished gold. The sight of it made her feel like a teenager again, longing for a man who wasn't real.

Flynn cleared his throat and swiftly dropped his hands. She found herself mourning the loss of them, missing the sensation of the rough edges of his fingers digging into her sides and the safe feeling it filled her with.

He had asked her a question, she realized. "Oh, I'm fine," she chirped, her voice unnatural to her ears.

"Don't you worry. You'll have your sea legs in no time." He went back to the rope he had been working with, tying it into a fancy knot. She sat down on what appeared to be an upturned bucket, trying to peer into the depths of the boat's cabin to see who else might be on board. Someone was moving about in the shadows, but she couldn't make out their face.

Flynn followed the direction of her gaze. "Oh, that's Rex. He's repairing some rigging. He takes care of the boat for me."

She nodded, still unsure what to say. On set, it had been so easy to hold her own against him, but here she was out of her depths. She was afraid to put a toe out of place, lest she fall overboard or signal something was off between them to the press.

"Sorry to disappoint you, if you thought you were going to have me all to yourself."

She snorted. "Why on earth would I think that?" But a rush of heat flared between her legs, and she cursed the effect he had on her.

He grinned, and she was glad she was already sitting down—because God help her, it was enough to make her swoon. The boys on shore would've loved that. She suddenly resented Rex, whoever he was. Because maybe, if it was just the two of them, he would take her down into that cabin and ravish her. She had never been ravished. But she would quite like to be. It was something she'd never admitted to herself before. At least not outside the confines of her bedroom in the dead of the night. But Flynn brought out something wild in her. Made her crave things that her mother would've said did not befit a lady.

Things that she knew should make her blush at the mere thought of them. But why would she be ashamed of such feelings? Eventually, she would make love to a man. That was the natural course of things. And she supposed there were few men with as much experience as Flynn had. He would know exactly how to touch her, how much pressure to use, where to kiss her... Her jaw went slack envisioning it.

He chuckled and she knew he had read her like a book. "You wouldn't be the first lady to dream of getting me alone." His English accent, sometimes clipped and straightforward, had melted into something softer and sexier. Like butter spread over a roll. Or, she supposed, in his case, clotted cream over a scone.

She scoffed, desperate to hide that she had been imagining exactly that. She'd been listening to Judy's flights of fancy too much. "That's not a dream, that's a nightmare." Livvy realized a moment too late how loud she'd been, and her head snapped back to the shore to make sure the reporters hadn't heard her.

He chuckled. "Don't worry, they didn't hear you. But I can kiss you passionately if you think it will help." She turned bright red at his suggestion, embarrassed not so much by her fantasy as by being caught out. This was exactly what she had to avoid. The man in her daydreams was a white knight. The flesh-and-blood figure before her was a cad. She reminded herself of Rhonda

Powers, the poor girl he'd jilted. That would be her fate too if she didn't pull herself together.

"Tell me about your boat," she said. Anything to change the subject.

He gave her a look, making it clear he knew exactly what she was up to, but he answered her question. "I've had her about two years. Bought her by accident."

She stared at him. "How on earth do you buy a boat by accident?"

"I was drunk." He said it so matter-of-factly.

"That is the answer to almost any story involving you, isn't it?"

He flashed her a smile, baring his teeth in a predatory manner that made a little shiver run down her spine. "That'd be a safe bet." She giggled in spite of herself. "Dash told me the next morning that I had insisted it was such a brilliant party I required a souvenir, so I wrote the host a check for his fifty-seven-foot yawl."

"Dash, as in Dash Howard?"

"Yes. He's my best friend. Used to sail with me. Before he fell in love." Livvy could tell just what Flynn Banks thought of love from his tone of voice. He'd spat out the word like he was swearing.

But beneath that, she sensed a loneliness. It was more the faraway look in his eyes than anything else, so subtle people would miss it unless they knew what it was to feel alone in this world. A look she was sure Flynn would deny. It was clear he missed his pal.

"Anyway, I tried to get out of it. But the wily bastard had cashed the check first thing. Worked out okay though. This boat's the only girl I'd want to tie myself to." He patted the strong wood beam of her mast lovingly. Flynn looked at the boat the way Livvy looked at her sister—with devotion and deep-seated care.

"And where'd you get the name?" Livvy was fairly certain she knew the answer, but she was afraid once they stopped talking about the boat, they would have exhausted all topics of conversation besides Flynn's tireless flirting. This relationship was as phony as the stuffed parrot perched on top of the boat's cabin—and it needed to stay that way.

"The *Sea Monkey*?" He grinned, more genuine and less predatory this time. "Surely you could tell from the drawing I've named her after Rallo. That little bugger might have turned coat and thrown his lot in with you, but I love him. I'm still convinced he's the reason my career exploded. People love a cheeky monkey."

"That they do." But Livvy wasn't talking about Rallo. She rather thought Flynn had a kindred spirit in the capuchin. They were both scallywags who seemed to love a good time and a pretty girl. "Has he ever been on the boat?"

"Rallo? No, I'm worried he'd scamper overboard and I wouldn't catch him in time. But sometimes I keep him for the weekend at my house in Malibu. Lionel trusts me with him. Rallo's good company. Doesn't steal my liquor or my women, and knows how to have a good time."

Livvy shook her head. Flynn was incorrigible. But damn if he wasn't also infernally charming.

She watched as Flynn methodically loosed the sail, hundreds of feet of material catching the wind and billowing to the side. The muscles and sinews of his arms flexed and stretched as he worked the fabric, and she found herself mesmerized by what he was doing, unable to take her eyes off the deft, sure movements of his hands. He uncoiled another length of rope and let it glide through his fingers as the thick pole running along the bottom of the sail swung to the right.

"Watch out for the boom," he called out. She had been so busy staring at him that she hadn't noticed the heavy pole was swinging in her direction. She scrambled to leap off the overturned bucket she was perched on and darted backwards. The pole stopped only a foot or so in front of her.

Her cheeks bloomed with irritation and shame. Did he know she'd been looking at him like he was a piece of fresh meat at a butcher shop? God, she'd practically been licking her chops. This wouldn't do. She was a nice girl. And nice girls didn't ogle notorious scoundrels as if they were a particularly tasty meal. Maybe the sea air was going to her head. She needed to pull herself together.

"I take it that's the boom," she replied dryly, striving to sound sarcastic.

"That it is," he told her archly, before giving her a wink. "You're a quick learner."

Oh God, now he was flirting with her again. "Look, I can leave if I'm in your way. We can go out to dinner tomorrow or something instead." She was already mentally planning the lunch she'd make and bring to Judy at the club. But to her surprise, he looked chagrined.

"What'll you tell those fellas?" He shrugged his shoulder in the direction of the press pool. A few of them were still watching them through the gate. The others were passing out life preservers between them, getting ready for their own voyage so that they could photograph the winners at the finish line. But before she could devise an excuse, Flynn crossed over to her and reached behind her, untying a section of rope that was tied taut to the dock. "Sorry. I forgot you're new to this, should've been more careful."

Well, that was...something. She didn't get the impression that Flynn Banks was a man who apologized very often.

Rex emerged from the cabin and moved to the front of the boat, dipping his head in her direction. "Miss," he said politely.

She watched as he unfurled a sail at the front of the boat. "What's that?"

Flynn craned his neck to see where she was pointing. "The jib, it's the secondary sail." Finished with his task, Flynn put his hands on his hips and looked at her. She tried not to stare at the way it made his biceps bulge beneath the tight line of his shirt-sleeve. He looked like he'd painted the shirt on this morning, but he wasn't remotely self-conscious. A peacock for the press, on his boat, he appeared comfortable enough in his own skin to have no need of showing off. It only made him more attractive.

He peered at her. "You've really never sailed?"

She shrugged. "My father was in the navy, and he was insistent that a ship was no place for a lady. Wouldn't even let me near the dock."

"Well, given that I'm the type of character you find round these parts, maybe he had the right idea." He chuckled. "But it's a shame he never taught you. Nothing calms the spirit like a day on the water. Let me show you." He offered his hand once more and helped her clamber over several coils of rope and the assemblage of pulleys and weights around the mast, before setting her in a small chair screwed into the boat. "This is how you control the boom, which you now know is what we call the pole that runs along the bottom of the mainsail." He wrapped his hands around a smaller piece of wood conveniently located in front of the chair. "This here is the tiller for the boom. It moves it from left to right." He demonstrated for her. "You'll be in charge of it during the race."

"What? I have no idea what I'm doing. We'll lose. And I told the press you were going to take first place easily."

He chuckled. "From your lips to God's ears."

"Look, if you want a prayer of winning this race, you should do it. Or make Rex."

"No, you'll be a natural, I can already tell. Besides, I'll be at the helm." He gestured at the captain's wheel that looked remarkably similar to the ones she'd seen him man in the pictures. She stifled a giggle and he gave her a queer look, as if assessing what exactly was so funny. "Rex is in charge of the jib. I promise, the boom tiller is the easiest job we've got. Try it."

She looked back and forth, from the small piece of wood to his face, but he only smiled at her encouragingly.

"What have I got myself into?" she muttered, taking hold of the wood and feeling it move easily with the weight of her hand.

"See? Told you." It was a lot simpler than she'd expected. The boom shifted with the lightest touch. "Just be sure that you duck if you bring it back in your direction."

She followed the line of the sail, noting that if she swung the boom back around to the left, it would careen directly into her unless she bent over. She gave Flynn a shaky thumbs-up, which made him smile.

"You'll be fine," he said. "The only other rule is to make sure you don't get overzealous, as that could make us capsize."

Capsize? She gave him a panicked look. That was not a possibility she had contemplated. What if she drowned? What would Judy do without her? Could her sister survive another loss? Their parents might have been gone four years, but there were days where the grief still felt like a fresh wound. She stood from the chair, terrified of the implication, but Flynn simply thrust a cream-colored life jacket in her direction. "You'll be fine. I've been sailing since I was a boy, and I've never capsized."

She raised her eyebrow at him. But he simply grabbed her hands, took the life jacket back, and pulled it gingerly over her head. "There. Now, even if we have an emergency, this will keep you safe."

Then, standing behind her, he took the ends of the cloth ties and tugged them until the life jacket cinched around her waist. His arms were around her. Purely for perfunctory reasons. But she was shocked at the care with which he held her, the featherlight touches he used as he checked each gap and tie to make sure the life jacket was secure. He came around to the front and tied off the strings in a little bow.

Livvy looked up into his eyes, and his gaze met hers. There was a moment of stillness where that mischievous twinkle in his eyes, so often his defining feature, was replaced with something more soulful. She studied his face and noticed a tiny scar in the corner of his eyebrow. She desperately wanted to reach out and touch it, feel the roughness of the hewn skin beneath the soft hair of his brows. She leaned toward him, as if pulled by some invisible force. She was certain she looked ridiculous doing so, trussed up in this floatation device.

But Flynn didn't seem to care. He appeared to be wrestling with something as he took a step toward her. She bit her lip, waiting, suspended in silent attraction. Would he kiss her? Even though no one was watching? Should she let him?

She lifted her head, turning her lips toward his face, offering herself up to him. Maybe if they did kiss, it would get this raging lust out of her system. She would fulfill her teenage fantasy and be done with it. Once and for all.

But as she waited for his mouth to meet hers, his hands dropped from her sides. He stepped back and reached down to fiddle with a pulley, readjusting his trousers as he stood. He gestured at the tiller again. "Just use a gentle touch and don't thrust it too quickly in one direction. Good life advice in general." He waggled his eyebrows and winked at her.

As quickly as it had come, the moment was gone. Flynn Banks, louche rogue, was back in full force.

Livvy refused to be embarrassed. Not by their near kiss, nor his double entendre. She might be an inexperienced slip of a girl, but he didn't need to know that. Instead, she stared him down and replied, "I'm surprised at you."

He smirked. "Am I too rough for your delicate sensibilities?"

"No, it's just that your reputation as a lothario precedes you, which would lead me to believe that you know ladies rather enjoy it when you thrust quickly in one direction."

He gaped at her and a sense of pride bloomed in her chest. She relished being able to surprise him. Hell, she'd even surprised herself. But Flynn Banks and his stupid devilish smile, his ridiculous sparkling blue eyes, and his adorable little eyebrow scar were not going to get the best of her. This relationship was for show, for the benefit of the press and the gullible public. She'd do best to remember that if she wanted to keep her job and help Judy achieve her dreams.

Livvy didn't break his gaze as she deposited herself back in her chair and seized the tiller with her hand, relishing the way Flynn's eyes widened as she purposefully and languidly wrapped her long fingers around the wooden handle.

He looked away, and she thought she heard him mutter, "Bloody woman is trying to kill me."

But Livvy ignored him and simply looked ahead at the harbor, admiring the fleet of sailboats taking their place in a line. She inhaled and relished the scent of the sea air. She had come to Hollywood for a fresh start. One filled with adventure and excitement and a bright future for Judy. So then, what was stopping her? Here she was, about to participate in a regatta with one of Hollywood's dreamiest stars, doing something she never would have imagined. She should seize the opportunity. She exhaled, giving herself permission to have a good time. To enjoy the day, rather than being on constant high alert for what could go wrong.

Judy had told her to have fun. Okay, she would—Flynn Banks and his dirty mind be damned. She craned her head at Flynn and nodded in the direction of the ships at the starting line. "What next, Captain Banks?"

CHAPTER 9

A FRESH WAVE OF SEA SPRAY HIT FLYNN IN THE FACE, AND he licked at the salt water at the edge of his mouth. He felt the best he had in days, on the water with the wind on his back. Out here, his troubles melted away, and it was as if he were Long John Silver or Jim Hawkins embarking on a grand adventure. It had been that way since he was a boy, since his mother had first read him *Treasure Island* and his father had allowed him to learn to sail on a tiny skiff on the estate pond.

He craned his head to the side. They were neck and neck with the boat in the lead—the *Santa Guadalupe,* a schooner that belonged to Johnny Weissmuller, the former Olympian who had found fame starring as Edgar Rice Burroughs's jungle hero in a series of films. Flynn would not be bested by bloody Tarzan. He'd been racing in the Catalina Regatta since he'd bought the *Sea Monkey,* and he had never won. Weissmuller had always beaten him. But not today. Especially not since Livvy had boasted to the reporters that he was going to win. It was cute, really, that she was so confident in him. He couldn't disappoint her.

He could see the isthmus of Catalina Island in the distance. At most, they had about ten miles to go. They were over halfway, and they'd maintained a steady pace in second place. But if they could overtake the *Santa Guadalupe* in the last leg, they could eke out a win (and he could save face with the press pool).

"Tack her to the left," Flynn bellowed. Rex quickly let out a string of rope to change the direction of the jib sail and let the wind flow to the opposite side.

"Olivia, tack the boom!" Flynn called. The girl furiously pulled at the tiller, and the boom swung across. She ducked and the sail flew clear over her back. He'd been right; she was a natural. It didn't matter that she'd never sailed before. She instinctively understood what to do. He never would've pegged her for it the first night they'd met, but she kept surprising him. First, with her fencing skills; then, her ribald sense of humor; and now, with her ability to take to sailing like a duck to water.

She looked back at him, making sure she'd done it right, and he gave her a huge smile. "Perfect!"

Her face lit up with pride, which made his stomach do something squiggly. Or maybe it was the choppy surf. It was particularly rough today. That must be it, because his stomach had never once somersaulted over a woman. The mere idea was absurd.

To be honest, he'd only invited her to join him because he was going to race regardless. No matter what Harry Evets or the Legion of Decency wanted, he would not have missed the Catalina Regatta. It was the biggest race of the year, and with the upgrades he'd made to the *Sea Monkey* over the last few months, he knew he had a real shot at winning. So, he'd told Harry that Olivia could come along if she liked, and they'd be sure to smile nice for the cameras. If Harry was going to foist dates on him for the next three months, Flynn wasn't going to skip out on any of the pleasures in his life, including sailing. He was certain the Legion of Decency would prefer he spent his weekends in self-flagellation, but that had never been his style.

Life was meant to be savored, and he'd never had any hesitation about showing up to the banquet of existence and gorging himself. Some might call that indulgent, even gluttonous. But what was it all for if not to be enjoyed? His mother had taught him that lesson. One he'd watched her learn the hard way.

Part of him had hoped Olivia would decline his invitation. Women were supposed to be bad luck onboard a ship, and in his experience, Hollywood dames preferred ballrooms to poop decks. Flynn knew this PR relationship was important, and he would've made up for it by taking her out every night the next week. But Olivia had agreed. And now he was glad she was here.

The bow of the *Sea Monkey* caught a surging wave, and the boat careened sharply to its starboard side. Shit, he hadn't been paying close enough attention. The wheel of the helm jerked in his hands and the sail swung in the wind.

"Watch out!"

The boom was careening backwards, straight in the direction of Olivia's temple. Flynn leapt without thinking, knocking her from the chair and tackling her to the deck.

"Oof!" She looked up and her eyes widened in terror as she watched the heavy metal pole pass directly over them, narrowly missing the curve of Flynn's back.

He didn't have time to enjoy the feel of her slight curves underneath him, because the next thing he knew, the mainsail tore from its riggings, fluttering in the wind.

Forget winning the race. At this point, Flynn was more concerned about staying afloat. He looked toward the bow and watched as Rex valiantly wrestled with the jib, keeping the *Sea Monkey* from going entirely horizontal into the waves.

Flynn rolled off Olivia and leapt up. He put his feet on the metal rungs along the bottom of the mast and started climbing.

He needed to fix the sail. He was scrambling for purchase when he felt a sharp tug between his shoulder blades.

Olivia called out, "Flynn! The pulley."

He craned his neck and noticed that the back of his shirt had wedged itself into one of the gears they used to hoist and maneuver the sail. He swore loudly and strained upward, trying to free himself in vain. His eyes darted between Olivia and the ragged sail.

He had to fix this. To hell with it.

He clung to the mast with his legs and one arm, while he used the other to pull the shirt over his head. Now shirtless, he finally reached the top of the mast and grabbed for the sail that had torn from the top side of the rigging. A gust of wind blew it from his grasp and the boom swung yet again, the force of its motion nearly knocking him from the mast.

He fought to right himself and looked down to see Olivia clambering over the midsection of the boat, crawling over the raised roof and skylight that covered the central cabin. What was the girl doing? She was going to get herself killed. And good luck to Harry Evets if he had to explain that to the press and the goddamn Legion of Decency.

But Olivia maneuvered herself to the front end of the boom. She grabbed hold of it with both her hands and, with what looked like an immense strain, held it in place.

"I'll keep her steady," she called. "Fix the sail."

He'd be damned. Olivia Blount, newly minted sailor, was saving his arse. And the mainsail of the *Sea Monkey* at that. He admired the way the sunlight caught her dark hair, how her violet eyes flashed with the intensity of her efforts. She was a sight to behold, a pirate queen if there ever was one.

"Stop ogling me and go!" she cried through gritted teeth.

Right, yes—their romance might be fake, but their current situation was all too real.

Shaken from his temporary brush with insanity, Flynn pushed himself forward to the sail and managed to grip the black fabric in his hands. It had torn loose from the rungs that attached it to the metal arc of the frame. He worked swiftly to tie it back together, using a halyard hitch to hold it taut. The entire thing would have to be refitted, but for now, this would have to do.

He hung from the top of the sail, finishing the last knot with one hand as he held himself to the frame with both legs and the other arm. *Now* who was the bloody sea monkey? But the sail swung wildly again, throwing Olivia back against the roof of the cabin and leaving him dangling from one arm.

He knew the moment Olivia saw him because she screamed. That caught the attention of Rex, who called out, "We need to tack the boat to the leeward side."

Flynn cursed, fumbling uselessly at the sail with his legs, trying to find some foothold. But he was hanging from the middle of the sail with a few feet of fabric between him and the mast. Olivia had no clue what tack or leeward side meant—he'd bet the *Sea Monkey* on it.

"Olivia!" he called out. She looked up at him. "Grab the helm and turn the back of the ship toward the wind!"

She nodded and ran for the wheel, which was spinning wildly without him there to captain it. Olivia twisted the helm sharply to her left and the sail swung to the right, leaving Flynn now hanging over open water.

"Not that way!" he yelped. She swore and turned it back to the right, bringing him back over the boat. "Now, hold it steady."

She did as she was told, grimacing as the force of the water and the wind fought against her. The bow of the boat turned into the wind, and the *Sea Monkey* righted itself, resuming a smooth sail now that its keel was once again aligned with the current.

Flynn breathed a sigh of relief and looked down. He was just above the roof of the cabin; if he timed it right, he would only fall a couple feet. It wouldn't be a soft landing, but it was better than staying stuck up here. He swung himself back and forth.

"What are you doing?" Olivia shrieked. The note of concern in her voice was adorable. He couldn't remember the last time a woman had cared much whether he lived or died. In fact, they seemed to usually advocate for the latter after about twenty-four hours.

He didn't answer but pulled his knees up and let go of the mast with both hands. His stomach swooped as he plummeted through the air, but he managed to land mostly on his feet, bracing himself with his hands to help him find his center of gravity. He then slid off the side of the cabin and back down to the deck.

Olivia was gaping at him, still holding the helm tight as Rex continued to man the jib at the bow. "What on earth were you thinking?"

"That my arms were getting tired holding onto that sail."

"You, you, you could've broken something. Or been seriously injured."

He shrugged. "But I wasn't." In fact, now that he'd escaped with nothing more bruised than his reputation as a sailor, he'd say that had been rather fun. Somewhere along the way he'd lost his hat, and he noticed it discarded near the helm at Olivia's feet. "Shall we share the wheel?"

He scooped up the hat and placed it on her head, pressing against her and slipping his arms around her to help her hold the helm in place. With his shirt still hanging from the pulley above, he could feel the sinuous shape of her, even beneath the bulk of the life preserver.

But before he knew it, she was gently elbowing him. "I've got it."

He chuckled and took a step back. "One successful rescue of the *Sea Monkey* and its captain, and now you're an expert?"

She twisted her head around to stick her tongue out at him. Christ, she was adorable with the brim of his hat sitting low on her brow. With every passing moment, he was less annoyed that Harry had chosen her for this charade. "No, but...I think we can still win this race."

She nodded in the direction of the *Santa Guadalupe*. In the flurry of fighting to keep the ship upright, he hadn't noticed Weissmuller's boat had hit the same rogue wave that they had. Somehow the *Sea Monkey* had pulled ahead, and the crew of the *Santa Guadalupe* was still getting their boat back on track.

By George, Olivia was right. The finish line was in sight.

He grinned at Olivia. "Stay there." Flynn sprinted to the front of the boat, where Rex was deftly handling the jib.

"Rex, we're in the lead." Flynn was breathless with excitement and felt like a boy again.

Rex looked over his shoulder at the *Santa Guadalupe* and gave Flynn a shit-eating grin. "That we are."

"Think we can do it? I had to tie the sail back to the frame."

Rex craned his head up to look at the top of the mainsail, studying Flynn's handiwork. "Those are good, strong knots. They should hold."

Excitement sparked in Flynn's belly. He hated losing. At anything. Cards. Horse racing. Women. But he especially hated losing out here on the water, a place that felt like his second home. "Let's go for it."

Rex smiled and turned the jib more sharply to the port side. The sail caught a fresh wind, gaining speed in the water.

Flynn whooped and hollered, sprinting back toward the helm. "Olivia, keep her steady, we'll do the rest."

She bit her lip and gave him a tight nod.

He ran to the rigging lining the side of the cabin on the port side, loosening it so that the mainsail billowed and ballooned with the force of the wind, once again picking up speed. He grabbed hold of the rigging and leaned over the side of the boat, looking toward the finish line. He raised his fist in the air and cheered, knowing in his bones that this was it.

"Flynn, look out!" He turned at the sound of Olivia's voice, only to see the *Santa Guadalupe* gaining on them. Weissmuller was leaning off his own rigging, giving Flynn a wicked grin and brandishing a cutlass as if he was mocking him.

If he wanted to make fun of Flynn's swashbuckling ways, so be it. Flynn would earn the title all the more by besting the apeman in this race.

Olivia seemed to read his mind. "Flynn, we need to pull to the left."

"What? No, that will put us in danger of capsizing again."

"Fine, suit yourself." She winced as the wheel of the ship tugged her arms to the right and she fought to hold it steady. "But if you want to win, your only chance is pulling to the left."

He looked back, studying the narrowing distance between him and the *Santa Guadalupe*, and the *Sea Monkey*'s path if they did as she said. Damn it, she was right. But what she suggested was madness. He'd done it only once. In a movie. He had no idea if it would actually work in real life.

Rex looked back at them both and called out, "Mate, you

can't seriously be considering that. It's potential suicide. The sail might not hold with that kind of wind pressure."

Flynn looked up at the knots he'd tied, the ends of the sail starting to fray. They only had a couple more miles to go. They could make it. They had to.

"What should I do?" yelled Olivia, a steely determination in her gaze.

"Pull to the left." He heard Rex swear loudly as he leapt from the rigging and crouched to the deck, allowing the boom and the mainsail to swing back to the port side of the *Sea Monkey*. He worked swiftly, retying the knots he'd only just undone and racing to the starboard side to undo the rigging there and change the direction of the wind in the sail. It was riskier with the current.

Olivia was pressed against the wheel, using all her weight to hold it steady. "It's too heavy."

"It's only a few more minutes." He stood. The *Santa Guadalupe* had stopped in the water. It had worked. They'd cut off the other ship's wind power with their sail.

They raced ahead as the crew of the *Santa Guadalupe* struggled to pivot, their sails flat and lifeless. Flynn crowed with excitement and extended a two-finger salute in Weissmuller's direction as the *Sea Monkey* made a swift clip through the water, drawing ever closer to the isthmus.

"Flynn," Olivia gasped. He looked over to see her bent over the wheel, her toes lifting from the deck.

He ran to her, placing his hands over hers and wresting the helm into place. "Hold on," he gritted out. She nodded and he felt her fingers tighten under his.

He heard a ripping sound and their heads snapped up to see the sail tearing from the makeshift knots he'd made. Shit. He looked ahead to the finish line; they were so close.

"I don't think we can make it," Olivia hissed. Her eyes widened as the next knot tore from the metal rung holding it in place. There were four more knots and they had a mile to go.

"We can make it. Just, whatever you do, don't let go of this wheel." They were committed now. It was too late to turn back. They'd all be pitched into the sea if they didn't stay the course.

Another tear, and Flynn watched in horror as one of the metal rings broke away from the frame of the sail and plunked into the ocean. Three more. There were still three more knots.

He looked out across the water. A half mile now. The *Santa Guadalupe* had gotten underway again, but if the *Sea Monkey* kept going, they had a comfortable lead.

He pressed against her more firmly, and she squeaked at the feel of him against her backside. "This isn't the time to be priggish," he growled. She didn't answer but squeezed herself ever closer to the wheel, putting space between them again. He could see her knuckles under his, white and straining with the tension of keeping the wheel in place. But she didn't let go. Instead, as another knot tore and the top of the sail began to flutter, she held on even more tightly.

Suddenly, she screamed as a buoy appeared out of nowhere in front of them, and she yanked the wheel to the right instinctually.

Flynn swore as everything on the ship lurched to the starboard side, including Rex, who wobbled and slid across the deck, struggling to keep his balance. Only Olivia and Flynn, clinging to the helm with all their strength, did not move.

He was about to scold her for her inability to control her shock when he looked up and watched as the port side of the *Sea Monkey* barely skirted the buoy that Olivia had spotted. She had saved them from almost certain shipwreck. If they'd held their course, they would've collided head-on with the buoy, and he didn't want to know what kind of damage that would've done to the hull.

He watched open-mouthed as the sail, seeming to understand its work was done, tore through its final two knots and fluttered down to the deck just as they crossed the finish line.

A small dinghy containing two men erupted into applause and cheers of "Congratulations." Flynn realized they were the line judges, there in the event of a photo finish. But they weren't necessary. The *Sea Monkey* had won handily, because of Olivia—her bravery and her quick thinking. He was stunned.

"Flynn, we won," Olivia murmured, clearly not sure of herself.

"We won." He said the words, scarcely believing them, letting the enormity of the moment sink in. Even with Dash onboard in a previous year, they had not managed to snag first place. But this woman—Olivia Blount, Liv De Lesseps, his phony girlfriend—had done it. Not only that, but she'd snatched victory from the jaws of potential disaster.

He erupted into loud cheers. "We! Won! We did it!" Flynn stood on an apple crate behind Olivia and whooped.

He smiled at her. "You won, Olivia! You saved us all!" Her pink lips, which had become thin white lines in the anxiety of the final minutes of the race, were glistening and plump once more as she broke into a broad grin and crowed with delight.

"I did, I really did it!" She lifted her arms. "Whoooo-hoooo!" She ran to him, and before he knew what was happening, she leapt into his arms and wrapped her legs around his waist, her arms around his neck. "*We won!*"

He fumbled to catch her, palming the curve of her ass and clinging to her to keep her from falling in excitement. He couldn't help it; he broke out into peals of joyous laughter. He quite liked this, the feel of her wrapped around him, her dainty hands clutching at his bare back. He liked it perhaps a bit too much. He suspected that, in spite of her ribald sense of humor, she was something of an innocent—and imagining her hands clutching at his back in a more horizontal position was not the direction his mind should be going. He didn't romance girls like Olivia Blount. For a host of reasons. But she felt so deliciously wonderful in his arms as he twirled her in a circle, both of them giggling with carefree abandon.

She kissed him on the cheek and then shrieked in exuberant surprise. "I can't believe I just did that."

"I can't either," he quipped, continuing to spin her, the loose curls of her raven hair streaming behind her.

He saw the spark of a flashbulb and noticed that there was a second dinghy, a larger one, that held the crop of reporters who had greeted them on the dock this morning. The press had sailed ahead, and now they were capturing his and Livvy's victory. Briefly, he thought how this photo would please Harry. It would really sell the supposed budding romance between him and Livvy. But truthfully, Flynn didn't much care. This wasn't like the lunch date the other day with its staged, ridiculous setup. This moment of unfettered joy was utterly and entirely real.

And it surprised him that the notion made him absurdly happy. Because he realized that ever since he'd hopped into the back seat of Olivia Blount's car, one thing was true—he was no longer bored.

CHAPTER 10

LIVVY LEANED AGAINST THE SHELL OF THE *SEA MONKEY*'S cabin and watched the sun creep toward the horizon. Avalon was charming, a little town of bric-a-brac houses nestled into the side of the hill on Catalina Island. At the edge of the bay was a large, round structure with a terra-cotta roof and a line of colonnades that made the building resemble an oversized carousel. She recognized it from a postcard a friend had once sent her—the Catalina Casino. The sun bathed the casino in warm oranges and soft pinks, transforming the circular building into a colorful, massive scoop of ice cream floating on top of the water.

They'd left Rex at Two Harbors, where he'd gone ashore to find the parts necessary to repair the sail. The *Sea Monkey* had a backup engine in case of emergency; they just hadn't been able to use it in the race without being disqualified. So while Rex scrounged for new parts, Flynn had motored him and Livvy over to Avalon and they'd anchored in the harbor. He was in the galley, scrounging up dinner, and Livvy almost jumped when he called out, "Food's ready."

"Oh, but you must come see the casino! It looks so lovely in the late evening sun."

He chuckled and came to stand beside her. "One of my favorite parts of sailing is getting to see the sunset on the water."

She could understand why. It was beautiful, peaceful. A lot calmer than running out of a nightclub with a scorned woman hot on your heels.

He bumped his shoulder against hers. "You ever been to the casino?" he asked, nodding in the direction of Avalon's most notable landmark.

She shook her head. "No, this is only my second time in Los Angeles, and I haven't been here very long."

"You have to go! They get the best bands. I've seen the Dorsey Brothers there three times! And Benny Goodman and his band last Christmas."

"It sounds wonderful," she said dreamily. It would be a long while before she could afford the luxury of something like going to a dance at the Catalina Casino. Not until she knew that Judy was secure, that they both could settle into their new lives in Hollywood. She couldn't remember the last time she'd gone dancing. Or done something purely for the fun of it.

"It is. I'll have to take you some time."

She turned to him and swallowed at the look in his eyes. She expected to see something hungry there, wolfish even. But instead, he was gazing at her with admiration and care. Her stomach somersaulted at the thought of going dancing with Flynn Banks, but she hated to admit it. The kiss she'd given him earlier twisted her in knots. She shouldn't have done that. It was only a peck on the cheek, but it had probably given him the wrong idea. At least the moment had been photographed. Harry Evets couldn't question that she was trying her hardest to follow marching orders, and if Flynn questioned her, she could claim it had only been for the cameras. "Oh no, I couldn't—"

He grinned and raised his eyebrows. "Why? We are dating, after all."

She blushed but held his gaze. "We're just playing pretend," she murmured.

He shrugged, as if to say, "Suit yourself," and ducked back into the ship's cabin. "Dinner's getting cold."

She followed him inside and smiled when she saw the table wedged in between a stack of his tackle gear, as well as a pile of shoes and shirts topped with a book on knot tying. He'd laid a red-and-white-checked tablecloth over the small round table and lit a candle inside one of those red glass jars she always saw at Italian restaurants.

"This is...romantic." She felt uneasy. There was no one here watching them, taking their picture. Who was this for?

Flynn bit his lip. She had never seen him look bashful before. She hadn't thought it an emotion he was capable of feeling. "It's nothing."

She didn't push him on the issue, taking it at face value as something nice he'd done for her, tidying up the space and trying to make it look presentable. Instead, she gave him a wan smile, pulled up a stool, and looked at the asparagus and fresh fish on her plate.

Flynn leaned against the galley countertop, crossed his arms over his chest, and waited for her to take a bite, staring at her like a puppy waiting for its dinner. She hardly expected Flynn to be a culinary expert. But he looked so hopeful. No matter what, she would say it was good.

But when she took a bite, she was surprised to find the fish was flavorful, the marinade of lemon and fresh spices sweeping over her tongue and its tart, acidic taste blending perfectly with the delicate breadcrumbs he'd topped it with. "This is delicious!"

A broad grin, one far more innocent than his usual roguish smile, spread across his face. "You like it?"

"It's superb, so much better than I was expecting." She picked up her napkin and held it to her face. "Shoot, I didn't mean—"

He waved her off, sitting down and digging into his own plate. "It's okay. You didn't think I could cook, did you?"

She grimaced and wrinkled her nose. "No, not really. I thought that—"

"That I'm a consummate bachelor who has a personal chef in his employ."

She swallowed the bite she'd just taken in a gulp, surprised by his candid response. "Well, yes, exactly."

"I'll admit, I rarely have time for cooking these days. I still can't make a decent cup of coffee. It's a lot of work to keep all the dames at my door happy. And all the Scotch in Hollywood isn't going to drink itself." He winked at her. There was the Flynn Banks she knew. "But I love it. Used to escape to the kitchens as a kid every chance I got."

She tapped her napkin to her mouth, self-conscious of crumbs that might have strayed onto her face. "Kitchens?"

Now it was his turn to grimace. "Yes, my father was a member of the British aristocracy, and I grew up on one of those dreadful crumbling estates."

"Like a castle?" She regretted it the instant she said it. She sounded like a child, wide-eyed at the prospect of a fairy tale.

He simply chuckled. "Less castle, more haunted house." Her heart panged at the note of bitterness in his voice. "It wasn't the happiest home, and when my father was in one of his moods, I would hide in the kitchens, where our cook would let me observe her work. By the time I left for Eton, I knew how to make everything from poached eggs to croquembouche. Used to entertain my mates at Oxford by sneaking into the kitchens and whipping them up a hot meal after a long night at the pub. I like feeling useful."

She rubbed at a small tear in the tablecloth. "My sister and I, we're like that too. I'm the eldest, so I've always taken care of her." Being useful and ensuring that Judy was safe and dry and happy made Livvy feel less guilty. "But lately, she's been doing the cooking while I've been at the studio."

"That must be nice. To have someone to look after who also looks after you." He said it so wistfully. Could it be possible? Was Flynn Banks lonely? The idea was laughable. And yet...something in his eyes once again gave him away.

"It is, mostly. Though she really shouldn't need to look after me. I'm the one who's meant to take care of her. Sometimes that's stressful though."

He set a glass of white wine in front of her, and she sipped it gingerly. She needed to keep her wits about her. "How so?"

"I love Judy. I'd do anything for her. But being responsible for someone means you're always worried. Will she be safe? Will she have enough to eat? It's hard not to feel like a mother hen."

Flynn chuckled. "How old is your sister?"

"Eighteen, but she'll always be a baby to me."

"Maybe you need to let that go."

The words sucked all the air from the room. It was true. Sometimes Livvy wanted to let go so much it hurt. But how could she?

"We're all each other has. If I don't take care of her, who will?"

"Ever consider that she might be able to take care of herself?"

Livvy scowled, and Flynn laughed. "All right, all right, Mother Superior. I'm sorry." She harrumphed at his implication that she was a nun. "Just seems to me that when you let yourself enjoy life a little bit more, you know how to have a good time."

The words were laced with a hint of something dark and suggestive. How could he go from making fun of her to eliciting sinful thoughts so quickly? It was dizzying—the way he could change the mood with a lift of his eyebrow or the tone of his voice. But she didn't want to think too hard about the way that his words made heat pool between her legs moments after he'd irked her with his mocking.

So instead of answering him, she took another bite of fish and savored it, letting the flavors wash over her tongue. He studied her, his gaze following the movement of her fork and fixating on her mouth as she chewed and licked the crumbs from her lips. It would be easy to be self-conscious, but part of her wanted to do it slowly, run her tongue around the edges of her mouth, if only to taunt him and put the shoe on the other foot. She relished having his eyes on her, the way she seemed to hold him in thrall. It made her feel powerful. Something she hadn't felt in years. Everything had felt too big, too hard, too impossible to ever get on top of.

"Careful, now." He growled. "It's not nice to tease. I've been known to bite." On the last word, he clicked his teeth together, like a shark devouring its prey.

Livvy choked on the piece of fish still in her mouth.

Flynn laughed as she scrambled for a glass of water, breaking the spell between them. "Oh, you should've seen the look on your face!"

He was still laughing, and all she could do was scowl at being caught out. She threw her dishcloth doubling as a napkin at him, but he ducked, and it landed in the sink. "You did that on purpose!"

His eyes flashed with a hint of the mischief that was always there, lingering at the edges of his existence. "And if I did? So what if I enjoy watching a lady savor"—he paused for effect, the silence implying something lewd—"my cooking."

She narrowed her eyes at him. "What is this? You light a

candle. You make me dinner. Are you trying to seduce me?" She leapt off the stool and leaned against the inside of the cabin, trying to put more distance between them. More for herself than for him. She was far too excited at the idea that anyone, particularly Flynn Banks, would want to seduce her. But it would be a mistake to let him see that. She made a show of clutching the neck of her blouse to her throat, silently praying he couldn't see the rising flush of pink at her neck that signaled her desire.

"A fella can't make his phony girlfriend dinner? Is there a law against it or something?" He leaned forward when he said it, bracing his hands against the too-small table between them.

If this was one of his pirate movies, he'd sweep the plates off the table, pull her onto it, and ravish her. The thought of it made her bite her lip and drop her hands.

The corner of Flynn's mouth curled up into a smirk. "You're thinking something naughty. I can tell."

She huffed, embarrassed that he could read her so easily. "No! I'm thinking which kitchen knife would be the best to defend myself with."

He laughed, then held up his hands. "I've learned from our fencing lessons not to trust you with a blade." The compliment made her smile in spite of herself. "In fact, I'm beginning to wonder if I can trust you all."

She scoffed. "And what is that supposed to mean? Between the two of us, I'm not the one who's untrustworthy."

"Oh, really? So you're not a bald-faced liar?"

Her mouth fell open and she stared at him, scarcely believing her ears. "Excuse me? I'm not the one who'd say anything to get a woman into bed."

"I don't need to say anything. I only need to smile." He

demonstrated his point, and in spite of herself, her knees wobbled. Jeepers, he was infuriating. And too handsome for his own good.

"It pains me to think what a better man could have done with your face."

He only grinned even more wickedly. "A better man would have wasted it."

"Ohhh, you're impossible."

"And you've done nothing but lie to me since the moment I met you."

"May I remind you that you jumped into my car?"

"That's no excuse for fibbing. Not only did you fail to enlighten me of the fact that you were my costar and not, in fact, a tourist—or whatever you wanted me to think you were—but you also pretended that you'd never heard of me or seen a single one of my films."

She didn't like where this was going. But in for a penny, in for a pound. "That isn't a lie. I haven't seen any of your films. I told you—I prefer to read. If I go to the pictures, it's to see a women's picture. Something like *Reno Rendezvous*."

She expected him to roll his eyes at her taste in movies, but instead his lips slashed into a wild grin, the look of an animal who had its prey right where it wanted. "Really?" His eyes sparkled, a touch of madness in them. "Then, where did you get the idea for that trick to cut off the wind to the *Santa Guadalupe*?"

Nuts. She had hoped he wouldn't notice that, what with trying to keep them all afloat and his efforts to prevent his mainsail from shredding to bits. "I, um, I read about it in a book."

He leaned further over the table, getting closer to her. "No, you didn't. You saw it in a movie. In *The Pirate's Folly*, to be exact.

It's the way my character, Captain William Roberts, manages to outrun the Spanish."

"That's, that's, that's—" she sputtered. She was out of excuses. And the way his forearms were rippling as he leaned all of his weight onto the table was extremely distracting. The corded muscles pulsed with the pressure of his weight, and her eyes moved up to the bulging biceps beneath the clean polo shirt he'd changed into after the race. "That's ridiculous."

"Oh no, it's not. What's ridiculous is this effort to keep pretending you haven't seen my movies."

"Fine!" she shrieked, surprised by the intensity in her own voice. "Fine." She cleared her throat, braced her hands on the opposite side of the table, and leaned toward him until their noses nearly touched. "What do you want me to say? That I've seen all of your films multiple times? That I watched *The Pirate's Folly* six times in a single weekend? That I haven't missed a Flynn Banks picture in years and could probably recite some of them from memory?"

He blinked at her. Whatever he was expecting her to say, it wasn't that. He began to roar with laughter, lifting his hands from the table and clutching at his belly. He fell back against the kitchen counter and laughed until tears began to leak from his eyes.

"What exactly is so funny about that?"

"Y-y-you—" He struggled to catch his breath, still laughing. "Here, I was thinking less of myself because some beautiful dame hadn't seen my pictures, thought them beneath her—and you're practically the president of the Flynn Banks fan club."

She crossed her arms over her chest and puckered her lips. "I am not."

"Ha, ha, ha. Yes, yes you are. It's absurd, really."

Livvy tried to process the fact that she'd revealed her most humiliating secret, thus eliminating any chance she had at keeping the upper hand with him. Not to mention that he seemed to care about her opinion. And he'd called her beautiful.

Her mind reeled. But as she tried to puzzle through it all, he finally recovered.

"Finished now?" she asked, her voice dripping with disdain.

He actually checked himself, feeling his chest and his face before responding. "I think so. But what I can't understand is why? Why would you lie about such a thing? Most of the country has seen a Flynn Banks picture."

For the first time in tonight's long list of ignominious moments, she blushed. She looked at the deck and toed a coiled piece of rope with her shoe. "Because I didn't want you to think I was some simpering schoolgirl. I wanted to be your costar, your equal. I thought if you believed I was an intellectual, you'd be intimidated. You have girls throwing themselves at you every day. The last thing you needed was another one. I wanted you to respect me, instead of seeing me like every other girl."

He barked out another laugh. "I assure you, I have never and will never think of you the same way I do any other girl."

She didn't know if he was teasing her or praising her, but the words made her insides ignite, curls of flame licking at the sides of her belly.

He worried his lip underneath his two front teeth, then looked up and nodded. "Well, I suppose that leaves only one more question."

"And what is that?" She braced for something provocative and lewd. Something befitting his reputation as Hollywood's number one rascal.

"Olivia Blount. Liv de Lesseps. You have a lot of names for such a slip of a woman. What should I call you?"

The sudden unexpected question caught her off guard, and she smiled. "My friends call me Livvy."

The corner of his lips tugged up into a crooked, close-mouthed smile that made her involuntarily take a step toward him. "And am I?" She stumbled on the coil of rope as he asked his question. He caught her by the elbow. "Your friend?"

She looked up and met his infernally blue eyes, sensing mischief and want and something unknowable twinkling there. She gave him one of his own infuriatingly confusing winks. "For now."

CHAPTER 11

"BUGGER. SHIT. DAMN IT ALL TO HELL," FLYNN MUTTERED through his teeth. He'd barely stepped one foot into the Blossom Room at the Roosevelt Hotel when Rhonda Powers swanned in his direction, making a show designed to grab everyone in the room's attention.

Only a week had passed since he'd won the Catalina Regatta with Livvy. Harry had nearly busted his buttons at the photograph of Flynn holding Livvy while she kissed him on the cheek. The studio boss had left a stack of the pictures in Flynn's dressing room with a note that said, "Nice work." But Harry was insistent that their dates weren't public enough. If this PR stunt was going to work, the pair needed to see and be seen.

In less than twenty-four hours, Harry's office had begun planning excursions for the two of them. So far this week, Flynn and Livvy had gone for a paddle in the swan boats at Echo Park, been photographed at the deli counter at Canter's, and staged several photo shoots on the lot in their costumes and rehearsal clothes. All wholesome grist for the gossip mill.

Tonight was Harry's biggest effort yet. He'd arranged for Flynn and Livvy to sit at the head table for some big Hollywood fundraiser. It was the first opportunity for them to be photographed as a couple in formal wear, and the first time they'd be seen dancing together. In short, it was the last place he needed to bump into Rhonda Powers. But she was only a few feet away now, and he couldn't exactly turn tail and run.

"Flynn," Rhonda drawled. "Darling."

He darted his eyes from side to side, searching desperately for an escape, but Rhonda draped her arms around him, drawing him in for embrace.

"Laying it on a little thick, aren't we?" he hissed in her ear.

"You catch more flies with sugar than with vinegar. Smile for the cameras." Rhonda pressed her cheek to his, and he blinked fiercely as a flashbulb went off right in front of his face. Shit. A cozy photograph with the woman the papers thought he'd jilted was a headache he did not want to deal with. But if he wasn't careful, Rhonda would make a scene and that would be worse.

Flynn reached for Rhonda's arms, attempting to extricate himself from her embrace. "You've had nothing but piss and vinegar for me for the last month." He was still looking for an exit route, or at least the nearest bar, when he caught Harry's eye in the corner.

Help, he mouthed.

But Harry simply shook his head and mouthed back, *Be nice*.

"What exactly did you mean by planting that cockamamie news story, anyway?" Flynn pressed Rhonda. "I jilted you at the altar? Poppycock! The closest I'd get to an altar is if I was in need of an exorcism."

She only squeezed him tighter and nipped at his ear. "You wouldn't answer my calls. You ran away from me at the Trocadero. How else could I get your attention?"

Rhonda finally dropped her arms as Henry Powell and Carmen Del Rio walked by and nodded at Flynn. "Good evening," Flynn answered them. He hoped it wasn't obvious he was grimacing, as he used the interruption as an opportunity to sidestep Rhonda and put some breathing room between them, but the woman was like a boa constrictor.

She reached out and wrapped her long, manicured fingers tightly around his wrist. Her nails dug into his skin, and he yelped, making every head within five feet snap in their direction.

"Stickpin accidentally left in my tuxedo," he muttered, pretending to pluck a pin from the inside of his jacket. He was seized with the desire to poke Rhonda with the sharp end of one of his cuff links, but he restrained himself.

Instead he leaned over and muttered in her ear. "Did it ever occur to you that I was trying to tell you I wasn't interested?"

She turned and gave him a beatific smile. "No." It was the most terrifying thing he'd witnessed. "And I don't like to be ignored. You kissed me in Joan and Dash's garden and then dropped me like a hot potato. You can see why a girl might be confused."

He gritted his teeth. Dear God, why did he always pick the clingy women? And where was Livvy? Shouldn't she be here by now? "I'm sorry to disappoint, Miss Powers, but a kiss from Flynn Banks means about as much as a handshake from someone else."

"Oh, don't sell yourself short. You just haven't met the right gal yet." From any other woman, this might be a maternal reassurance, but the way Rhonda said it sounded more like a spider coaxing a fly into its web.

He wanted to tell her that it wasn't personal. That for Flynn Banks, there would never be a right gal. That was how he liked it. But at that moment, Livvy came in the other door of the Blossom Room, looking absolutely resplendent in a deep-lavender gown, and he lost the thread of his response.

Rhonda followed his eyeline to his costar, and he almost

laughed at the strange sound she emitted in response, a cross between a squeak and a harrumph.

But then Rhonda used her iron grip to tug his forearm behind her back and wrap it around her waist. If she didn't make it in Hollywood, Rhonda Powers had a real future as the first human iron lung.

Livvy raised her eyebrows at him, and Flynn tried to shake his head subtly to make it clear he was not a willing participant in Rhonda's antics. That, in fact, he was rather in need of Livvy's assistance. He grinned at her like a madman and nudged his head in Rhonda's direction, trying to tell Livvy he needed rescuing. But Livvy merely winked at him and walked to the bar. Damn it. She was supposed to be his date tonight so they could show the whole world he was a reformed man. But how could they pretend he'd turned over a new leaf if Rhonda clung to him like a barnacle the entire evening?

His attention was soon diverted when Rhonda called out, "Uncle Stan! Uncle Stan, over here!"

Flynn looked to see who she was calling and caught sight of a squat man with such a substantial pair of mutton chops that he looked like an aging walrus. The expression on the man's face suggested he was perpetually irritated. But Flynn almost swallowed his tongue when he noticed who dear old Uncle Stan was standing next to—Will Hays, the president of the Motion Picture Association of America and the namesake of the Production Code, a.k.a. the Hays Code. Simply put, he was the man who decided what was acceptable or not in Hollywood films and the lives of their stars.

Maybe the two men would give him and Rhonda a friendly nod like everyone else and keep moving. But Flynn knew it was too much to ask for when they began to approach.

"Flynn, this is my uncle, Stan," Rhonda said. "Uncle Stan, this is Flynn Banks."

Uncle Stan gave Flynn a disdainful look, his eyes darting to Flynn's hand that Rhonda had plastered to her waist.

Flynn curled his fingers inward, trying his best to remove the offending extremity despite Rhonda's steel grip. "Pleasure." He gulped, making it egregiously obvious it was anything but.

Uncle Stan simply glared at him, leaving the foursome standing in awkward silence until Will Hays interrupted. "You'll have to excuse Stanley. He spends too much of his time looking for things that offend him."

Stanley huffed, sounding rather like a bull seal about to give birth. Hays ignored the man and extended his hand. Flynn used the opportunity to free himself from Rhonda.

"Jolly good to meet you, Hays," Flynn barked, shaking Hays's hand perhaps a little too vigorously. Lord, he sounded like an ass. Or worse, his pompous prick of a father. *Jolly good.* He didn't think he had ever said those words before in his life. But shove him in the path of Hollywood's most moralizing crank and suddenly he was turning on the noblesse oblige. Hays at least seemed more personable than this mysterious Uncle Stan.

"Nice to meet you, Banks. As Miss Powers has already hinted, this is Stanley Devlin, one of my top men in the PCA office."

"Pleased to make your acquaintance, Mr. Devlin." Flynn extended his hand, but Stanley Devlin looked down at it as if it were something foul. The Production Code Administration's sudden and unrelenting zero-tolerance policy for Flynn's profligate lifestyle was becoming clearer by the second. Rhonda wasn't only the daughter of a Hollywood legend. She also had a direct line to the studios' moral arbiters. From a certain angle, it was flattering, really. Rhonda was so offended by his kiss-off that she'd called in Uncle Stan to do her dirty work. And Devlin had brought in the artillery with Hays in tow. Though Hays at least seemed to have a personality—a fact which surprised Flynn.

Under normal circumstances, annoying a pair of stuffed shirts like these two would have delighted Flynn to no end. In fact, he would've taken particular glee in finding more ways to peeve Devlin and Hays throughout the night. But even Flynn knew that was a bloody stupid idea given the circumstances. Flynn added "not being able to relish the look of disgust he engendered on Stanley Devlin's face" to the column of reasons he disliked Rhonda Powers.

Devlin finally spoke. "I hope you're treating our little Rhonda here well." There was no paternal concern in his voice. It was a rote delivery, as if he had been given a script to read that he found lacking.

But Rhonda was clearly prepared. "Oh, Uncle Stan." She swatted her hand at the man playfully and giggled like a schoolgirl.

"Er…" Flynn was struggling to come up with a response to Devlin's query. In part because, well, what could he say to a man who thought he was a scourge on society just because he liked to drink whiskey and chase skirts? Flynn's eyes darted frantically around the room, searching for a way out, when Rhonda interjected.

"He gets so tongue-tied around me. Isn't it cute?" Then she stood on her tiptoes and planted a kiss on Flynn's cheek. He could feel the ghost of her lipstick leaving its mark on his skin. This situation was going from bad to worse by the second.

He looked back at the bar for Livvy, shoving his hands in his pockets to avoid scrubbing at his face. He wanted a napkin to wipe off the lipstick print this instant. If the press saw him like this, with the outline of Rhonda's ruby-red pucker seared onto his face like a cattle brand... Well, the thought gave him hives. But he couldn't exactly rub it off in front of Will Hays and Rhonda's uncle like it was something contagious.

Livvy wasn't standing at the bar anymore. Damn it, where had she gone? Where was Harry, for that matter? Didn't he see that disaster was about to strike? If the studio boss wanted tonight to be a success, he needed to intervene. And quickly.

Could Flynn make a run for the toilet? Before he could feign illness, Hays gave him an appraising look and began to speak. "I must say, Mr. Banks, it's nice to see you out on the town for a reason other than getting your kicks."

Flynn bristled. Jesus Christ, didn't anyone know how to have a little fun around here? "Yes, well, I never would have picked you for a supporter of—" Bollocks. What was the name of the charity they were supposed to be here raising money for? He'd already forgotten.

He grabbed at the collar of his shirt, suddenly finding it much too tight. Devlin was staring him down, his beady black eyes practically boring through his skull.

"Yes?" Hays raised one eyebrow. It was obvious Hays knew Flynn had no idea what charity they were celebrating tonight. Hays clearly found it funny and was enjoying making Flynn sweat, while Devlin stared at him with the intensity of a jaguar stalking its prey. If Flynn so much as blinked or, heaven forbid, turned to read the banner hanging over the dais at the front of the room, he'd give himself away.

Nuts. What had the invitation said? Juvenile delinquents? Widowed mothers? No, neither of those was right. Devlin pursed his lips, and Flynn could feel a bead of sweat trickling down his spine. Damn it.

"Darling, there you are, I've been looking all over for you." In the nick of time, Livvy swanned into their circle, wrapping her hand around Flynn's arm and tugging him ever so slightly in her direction. Rhonda glared daggers at them both.

Flynn used the moment to edge a little further from Rhonda. Livvy reached up to kiss his other, unblemished cheek, and he hissed in her ear, "Impeccable timing, Blount."

Livvy smiled at him, the portrait of false innocence, and passed him a cocktail. "I thought you could use a drink," she murmured. He could use about four. He yearned to down the drink in one gulp. It was only the knowledge that Devlin would mark it in his list of Flynn's sins that kept him from knocking it back. Instead, he sipped at it while Livvy turned to face the rest of their semicircle.

Flynn said, "Miss Powers, Mr. Hays, and Mr. Devlin. I'm afraid there must be some confusion as to who's company I'm keeping tonight. I'm here as a guest of Evets's Studios. Might I present my costar and my date for the evening, Miss Liv de Lesseps?"

If looks could kill, Rhonda Powers would be tried on charges of homicide with the glare she shot Livvy. But Devlin's expression of disgust twisted into something leering when he regarded Flynn's costar.

Flynn fought the urge to possessively wrap his arm around Livvy's shoulder. She wasn't his; this relationship was a farce. Besides, he didn't do possessive. But he didn't like it when a Hollywood suit looked at a lady like she was a particularly delicious item on the Brown Derby menu. Flynn stepped in front of Livvy slightly, trying to shield her from the lascivious gleam in Devlin's eye.

The man seemed to take the hint and glanced at his niece with bored distaste. "It seems I was…given faulty information about who was meant to be on your arm for the evening."

Rhonda's cheeks heated as Devlin cast her a withering look. She looked ready to say something nasty when Livvy broke in. "An innocent mistake, Mr. Devlin. Flynn is so popular, after all. Thanks for keeping him warm for me, Miss Powers." Devlin's mouth twisted into a moue of repulsion at the reminder of Flynn's profligacy, but Livvy didn't falter and merely yanked Flynn a little closer and placed her hand over his, patting it gently. "I'm new to Hollywood, and he's been ever so attentive in making sure I'm not lonesome as I get accustomed to so many fresh places and faces."

"'Attentive' is one word for it," Rhonda grumbled under her breath.

"Don't start, Rhonda," Devlin growled.

The rest of them pretended not to hear the exchange.

"I must say," started Will Hays, who appeared eager to gloss over the uncomfortable situation with Rhonda. "I'm delighted to meet the woman who has tamed Flynn Banks."

Tamed? Jesus Christ, the notion was absurd. But Flynn pasted on a smile, knowing that Will Hays's belief in his reform was the entire point of their being here. If it meant Flynn had to give the performance of his life, he would do it. He thought of the *Sea Monkey*, his house in Malibu, the doors that opened at the sound of his name—and all the pleasures he had worked so hard to win for himself. All of that would be gone in the blink of an eye if Flynn and Livvy couldn't pull this off.

Livvy, bless her, didn't address Hays's comment and instead asked, "Mr. Hays, are you a great lover of the symphony?"

The symphony! The Southern California Symphony Association. That was what this whole shindig was about.

Hays brightened, and Flynn marveled at Livvy's ability to put anyone in a good mood. "Why, yes. I'm a particular fan of their Hollywood Bowl season."

Livvy lit up like a Christmas tree. It filled Flynn's chest with a warmth akin to the effect of his favorite Scotch. "Oh, I love the Bowl. That's where I got my start. I was Lady Macbeth in their production last year."

Flynn hadn't known that. He was impressed. The dame could fence, sail, *and* she'd starred in bloody Shakespeare. Was there anything she couldn't do?

Devlin wrinkled his nose as if he smelled something noxious. "That was you? Miss De Lesseps, that was one of the most depraved, bloody, immoral things I have ever seen."

Flynn gritted his teeth. Olivia Blount was earnest, wholesome, and winsome. Not to mention respectable. And infuriatingly gorgeous. How dare Stanley Devlin impugn her character when he didn't even know her?

"There's a reason it's called acting," Flynn growled, at the same time that Hays interjected, "I loved every minute of it. You were a fearsome Lady Macbeth. Mr. Banks should watch out."

Was that...? Had Hays winked at him?

Devlin scowled at his boss, clearly annoyed by Hays's encouragement.

Livvy smiled, holding in a laugh. "Thank you, Mr. Hays."

Devlin tried to save face, adding, "If you ask me, Hollywood could use a bit more Shakespeare. Now that's art. Not the swashbuckling Banks does."

"Oh, I don't know. I think Flynn might surprise us all," Livvy trilled. "Swashbuckling is harder than you think. I'm lucky Mr. Banks has been here to show me the ropes. I've had to learn an awful lot since coming to Hollywood—and he's an expert at what he does."

"I'll take your word for it," Devlin demurred, at the same time that Hays muttered, "Often to his own detriment."

A burst of pride bloomed in Flynn's chest at Livvy's defense of his work. A few weeks ago, she'd claimed that she'd never seen one of his films. Now she was championing them to strangers. Perhaps it was for the sake of appearances, but the note of sincerity in her voice touched him.

Still, he didn't need her to fight his battles. He could perform bloody Shakespeare too. "I'll have you know, Devlin," Flynn interjected, "that I played in *Hamlet* at university, and there wasn't a dry eye in the house when I did my Desdemona."

"Mmm, yes, well, in that instance, I could probably understand Othello's desire to strangle you," Hays quipped.

Flynn and Livvy blinked in surprise, first at each other, then at Hays.

"Don't look so surprised, I'm not a complete bore. I do have a sense of humor, you know."

Flynn almost guffawed from sheer shock, but Livvy didn't miss a beat. "Maybe remember that the next time you're evaluating a film."

Hays gaped at Livvy's censure, but then he chuckled.

"That goes for you too, Mr. Devlin."

Good old Uncle Stan turned beet red and looked as if he'd swallowed his necktie. Livvy stared him down, refusing to blink. Flynn was impressed. Hays and Devlin were intimidating, even to him. Particularly when this entire scheme rested on their believing it. But Livvy was easily using their fake romance to advocate for him. Whether or not he deserved it.

Hays clapped Flynn on the back—a friendly gesture that Flynn had never conceived the enforcer of the Production Code giving him. "I like her, Banks. She's good for you." Flynn happened to agree, but he wasn't going to tell Hays that. Or Livvy, for that matter.

"Too good," Livvy agreed. "But he has a nice face."

At that, Flynn genuinely laughed. Who was this woman? She was prim and proper. A lady in every sense of the word. Her raven-black hair and Cupid's bow mouth made her seem as fragile as a porcelain doll. In short, the antithesis of everything Flynn was drawn to in a woman. But she ripped the rug from beneath him so frequently, he supposed he should get used to standing on hardwood floor. Every answer she gave only led to more questions. He wanted to read an *Encyclopedia of Olivia Blount* and commit it to memory so he could understand every bit of her.

Rhonda looked as if she was going to blow her top at any minute. Her arms were crossed over her chest and her face was so scrunched up in frustration that she resembled a pug. She tapped her foot in irritation, and Flynn thought she might only be moments away from a full-on temper tantrum.

"Uncle Stan, I'm thirsty," she whined. Jesus, how had Flynn been remotely attracted to her for even a second? She was a petulant child.

"Rhonda, you are perfectly capable of getting yourself a drink. I am not your babysitter."

Flynn almost swallowed his tongue at Devlin's retort, while Rhonda harrumphed and stomped off in the direction of the bar.

Devlin shot one last look of disdain at Flynn. "You're on thin ice with me, Banks. Don't you forget it."

Before Flynn could reply, Devlin followed his niece to the bar, leaving Flynn and Livvy with Will Hays.

Flynn needed to try to clear the air. "Mr. Hays, whatever Mr. Devlin or Miss Powers told you—"

The president of the Motion Picture Association held up his hand, signaling Flynn to stop. "No need to explain, Banks. Clearly, Rhonda was confused. If I've heard Stanley say it once,

I've heard it a million times. Besides the moral turpitude of the motion picture industry, his chief complaint in life is how much Rhonda's mother coddles that girl. She never learned how to take no for answer. And now Rhonda expects Uncle Stan to be her champion." Hays looked over his shoulder in their direction and sighed. "But I better go follow them all the same. Lovely to meet you, Miss De Lesseps."

Flynn stared after them in disbelief. Had it really been that easy? If so, Harry was a genius. Rhonda had tried to ruin his life, to get Will Hays and the lackeys of the Production Code Administration to blow up his career. But her little ploy to humiliate Flynn in front of her Uncle Stan had blown up in her face.

Because Rhonda Powers hadn't accounted for Liv de Lesseps. Hell, neither had he.

Flynn picked at the dry piece of chicken on his plate in dismay. He could count on one hand the number of decent meals he'd eaten at a Hollywood fundraiser. When events were responsible for feeding over one hundred people, the food was always bland and flavorless. It was yet another reason he found nights like this tiresome, preferring instead to spend them in the back room at Musso's or watching the sunset from his house.

He cast his eyes at the program lying next to his fork. This fundraiser was interminable. Was this still the same piece the Philharmonic had been playing for the last fifteen minutes? "Variations for Orchestra" by Arnold Schoenberg? It was hard to tell, given the entire thing was a morass of chaotic noise. He'd enjoyed the Bach. He'd spent most of the Stravinsky staring at Livvy, enjoying the way the undulating line of her body, clad in her purple chiffon gown, practically shimmered with excitement. He'd sworn she'd been tapping her toes. At a classical piece!

Hell, he had even endured the droning speech from the Symphony Association's president, asking every guest to open their hearts and their wallets to help save the orchestra. When they'd passed around a plate, the expectant grin on Livvy's face had him reaching for his pocketbook and placing a crisp hundred-dollar bill on the collection platter. She'd given him a look of such pure joy at this act of generosity that he'd turned his wallet upside down and emptied the rest of its contents without thinking twice.

The thought that he would do anything to make her smile like that flitted through his mind. But he dismissed it as gratitude for how she'd saved his hide with Devlin and Hays.

He flinched as the violins and French horns clashed in a cacophony of notes. This was grim. He was shocked his ears hadn't started to bleed yet.

He glanced at Livvy, expecting to see the same blissful rapture on her face that he had committed to memory throughout the previous two numbers. But instead, she was studying her napkin. If he dipped his head just so, he could make out a grimace pulling at the edges of her mouth. She hated this song as much as he did. It was strangely satisfying.

He looked at her plate, where her chicken also remained largely untouched. She'd made her mashed potatoes into two mountains and mixed in flecks of the broccoli to make it look like a snowy forest. It was whimsical and lovely and unexpected. That was Livvy, to a T.

He leaned over. "Would you like to go somewhere a little less…atonal?" he murmured in her ear. She grabbed at the napkin in her lap, disguising her laugh as a cough. Her eyes darted to the table next to theirs where Harry was seated, flanked by Hays and Devlin. "Won't he—"

Flynn shook his head. "We came, we've had our picture taken. You won over Will Hays. He should be more than satisfied."

She furrowed her brow and bit her lip. "I don't know..." She kept looking between him and Harry. "I should probably stay; I wouldn't want to give Harry reason to scold me. Besides, the studio car is supposed to pick me up here. How will they find me?"

"Shhhh," hissed another guest at their table, a woman with gray hair piled into a mass of curls in a style that hadn't been popular in this century.

Livvy looked at Flynn as she shook with giggles and rolled her eyes. He could just make out the tip of her delectably pink tongue behind her napkin as she stuck it out in the direction of the shusher.

"I'll drive you home," he whispered. She still looked uncertain, her desire to leave clearly conflicting with her need to please Harry.

As if to punctuate the urgency of his offer, the clarinets and piccolos joined in a discordant trilling of chords that had Flynn fearing for the durability of the crystal goblets at each place setting.

Livvy winced at the sound and nodded. "Okay, I can't stand it any longer."

She put her hand in Flynn's. It felt right—small, yet so strong—and her fingers knotted between his. His stomach lurched with excitement at the press of her palm. Or maybe he was woozy after three cocktails and just a bite of dry chicken and flavorless broccoli.

They stood together and he pulled her to the door, ignoring

the mutters and gasps that erupted. He looked over his shoulder and stifled a laugh when he watched Livvy hold her hand to her head in Harry's direction, feigning a headache.

"You know he won't believe that for a second," he growled in her ear.

"Yes, he will." She looked quite pleased with herself. "Because I'm not you."

She had him there.

CHAPTER 12

FLYNN REVVED THE ENGINE AND LIVVY SCREAMED, laughing as he pushed his foot to the gas and they peeled away from the intersection. Her hair was streaming behind her, a snarl of curls in the wind, and for the first time in her life, she didn't care. That realization itself was thrilling—even more than the purr of the engine or the rush of adrenaline she felt as Flynn darted in and out of lanes and around slower cars.

"Where are you taking me?" she called over the roar of wind that whipped past them as he drove down neon-streaked streets, past blinking lights.

"Do you like Mexican food?" he asked, his voice similarly raised.

"I've never had it."

He turned, his jaw hanging open in an exaggerated gape. "You what?"

"My parents didn't like spicy food. And at any rate, we hardly ever ate out."

He made a sharp left turn, and she slid toward him on the bench seat, the edge of her thigh colliding with his much firmer, more solid leg. She liked the feel of him pressed against her far too much. The embers of her girlhood crush were too easy to fan back to a raging fire.

Just as she was about to scooch back to her side of the car, he pointed ahead. "See that sign in the distance? That's the El Cholo Café." She squinted and could just make out the hot-pink neon sign that burned the name of the restaurant into the night sky. "I promise you, it'll be the best meal you'll ever eat."

"You have an exaggerated opinion of everything, don't you?"

He turned and gave her a gleaming movie-star smile. "Only of myself. But I have a feeling you might just cure me of that."

The confession stole her breath away. He was teasing, right? This was all for fun, for show, to get him in good with the Production Code Administration and the Legion of Decency. A task she hoped they'd accomplished tonight.

She had been too impudent with that Devlin man, but she didn't like the way he had looked at her. She liked the way he'd spoken to Flynn even less. Was Flynn a playboy who lived life too hard? Probably, yes. But at least he didn't pretend to be something he wasn't. That was rarely the case when it came to men like Devlin—moral arbiters with a sense of rectitude so stiff they could choke on it. She'd be lying if she said Flynn's reputation didn't make her slightly afraid of him, but it was also part of one thing she admired about him—he was true to himself. And how many people in this world could say that?

Except there was one thing that was false: this sham of a relationship and the pretense they had to maintain at Harry's orders.

She glanced at Flynn, and her stomach twisted at the outline of Rhonda Powers's lipstick still on his face. When she'd arrived at the Roosevelt, he and Rhonda had looked pretty cozy. He'd even smiled for a picture with her. He and Livvy were supposed to be a team, and if Flynn messed up her job at Evets's Studios by running back to Rhonda, she and Judy would have no other options in Hollywood. What was he thinking, letting Rhonda kiss him?

Was it because Flynn still had feelings for Rhonda? Ones Harry had forbidden him from pursuing for some reason?

Before she could spiral any further, Flynn pulled into the parking lot of the El Cholo Café and tossed his keys to the valet, who said, "Señor Banks, good to see you again. It has been too long."

"José, even a week without El Cholo is too long. But I'm making another picture. You know the studio, they keep me running ragged."

"*Sí, sí,*" the valet replied, opening the passenger door for Livvy. "And who is this lovely señorita?"

"My new costar, Liv de Lesseps."

The fake name still sounded odd to her ears. Liv de Lesseps was something the studio had created, and she couldn't make the glamorous image that name projected jive with the practical, studious girl she'd always prided herself on being. Back when she'd intended to become an author, she'd planned to write under her own name. José extended his hand to help her out of the car, and she took it. "I'm Olivia Blount."

"Miss Blount, it is a pleasure to welcome you to El Cholo." José made a show of sweeping into a bow and pressing a chaste kiss to the top of her hand.

"Now, don't you steal my girl," Flynn joked.

José looked up at Livvy and grinned. "I think we should let the lady decide."

Livvy bit her lip, pretending to debate the issue. But butterflies were taking wing inside her at the sound of Flynn Banks calling her his girl. "Hmm, I'm not sure."

Flynn laughed.

"Can I try the food first?" Livvy went on.

"Absolutely not," Flynn replied.

She pretended to pout. "Why not?"

"Because no one would ever choose me after tasting an El Cholo enchilada."

José shrugged and said, "He is right, Miss Blount."

"But don't take my word for it." Flynn held out his arm for her and she gripped his bicep, enjoying the taut strength of his muscle beneath his impeccably tailored suit. "C'mon, Livvy, I'm starving."

He led her up the terra-cotta steps into the cozy bungalow that had been transformed into a restaurant. El Cholo Café was a feast for the senses. Delectable spices and bubbling cheese greeted her nose, making her stomach growl. The bungalow was decorated with colorful wall hangings that welcomed its guests in to sit at high-back wooden booths.

"Banks!" proclaimed the man behind the cash register.

Flynn clapped his hand to the fellow's and gave him a hearty handshake. "George, it's good to see you. May I introduce you to Liv de Lesseps? Hollywood's newest and soon-to-be brightest star."

She blushed at Flynn's praise and extended her own hand to greet the tall, dark-haired, handsome man working the counter.

"Livvy, this here is George Salisbury. He owns the restaurant with his wife, Aurelia."

"Pleased to meet you," she replied.

"George, she's never had Mexican food before."

The restaurant owner's eyes bulged. "I'll tell Joe to give you the works then. Banks, you haven't been back since we changed the menu. Joe's got us selling combination plates now. Rice and beans with your enchilada."

Flynn appeared absolutely ravenous at the news that there was something new on the menu. He looked like something out of a cartoon. Livvy tried to hold back her laughter, but Flynn heard her.

"What's so funny?"

"You. You're practically drooling."

"Food is a serious business," he retorted, before leaning over and whispering in her ear. "Besides, what makes you think it's merely the food that's got me all worked up?"

The words made something warm and wet pool between her thighs. He couldn't mean her? No, that was…indecent. Besides, she was not the kind of girl that Flynn Banks would go for—not outside this charade they were committed to. That's all the words were: part of the game they played.

George gestured to a waiter lingering behind them. "Pedro, put them in Mr. Banks's favorite booth."

As Flynn led her into the room behind the register, Livvy clung to him tightly, horrified to discover that his whisperings had turned her knees to jelly. But he didn't seem to care. He held her hand, steady and solid in his own, and brought her to a cozy wooden booth in the side room. He extended his arm, helping her slide onto the bench as she swept the fuller skirts of her chiffon gown beneath her.

Flynn crossed to the other side of the table and took his seat as their waiter laid a cloth napkin on Livvy's lap. "Now, Pedro, this isn't a fine dining establishment, let the lady have the authentic El Cholo experience."

Pedro chuckled and nodded. He held out menus for both of them but Flynn waved him away. "Dos combination plates, the cheese enchilada," he ordered. "And I'll have a beer. Do you want a drink?"

Livvy shook her head. "No, water is fine, thank you."

When Pedro walked away, she scanned the room, soaking in

all the fine details, from the beautifully painted tile pattern that wound its way around the top of the room to the family photos framed and hung on the wall. A fire crackled in a hearth that split the room in two, and she relaxed, letting the warmth seep into her bones.

She turned back to Flynn and was surprised to see him grinning at her. "What are you smiling at?"

"You. Watching you take it all in. You're beautiful when you're curious."

She blushed. "I've never seen any place like it. It's so...homey."

"That's what I love about it too. None of that fake glamour or attempts to impress. Just good people making good food. There's not a lot of folks who understand how special that is."

Livvy rolled her eyes. "I'm sure that's what you tell all the girls."

Flynn smirked, his left eyebrow arching in a fashion that reminded her of his role in *The Fighting Swan*. "I don't bring other girls here. The type of girls I usually go for want champagne and a night on the town. You're different, Livvy."

"You mean provincial." She was well read and her father had been well traveled. Flynn Banks was the son of an aristocrat. They did not inhabit the same universe.

"No one could ever describe you as provincial. I saw how you soaked in the Bach and the Stravinsky tonight. Everyone else was pretending to enjoy it because they think it makes them look smart. Hollywood's full of philistines pretending to be dilettantes. But you're the real deal. You actually appreciate the symphony. I can tell by the way every note hits a different part of your body or the slight smile that ghosts across your face when the strings get particularly melodic. You even try to hide your flinch when they hit notes that don't belong. You can't fake that."

A strange sensation passed over her, some mixture of pleasure and embarrassment. She hadn't realized he'd been watching her that closely. Until that last piece, the music had been so lovely, so moving that it had been impossible not to get swept up in it. "I love music. I always have. My parents used to take my sister and me to hear the local symphony. But I haven't been out to see a live orchestra since—" Her voice caught as she was suddenly flooded with memories of her parents and the swirl of emotions that came with their loss.

"Since?" Flynn raised his eyebrows.

Livvy couldn't give him that piece of herself. He hadn't earned the right to it. And if he knew the truth… She didn't know what would be worse: if he met her with disappointment or with pity. So, she swallowed back the rising tide of grief that threatened to overwhelm her. "Well, it's been a very long time, anyway."

Flynn looked as if he wanted to push her to say more, but their drinks arrived, and she sipped at her water, trying to banish the emotions that Flynn's words had stirred in her. Flynn sipped at his beer, a brush of foam giving him a fake mustache. Livvy giggled, breaking the spell of the tension that had sprung up between them. "You look like Dash Howard."

He scoffed and swept at his upper lip with the back of his hand. "Never insult me like that again."

It only made her laugh harder. "I thought he was your best friend."

"He is! But everyone knows that of the two of us, I'm the better looking one."

She rolled her eyes at that. He was teasing, but there was still a hint of vanity there. Flynn Banks was a bit of a peacock. "Oh, I don't know. I think he's rather handsome. I've always preferred his pictures."

Flynn narrowed his eyes at her. "You minx. That's a lie and you know it. No one who learned how to sail a ship from watching my movies prefers Dash Howard."

She threw back her head and laughed. He was so unexpected. So playful. Kind and funny.

"Would you rather be sitting here with Dash Howard right now?"

She bit her lip and pretended to think about it, and Flynn took another pull on his beer.

"Oh, c'mon, Livvy."

"Well," she teased, drawing out each word, "he is madly in love with his wife, so…"

Flynn snorted, and Livvy heard him say what sounded distinctly like, "Poor bastard."

Her eyes caught on the ghost of the lipstick stain Rhonda had left on his face earlier this evening. A pang of hurt and jealousy flared again. She resisted the urge to reach across the table and scrub it from Flynn's face. To Flynn, this was a big game. If he didn't rehabilitate his image, what would actually happen to him? A slap on the wrist? He was a member of the British aristocracy. His movie-star salary was probably mere gravy compared to what his family was worth. *He* wouldn't be destitute if the press got wise to their ruse. She shouldn't have let him bring her here tonight; she should've insisted they stay at the fundraiser and play up their budding romance. What good was sitting alone in this booth with him?

But when she met his gaze, she gasped. He was studying her, his usually twinkling blue eyes deeper and darker, full of something that looked an awful lot like hunger. What did he see when he looked at her? An innocent? A try-hard? Or something else? A girl who loved music and books, who wanted desperately for someone to take her seriously? People described Flynn Banks as a man who could undress women with his eyes, but this wasn't that. It was something more...intimate. Like he could see her innermost thoughts.

This. Is. Not. Real. She recited it in her head like a mantra. So what if he noticed the way she loved music and called her beautiful? It was all part of the act. Maybe Flynn was one of those actors who preferred to stay in character throughout the course of a production. He could charm the habit off a nun, and she couldn't let herself get caught up in the fantasy of their pretending.

Her hand was on the table, and he reached out as if he was going to take it. She drew back, afraid of what his touch might do to her. That it might unravel her.

"Livvy," he growled, his voice low and warm like a shot of whiskey. Not that she made a habit of taking shots of whiskey.

Suddenly, the room felt very hot. Was that fire really necessary? It was Los Angeles in October, for heaven's sake. Maybe she should go to the bathroom and put a wet paper towel to her face?

She grabbed her water and savored the cool press of the glass against her lips. Flynn followed her movements with his eyes, seeming to lock into the bead of liquid that clung to her mouth. She darted her tongue out to lick it away, and the black circle of his pupils swelled, nearly drowning out the cool ring of blue of his irises. She couldn't look away.

"Dinner is served." Pedro broke the hypnotic power of Flynn's gaze as he returned with a tray of two steaming-hot plates. Using a pot holder, he slid them onto the table. The smell of warm, delectable spices and melted cheese assaulted Livvy's senses, and her mouth began to water for entirely different reasons. She turned her gaze to her plate, the deep brown of the enchilada sauce and golden hues of the cheese swirling into each other.

Flynn laughed, breaking her focus.

"What's so funny?"

"You. You look like a wolf licking its chops."

"I do not!" But she knew she probably did. "It just smells incredible, that's all."

"I hope you don't think I meant that as an insult. If anyone studied a plate of El Cholo enchiladas any other way, I'd send them to have their head examined. Taste them. I want to know what you think."

Livvy obliged, picking up her fork and cutting a small bite of enchilada with the edge of the tines. She raised it to her mouth, trying not to drip sauce on her gown, and as the blend of peppers, spices, and cheese collided with her taste buds, she tried not to moan. Flynn had not been exaggerating; this was the best thing she had ever tasted. Maybe leaving the fundraiser hadn't been the worst idea after all. The food was an explosion of flavors inside her mouth that were both entirely unfamiliar and reassuringly satisfying. How could something taste like home when she'd never had it before?

After swallowing, she glanced at Flynn, and his eyes danced with merriment. "Good?"

"The tops." She wanted more right now. And not just the prim ladylike taste of her first bite. She looked down at the plate and then back up at Flynn, who had yet to touch his own food.

"Swirl together the beans and the rice and the enchilada." She did as he said, scraping all three items together onto her fork with the back of her knife. "There's no need to be a lady for my sake."

He seemed to read her mind, and the words hit Livvy in the gut. Why was that the most attractive thing in her life that a man had said to her? She was eating dinner, for Pete's sake, not doing a striptease. Yet that permission to let go, to enjoy herself without judgment, made her feel free in a way she so rarely did.

But she seemed to experience that sense of freedom more and more in Flynn's presence—on the boat during the race, acting opposite each other in a scene, tonight listening to the orchestra, and now here, eating this divine meal. Ironically, all those things had happened because of this publicity dating scheme—but Flynn made Livvy feel authentic and alive in a way she never had before. Except when she was reading a book or watching a movie. Frankly, she hadn't known people could simply experience this freedom in their daily life.

Flynn tucked into his meal and they ate in companionable silence, as Livvy resisted the urge to scarf down everything on her plate in under a minute. Still, it seemed as if no time at all had passed before her food was gone. Flynn laughed as she used the edge of her fork to scrape up the remaining sauce on the plate. She stuck her fork in her mouth and crinkled up her nose in a teasing gesture, making a show of enjoying every last bite.

"You've shown me a different side of you tonight, and I like it," Flynn told her. "I like watching you savor things."

His words were laced with a double meaning, and a white-hot pulse of want shot through her. *No, no, no.* He was a lothario. This was how he got starlets into his bed on a nightly basis. She could not allow herself to fall for it. If she and Flynn weren't doing this for the sake of an audience, they weren't going to do it at all.

As Pedro cleared their plates, George Salisbury came over, twisting his hands together nervously.

"Why the long face, George? I told you it'd be impossible for someone not to enjoy your food." Flynn nodded at the empty plates that Pedro was carting away, both of them licked so clean you might never have known there was food on them.

"It was the best meal of my life," Livvy declared. She wasn't exaggerating either.

George gave her a weak smile. "No, no, nothing like that. But thank you, Miss De Lesseps. I'm glad you enjoyed it. Banks, there's a man out front, a photographer. He arrived here about five minutes after you did. He won't leave, says he wants a picture of the two of you coming out of the restaurant. I just wanted to warn you."

"No trouble, George. Could you maybe have José take the car round the back?"

Livvy was relieved at first. But then she realized this was the perfect opportunity to make tonight a true success. "Wait, Flynn. Let's go out the front."

He tilted his head and looked at her in confusion. "Why? George has an easy enough escape route for us."

"Yes, but…" She looked leerily up at George Salisbury. She couldn't drop the ruse that she and Flynn were an item in front of some random stranger. She needed an excuse. "The Evets publicity department said the more photos people take of me when I'm out on the town, the better. That it's good for my career." She gave Flynn a pointed look, trying to get him to understand what she really meant. Livvy could hardly believe what she was saying. But tonight had been so strange. Her growing feelings for Flynn unsettled her. She needed a firm reminder that this was all for show. What better than a run-in with a photo bug?

Flynn looked back at her, clearly mystified at her sudden desire for publicity, and she stared even harder at him, raising her eyebrows. George Salisbury looked confused. But then something clicked. "Oh. Ohhhh. Yes, absolutely. We should get you that camera time. That's a brilliant idea. Wish I'd thought of it myself." He winked at her, and she resented her stomach for the butterflies it generated in response. He stood and proffered his arm, which she took, and they started for the door.

"Thanks for a wonderful meal, Mr. Salisbury. I hope to be back soon," she called over her shoulder at the restaurant's owner, who still looked perplexed at what had just transpired. She and Flynn stepped out the heavy carved door of the restaurant, only to be temporarily blinded by a flashbulb.

"Banks, is this your new flame? What about poor Rhonda? Did you really jilt the dame at the altar?"

Livvy blinked furiously, trying to clear the stars from her eyes that hovered from the aftereffects of the flash. Maybe this had been a mistake. She'd wanted to play the game, to give Harry what he thought Flynn needed. Particularly after they'd flown the coop from the fundraiser.

Flynn responded dryly, "Rubbish. Utterly and completely. Me near an altar? It would spontaneously combust." Livvy gently stepped on his foot, reminding him that he was supposed to be selling the notion that he was a reformed man, currently falling in love with her. She covered Flynn's yelp with a hollow laugh that she was certain even the photographer could tell was fake. But Flynn got the message.

"Well, it would have in the past," he amended. "But I never made Rhonda Powers any promises. How could I when my new costar is everything I could have ever dreamed of?" He nudged Livvy forward a bit, as if he were presenting her to the cameraman. "This is Liv de Lesseps. My new partner, on-screen and off. The girl I never knew I'd been waiting for. Mark my words, she's going to be a great star."

Livvy's heart beat faster at Flynn's description of her as the girl he'd been waiting for. Once, such a thing had been her greatest fantasy. She watched as the reporter scribbled her name in his pad. This was her life now. How very odd. To have a complete stranger take your picture and write your name down in his notes. But it wouldn't do to stand gaping like a codfish, when it had been her idea to go out the front and put on a show. She needed to do something to sell this quickly.

She leaned over and hissed in Flynn's ear, "Kiss me."

His eyes widened and he turned his head to meet her gaze. Surprise and lust mingled in his sparkling blue eyes. "Are you sure?" he whispered.

She didn't answer him, but simply leaned forward and gently pressed her lips to his.

"Hoo boy, it's my lucky night," the photographer crowed. The white light of the flash was hot on her face, but not nearly so hot as the rush of want that traveled from where their lips met to the apex of her legs. She clenched her thighs together and stood on her tiptoes, increasing the pressure of her mouth upon his.

He followed her lead and deepened the kiss, his tongue licking at the seam of her lips. She opened for him and the place between her legs pulsed with desire as he explored her mouth, flicking at her teeth and tangling with her tongue. It was playful and dangerous and oh so sexy. Just like Flynn.

This was meant to be for show. To remind her this was all make believe. But right now she was having trouble remembering that—because in all her life, she'd never felt anything so real, so alive as this kiss. It was a zap of electricity to her system, waking her up when she hadn't even realized she'd been asleep. Flynn Banks was rearranging every molecule in her body with a mere kiss.

It was too much. She broke away from him, dizzy with desire and scarcely able to see straight.

"Thanks for the picture," the reporter cooed.

Flynn didn't answer, simply grabbed her hand and pulled her off in the direction of the valet, where José was waiting with their car. Livvy was in a daze as Flynn opened the door and ushered her into the bench seat. They said nothing as he pulled out onto Western Avenue and headed north.

"I'm at the Garden of Allah bungalows," she murmured eventually.

He nodded and wound his way through the middle of the city toward Hollywood, where her residence lay nestled at the foot of the hills. The silence resumed as she replayed the events of the evening in her mind. The way Flynn had looked at her while she ate her meal, like he was anticipating her reaction to every bite. His delight at sharing the restaurant with her. The way his eyes had flared with something she couldn't even identify when she'd told him to kiss her. The press of his lips against hers. The sweep of his tongue as he plundered her mouth like she was the pirate's treasure in one of his films.

His car hit a bump, jostling them in their seats and sending his glove box flying open. A small black book fell out of the compartment and slid into her lap. She picked it up, flipping through its pages, a sickening sensation overtaking her as she realized what it was: Flynn's little black book. She paged through it, scrutinizing the various stars, hearts, and strike-throughs he'd scribbled in, realizing that it was some sort of code for the women listed inside the book.

Suddenly, he reached over with one hand and clapped the book shut. "I'm sorry. It fell out when we hit the curb," she said.

"A girl like you has no business examining a book like that." She couldn't tell if he was complimenting or insulting her. Did he think her too delicate to see such a thing? He gently patted the top of her hand, still holding the book. "Put it back where you found it."

She did as she was told while white-hot flames of shame licked at her. She had never felt so foolish. Minutes ago, she'd been reliving their kiss, and now he was treating her like a kid caught with their hand in the cookie jar. Their kiss had been no different from the hundreds she'd watched at the movies. That was why Flynn made every woman over fourteen and under one hundred weak at the knees. Because he was a fantasy, good at making love for show. She had to remember that. She thought of Rhonda and the way the woman had wound herself around Flynn.

"Why did you jilt Rhonda Powers?" She blurted it out before she even realized what she was doing. Oh God, why had she asked him that? Wasn't it bad enough that she'd pawed through his book of assignations? Now, she had to go interrogate him about Rhonda. And what did Rhonda matter? She and Flynn were playing a game, two roles for the benefit of Flynn's reputation and the success of Evets's Studios. When they were done making their picture, this whole farce would be over with and he could do whatever he liked.

His face was stony as he kept his eyes on the road. "You shouldn't pay any mind to the questions reporters ask us." There was no mirth in his response. The roof of the car was still down, and yet the temperature seemed to have dropped ten degrees.

"I don't. But you seemed pretty cozy with her at the fundraiser before I got there. And the papers said—"

"Ah, so you not only watch Flynn Banks movies, but also read the gossip columns." His tone could have frozen a tray of ice. She'd really put her foot in it now.

"Connie in wardrobe showed me," she admitted. "She saw us leaving the lot holding hands... You know, the first little publicity stunt we did? She thought she should warn me."

He ran a hand down his face. "Damn meddling woman." He turned his head to look at Livvy, briefly taking his eyes from the road. "That story isn't true. Not a word of it."

"How should I know? The first night I met you, you were trying to escape from some woman who wanted to cause you bodily harm."

"Yes, and you pretended to have no idea who I was, so we both weren't at our best, were we?"

Livvy blushed, remembering the haughty act she'd put on that night. But that wasn't what they were arguing about. "Well, whoever she was, I have no doubt that wasn't the first woman to chase you out of the Troc like that, if your little book is anything to go by."

He grunted in response, so she barreled on. "And you didn't look too upset when Rhonda kissed you tonight. I had to intervene before you remembered I was meant to be your date."

"That, that's not true!" Flynn struggled to get the words out. "She cornered me. I was trapped. I couldn't exactly cause a scene in front of Will Hays, when the whole point of our being there tonight was to show off how much your steady presence has reformed my wicked, wicked ways. It's that woman's fault you and I are stuck in this mess in the first place." There was something bitter in his voice, and she realized for the first time that maybe Flynn had been as reluctant to agree to this farce as she had.

But then, something in him softened, the fight going out of him. "Look, if you want to accuse me of sleeping with a different woman every week, of being a scoundrel and a cad, fine. I'm not going to lie to you and try to pretend like that little book isn't exactly what you think it is. But don't accuse me of being something I'm not. I've left behind my share of broken hearts, but I don't promise anything I'm not willing to give. I don't jilt women.

I don't lead them on. If you sign up for a ride on the Flynn Banks merry-go-round, you'll know exactly what you're getting. Is it my fault if a dame loses her head every once and awhile? Everyone knows who I am, and if some wacky doll gets stars in her eyes, I certainly didn't put them there."

Something occurred to her then. "That night, when you jumped in my car, you were trying to get away from Rhonda." He didn't answer, but the firm clench of his jaw told her she was right. From the moment they'd met, he had been outrunning Rhonda Powers. And despite this fact, Livvy had been jealous.

It was ridiculous. And hilarious. Because he was right: He was honest about who he was. That was why she was reluctant to give him even an inch when it came to letting him into her life and her heart. She knew what that would mean: heartbreak. Flynn Banks was not the marrying kind, but Livvy was. There was no sense in falling for someone who made it abundantly clear that he could never be what she needed. Maybe hitting that bump in the road and finding that book had been the work of her guardian angel.

"I'm sorry I thought that there might really be something between you and Rhonda," she murmured. "But I have to get this right. My job—no, my life—depends on us convincing everyone we're falling in love."

"Well, it's you who has the tougher acting assignment," Flynn retorted.

"And what is that supposed to mean?"

"You've made it quite obvious since the first moment we met that I'm beneath you. That any association with me was unacceptable because it might tarnish your lily-white, stick-up-your-arse reputation. And maybe it will. I'm the son of an aristocrat and went to the best schools that money can buy, but you can't dye a black sheep white. I don't have a problem acknowledging that

I'm a womanizer and a booze hound and that my greatest asset is my pretty face, not my intellect. I like stiff drinks and beautiful women. Never pretended otherwise. You wanted me to think you were too good for pirate movies. But you know something? People like pirate movies."

Livvy felt like a grade A heel. She'd been trying to protect herself, but she'd ended up making Flynn think she disdained him. When her problem was quite the opposite. "I like pirate movies."

"And books and fencing. I know you do, Livvy." His voice had moved from accusatory to a gentle vulnerability, a softness she almost couldn't bear in the face of how rude she'd been.

"I like that you like those things," Flynn continued. "Once we got past that rocky start, I realized that you might play your cards close to the vest, but you're every bit as true to yourself as I am. It's something I admire in you."

His words took her breath away. Everyone always wanted her to be something she wasn't. Her father and mother had stifled her, insisting she always be the portrait of propriety. Judy never asked anything of her, but Livvy knew she had to be the mother hen for the both of them. And the studio didn't want Olivia Blount; they wanted Liv de Lesseps, worldly star with a name they had invented and Flynn Banks's arm candy. But what did she want? Had she thought of her own wants even once in the month and a half since she'd come to Hollywood?

They pulled up to a stoplight, and she turned to find Flynn studying her. A burst of yearning tugged at her heart, and she leaned ever so slightly closer to him, wondering if he might kiss her again. This time without an audience.

Flynn said, "Livvy, this thing between us might be falser than Joan Davis's eyelashes." The reminder was like having a bucket of water pitched over her head. But then he said something that slipped into the corner of her heart, a corner she realized she had earmarked for him. "But you... You're quite possibly the realest person I've ever met."

CHAPTER 13

FLYNN WAS SHOCKED TO DISCOVER HOW RUN-DOWN THE Garden of Allah Hotel had become. The stories of its opulence and its notorious parties were the stuff of Hollywood legend. But now it was a dingy collection of buildings that had seen better days. The only remnants of its greatness were the algae-filled water features burbling in the shadow of the looming estate.

He followed Livvy's directions to the small bungalow where she was staying. She moved to open the door of the passenger seat and he stopped her. "I may not be a gentleman, but I always walk a lady to her door."

She looked ready to protest, but he reached across her and opened her door, before hurrying out of the car and offering his hand once he was at her side. She bit her lip and gripped his fingers.

Something had changed between them in the last few hours. Every touch, every interaction was charged with the promise of something more. What had been fun and games was suddenly the most serious thing in the world. And he didn't know what to do with that. He was not and had never been a serious person.

As they walked to the front door, Flynn wondered if he should kiss her again. Good God, what was happening to him? He'd never once questioned the wisdom of kissing a woman in his life. But he knew he wasn't the type of man that Livvy deserved. She was vibrant, infuriating, fascinating, and funny too—but above all, she was kind and smart and good. The antithesis of all that he was.

But when he stood next to her on the stoop, her face turned up to him in the flickering beams of her porch light, he found it hard to remember any reason not to kiss her.

"Well, I suppose this is good night," she huffed, something breathless in her tone.

"Suppose so." He shrugged. Jesus, he was acting like a fumbling schoolboy. "But Livvy..." She looked uncertain, her eyes flicking back toward the car. He silently cursed his stupid black book. He'd locked it in his car weeks ago to avoid its temptation for the duration of this PR stunt. He'd honestly forgotten about it until it fell into Livvy's lap. He'd never felt the least bit of shame about that book. Until tonight. Watching Livvy page through it made him feel dirty. Like he had let her down before he'd ever met her. It unsettled him.

He didn't know what to say, so he placed his hand under her chin and tilted it up to study her face—her open, searching violet eyes, the freckle darker than the rest on her right cheek, the pert little curve of her nose, and the perfect Cupid's bow of her lips.

He leaned down to kiss them, and the door opened behind them.

"Livvy, you're home! Oh, er, sorry."

Livvy practically leaped off the porch in her rush to put distance between them. "Oh, don't worry, Judy. Mr. Banks was only making sure I made it to the door safely."

The kid behind the door gave her sister a look that said she didn't believe that for a second. But Livvy was back to calling him Mr. Banks. Whatever spell had been cast over them tonight had dissipated the second that girl had opened the door.

Flynn looked up and studied the kid. Livvy had said the girl was eighteen years old. But she still had the lean, feral build of a teenager. Judy was blond, the opposite of Livvy's dark curls, and while her eyes were the same shape, they were hazel, not the ravishing gray-violet that made Livvy so unique.

But was that…? Judy stepped back to let her sister in, and Livvy saw it the same time that he did. It had been hidden by the shadows of the porch.

Judy Blount was sporting a massive black eye.

Livvy gasped. "Oh my God, Judy. Are you all right?" Livvy rushed into the bungalow and immediately dragged her sister into the light of the living room. "What happened?"

The girl was clearly uncomfortable with Livvy's ministrations. She shook Livvy off and moved to the other side of the couch. "I'm fine. I messed up my number tonight, that's all."

Livvy looked stricken. "Tonight was your first night dancing in the floor show! Oh, Judy, I forgot. I was supposed to be here when you got home. I'm so, so sorry."

Judy eyed Flynn with a mixture of suspicion and interest. "That's okay. I knew you had other plans tonight."

Livvy still looked horrified. If she'd been wearing pearls, she would've clutched them. "I knew this club was a bad idea. First you injure your wrist, then you sprain your ankle, and now you've got a black eye. They don't seem to care much about the safety of their dancers. Can't you get a job at Schwab's or something instead?"

Judy stuck out her chin in a gesture of defiance Flynn knew all too well. He'd made that face at least ten times a day when he was Judy's age. "Stop fussing, Livvy. I'm a big girl. Mr. Wilkes said that if I want to be a dancer in the pictures, this is the best place to start."

"I'll bet he did," Livvy muttered.

Flynn's ears perked up at the mention of Mr. Wilkes. He'd put some money in the man's nightclub a few years back—the Sphinx, he recalled. Flynn had never been there himself. Billy Wilkes was an unsavory fellow, and his joints were known for being on the seedy side, but throwing money at the man's business aspirations had been the easiest way to settle a gambling debt after a poker game at Dash Howard's house had gotten out of hand.

Flynn looked at Judy more closely, noticing the purple bruising around her eye and the imprint of a small stone. He thought it was about the same size as the ruby ring Wilkes always wore on his pinkie finger. "How'd you say it happened?"

Both Judy and Livvy looked up at Flynn as if they'd forgotten he was even there. Judy chewed her lip nervously. "I told you, I messed up my number. I wasn't looking where I was going when I was kicking my way into the wings, and I ran into a flat used in the bubble dance routine."

Flynn's eyebrows rose at that. This kid didn't belong working in a club where there was bubble dancing going on. Hell, neither of the Blount girls belonged in a place like that. Besides, he could tell Judy was lying through her teeth. He'd lay down twenty bucks right now that the kid had got in Billy Wilkes's way and he'd back-handed her, leaving a mark with his ring. And it sounded like this wasn't the first time. He had a sickening feeling the injured wrist and sprained ankle hadn't been accidents either. Billy Wilkes preferred to communicate with his fists, not with his words.

But Livvy bought Judy's lie, scooching over to her sister on the couch and holding Judy's face under the light of the lamp. "Oh, Judy, it's turning green."

"That's good, means it's already starting to heal," Flynn told them. He shouldn't be here. This was none of his business. But he wanted to help. To prove he was more than that book of women's names and his stupid rating system.

"Oh, thank goodness it's already on the mend." Livvy continued to cluck and fuss over Judy, examining her face. "I should never have gone tonight. I should have been here for you."

Judy grimaced. "What good would that have done? Were you going to come to the club and stop me from running into the set? I'm not a child, Livvy."

"That may be, but I'm still responsible for you. I should've been here to help take care of it. Not off somewhere eating enchiladas."

Judy immediately disagreed, and Flynn left them bickering while he wandered into the kitchen—if the tiny range and icebox shoved into the corner could be called that. He opened the icebox door. There was nothing in it. Not even a jar of mayonnaise or mustard. What was the studio paying Livvy? Flynn made a mental note to talk to Harry. She was new and unproven, but Livvy should be able to afford groceries. Hell, she should be able to afford a better place to live than this dump. At the very least, she should be making enough so that her kid sister didn't have to lie about working for one of the most abusive club managers in town. The Sphinx wasn't the only spot that had a reputation for roughing up their showgirls, but there were spots where Judy would be safer and happier, though poorer.

The freezer's offerings weren't much better than the fridge's, but there was at least a frozen clump of chuck roast that looked like it'd been there since the Harding administration. He chipped it out of the freezer, took the single dish towel from the oven door, and wrapped it up.

When he returned to the living room, the girls were still arguing. He cleared his throat. "Er, sorry to interrupt." They snapped their heads in his direction. "But you should put this over that eye for a bit. Will help keep it from swelling."

"You sure know a lot about how to tend a black eye," Livvy quipped.

"It's common knowledge." Flynn shrugged, unsure if she had meant it as an insult. "But if you want the real reason, well, that's a story for another night." He winked at her. "Judy, keep that pressed on your eye for at least fifteen minutes. Livvy, if it looks worse in the morning, give me a ring. I'll have my doctor make a house call."

Livvy looked ready to kiss him, her eyes welling with tears. But this wasn't the time for that. His head was spinning with ideas about how to help Judy. Could he call Billy and threaten to pull his investment if the club manager didn't go easy on her? No, that would only make things worse. "I should be going."

He headed for the door as Livvy called out her thanks after him. He was climbing into his car when Judy rushed out after him.

"What's the matter?" he asked.

"Nothing. I just wanted to thank you—for not telling my sister the truth about my eye."

He chuckled. The kid was smart. He'd give her that. "I'm gonna guess the wrist injury and sprained ankle weren't accidents either?"

Judy bit her lip, chagrined. She shook her head. "Please don't tell Livvy. We need the money, and this pays better than any other dancing gig in town."

He should march back in there and tell Livvy the truth right now. He saw the way Livvy fretted over her sister; she would want to know what was happening. And Livvy wouldn't think twice about the money they lost if Judy quit—not if it was a choice between that and keeping Judy safe. He ran a hand down his face. "Can't you get a job at a soda fountain or something?"

Judy squared her shoulders and jutted out her chin, trying to look braver than he knew she was. "No. I'm a dancer."

"Ah. Can't get in the way of your dreams, now can we?" Flynn was annoyed on Livvy's behalf. He'd seen how much she had given up for Judy. How she made herself smaller, all in the name of protecting her sister. And the kid didn't even appreciate it.

Something fiery flashed in Judy's eyes. "No, it's nothing like that," she fumed. "It is my dream to be a dancer. But I'd give it up tomorrow if that would make Livvy happy."

"And what makes her happy is seeing you happy." He could almost hear Livvy saying the words herself, as if she were there in the drive with them.

"No. I mean, yes. But if you tell Livvy, she'll have us packed up as quick as if we were running from a house fire. She'll move us back to Saratoga if she thinks that'll keep us safe. Livvy never wanted to be an actress. She only said yes to the audition for the Hollywood Bowl talent scout because I begged her to. But since we got here, Livvy's changed. She's happy. I haven't seen her like this in a long, long time. Since before our parents died."

The words crashed into Flynn like a tidal wave. Suddenly, all the puzzle pieces were falling into place. The reason for Livvy's overprotectiveness. Her wariness around Flynn. The strange mix of disgust and fascination she seemed to hold for him.

Judy's eyes filled with tears. "Livvy brought us here because I begged her to. Because I knew if we didn't come to Hollywood, I'd never get my shot. Sure, I don't want to give up before I've even had a chance. But more importantly, I don't ever want to see Livvy go back to the way she's been these last four years. She was a shell of the sister I grew up with. So, please don't tell her. I promise I can handle it."

"Well, I'll be a monkey's uncle. You're not what I expected, kid." Flynn had been far more narcissistic when he was eighteen than this slip of a girl. But Livvy and Judy were two peas in a pod, loving each other into martyrdom. He sighed. "Fine, I won't tell your sister. It's your business anyway. But Livvy's right, you know. Billy Wilkes is bad news. You should find a job elsewhere. I can call some people for you if you like, try to pull some strings."

Judy's eyes widened and she shook her head with shocking vehemence. "No, don't go out of your way for me. Livvy would find out, and then she'll know I've been lying to her. I can take care of myself. Really, I can."

If he had any sense, he'd march back in there and tell Livvy exactly what was happening. Not only because he was skeptical Judy Blount could handle a man like Billy Wilkes, but because he knew, without question, that this was not what Livvy wanted for her sister. But he'd heard what Livvy had said—that she shouldn't have been off eating enchiladas.

Selfishly, he needed Livvy to stay in Hollywood too. If it weren't for her tonight—first rescuing him from Rhonda's clutches at the fundraiser, and then her quick thinking with that kiss in front of El Cholo—he'd already be on his way to becoming Hollywood's chief persona non grata. He'd been reluctant to participate in this charade, but if anyone could turn his reputation around, it was Livvy. What's more, he liked spending time with her. Talking to her. Making her so peeved that she got a little wrinkle between her eyes. Sparring with her—metaphorically and literally.

Flynn absolutely loved life. Maybe a little too much. Good food, good drinks, good fucking. They were all things he could never get enough of. But tonight, for the first time, he'd discovered the pleasure of watching *someone else* absorb the best this world had to offer—both things he loved, like an El Cholo enchilada, and things he'd never had time for, like classical music. He had friends, sure, and they knew how to have a good time. But this was different. Livvy was becoming someone he wanted to ensure was enjoying herself.

Judy said this was the first time she'd seen Livvy happy in a while, and part of him hoped it was because of him. He was certainly happier with Livvy in his life. He had scarcely even thought of his brother's last telegram lately. Instead, he'd thought of Livvy. The way she'd jumped on him when they'd won the regatta. The glimmer of want in her eyes when he flirted with her. And tonight, the way she'd responded to his kiss. How she'd turned pliant and passionate in his arms. Tonight had been special. And if Livvy knew the truth about Judy's black eye, there wouldn't be another night like this.

He turned the key in the ignition and looked at Judy, her bruise a deep plum in the shadows of the moonlight. "It'll be our little secret."

CHAPTER 14

"I LOOK RIDICULOUS." LIVVY GLARED AT THE MIRROR AS she tried to pin her hat in place.

"Don't be silly, you're the prettiest Peter Pan there's ever been," Judy trilled. She took the hat and affixed it jauntily to Livvy's head. "There."

Livvy studied herself in the bathroom mirror. Judy had pinned her black curls up into a sort of bob, so it looked like she had a pixie cut. She turned her head from side to side and fingered the collar of the green suede blouse Evelyn in wardrobe had lent her. "I do look quite fetching, don't I?"

Judy giggled and hugged her from behind. "Of course you do."

"I wish you were coming with me tonight. It's supposed to be the biggest Halloween party in town."

Judy squeezed her tight. "I know, I wish I was too. But I have shows at eight, nine thirty, and eleven tonight."

Livvy sighed. The bruise on her sister's face had faded to a sickly yellow, even if Livvy's guilt was as potent as ever. The bruise was practically invisible with the aid of a thick foundation. Since then, Judy hadn't sustained any further injuries. At least not any that Livvy was aware of. But she still didn't like Judy working at the Sphinx Club.

"Besides," Judy said, "you'll have more fun without me."

"I doubt that very much. I'm only going because it would look very odd indeed if the gal who was rumored to have captured Flynn's heart didn't make an appearance at his party." If Judy was going tonight, she'd have someone to talk to. Someone to distract her from Flynn Banks and the way her heart beat faster whenever she caught him looking at her.

Leda Price had once dubbed Flynn's house "Cirrhosis By the Sea," so notorious were the drunken exploits of his house parties. Having to face that alone… Well, she was going to need all the faith, trust, and pixie dust she could muster. Maybe she could feign a headache after she convinced the other guests that she and Flynn were together.

Judy opened a lipstick tube and rotated it before passing it to Livvy, who applied it carefully. Judy sighed dreamily. "No one at the party will be able to keep their eyes off of you. Least of all Flynn Banks." She waggled her eyebrows at her sister in the mirror.

Livvy rolled her eyes. "If I've told you once, I've told you a hundred times that it's an act. It can't be more than that."

"That was until tonight."

"And what's so different about tonight?"

"Before tonight, there's never been a Peter Pan with such a cute butt." Judy grabbed for a magazine near the sink and playfully whacked Livvy on her backside, making Livvy jump and clutch her bottom. Livvy gave her sister a look, but she couldn't repress a giggle. She turned and snatched the offending periodical from Judy's hands, realizing it was the latest issue of *Silver Screen Secrets*. The one featuring a photo of her and Flynn kissing outside of El Cholo and a feature story about their romance. Harry had been so delighted that he'd personally called to congratulate her. She'd have preferred he raise her salary so she and Judy could get out of this dump. But at least Harry saw that she and Flynn were trying their best.

Livvy herself should be thrilled the setup had worked so well. Yet every time she thought of it now, her hands got clammy and she lost her appetite. Because she couldn't forget the way that kiss had felt. How much she'd wanted to lose herself in Flynn's arms, right then and there. How it had made her want more. How those feelings had failed to dissipate. Even after holding the evidence of his conquests in her hands.

Livvy left the bathroom and wandered into the living room, tugging on her matching green shoes over her tights while holding onto the couch. Judy followed her and held up the issue of *Silver Screen Secrets* to wave under Livvy's nose. "This doesn't look fake to me!"

Livvy shook her head. "It's called acting, Judy. We both are being paid to do it professionally. I would hope it doesn't look fake, or our move to Hollywood might turn out to be a quick visit."

Judy turned her sister around to face her. "What do you mean?"

"If I can't convince the world that Flynn has mended his ways and fallen for me, I'll be out of a job. We'll have to go back to Saratoga."

Judy blanched. "No, we won't. We're not going back. There's nothing for us there."

Livvy sighed, the weight of all she was carrying bearing down on her. "We wouldn't have a choice, Judy. I don't want to leave either. Believe it or not, I'm actually starting to enjoy life on a movie set. But we can barely afford this dump with my studio salary and your income from the club."

"I could take on more," Judy protested. "Billy Wilkes told some of the other girls he's looking for dancers to perform at studio parties. I could do that."

Livvy felt a sickening sense of dread at the suggestion. "It's clear that Mr. Wilkes has no regard for your safety. I don't want you doing more work for him."

Judy looked as if Livvy had slapped her. "Those accidents were all my fault."

Livvy peered at her. Something about this whole situation still seemed off. "I've never known you to be accident-prone before. In all your years of dancing, the worst you had were broken toenails from your pointe shoes."

"I'm not used to dancing in a nightclub, and there's a million things happening backstage that I've had to adjust to. I promise, Livvy, now that I have my feet under me, I'll be fine."

"If you get hurt again, I won't let you go back there."

Judy gasped. "I'm not a child, Livvy. You can't stop me. Besides, you know we need the money."

Livvy hated that her sister was right. "Fine. But none of this studio party business."

"But it could be my chance. Billy says girls get discovered there all the time."

Ah, so that's what this was about. Judy's career. Livvy's heart went out to her sister, and she pulled Judy in for a hug. "You'll get discovered, Judy. If I make good at the studio with this PR stunt, maybe Harry will let me ask for a favor. Or we'll think of another way. You don't need Billy Wilkes. I shouldn't have agreed to make this picture. I should have made them hire you instead."

Judy squeezed her tighter. "But I'm so glad you agreed to make this movie. It got us here, didn't it?"

"Where? Me trapped in a fake romance with Flynn Banks concocted by a publicity department? Constantly living in fear of being caught? You working in a club where you keep getting hurt? I want you to have everything you've ever wanted, Judy. But maybe Hollywood was a mistake."

"No, Livvy. It's not a mistake. When I see how you've been these last few weeks, I know it could never be a mistake. Tell me the truth—are you so unhappy acting? I know it was never your dream. But lately, you've seemed…different. Lighter."

Livvy considered Judy's question. She had never wanted to be an actress, that was true. She'd loved movies, yes, Flynn's in particular, but ever since she was a child, all she had wanted to do was write books. When their parents died, she set that dream aside to take care of Judy. Acting had been an accident. But did she dislike it? She'd been so busy fretting over this business with Flynn that she hadn't stopped to consider whether she was happy in her work. She seemed to have a knack for it, and she loved the more physical parts of her job, like the fencing scenes. "I'm not unhappy acting. It's rewarding. A different way to approach storytelling than writing, but fulfilling all the same. And I'm having a lot more fun than I anticipated."

"Are you sure…" Judy's voice trailed off. "Never mind."

"No, say it. What is it?"

"Are you sure that part of it isn't Flynn?"

Livvy chuckled and shook her head. "You're impossible."

"I mean it, Livvy. You haven't dated anyone since before Mom and Dad died. Flynn has brought a spark back to your eyes that I haven't seen in a long time. He's good for you."

"Flynn Banks is good for absolutely no one." So what if he made her laugh? So what if every time that she was with him, she worried less? That was probably what Judy was sensing.

Judy wrinkled her nose. "That doesn't mean you can't enjoy your time with him."

Livvy drew her sister into a hug. "How'd I get so lucky to get you for a sister?" She kissed Judy on top of the head. "Promise me you'll come right home after the last show."

"Yes, Mother," Judy drawled. Livvy gave her a look. "Fine, fine. I promise. But only if you promise not to rush home from the party like a hen returning to her nest. You deserve to have some fun, Livvy."

That was the trouble though, wasn't it? Every time she was with Flynn Banks, she had more fun than she'd ever experienced in her entire life—and she was becoming entirely too accustomed to it.

"Ovrrrr therrrrrrre." Flynn gestured violently with his arm toward his deck, trying not to move his upper lip. He was sitting on a barstool in his kitchen while his friends helped him put the finishing touches on the house for his annual Halloween party.

"Stop talking! You're going to spoil your mustache." Arlene Morgan, Joan's former assistant and now celebrated Hollywood screenwriter and director, was attempting to draw a mustache on Flynn's face with a charcoal pencil.

"Good, then I won't look like that idiot." Dash Howard flipped him off as he carried a jack-o'-lantern out the door to deposit on the deck where Flynn had pointed.

Joan, who was engrossed in making punch that was a neon shade of green, looked up and tilted her head, resembling a cocker spaniel considering its master. "I don't know, Flynn. I think it suits you. It's very handsome."

"You *would* say that."

Joan shrugged as Dash reentered the house and pressed a kiss to her temple. "I like what I like." She finished pouring a bottle of what smelled like eighty-proof liquor into the punch bowl and turned to kiss Dash properly. Don Lamont, musical star and Arlene's husband, then emerged from the bathroom down the hall.

"Do they look right, Arlene?" He grinned, revealing two pointed fangs that he'd applied to complete his Dracula costume.

Arlene looked up from drawing the curled tip of Flynn's mustache and gasped. "Ohhh, darling, you look positively terrifying." She turned back to her handiwork and stuck her tongue in the corner of her mouth to concentrate. Flynn tried not to sneeze. "There, you're done."

"Finally," Flynn growled.

Arlene set down her pencil and ran to hug Don, who picked her up and spun her into a hug before pretending to bite her neck. "I vant to suck your blood."

"Disgusting, all of you," Flynn muttered.

"You're just jealous," Arlene huffed, yelping as Don tickled her neck with his fangs.

"*Pffft*, jealous. I'm quite content to go through my life without ever looking as ridiculous as you all do right now." But Flynn couldn't help thinking of Livvy and wondering what she would wear tonight. Lately he'd been imagining her wearing nothing.

That way lay madness. Livvy was supposed to improve his reputation, not make it worse. Seducing her was not going to help his cause. But she filled him with foreign feelings, ones that jumbled his insides as if his internal organs were potatoes in a sack. He hadn't seen her outside the studio all week, though he had often found himself thinking about her, wondering how she'd react to piece of music he heard on the wireless or what she read at night before falling asleep.

"You looked fairly ridiculous kissing that new costar of yours outside El Cholo," Dash drawled.

"Harry didn't think so. He's never been happier to see me linked to a dame in the press." Flynn usually told his friends everything, but in this case, he figured the fewer people who knew the truth, the less likely they were to get caught. Before Dash could probe further, Flynn reached for the ladle in the punch bowl and poured its contents straight into his mouth, choking down the heinous concoction Joan had made. He coughed, his throat catching fire as the punch filled his stomach. "What the hell did you put in that?"

Joan smiled, looking more mischievous than ever. "Zombie elixir—so strong it could raise the dead."

Flynn chuckled. "You could say that again. This stuff tastes like gasoline."

Dash interjected on his wife's behalf, "I'm sure it's wonderful, darling." He nuzzled her neck and wrapped his hand around her waist. Flynn wasn't sure if it was the lighter fluid he'd consumed or the sickening sight of his best friend so visibly in love with his wife, but he fought back the urge to retch.

Joan leaned into Dash's kiss, but she murmured, "No, it's probably terrible. But I'm a movie star. Flynn should get his staff to make punch if he wants it to taste good."

"I gave the staff the night off," Flynn said. "I find people enjoy the party more if they don't feel like there's someone surveying their every move."

"Well, they might enjoy the party more if someone besides me made the drinks, but it's your funeral." Joan shrugged.

Don and Arlene laughed, still clinging to each other like

barnacles on a rock. "I'm so glad love hasn't changed you, Joan," Arlene trilled.

"Darling," Joan replied, "there are some things a woman simply cannot change. My ability to cook is one of them. Besides, after one drink, everyone will be so plotzed, they won't be able to tell the difference."

Everyone laughed, and Flynn had never felt more like the odd man out. What the hell was the matter with him? The people in this room were his best friends. Why did he suddenly feel like a sock without its mate? He checked the clock hanging on the wall, wondering what time Livvy would arrive.

"Is it just me, or is this kitchen hot as Hades all of a sudden?" He tugged at the ruffled cravat around his neck, trying to loosen it.

Both couples exchanged meaningful looks with each other.

"What?" Flynn asked. He'd about had it with them.

"Nothing," they answered in unison.

"It's not nothing; you're all eyeing each other like owls, so what is it?"

Arlene and Joan looked at each other and sighed heavily. "Well, it's just...you're not jealous."

"Isn't that what I just said?"

"No, it's much worse than that," Joan added. "You're in love."

Of all the ridiculous things he'd ever been accused of in his life, this took the cake. "Me? In love? Rubbish. I'd expect this from Arlene, but from you? Joan Davis? You who once swore you didn't believe in love? Maybe you've been sampling your own punch too much. Dash, tell them, it's absurd. Flynn Banks in love—what a preposterous suggestion."

Dash merely stared at him, a look of pity on his face.

"Oh, not you too!"

"I would've said it was impossible," Dash admitted.

"It is!"

"But Flynn, have you ever brought a girl to El Cholo before?"

He had to admit that Dash had him there. He took girls to the Trocadero, the Brown Derby, the Cocoanut Grove, or back here to his house. The one place he did not bring them was El Cholo. Because El Cholo was about good food and drink and nothing else. He didn't want it tainted with the memory of some blowsy aspiring starlet. Most of all, he didn't want to sneak out through the El Cholo kitchen to escape a scorned woman. "No, but that's different. Livvy isn't a girl."

"She looks an awful lot like a girl to me," murmured Arlene.

"That's not what I mean! It wasn't like that. We were tired of the dog-and-pony show at the symphony benefit, and she'd never had Mexican food, and I wanted to show her a real piece of Los Angeles. I wouldn't take a girl there. But Livvy, she's not just some dame I'm making whoopee with. She's, she's..." He hunted for the right word to describe her. What was Livvy? A costar? That was too anodyne a description. A friend? That was far too familiar, was it not? As he racked his brain, hunting for the perfect word to describe her, his four friends crossed their arms and shook their heads, clearly judging him.

"Ohhh, you've got it bad, buster," Don said, chuckling.

"You're all off your nut," Flynn growled. He snatched the gloved hook that he'd left on the tiled kitchen counter and turned to go. "If you'll excuse me, I need to put on my wig."

CHAPTER 15

WHEN THE STUDIO CAR DROPPED LIVVY OFF AT FLYNN'S Malibu mansion, she could hardly believe her eyes. The entire stone driveway was lined with glowing jack-o'-lanterns, and a flurry of construction paper bats were taped to the stucco wall of the house. The jack-o'-lanterns continued around the perimeter of the property, and she had no doubt that if she followed them, they would lead all the way to the beach. She suddenly felt very small and out of place in her green Peter Pan costume, the gravel of the driveway pressing through her elfin shoes.

"'Second star to the right and straight on till morning,'" she muttered, taking a breath and squaring her shoulders.

She passed through the arched doorway lined with colorful tiles and approached Flynn's oak front door, which stood open. A breeze blew in from the water, and she hugged her thin little cardigan more tightly around her as she scurried inside.

"May I take your coat—er, sweater?"

Livvy was shocked to find award-winning screenwriter Arlene Morgan, dressed as a rather fetching witch, working the unofficial coat check. "Miss Morgan?"

"Technically, it's Lamont now. But on scripts, it's still Morgan."

That was right. Livvy remembered now. Arlene Morgan had married rising star Don Lamont earlier this year in a quiet ceremony in her parents' backyard. She'd read about it in one of Judy's copies of *Silver Screen Secrets*.

"Oh, I just wanted to say how much I admire your work," Livvy stammered, so nervous she could barely get the words out. "I love to read, and your script for *Reno Rendezvous* made me realize that movies are just as much a storytelling art form as novels."

Arlene darted her head around, making a show of looking for onlookers. "Don't say that too loud in here, the house that piracy built." Livvy laughed. It should come as no surprise that Arlene Morgan was a quick wit, but it caught Livvy off guard all the same. "Besides, aren't you starring in a swashbuckler right now?"

Livvy blushed. "Yes, it's my first picture. I'm Liv de Lesseps, but you probably already know that."

"Well, let me tell you a secret, Miss De Lesseps. Swashbucklers are my favorite!"

Livvy giggled and handed over her sweater. "They're mine too." They tittered together. "I hope my movie won't disappoint."

"Based on what Flynn's said, I'm sure you won't." Livvy wanted to ask what Arlene meant by that. She'd said *you*, not *it*. Had it been a slip of the tongue? Or was Arlene hinting at something? How much had Flynn been talking about her with his friends? It was a terrifying and thrilling thought.

"Um, has he told you—"

"That he's in love with you?"

Livvy froze in her tracks. So Flynn hadn't told his friends about the PR relationship. He'd kept them in the dark and protected the ruse. But saying he was in love with her? That seemed to be laying it on a bit thick. Arlene carried on, not noticing that she had rendered Livvy mute.

"Of course he didn't tell us that. But it's obvious to those of us who know him well. Enjoy the party!"

Arlene turned and hung Livvy's sweater in the foyer closet, clearly signaling that this conversation was over.

Livvy slipped into the living room, feeling like she'd bumped her head on something on the way in. *Flynn was in love with her?* Or at least his friends seemed to think so. That couldn't possibly mean that the man had real feelings for her. The idea was preposterous. Perhaps he was just *really* convincing whenever he talked about her.

Not looking where she was going, she accidentally bumped into someone's back. "Oh, I'm so sorry," she started, only to nearly swallow her tongue when Joan Davis turned around to face her.

"Oh, you must be Livvy!" Joan grabbed Livvy's shoulders and held her at arm's length, taking her in. "Oh my goodness, are you Peter Pan?"

Livvy nodded, unable to find her voice as she let the scene around her filter into her brain. Dash Howard stood behind Joan; they had been dancing until Livvy collided with them.

"Dash, go get Flynn. This is too good." As Dash stalked off, Joan returned her attention to Livvy. "Wait till you see him, darling. Did you plan this together?"

"Uh, no." Livvy hadn't the scarcest idea what Joan was talking about.

She let herself take in the rest of the room. A live band was in the corner, playing a rollicking rendition of the Charleston. She did a double take. Was that Benny Goodman on clarinet? Flynn hadn't been joking when he'd told her his Halloween party was the event of the season. Everyone who was anyone in Hollywood was packed into this room, drinking a ghastly looking green beverage out of punch glasses, smoking, and having a hell of a great time. It was shockingly normal. Except that you could spit in any direction and hit someone more famous than God.

"*Pan!*" bellowed a British voice that made Livvy feel like she'd swallowed an entire bottle of pixie dust, a shimmery, fizzy sensation suffusing her whole body. She looked down to make sure her feet were still on the ground.

The owner of the voice rounded the corner from the kitchen, and in the place of Flynn Banks was Captain Hook in all his mustache-twirling glory.

Flynn was sporting a massive curly dark wig, on top of which was perched an ostentatious hat with a large black feather protruding from the brim and curling down into Flynn's face. Above his full lips, he had painted a false mustache. The only way she recognized him was by the unmistakable twinkle in his blue eyes and the mischievous smirk in the corner of his mouth. And the live capuchin monkey perched on his shoulder, whose eyes lit up at the sight of her.

The monkey leapt to the floor and sprinted to her, climbing her leg until she made a perch for him with her forearm. "Hello, Rallo, I didn't expect to see you here."

The monkey grinned, and she giggled at the awful sight of his bared teeth as he climbed her arm and planted a kiss on her cheek.

"Don't you steal my girl," Flynn called out. It made Livvy laugh, and she patted Rallo on the head. She was overcome by the sensation of bubbles floating through her chest.

It was ridiculous, really. She'd been so frightened of coming tonight. Doubtful that she could control whatever she felt for Flynn. Uneasy about the party guests' wilder side. Or worse, that Flynn's friends and Hollywood acquaintances would find her lacking in some way. Or that they'd immediately see through their charade, and the jig would be up. Arlene Morgan seemed absolutely convinced Flynn was head over heels for her—a thought perhaps even more terrifying than the notion of being found out. But all her anxieties vanished at the sight of a little monkey.

Flynn ran to her and swept her up into a hug, twirling her in a circle. Livvy had the stray thought that this must be what flying felt like. Rallo gnashed his teeth and leapt down, scurrying out of the room.

"Oh, this is marvelous!" crowed Flynn. "Brilliant! Who told you?"

"Who told me what?" He set her down and kept his hands on her waist.

"That I was going as Captain Hook tonight. Your costume is too, too perfect."

"No one told me anything. Judy suggested that I be Peter Pan, and Connie in the wardrobe department offered to help with my costume."

"So it's a coincidence?" Flynn marveled. "Splendid!"

A kaleidoscope of butterflies took flight in Livvy's chest as Flynn continued to hold on to her, clearly delighted by their accidentally coordinated costumes.

"Clearly a sign that we're meant to be," she joked, her voice warbling a bit with nerves. All those around them laughed, including Flynn. Livvy heard someone mutter something about Flynn being "a changed man" behind her and silently patted herself on the back.

Then Flynn assumed a fighting stance, brandishing his hook as if it were a rapier. "En garde, Pan!"

Livvy felt every set of eyes in the room that wasn't already looking in their direction turn to them. She'd intended to make a brief appearance at the party, smile for some photos, and go home to wait for Judy. But something told her the night had just taken a turn.

"Um…" She removed the tiny faux dagger from the belt around her waist and brandished it limply.

But before she could blink, Joan Davis wrested a rapier from a display on the wall and tossed it at Livvy. "Catch!"

Livvy lifted her arm just in time to grip the fine brass handle of the sword. Its firm, cool presence in her hand filled her with a renewed courage. She grinned, winked at Joan, and mirrored Flynn's stance. "Might I remind you, Hook, that it is Pan who always wins the battle?"

"Not this time." Something wicked flashed in Flynn's eyes as he drew out a rapier hanging from the belt at his side. She attacked, but he parried with his hook, sliding it down the length of the metal blade as it shrieked at the contact.

The other guests parted, making a wide circle around Flynn and Livvy so they could watch. But Livvy only had eyes for Flynn, his ridiculously oversized hat feather taunting her. With one swift movement, she swirled her rapier out of the curve of Flynn's hook and raised it in a circular motion, slicing off the tip of the obnoxiously large feather. She zigzagged back to knock his hat all the way off with the point of her blade.

The party guests broke into a combination of gasps and applause.

"You do like removing my wardrobe with your sword," Flynn teased. She blushed, realizing that the tittering jocularity spreading through the room had just been amplified by his comment. She needed to answer him.

"Hush! You've managed to convince the press that I've reformed you. You don't want them getting the wrong idea, do you?"

The crowd roared with laughter, and she breathed a little easier. She'd intended it as a warning to Flynn, a reminder that they were supposed to appear chastely in love. He should avoid referencing scandalous activities that hadn't even occurred between them. *And never will,* she thought a bit mournfully. But the guests were enjoying this dance between them. Perhaps she should give them the show they so clearly wanted.

Returning to the basics of her fencing training, she furiously attacked, backing Flynn up until he was nearly against the wall of the living room. Then she produced the tiny dagger she'd slipped back into the holster of her belt and threw it at him, pinning his red velvet coat to the wall.

"I did try to warn you that Peter Pan always wins," she crowed, enjoying the admiring murmurs that were traveling around the room.

He attempted to tug the handle of the blade out with his hook to no avail, then raised his hands in surrender. "All right, all right."

But she continued to advance on him, extending the point of her blade until it notched itself in the dimple in his chin.

He gulped. "B-bad form," he choked out. She smiled. Those were Hook's exact final words in J. M. Barrie's novel. It wasn't something she'd expected him to know. But then she remembered the night they'd first met. He'd said that *Treasure Island* was his favorite novel. It wasn't much of a stretch to imagine he had a fondness for *Peter Pan* too.

She gently moved the tip of the blade up, caressing his cheek with it. A little zip of electricity ran down her spine at how unexpectedly intimate the gesture was. He raised his eyebrows, but he still looked unsettled. "Livvy...remember, it's the crocodile, not Peter Pan, who kills Hook."

The room laughed at that, but he looked more nervous than she'd ever seen him, and she wanted to relish this moment. She'd regained the upper hand, if only for this brief interlude, and she wanted to bask in it.

"Oh, I know, but there aren't any crocodiles to be had in Malibu." She increased her pressure on the blade ever so slightly, watching as it bit gently into his cheek, not hard enough to leave a mark, but enough to change the color of his complexion. "Besides, I like you better as Flynn Banks." She slid her blade under the center part of his wig and pulled it off his head, flinging it into the crowd. Someone whooped with excitement as they reached up and caught it. "Piracy looks better on you as a blond."

His jaw dropped at her words, and she threw her blade at his feet. She put her hands on her hips and struck the pose that hundreds of actors playing Peter Pan on stages around the world had assumed.

But the false bravado that had overtaken her while she was dueling Flynn was quickly dissipating. She resisted the urge to clock the number of extremely famous faces in the crowd who were very likely staring at her. She was entirely uncertain what to do now.

But Joan and Arlene, who had apparently abandoned her duties at the front door, wrapped their arms around her. "Congratulations!" Arlene cooed, while Joan pulled her toward the kitchen, adding, "Let's get you a drink."

CHAPTER 16

AS JOAN AND ARLENE CARTED LIVVY OFF TO THE NEXT room telling her God knows what, Flynn stared after her. He knew better than to challenge Livvy with a sword. But when she'd entered the party dressed as Peter Pan, the green suede of her costume hugging the pert little curve of her butt, he hadn't been able to resist putting on a show. Besides, wasn't that what he was supposed to be doing? Showing the world how impressive Livvy is? Flynn was beginning to realize it wasn't just Livvy's unstained reputation that had convinced Harry to entrap her into this publicity stunt. No, Harry had seen something extraordinary in this bookish beauty. Something that made her a more believable match for Flynn than he'd ever thought she could be. Flynn was just doing his job to keep up the ruse by helping people see that.

He was still gaping after that irresistible, retreating backside when Dash approached and clapped him on the shoulder. "That is one hell of a woman."

"Don't I know it," muttered Flynn. He realized that he was still pinned to the wall with the point of her dagger. The rest of the crowd, sensing the show was over, had turned away to chat with each other. Flynn picked up snatches of their murmurs, some marveling at Livvy's skill, others calling it unladylike. Bugger, had he cocked this up? He'd gotten carried away by the delightful coincidence of their costumes. And he'd never been able to resist making a bit of a scene.

The band resumed playing. He continued to tug at the dagger to no avail, barely able to twist his trapped arm to wrap his fingers around it.

Dash gave him a look.

"What?"

"Nothing, nothing."

Flynn continued to wrestle with the stupid dagger until Dash drawled, "Might help if you lost the hook."

Flynn sighed, a bit irritated he hadn't thought of it himself. But his mind was spinning off in a million different directions, fretting over whatever Joan and Arlene were telling Livvy in the kitchen. Or worse, what Livvy was telling them. He dropped the hook, resigning himself to the fact that the portion of his evening with a complete costume was now over. With his other hand free, he easily pulled the dagger from the wall and rotated his shoulder a few times to wake up the muscles that had been starting to tingle from being trapped in place.

Dash nodded to the porch and Flynn followed him outside. The air was crisp and cold, and it smelled of the briny tang of the ocean. Flynn took in the deck, the line of meticulously carved jack-o'-lanterns that stood like sentinels guarding the stairs leading up to a second patio outside the master bedroom. The old friends climbed up there together in silence.

"Thought you could use some air," said Dash.

"Thanks," Flynn grunted.

He was thrown back to the memory of another night on this deck a few years ago, when Dash had come over in a huff, having learned that one of his pranks had accidentally led to his marriage to Joan. Now, Dash was blissfully (re)married to his costar, and Flynn was still a happy bachelor who shuddered at the mere mention of an engagement. Even though the thought of waking up next to Livvy every morning was far more tempting than he cared to admit.

He and Dash leaned against the stucco wall of the upstairs patio and stood in silence, listening to the waves crash against the rocks below. Then Dash turned and studied Flynn with a look of consternation. "What are you doing with that girl?"

Of all the questions he'd expected to hear from his best friend, that wasn't one of them. Dash hadn't exactly cultivated a sterling reputation before he'd married Joan. "What do you mean? You know what I'm doing. We're having some fun."

Dash rolled his eyes. "No. I know your version of having fun, and that little exhibition in there wasn't it. That girl isn't your usual worldly dame; her earnestness is written all over her face. So I ask you again, what are you doing?"

"I don't know what you mean."

"C'mon, Flynn. When I didn't want to admit I was in love with Joan, you told me how stupid I was. What are friends for, if not to point out the obvious things we refuse to admit to ourselves? You brought her to your favorite restaurant, somewhere you've never taken a doll. You challenged her to a sword fight in front of half of Hollywood, knowing full well she'd probably embarrass you."

"I didn't know—"

"Don't tell me that what she did in there was surprising to you. You weren't shocked at how good she was. You were goddamn delighted. It was written all over your face how much you enjoyed going toe-to-toe to her. How much you like that she's better than you with a sword."

The words hit Flynn like a bucket of cold water. "No, I just thought it was funny that our costumes went so well together. If the host of a party is dressed as Captain Hook, is he not morally obligated to duel the first person to arrive that's dressed as Peter Pan?"

"Even for you, that's a ludicrous argument." Dash reached for the bottle of wine someone had left on the patio table and took a swig from it before passing it to Flynn. "Look, maybe that excuse would fly with Benny Goodman or Bing Crosby or half the other fellas in that room. But you can't fool me. You wanted everyone to see her, to be awed by her."

"She was rather spectacular, wasn't she?" Flynn grinned. He took another swig from the wine bottle.

"She was," Dash admitted. "But that's not my point. My point is that you've been acting strangely for weeks now. When Joan and I saw that picture of you with the girl outside of El Cholo, we couldn't believe it. So what the hell is going on?"

Flynn sighed. "Fine. I'll level with you. But you can't tell anyone. Not even Joan." Dash looked ready to argue, but Flynn glared at him. "If our friendship means anything to you, you'll keep this to yourself."

"Fine," Dash growled.

"Livvy and me, it's not real. That business with Rhonda Powers put me on thin ice with the Legion of Decency, so Harry decreed that Livvy and I should pretend to fall in love for publicity. Make it look like the influence of a good woman reformed me. Everything the last few weeks has been about convincing people of that fact."

"I think the only person you're convincing of anything right now is yourself." Dash gave him a pointed look.

Flynn scoffed. "Hardly. We're just good at pretending. Every relationship—or marriage, for that matter—that the publicity department arranges isn't destined to become true love. We're friends, that's all. Friends doing our job. You think there's something there because that's what we want you to see, but none of this is real."

"Does she know that?"

The question caught Flynn off guard. Was Livvy developing feelings for him? No. It was impossible. She was far too smart for that. Besides, what had she said the other night? She should have been home with Judy instead of eating enchiladas with him. She was doing this because Harry Evets had told her to. And that was that. Wasn't it? "Of course she does."

Dash raised an eyebrow and snagged the bottle of wine back for another swig. "You don't sound convinced."

"Oh hell, Dash, what do you want from me?" Flynn was getting annoyed. His Halloween party was his favorite night of the year, and here he was arguing with his best friend about a dame. "I wouldn't be in this mess if you and Joan hadn't invited Rhonda Powers to your party."

Dash rolled his eyes. "Neither of us told you to kiss her in the garden. In fact, if you had asked, we would've warned you off her immediately. Which we did as soon as we realized what you were up to. You couldn't keep your hands to yourself for one evening."

"I wasn't aware that the Howard and Davis residence came with a celibacy policy," Flynn bit out.

"It doesn't—" Dash started.

"Give me a break, Dash. You act like you've never kissed a girl and regretted it. I always knew you were a better man than me, but you're not gonna be applying for sainthood anytime soon."

"I am not a saint, but you're also not the villain you've convinced yourself you are."

"Rhonda seems to think I am."

"And what? You want to prove her right? The only thing Rhonda Powers proves is that sometimes you're an idiot. For once in your life, think with your head and not your dick. You wouldn't be in this mess if you did, and now people are going to get hurt. You don't need to reform, but you could exercise some better judgment once in a while!"

Flynn had never heard his friend sound so disappointed. It reminded Flynn of the way his father used to speak to him, the way he always seemed to imply that he'd fallen short. The tone of voice that had made him decide that since he would never be good enough, he would rather be wicked instead.

"Don't speak to me like that," Flynn snapped. "I don't understand why you suddenly want me to be something I'm not. I'm never going to be Prince Charming, Dash. I'm a rogue through and through, and that's how I like it. Livvy knows that. She's just helping me try to convince the public otherwise until this Rhonda mess dies down. Why is that a problem?"

Dash looked at him then, a profound sadness in his eyes. It stopped Flynn in his tracks. "It's not. Not if that's really who you are. But what I'm asking you to do is stop and think about whether you are still the same Flynn Banks you were on the night we met at Musso and Frank's Grill six years ago. When I beat you in that drinking contest."

"Excuse me, *I* beat *you*."

That made Dash chuckle, and the weight of the stone that had dropped into Flynn's stomach lessened ever so slightly. But he seriously considered what Dash had said: Was he still the same Flynn Banks? He thought so. He drank as much, swore as much, seduced women whenever he felt like it. Sure, he'd curtailed all that these last few weeks. But it was an act. When all this was over, he'd go right back to who he was before.

"The Flynn Bankses of this world don't change," Flynn retorted, trying to find some of that caddish spark that had never seemed far out of reach. But his heart wasn't in it—and Dash could tell.

"I don't think that's true. But even if it is, you need to figure out your intentions before you break that girl's heart."

Dash might as well have plunged Livvy's dagger into Flynn's gut and twisted. "I am not going to break her heart. She's faking it. Just like me."

"It might have started out that way, but I think you should ask her if that's still true. But first, you should ask yourself."

Flynn stared out at the sea, the stars and the full moon twinkling off the vast inky water that was his backyard. He thought about the ways his life had recently changed. The way he'd swum through that water until he was exhausted, trying to banish the memory of a girl he'd only just met. The guilt he'd felt when his little black book fell into Livvy's lap and her hurt had been scrawled across her face. Livvy had turned him upside down, shaken him, and left him completely jumbled.

Had he righted himself since the first night they met? Or had he only grown more confused, more desperate to convince Livvy that he was worthy of her smiles, her attention, and her tinkling little laugh? That laugh. Every time he said or did something that made it come out of her mouth, he felt like he'd won a prize at the fair. He thought about *Treasure Island,* the dog-eared pages of his copy that he'd read a hundred times. How it was Livvy who helped him remember how much he'd once loved to read. He'd been enjoying revisiting it these last few weeks, reading a little each night before bed.

Was Dash right? Was Livvy different? Was *he* different with her?

Dash startled Flynn from his thoughts with a clap on the back. "I saw the way that girl looked at you tonight. What's more, I saw the way you looked at her. Like she could hang the moon. All I want, hell, all any of us want—Joan, Arlene, Don—is for you to be happy. But first you have to be honest."

Dash let the words hover there, and Flynn mulled them over. He thought about Livvy, the ecstatic joy on her face when they'd won the regatta and how she'd jumped into his arms without thinking. The look of sinful bliss she'd worn when the first bite of enchiladas had touched her lips.

When they first met, he'd tried seducing her. While reminding her that he never played for keeps. Then, they'd agreed to be friends. But the woman who had answered his challenge tonight with her eyes blazing, who had driven him into a corner with her sword and pinned him to the wall, had scorched his soul with her inner fire. And Flynn? He had liked it. He'd liked it ever since their duel at the soundstage, and he'd invited her to do it again tonight. In front of his closest friends and enemies, so that they could all see what he saw. That she was marvelous; a goddamned pirate queen.

She made him, and every single thing in a room, glitter in the reflection of her brilliance. She was a jewel, one that he was realizing would be unbearable to lose. Somewhere along the way she'd stolen past his defenses. Defenses he usually never even had to worry about maintaining. Besides, Livvy was not the type of girl to fall for a committed scoundrel like him. So, there was no way that she could possibly have real feelings. Yet Dash seemed to think otherwise. Was his oldest friend imagining things? Or could there truly be something there?

"I need to talk to her," Flynn muttered, sprinting over to the steps.

"Attaboy," called Dash.

Flynn took the stairs two at a time, running toward the kitchen, praying Livvy was still safely ensconced there with Joan and Arlene. But when he entered, Joan was merely humming a song, while Arlene and Don danced in the corner.

"Livvy. Where is she?"

Joan shrugged. "I don't know. She hightailed it out of here when Johnny Albright came in looking for a partner to bob for apples with. Said she needed to find you. Smart girl."

Flynn was shocked to find a white-hot flame of jealousy flare in his chest. Before he could hear more, he was through the kitchen door, into the tiled hall, and back to the living room. His guests were a swaying mass, crushed against each other while Benny Goodman played "Begin the Beguine." His eyes darted around the room, looking for Livvy's green felt hat or her telltale pitch-black curls. She wasn't anywhere to be found.

His heart sank. She must've left. Why had he let Dash pull him away for so long? Livvy didn't know many people in Hollywood yet, and he'd left her there to mingle. He knew she could more than hold her own, but that didn't mean that she wanted to or should always be expected to.

Suddenly, he wasn't very interested in this party either. He wanted these people out of his house. He craved the quiet—just himself, a glass of whiskey, and the crash of the waves against the sand. He needed to think. But he couldn't exactly kick them out.

He stole a glance at the clock on the wall. Christ, it was barely ten o'clock. If he asked everyone to leave, they'd probably think he needed his head examined. Flynn Banks ending a party at 10 p.m.? It was unheard of.

But he needed to think. To figure out whether anything Dash

had said was true. Was Livvy not merely pretending? He dodged a couple so drunk he had to wonder how they were keeping each other upright, and headed for the long hallway to the only place in this house he was guaranteed to find solitude—the library.

CHAPTER 17

THE SECOND SHE ENTERED THE LIBRARY, THE CONSTRICTED feeling in Livvy's chest released.

Joan and Arlene had been so kind, hurrying her away to the kitchen and plying her with punch and toffee. But it had been hard to breathe in their company. All she could think was how they had three Oscars between them. They fretted over her, never prying or asking a single question about Flynn, trying to put her at ease. But when a dreadful man with hands that wandered more than Christopher Columbus had come in and tried to cajole her into bobbing for apples with him, she couldn't take it anymore. She'd made an excuse about needing to find Flynn and scampered off.

She should have gone home. But while looking for Flynn, she'd happened upon the library at the end of the hall.

The thick door turned the music in the living room into a muffled din. She turned in a circle, marveling at the room before her. Every wall was covered with floor-to-ceiling shelves, books of all shapes and sizes spilling out of them. She inhaled, taking in the scent of the dusty tomes, the distinctive tang of the glue holding the pages together in each of the individual treasures. She was inclined to think they were for show, except that she could tell the difference between untouched books and a well-loved library. This was obviously the latter, with books haphazardly stuffed into crannies where they clearly didn't belong and busts of authors like Shakespeare and Oscar Wilde serving as makeshift bookends.

A lumpy armchair covered with burnt-orange velvet was stuck in the corner, and Livvy wandered toward it. Her eye caught on the book hanging over the arm of the chair, a well-worn copy of *Treasure Island* whose spine had more cracks than an unlucky piece of pavement. Livvy admired the pair of slippers stuck under the chair and the tartan blanket tucked over its back. Everything about the space was cozy and comforting.

On one side of the chair was a globe. Livvy pressed a small wooden button hidden in the grain of the wooden stand, and the top of the globe snapped open, revealing a collection of liquor bottles, ice tongs, and crystal glasses. She picked up a crystal tumbler and sniffed it. It reminded her of Flynn's favorite Scotch, which she hadn't even realized she'd known until this moment. It was smoky and warm, a strange blend of cinnamon and pine. It smelled like him.

"Pilfering the good stuff?" The voice in the doorway startled Livvy so much that she bobbled the glass in her hands, struggling not to drop it. She could tell that it was expensive from its heft and clarity.

"No, I was just—" She turned and lost her train of thought at the sight of Flynn. He was leaning against the doorjamb, his blond hair messy from its time spent under his Captain Hook wig. He must have rubbed his mustache; it now looked like a smear of soot across his face. But the kohl around his eyes was still perfect, and her knees turned to jelly when he gave her a smolder.

"I was only teasing. What are you doing down here? I was worried you might've left."

She set the glass down, suddenly awkward in the room that had been so comforting only moments before. "I was...looking for the bathroom." She surprised herself with how quickly the lie came. "But I was leaving."

"Oh." His face fell. "But you can't leave yet."

"Why is that?"

"Because I want you to stay. Please."

His plea made her warm and tingly, like she'd knocked back a glass of that whiskey in the globe. "I didn't think you'd miss me. You have so many guests. And your friends. You'd hardly notice if I left."

His eyes flared with something dangerous. "I assure you, I would notice. And I would feel the loss of your presence most keenly."

Had someone turned a radiator on in this room? It was suddenly sweltering. A bead of sweat dripped down her back, and she resisted the urge to fan herself. "Well, I...got overwhelmed."

"So you decided to find some reading material?" He grinned, something wicked and irresistible there, and she found herself taking a step toward him as if pulled in his direction by an invisible force.

"This library is incredible."

"Being an aristocrat oughta be good for something." He pushed off the doorway casually, stalking into the room, and she prayed he didn't hear her gulp.

"You inherited all this?" she squeaked.

"Some of it. Other parts I bought myself. I know you think I'm a philistine—"

"I don't!"

"But 'the person, be it gentleman or lady, who has not pleasure in a good novel, must be intolerably stupid.'"

She had not expected this evening to involve Flynn Banks quoting Jane Austen to her. "You've read *Northanger Abbey*?"

"And *Pride and Prejudice*. Though *Emma* is my favorite." He started trawling the shelves, dropping leather-bound volumes gently to the floor as he hunted for something. He turned his head to her. "Always a fan of the cheeky ones, you know."

He winked at her, sizing up her costume and the fuchsia blush that had suffused her neck and face. "You know green and pink is my favorite color combination."

She barked out a laugh. "You're making that up."

"No, I'm not. I just decided right now that it's my favorite. I'm allowed to do that. My library, my rules." He returned to rummaging through his shelves. "You're a fan of Austen, I take it?"

"Would you believe me if I said no?"

"No," he murmured drily, twisting around to give her a withering glance. But the twinkle in his eyes made it obvious he was teasing.

"Good. Because she's my favorite author. She's why I wanted to be a writer."

Flynn peered at her as if he was seeing something clearly for the first time. "I didn't know you wanted to be a writer."

She raised one shoulder to her ear. It had been years since she'd expressed this dream to anyone. Judy was the only one who knew. And Livvy had tried her darndest to convince her sister that she didn't want it anymore. "It was a childish dream. And sometimes being a grown-up means setting aside such things. Things like...crushes on silver screen swashbucklers."

Flynn gave her a look that she felt all the way down to her toes. "Personally, I believe in indulging your childhood dreams."

She stared at him as he ransacked his shelves, trying to work out the puzzle that was Flynn Banks. An hour ago, he had challenged her to a sword fight that he knew he would lose. Now, he was climbing ladders and pawing through books in search of something he wanted to show her. What did he mean by encouraging her to indulge in childhood dreams? That he wanted her to have a crush on him?

He was charming and roguish and all the things she knew him to be, but there was something different too. Something, dare she say, unsure? Maybe even something...sweet? "I'm surprised more of your guests don't hide out in here."

"Well, as you so aptly pointed out the night we met, Hollywood isn't exactly known for its literary luminaries."

She cringed, remembering how priggish she had been. But he wasn't paying attention to her as he continued rooting through the shelves.

"It has to be here somewhere." He returned to the floor and crossed to a shelf on the far side of the room. "Ah, here we go." He climbed the ladder again and blew the dust off a leather-bound volume. It had been nestled in a stack of books that appeared to be at least fifty years old. He held it out to Livvy while he grabbed for two more volumes still on the shelf.

She approached him gingerly and reached up to take it. Her hands were shaking, and she didn't think it was only because of what she suspected he was handing her. She clasped the honey-bound book in her hands, turning it over to study the spine with a red leather-embossed *I*. An involuntary gasp escaped her lips as she read the title, embossed above the *I*, this time on black leather. *Pride and Prejudice*.

"Is this what I think it is?" she whispered, her voice hushed.

Flynn jumped down with the grace of an acrobat, holding the other two volumes, which he presented to her with a mock bow. "That depends. Do you think it's a first edition of *Pride and Prejudice*? Because then, the answer is yes."

"I can't believe you have this. In your house."

"Not like I earned it or anything," he muttered, suddenly looking a bit bashful. "It's been in the family since 1813."

She nearly dropped the book at that. Only her sense that she was holding a precious object kept her clinging tightly to it. "You mean, someone in your family bought this when it was first published?"

He shrugged. "That doesn't mean anyone in my family read it, mind you. The Banks family has always been more interested in stocking their shelves with impressive tomes than it has been in reading them."

"Until you, you mean." She gestured around at the well-loved library.

He did blush then, and she was shocked at how much it pleased her to make him feel as unsettled as he did her. "My mother loved to read to me as a boy. Whenever I was looking for her, she'd be in the library. And she read to me every night before bed. Never mind that my father raised hell about it. 'The nanny can do it,' he always said. But my mother never missed a single night. Not until they sent me off to boarding school. And then, well, she—" He paused, his voice choked with emotion, and her heart sank.

She reached out her hand and gently placed it atop his. "I'm so sorry, Flynn." She knew the stricken look on his face well. It was one she'd seen on Judy and herself these last four years. No matter what your relationship with them, losing a parent was hard.

He swallowed. "It's all right. It's been over twenty years. You remind me of her sometimes. Her name's Violet, just like your eyes." He gave her a weak smile. "She's happier now, anyway."

"Yes, she's in a better place, I'm sure of it." Livvy tried to reassure him, squeezing his hand.

"I suppose. If you call the Left Bank of Paris a better place."

"Is that where she's buried?"

Flynn's eyes widened to saucers. "Good God, no! Did you... Oh bloody hell, you thought... I can see now how it might sound that way. No, no, she's not dead." He ran a hand through his hair, making the blond locks that drove women around the world mad fall into his eyes. He began pacing, caught up in a memory. "Dead, ha. Father wishes. Or perhaps not, since he'll be shuffling off his mortal coil any day now. Though God knows they won't end up in the same place."

Livvy gasped at how casually Flynn mentioned the fact that his father was on his deathbed. But Flynn didn't seem to notice. "As soon as I was out of the house, she ran off with an opera singer. Moved to Paris with him. Has been there ever since. I was angry at first. But she'd had no choice. She couldn't have lived she stayed. It made my father apoplectic with rage when I told him I was moving to Hollywood to pursue a career. 'You'll end up just like your mother,' he warned. Shame he didn't realize that was what I wanted all along. To be happy like her. My mother knew the truth—that being 'wicked' is the only way to be happy. Reputation be damned. She taught me that the only way to be content in this world is to free yourself from the yoke of a title and the damned aristocrats who all have sticks up their arses."

She giggled at that, and her laugh broke Flynn out of the rant he had started. "I'm sorry, got lost a bit. You don't need to hear me mutter on about old family scandals."

"No, I like hearing it, really." She liked learning about who he was before he'd become Hollywood's favorite swashbuckler. "Getting to know you... It's nice."

"There's not much to know. I was born a spoiled toff, and I grew up to be a spoiled toff with a bit more self-awareness."

"You're selling yourself short." A month ago, she would've

agreed with him. But now? The way he had been with her. With Judy. He might have a lot of resources, and things might come easily to him. But she would hardly call him spoiled. Confusing? Infuriating? Roguish? Sure. But never spoiled. "You're the most generous man I've ever met. You want everyone around you to enjoy themselves. You're not happy unless we're all having a good time."

"I think the term for that is 'incurable reprobate.'" He smiled a devilish grin that enhanced his words. While he'd been pacing, he'd ended up on the other side of the room, next to his velvet armchair. She took a step toward him, not even realizing what she was doing. "But if you want to call it generosity, so be it. Would you like to borrow that?"

"What?" She realized then that she was still holding the first volume of *Pride and Prejudice.* "This? Oh no, I couldn't. What if something happened to it? The Garden of Allah doesn't exactly have exemplary anti-theft measures."

He frowned at that. "I don't like thinking about you living somewhere that's not safe."

She waved it off, even as her tummy flipped at the concern in his voice. "It's fine, just not the best place for a priceless first edition."

"Then you should come here and read it whenever you like. Or any other book. My library is open to you anytime you wish to visit. I'll have the staff make you a key."

She almost fainted at that. This room was full of untold treasures. More books than she could likely read in a lifetime—and he was offering her unfettered access. "Flynn, I don't know what to say. That's too kind."

"It's truly the least I can do in exchange for your pretending to be madly in love with me and saving my hide with the studio."

She blushed and searched for a sufficient way to say thank you, hugging the precious book to her chest. She was certain he was just being nice; this room was proof that even if he did lose his job, he'd still have his family's money. But there was no way to express that without sounding rude. Ironic really. She was surrounded by words but unable to come up with a single one that could convey what this meant to her. Before her parents had died and she'd put all her energy into looking after Judy, books had been her refuge. The stories they held. The worlds they opened. The adventures they promised. But the public library in her small town had been meager compared to the riches here.

"Thank you," she murmured, finding that nothing else would do. She nodded in the direction of his comfortable armchair. "I see you're reading *Treasure Island* again."

"I've read it twice since the night we met." He grinned. "It helps me when I'm having trouble sleeping. Getting lost in the world of Jim and Long John Silver. It's more effective than a nightcap lately."

Her eyes darted to the bottle of whiskey enclosed in the globe.

He followed her line of sight and chuckled. "I didn't say I was reading in place of a nightcap, mind you."

She shook her head. "I'm glad that it still captures your imagination the way it used to." She inched toward him, again drawn by the invisible force she couldn't name. She was standing so close she could touch him now. "Books have always been my salvation. When everything else goes askew, my favorite stories are there to comfort me."

He nodded and reached for her, gently stroking a finger down the back of her hand that still clutched the book. His touch was light as a feather, and yet it set her on fire. "You reminded me," he murmured, gazing at her with what looked an awful lot like adoration, "how much I love stories. And the reason why I had all these books shipped here from England in the first place. I hadn't spent much time here the last few years. But you made me want to read again. If only to prove to myself I wasn't the dunderhead actor you pegged me as."

She scrunched up her nose and closed her eyes. "I was such an ass that night. I was terrified when you jumped in my car. You do have a bit of a reputation, you know." He grinned, looking positively wolfish, and she tingled in response. "I acted that way because it was the only thing that I could think of to protect myself. After years of mooning over you on-screen, suddenly, there you were, flesh and blood in my car. I didn't want to lose my head, so instead I tried to fool you into thinking I was a worldly creature slumming it in Hollywood."

"Oh, you are." His voice was so quiet now that she knew she wouldn't be able to hear him if she wasn't standing so close. He gripped the book in her hands and withdrew it, gently setting it on the chair behind him without even turning around. "You're much too good for any of us. Me in particular."

He held both her hands now, and she was struck by how much taller he was than her. The way that the top of her head barely grazed his chin. She tilted her head up to him. "Was that why you challenged me to a duel in front of all your friends, knowing full well you would lose?"

He smiled, his eyes crinkling as he held in a laugh. "You see, you're far too smart for me. You know you're better than me, and you're not afraid to tell me so."

"It's a defense mechanism, that's all." She swallowed, suddenly parched. But she didn't want to break this moment. This spell. Whatever it was. He wrapped his hands around her wrists and pulled her toward him, closing the gap between them. Through the thin suede of her costume, she could feel the muscled contours of his body. She wished to run her fingers over every stern line and rippling inch. To study him like one of the books in this room.

"Be that as it may, it's irresistible." He leaned down and ghosted the lightest kiss to her lips, pulling back a hairsbreadth to look in her eyes, searching for a signal that this was all right.

"There aren't any photographers here," she murmured, thinking of the kiss they had staged last week on the steps of El Cholo.

"Good," he growled. "That means I can kiss you the way you deserve."

She nearly swooned at that and pressed her lips fiercely to his, clinging to him to keep herself upright. He started in surprise at her initiative before wrapping his arms tightly around her and holding her closer than she thought was possible. He deepened the kiss, teasing at her mouth with his tongue until she opened for him. She moaned as he tangled his tongue with hers. In Flynn's arms, she felt like an oasis happened upon by a man dying of thirst. It was better than anything she'd imagined as a teenager watching him at the movies. He devoured her as if he couldn't get enough. She saw stars as he tugged at her bottom lip.

They broke apart, and he nuzzled at her ear with his nose, sucking on her neck. She whimpered and pressed into his mouth, letting him suck and swirl his tongue across the sensitive spot right below her ear. A sensation of pure liquid heat shot through her and pooled between her legs. Was this what it felt like to want a man so desperately you would do anything?

She clung to him, and he stopped for a moment, pressing his cheek to hers. "Livvy, I don't want this to be just a game, a charade for people who don't know better."

She had to be dreaming. Was Flynn saying that he wanted her? As more than a patsy for the Legion of Decency? More than a friend? She didn't know what to do with that. The idea frightened and thrilled her in equal measure. She hadn't let herself want something, yearn for something in so long. But what good was it when she knew she couldn't have it? But oh, how she wanted Flynn. Was it possible to let herself give in to it? She needed it to be. If only just for tonight. So she turned toward his lips and kissed him again.

All she wanted right now was not to think. To live in this moment where he plundered her mouth as if she were one of the ships he pillaged in a film. He eagerly responded to her, and she thought she might explode into stardust from the pure sensation of it all. Every nerve ending in her body was alight with desire. Every other kiss she'd experienced—and the list was not long—was a pale shadow of this one.

This was a proper embrace from a man who not only knew what he was doing but took immense pleasure in doing it. Maybe there was something to being with a notorious scoundrel after all, if it meant they would kiss you like this.

He pushed her up against one of the bookshelves and tangled his hands in her hair. She giggled as a book near her head fell from its spot, knocked out of place by his vigorous ministrations.

He kissed the tip of her nose. "I love hearing you laugh."

She sighed in happiness.

His hand fumbled with the bottom of her blouse. "Is this all right?" he asked, a hungry look in his eyes. She bit her lip and pondered it, before kissing him in answer. Her skin pebbled as he reached under her thin green blouse, finding the line of her cotton bra. He found her left nipple and brushed it gently with his hand, while he continued to dot her jawline with kisses, taking her earlobe in between his teeth and nibbling at it ever so gently. She arched in to him as he plucked at her breast, feeling him stiffen at her movement as she tried to find a place on the shelf to rest her weight without tipping it over.

He seemed to read her mind and told her, "They're bolted into the ground." Then, he gripped her bottom and lifted her up as she swept madly behind her, clearing a space as books cascaded to the floor. She winced, silently hoping they were not more first editions. But the feeling of his hands on her backside was enough to distract her from the thought of potential biblio-violence.

He sat her on the shelf and she widened her legs, allowing him to make himself snug against her. Her hands pulled at his shirt, trying to find the buttons under the heaps of ruffles. He huffed in frustration and tugged the shirt out of the ridiculously tight breeches that made his butt look absolutely irresistible.

With the fabric loosed from his pants, Livvy was able to place her hands under his shirt. The juxtaposition of his hard muscle and his warm skin was intoxicating, and she ran her palms over his chest as he reached around to unsnap her bra. He fully cupped both of her breasts, and she shivered at the rough scrape of the calluses on his hands. She gasped and threw her head back in pleasure, exposing more of her neck, which he readily took advantage of kissing.

A sudden trill of giggles broke them apart, as the door to the library burst open and Arlene tugged Don into the library by the edge of his black cape. Livvy's cheeks felt like they were bursting into flame as she looked up at the shocked couple, realizing that Flynn's hands were still under her blouse.

Flynn quickly adjusted himself in his breeches before turning to shield Livvy from their prying gaze, as a wide smirk spread across Don's face. "Looks like someone else had the same idea as us, Lena."

Arlene smacked Don gently on the back side of his head.

"Don't be so crass." She looked back at Livvy and Flynn, an apologetic smile on her face. "We didn't mean to interrupt."

Livvy jumped up off the shelf, struggling to reach under her shirt and redo the clasp of her bra. "Oh no, that's, uh... We should... I was just leaving."

Flynn's head snapped to her. He looked hurt. But what was she supposed to say? *Could you two leave and pretend you didn't see anything so Flynn can go back to ravishing me?* The mere thought of it made her blush from head to toe.

Arlene's face dropped. "No, please don't go on our account."

Livvy knew she must look a fright. She gave up on getting her bra back on and frantically smoothed her hair back into place. "No, really, I need to be getting home. My sister will worry if I stay out too late."

Confident that she could at least find her way to the front door and her car without too many strange looks, Livvy awkwardly stepped around Flynn, trying to avoid tripping on any of the books they had knocked from the shelves in their passion. "Thank you, Flynn, for a...lovely evening," she stammered.

Don chuckled under his breath and Arlene smacked his arm and hissed, "Behave." Livvy would've found it hilarious if she wasn't so mortified.

She squeezed past Arlene and Don to get out the door, and as she passed, Arlene whispered, "I told you he was in love with you."

Livvy acted as if she didn't hear her and kept going, swiftly making it to her car without further incident. The words echoed in Livvy's head her entire drive home. If he wasn't pretending, then what did he want? A short-lived love affair like all the rest? She didn't know if she could survive that.

But what if he wanted something else? That thought

frightened her. But the thing that scared her most of all? She couldn't shake the feeling of his mouth against hers and the sensation of his hands on her body. Worse, she didn't want to. What she wanted was more. But that wasn't something she could allow herself. Was it?

CHAPTER 18

FLYNN HAD TO LAUGH AT GOD'S SENSE OF HUMOR. AFTER going to bed early and letting Dash and Joan see the last guests out in the wee hours of the morning, he woke refreshed and eager to see Livvy on set. Because he'd watched her flee from the library, standing there like a dodo bird. When what he should've done was go after her and tell her that he didn't want this to be just a publicity stunt anymore. Against all odds and the promises he'd made himself, he'd developed feelings for a dame. And stranger still, he couldn't wait to tell her. But when he'd practically skipped downstairs to retrieve his morning cup of coffee, all the wind went out of his sails.

Hugh had left a telegram sitting ominously on the kitchen counter, its inky black address mocking him. Flynn stared at it. Considered tossing it in the rubbish bin without opening it. Nothing was going to dampen the spring in his step. The last thing he needed was another request for funds from Edgar. Until he was in the clear with the Legion of Decency, Flynn was keeping his bank vault locked and bolted. But curiosity got the better of him while he sat there staring at the telegram, sipping his too-hot coffee. It contained only three words:

HE IS GONE

It was done then. Lord Banks, the seventh Viscount of Nottsworth, had shuffled off his mortal coil once and for all. Flynn expected to feel nothing. Perhaps a sense of relief, of a weight being lifted. Even outright glee at the thought of his father rotting in hell like he deserved. He'd certainly taken enough beatings from his father to have earned the right to dance on his grave. But a peculiar pain hit him square in the chest as he read the words over again. Was this grief? How could it be? How could any part of him mourn for this man?

He'd never know what his father had so desperately wanted to tell him on his deathbed. But there was nothing his father could have said that would've mattered. Flynn's only regret was that he'd never confronted the bastard about the fact that he knew his father's worst secret. That he had never exposed the old man for what he truly was. Flynn had hoped that his profligate lifestyle had been punishment enough. The best revenge was living well, after all. But should Flynn have told him? Had he caused more harm by choosing to run away rather than confront him? And did it matter now that his father was dead?

All of this roiled in his mind as he ghost-walked through his morning ablutions, washing his face, shaving, and pomading his hair. His plan to rush to the studio, visit Livvy's dressing room, and confess how he felt was forgotten, washed away by a sea of confusion and unease.

Two hours later, Flynn was on set. But his mind was still back at home with that blasted telegram. He alternated between a deep sadness that his father had never loved him, had never been capable of such affection, and an anger at himself for feeling so shaken by this news. *Choose joy.* He recited the words to himself over and over in his head, hoping they would dispel this foreign emotion of guilt. Absentmindedly, he wondered if he was in the will. Likely not, if Edgar was reduced to begging him for funds. A shame, as Flynn could've used the extra cushion right now.

Livvy gave him a weak smile, but he didn't return it. She frowned, but he scarcely noticed, being so lost in his own thoughts. She was in a billowing gown, looking nervously up at the scaffolding she needed to climb to reach her perch. His character was meant to scale the walls of her home, climbing to her balcony and stealing a good-night kiss. All very *Romeo and Juliet*. He ran his hand down his face. He didn't have the stomach for this today. Not with his thoughts a jumble. He couldn't pretend to make love to her until they had a chance to talk about last night. It felt...wrong. But by the same token, before he could confess to her, he wanted to shake off whatever this sudden pall was. How would she respond if he admitted he was developing feelings for her with this hangdog expression?

Livvy gently nudged him, and it made him jump. "What was that for?" he growled.

She looked hurt. Fuck. Here his father was again, ruining his life. This time from beyond the grave.

"I was trying to be friendly," she muttered. She bit her lip and rolled her shoulders back. "I thought...last night..." Her voice trailed off and he had no idea whether she intended to tell him it was a terrible mistake or the best night of her life.

He snapped at her when she didn't continue. "What?"

"Never mind. Let me be. I need to focus."

He was in a wretched mood. He should have called in sick. But Harry knew that his Halloween party had been last night. He would have assumed Flynn was hungover and docked his pay. Now Flynn was taking it out on Livvy instead. For the first time, he thought perhaps there were some parts of himself that could use improving. "Sorry. I just... I'm not feeling myself this morning."

Livvy's face fell as she stared at him. Oh. No. She thought it was because of last night. He was digging this hole deeper. He started to apologize and try to explain when a production assistant came to escort her to the scaffolding.

He slumped in a chair behind the camera, waiting for her before taking his own post. Rallo, who had been at Lionel's foot in the shadows, sprang into his lap and sat there. Flynn watched as Livvy balked at the directions to climb up to the tiny wooden balcony the crew had built for the scene. He petted the tiny monkey and muttered, "At least she has solid ground beneath her. I have to stay on the edge of the balcony with only a foothold and my own strength."

The monkey cocked his head, seemingly listening to Flynn complain, taking in his monologue. It occurred to Flynn that his position in today's scene was a fitting metaphor for his mental state, but he didn't particularly like the implications of that.

"You understand me, Rallo. Hell, you might be the only one in this entire town who does."

The monkey chittered in agreement, and man and beast both looked across the soundstage to watch Livvy scale the scaffolding in her voluminous skirt. She was one hell of a woman. And still he couldn't shake himself from this hollowness that had descended on him when he read that telegram. It was infuriating. He hated his father. Why should he feel this so keenly?

At long last, Livvy was ready. The director, Mickey Curtis, whom Flynn had worked with several times, pulled Flynn aside. "Okay so, we'll film you jumping into the tree beneath her window, scaling its branches, and climbing onto her balcony," he explained in his thick Irish brogue.

Flynn nodded. "Got it, Mick." Frankly, he wanted to get this over with. Then, he could get his head on straight and explain himself to Livvy.

"All right then, if everyone is ready, places!" Mickey called out. "Action!"

Flynn crossed from behind the camera into the frame, scaled the tree easily, and took his spot hanging onto Livvy's balcony. "Lady Margaret," he called. "What ho, Lady Margaret."

"Who goes there?" Livvy emerged, her eyes sparking and her black hair looking even richer and glossier under the intense lighting. He almost lost his balance.

He gripped the edge of the concrete balcony, holding on for dear life. Jesus Christ. He'd never been unsettled by a woman like this before. He hadn't really given her a good look this morning until now. If it was possible, she was even more beautiful than she had been in the library last night, with her lips swollen and her breasts straining at her blouse. "It is I, your lovelorn suitor," he squeaked.

"Cut," called Curtis. "Banks, you all right?"

Flynn pulled himself up, trying to ignore the queer look Livvy was giving him. "Yes, yes," he huffed out. "I'm fine, just lost my footing a little."

"All right, back to one."

Flynn sighed and climbed down from his perch as Livvy retreated through the archway, into what was meant to be Lady Margaret's bedroom. Again, he regretted not skiving off for the day.

Soon enough they were rolling again, and Flynn masterfully scaled the wall, this time keeping his wits about him as Livvy strode into the scene.

"Jamie Brandt," she hissed. "What are you doing here? Are you mad? If my father's guards find you here, they'll kill you."

"It's a risk I'm willing to take." He winked at her. Fine, this was fine. The scene was moving along now. "If it means I can say good night to the woman I love."

Livvy blinked at him, seeming to forget her lines for a moment as she took in what he said. But the moment passed as quickly as it came. "You're a fool, Jamie Brandt. You must go. Besides, I don't love you." The words weren't real, but they bruised Flynn's heart all the same. He needed to get ahold of himself.

"Ah, well, then I suppose my life means very little." He swung out from the balcony, hiding himself in the faux ivy covering the exterior of the house.

Livvy gasped. "Jamie, no!"

He swung back to her. "Ah, so you do care." He winked at her. The scene felt real. Alive in a way no love scene he'd done before ever had.

"Oh, darling." She reached for him, pulling at his woolen cloak to draw him closer. "I do love you. I love your bravery. I love how headstrong you are. Most of all, I love what you are doing for the people of this little island. But you must go. Every minute you linger, you are in greater danger."

"I will. But, Margaret, won't you come with me? Be my pirate queen. We could liberate all the people of this island. Together." Livvy's eyes flashed at the word *together*. He didn't know if she was that good of an actress, or if last night was still on her mind. He cursed himself for reading that bloody telegram. For standing in the library and watching her go. If he'd run after her last night, maybe he would've have been too preoccupied to read his father's death notice.

"If I do that, I will as good as sign your death warrant," she continued, in character. "My father will say you kidnapped me."

He made a show of sighing. "You are right. I know it. But that shall not stop me from trying to convince you."

Members of the crew behind the camera were starting to make a loud noise, as if they were carousing. Livvy's head snapped back, looking through the archway. "Go, my darling. They cannot find you here."

"Kiss me goodbye." He leaned forward over the balcony, bracing himself to feel her lips against his, even if only for the benefit of the camera this time.

She placed her hands on the railing and wrapped her arms around his neck, honoring his request for a kiss. It was meant to be chaste and brief enough to skirt the rules of the Production Code, but Livvy flung herself at him with so much force that if she hadn't been holding onto him, he might have tumbled backwards. She kissed him so fiercely it hurt. It was the first time in hours he'd thought of anything but his own self-pity. He found it invigorating, and he returned the kiss with equally bruising passion.

"Cut!" bellowed Curtis from below them.

They broke apart, Livvy's chest heaving as she tried to catch her breath. She stared at Flynn, and he was desperate to know what was running through that brilliant mind. She frowned at him, seemingly even more confused now. Damn it. If he could just ask for a break to take her aside and explain things... But then Livvy would have to climb down the scaffolding again, *and* back up it. By then, she'd probably be so peeved she wouldn't care what he had to say.

"Miss De Lesseps," Curtis called up. "That was fantastic, but perhaps a little less, er, eager this time?"

Livvy nodded. "Sorry, Mr. Curtis. I, uh, wanted it to feel real. Suppose I got carried away by the scene."

The scene. Sure. Flynn tried not to scoff. There was more than the scene simmering between them. Unless he was truly losing his mind, which was not outside the realm of possibility.

They performed the scene again, starting from the dialogue so that Flynn didn't have to keep climbing up and down. But when they got to the kiss, Livvy barely touched her lips to his, puckering up in an exaggerated fashion and then breaking away before he'd had the chance to do more than breathe against her mouth.

Curtis cut again. Flynn could hear the man trying to hold in a laugh. "Uh, Miss De Lesseps, you overcorrected," he called up.

Flynn chuckled. You could say that again. He'd shared better kisses with the offerings at the fish market.

Livvy bit her lip. "Sorry, Mr. Curtis. I promise to get it this time."

She turned to return to her place out of the camera's line of sight, and Flynn called after her. "Livvy."

She whirled to face him.

"It's natural to have nerves. Let me guide the kiss this time." He felt like an ass for saying it, but his arms were getting tired clinging to this balcony.

He expected her to argue, to tell him she knew how to do a stage kiss. But she merely smiled and nodded. She gulped, and he realized the poor girl was nervous. Because of him. And his bloody mixed signals. This was the first time they'd filmed a love scene together. And he was making it harder on her. He really was an arse sometimes.

This time, the kiss was perfect. She did as he'd suggested and let him lean in, leading the moment. He pressed his lips to hers, resisting the urge to ravish her, and wrapped his arms around her as she tilted her head slightly.

They stood there, holding the kiss, and though it wasn't as passionate as the first, Flynn was alarmed to realize he found it arousing. The fact that he was wearing breeches tightly tailored to his form meant that if this went on much longer, it would be rather evident to the whole crew what was happening. God, he really was losing his touch, wasn't he? He'd never had an issue controlling Little Flynn on a set. Possibly because he usually got a good enough workout in the evening. Flynn withdrew from the clench a little, trying to quell his desire, but Livvy made a sudden jerking moment and bonked her forehead into his.

"Ow!" Flynn yelped and clapped one hand to his face, holding onto the balcony with the other.

"Cut," yelled Curtis, frustration mounting in his voice. "That was a medium shot, so we won't be able to cut around the injury."

Livvy looked penitent. "I'm so sorry. Flynn changed the timing." She looked at Flynn, knitting her fingers in the satin of her gown. "Why did you break away so suddenly? You startled me."

He swallowed down a retort and instead gritted out, "This scene seems to be a hard one."

She looked pointedly at his crotch at the word *hard*. Had she just? No, it couldn't be. Lord, he had a dirty mind. He briefly wondered if they could create a mouthwash for the brain. But no, there it was again. Livvy darted a meaningful glance at his crotch, before calling out to the director below him. "I'll do better this time. Wouldn't want our performances to get stiff."

That had to be on purpose. She gave him a look, and once again he was startled to find his heart swelling with affection for her. Usually only one part of him tended to swell when it came to dames. Though he'd take his heart over the alternative at this exact moment. At least that wouldn't be visible. He had nothing to be ashamed of in that department, thank you very much. But he didn't think the censors who were trying to blackball him would take very kindly to the sight of his erect cock on the screen. Not really the mark of a reformed scoundrel.

Livvy wrapped her arms around him and tangled her hands

slightly in his hair. He kissed her, and they stood locked in an embrace for a few seconds. She deepened it slightly, darting her tongue across his lips, and he was ready for her. Two could play at this game. He'd lay a kiss on her so intense that she'd be seeing stars. See how she liked it if she was the one ruining a take. He parted his lips, sucking her tongue into his mouth. Satisfaction flared in him as a tiny squeak erupted from her. Message received, loud and clear.

But he'd miscalculated. Little Flynn was making his presence known again.

He tried to think of the most unerotic things he could muster. He would not cause them to flub another take. What was something decidedly unsexy? Flannel nightgowns. That was a good one.

But then an image of Livvy wearing a flannel nightie popped into his mind, and he stiffened further. *Shit, shit, shit.* He moved his head slightly, releasing the pressure of his mouth and lessening the beguiling sensation of *her* tongue sweeping across his lips.

He needed to think of something comforting, something maternal. Like his mother reading him a bedtime story. He focused on the memory and locked it in his mind.

Suddenly, without warning, his mother transformed into Livvy. She was reading to him now. And she was naked.

"No!" he cried out, breaking the kiss. He did not want to touch that Oedipal nightmare with a ten-foot pole. He realized a moment too late that he'd disrupted the take.

"Everything all right up there, Banks?" Curtis asked.

"Yes, uh, it's fine." He needed to come up with an excuse. "I felt myself...starting to slip off the balcony."

Livvy looked at him, one eyebrow raised. "Slipping off the balcony, huh? Maybe you should try to be less enthusiastic." She winked at him, and he didn't know whether to be irritated or turned on by her teasing.

"No one's ever complained about my enthusiasm," he growled under his breath.

Curtis interrupted their back-and-forth, calling up, "Everyone set?"

"Yes," they both replied.

Livvy stuck her head out from her hiding place, her eyes sparkling with mischief. "Think you can manage to hold on to the railing this time?"

"You worry about your blocking and I'll worry about mine."

This time, when they got to the kiss, it was Flynn who escalated things first. He tangled his hand in her hair and turned her head to face his so he could get a better angle on her mouth. He sucked at her bottom lip and her eyes flashed open, flaring with want and surprise. From this angle, no matter what Little Flynn did, the camera wouldn't be able to see it.

He knew better than her how to hide a passionate kiss behind the limitations of the Production Code. He nibbled at her, sucking her bottom lip into his mouth until two pink circles came to her cheeks. He knew he was pushing things with how long this was going on, so he swept his tongue into her and pressed his lips so firmly against hers that she released a guttural whimper.

He broke away, and this time she was so breathless, she could barely tell his character good night.

"Perfect, I think that was the one," Curtis called from his post beneath them.

Livvy didn't break eye contact with Flynn, studying him like he was a difficult puzzle she had yet to work out. But she called down to Curtis, "Really? That wasn't too much? I got lost in it a bit. I could try it again and hold back a little more." The entire thing came out on a huff of breath, and Flynn took in the heaving rise and fall of her chest with delight.

"No, Miss De Lesseps, that's not necessary. The angle will hide any overeagerness."

She flushed at the director's words, and Flynn tried to memorize the sight of her porcelain flesh turning a titillating pink as it disappeared into the neckline of her bodice.

He leaned over the railing of the balcony so that his head was right behind hers. "I don't think you can hold back. What's more, I don't think you want to. And neither do I."

Livvy's head snapped back at the words. But he was leaning so close to her that he didn't have time to get out of the way. The back of her head smacked him in the face, connecting with his nose.

Holy hell, that hurt. Livvy gasped. Flynn's upper lip was suddenly warm and wet with a profusion of blood pouring out his nose.

He clapped his hands to his face, forgetting for a moment to hold on. Livvy screamed as she grabbed onto the front of his shirt and tugged him over the balcony, saving him from falling but pulling him down on top of her. His face collided with the ornate bodice of her gown, his blood smearing across the delicate embroidery.

The fleeting realization that his face was pressed into her chest flitted through his mind. Then she moved, sending another searing shock of pain through his face and banishing any vaguely erotic thoughts.

"Oh God, Flynn, Flynn, are you all right?" She tried to scramble backwards so he could sit up, but the result was only that his face dragged down her gown, bringing a smear of blood with it. He looked up, still holding his hands to his nose, and watched as she pressed her hands to her bodice and drew them away in horror. "Oh, no." Her face turned a pale shade of green and she started to wobble. Oh Christ, she was going to—

Clunk. She hit the balcony floor, collapsing at the sight of his blood smeared all over her. He managed to roll off her, hoping that if he gave her some space, she might regain consciousness.

From below them, he heard a cry. "Rallo, no! Come back here."

Suddenly and without warning, the little monkey sprang onto Flynn's head, chittering and moving.

"Rallo, stop," Flynn begged, sounding like he had a cold.

The monkey jumped off Flynn's head, mercifully, and began gently slapping its hands against Livvy's face, apparently trying to revive her.

"I see that you only have eyes for the lady as usual," Flynn muttered.

Livvy's eyes fluttered open. She noticed the monkey sitting on her chest, and her eyes rolled back into her head as she fainted once more.

Flynn sure as hell hoped they could cobble something together from the footage they had, because it was abundantly clear that filming was over for the day.

CHAPTER 19

AFTER THE BLEEDING FINALLY STOPPED, FLYNN PULLED THE two twists of tissue out of his nostrils and studied his face in the dressing room mirror. A few spots around the edges of his nose were starting to turn black and blue. He gingerly pressed at them, and they were sore, but nothing seemed broken or out of whack. Thank God. Though he supposed maybe he'd look more rugged with a broken nose. It would add to his appeal as a scallywag.

There was a soft knock at the door. "Can I come in?" trilled a voice he realized might be his favorite sound. Even if its owner had nearly misaligned his face.

"As long as you haven't come to finish the job," he called out.

Livvy entered, freshly changed out of her bloody costume into a ribbed sweater and pencil skirt. Her hair looked a bit damp, as if she'd showered. He couldn't blame her. He probably would've done the same had he found himself unexpectedly covered in someone else's blood.

She looked sheepish, her head hanging down. "I came to apologize and to make sure you're all right."

"I'll live." He shrugged and turned around, which led her to gasp at his freshly blooming bruises.

"Oh, Flynn, I'm so sorry. Does it hurt?" She rushed toward

him and turned his head from side to side, studying his face in the light of the dressing room's mirror bulbs.

Well, he might as well milk this moment. "Terribly," he muttered. "I think it might be broken." He'd give her credit for one thing. The pain had driven away the strange specter of grief that had taken hold of him this morning.

She sat down in the chair opposite his and dropped her face in her hands. "I'm a fool. How long will it take to heal? Did the doctor say you can keep making the picture? Will it leave a permanent mark?"

She was rambling, and it was adorable to hear her so concerned. "Careful, keep going and I might begin to think you care about me."

She snapped her head up and caught the wide grin spreading across his face. Realization dawned. "You're lying. It's not broken at all." She reached for one of the makeup towels on the dressing room counter and threw it at him. "You wicked, horrible man. Here I thought I'd permanently damaged the source of your income."

He chuckled and clasped his hands to his chest. "You wound me. I'm worth more than my pretty face."

"I was beginning to think so. Until this morning."

"What happened this morning?" He was fairly certain he knew the answer.

She bit her lip, looking fearful. "Nothing. I'm a fool, that's all."

"You're not a fool. You just didn't know what to do with me when I was being so hot and cold." Her mouth fell open and he reached forward and gently tipped it shut. "What, you think I didn't realize I was being an arse?"

"I wasn't sure you were capable of being that self-aware."

"Trust me, love, I know exactly who I am." Or he had once. Lately, he wasn't so sure. Livvy and this business with his father had turned him topsy-turvy. No, it had started before that. He'd been bored, distracted, dissatisfied. But until now, he hadn't been able to fathom why.

"I was rude, snapping at you like that. I've been a bit...distracted this morning." He didn't know why, but he didn't want to tell her about his father. Not right now, when he felt like they were on the brink of something important. "But I wasn't the only one who was distracted, was I?"

She turned bright red.

"What happened out there?" he nudged her. "You've been perfect every other day of shooting. You can do rings around with me a rapier. You're the fastest study I've ever known. But all of a sudden, you can't get through a love scene?"

She crossed her arms over her chest and huffed. She looked damnably cute, and Flynn was possessed with the urge to lean over and kiss the tip of her nose, but he resisted. "I wasn't doing it on purpose. You made your own fair share of mistakes."

"I did. But, love, I didn't say you did it on purpose. I just asked you what happened. Now I'm quite interested to hear more." He raised his eyebrows and gave her a look he'd once spent a week perfecting in the mirror.

"It wasn't intentional, I swear." Her shoulders fell and she leaned back in her chair. "Maybe it was. I don't know. I'm new to all this, and I want to get it right. I don't want this to be my only picture. I like acting, Flynn. I really do. Even if it wasn't my dream to begin with, it's starting to feel good. Like something I could keep doing and maybe even become really good at one day. But I'm all mixed up."

He scooted his chair closer to her and reached for her hand. "About what?"

"You. Us. This is supposed to be pretend. But last night, the way you kissed me, the things you said... They made me think, well, you know. Then this morning, you were so different. I thought maybe you'd changed your mind. Or been too drunk to realize what you were saying yesterday. I realized this scene we were filming was an opportunity. To see if any of this was real. You kissed me, and I couldn't help myself. I wanted to keep kissing you. To let myself have this one thing. Because it was safe. It was part of the scene. I didn't intend to keep ruining takes, but I panicked. I've gone haywire."

He couldn't stop a lazy, self-satisfied grin from spreading across his face. "I tend to have that effect on people."

She wrenched her hand from his. "This is exactly what I mean. Are you toying with me? You kiss me breathless at one moment and ignore me the next. How could I know if you were high on the atmosphere last night and regretted what you said when you woke up this morning?"

He reached for her again and stilled her fluttering hands. "I don't know if I can give you an answer that satisfies you. But I will never, as long as I live, regret the way it felt to hold you in my arms and kiss you senseless last night."

She gulped and sat up straighter in her chair.

"I can tell you that I'm as mixed up as you are. Maybe more so. But this morning, the way I behaved—that had nothing to do with you. I'll be frank. I don't know if I'm capable of having more than a short-lived love affair. I've never tried. All I know is that, for the first time in my life, you make me want to."

She slowly exhaled, shuddering at the weight of what he had said. She leaned forward and kissed him hard on the mouth, his nose stinging at the gentle press of her face against his.

He whimpered, and she broke away. "Oh, you poor dear, I've hurt you. Again!"

But Livvy kissing him was worth a hundred broken noses. "I know a way you can make it up to me."

"Yes?" Her eyes sparkled.

"Come to my house for dinner tonight."

Her face fell. "I can't."

"Why not?"

"Judy has an important gig tonight. Her first time dancing in the background of a picture. I have to make sure she gets off all right. I promised to help her with her hair."

"So come after that. We can eat whenever you like." He thought of Judy's black eye and their mutual secret, knowing that it had been the handiwork of Billy Wilkes. But Livvy hadn't told him about any incidents since. He hoped the kid had found her footing. "Besides, the kid will be fine. She's far more capable of taking care of herself than you give her credit for."

Livvy chewed on her lip. "I don't know. I should probably wait up for her."

Flynn pressed his fingers to his nose and gave Livvy a hangdog expression, laying on the full guilt trip.

"You know, maybe I should've broken your nose after all."

He scoffed in indignation. "And ruin the most beautiful face in all of America?"

She rolled her eyes. "All right, fine. I'll let the little chick fly the coop solo."

Flynn smiled. "I promise you won't regret it. You deserve to live your life, Livvy. To suck the marrow out of the bones of this existence. And it would be my privilege to give you a taste of what you've been missing."

CHAPTER 20

LIVVY DIDN'T THINK SHE'D EVER BEEN THIS NERVOUS. IT was the good kind of nerves—the fizzy, shaken-champagne-bottle ones. But still, she wished the courage she'd found earlier that day in Flynn's dressing room hadn't suddenly deserted her.

She held her bottle of wine and rang the doorbell, once again marveling at the tile lining the archway and porch outside Flynn's front door. It was colorful, full of rich blues, oranges, and reds, and she pondered who had done such lovely, delicate work.

Flynn yanked the door open and leaned against the doorjamb. He was dressed casually in a simple pair of brown trousers and a knit, short-sleeved V-neck sweater that brought out the blue in his eyes. She liked this version of him. Handsome, but plain. Not trussed up like a movie star or a pirate. Just Flynn, in his most natural state.

"Aren't you a sight for sore eyes." He whistled as he took her in.

She felt self-conscious then, afraid that her chiffon polka-dot dress was too much. "I'm sorry, I guess I overdressed."

He shook his head. "Nonsense, you look beautiful. Besides, in my view, a woman wearing any clothing at all is always overdressed."

Her jaw fell open at his saucy remark, and she couldn't

suppress a shocked huff of laughter. "Is it safe for me to come in?" she teased.

He winked at her. "Never. But I think you like that."

She had to admit she did. She'd been so afraid of Flynn. The truth was, her fears had nothing to do with him and everything to do with the fact that in the dark of movie theaters, it was his wicked ways that had always thrilled her. The nights she'd spent reading about his exploits in a movie magazine had made her feel things that she didn't even have words to describe. It scared her how much she was attracted to his foibles and cheeky sense of humor. How curious she was about the way he went through life, savoring each moment without shame or regret. It was admirable, really. Setting aside the notion of worrying about what other people thought... How freeing that must be. Was that something she could allow herself to do? Well, she was here.

"I don't hate it." She winked at him. He laughed and reached for the bottle of wine she brought, studying the label. "Um, it's a local fortified wine. The man at the shop said it was good." She winced, realizing how much that made her sound like a country bumpkin. Flynn probably had a cellar full of wines from France and Italy. But her parents had taught her never to arrive at someone's house empty-handed, and she certainly wasn't going to start now. It was the least she could do to honor their memory.

"I'm sure it's delicious, but you didn't need to bring anything. Tonight is about treating you." He stood aside and held out his arm, gesturing for her to come inside. "I told you, I want to show you what you've been missing."

She stepped inside timidly, remembering the way through the foyer from the party, but not wanting to be presumptuous. She awkwardly stood there, waiting for him to take charge.

He snuck up behind her and whispered in her ear, "Make yourself at home. There's no need to be so nervous."

She wanted to lean back into the feel of him pressed against her, let him take the edge of her ear between his teeth and nibble at it again. But she resisted. She was barely two feet inside his home and she was already losing her head.

She racked her brain for a safe topic. "The tile in your entryway is gorgeous. I've never seen anything like it. Is it from Spain?"

He grinned. "Actually, it's from right here in Malibu. A place called Malibu Potteries. Alas, they never recovered after a fire a few years back, but they did some marvelous work. Here, let me show you."

He took her hand and pulled her into a more formal dining room down the hall. It was a room she hadn't seen during the Halloween party. Setting her bottle of wine on his hefty oak table, he reached for a light switch in the corner. The sun was low in the sky and the room was bathed in afternoon shadows. When the light flicked on, it illuminated the tile floor beneath the table. But no, wait, was that a rug? She kneeled down and touched it, gasping in delight. "It's a rug made out of tile."

"It is!" He watched her, a look of delight dancing in his eyes. "This was one of their specialties. They did the whole house. All the fountains in the gardens and the details on the terrace both upstairs and downstairs."

"Your house is a work of art." She craned her neck to peer under the table, enjoying the rich maroons and yellows that made the tile imitate the threads of a Persian rug. It was breathtaking.

He shrugged. "I grew up in a stodgy house full of antiquities. I wanted this place to feel cozy and Californian. It's a home, not a museum. But I couldn't resist the artistry of the tile."

She stood back up. "It's marvelous. It's not stuffy at all either.

It feels like it belongs here, with the surf and the sand." She gestured her chin at the set of floor-to-ceiling windows that lined the dining room, granting a breathtaking view of the California coast—the rugged rocks and the crashing waves, the wooden beams of the Malibu Pier in the distance, and beyond that, the undulating brown curves of the hills.

He followed her eyes, and she could feel the heat of his gaze, studying her as she took in the natural beauty that surrounded them. "It's stunning, isn't it?"

She nodded and walked closer to the window.

He chuckled when she pressed her face to the glass. "You know, we can go outside."

He extended his hand and drew her back into the hall, down past the foyer, and into the large room where the party had been. It was so different now. A large stone hearth dominated the space, and there were timeworn, velvet-upholstered chairs and a sofa that looked plush, if also a bit stiff.

She barely had time to take it in before he opened a door on the side of the room and ushered her onto the terrace. Her gaze caught on one of the fountains he'd mentioned, a beautiful pattern of a peacock's tail emerging from the panoply of turquoise, greens, and blues.

But the fountain paled in comparison to the view. His deck sat atop the beach, the waves lapping at the bar of sand that extended from a set of wooden stairs in the corner. The center of the deck boasted a glass table decorated with a red-and-white checked tablecloth, which was held down with a candle in a red glass. A single red rose in a small vase sat next to it.

It was just like the way he'd set the table after the Catalina Regatta. That had only been a month ago, and already, it seemed like an eternity.

Her heart panged in her chest. Had he done this for her? He looked at her sheepishly, and she could've kissed him right then. She'd never seen him like this. Unsure of himself.

"Do you like it?" he asked.

She nodded, a bit overcome. "It's like the—"

"Dinner on the *Sea Monkey*. I know. I was rough and a bit rude that night. I wanted a do-over."

She smiled up at him. "You might have been a little gruff, but it was still a lovely evening. The fish you made was divine."

He gave her the most radiant smile she'd ever seen. "I'm glad you liked it. But I hope this is even better. Alex over at Perino's gave me the tablecloth and candle. I thought it was warm enough tonight to eat outside."

"It's perfect." It may have been early November, but it was still unseasonably nice, even for Southern California. She was warm in her dress. She marveled at the contradictions of Flynn Banks. His swashbuckling nature and brash persona so at odds with his quiet intellectualism and this unexpected streak of romanticism.

She walked to the edge of the deck and rested her hands on the railing, leaning forward and taking a deep breath as she let the sea air steady her. She loved the way the beach smelled and felt. The warm, radiating heat of the sand; the briny smell of the air damp from the spray of the waves; the bright reflection of the sun on the water; and the ever-changing colors of the ocean—sometimes a sparkling green, other times a blue so deep it was almost black. As a girl, she had loved taking trips to the shore. Other than a library or a movie theater, the beach had been the only place she could find peace.

She closed her eyes and took another deep breath, sucking in air when she felt Flynn's hands circle around her waist and his chin rest against her shoulder.

"Is this all right?" he murmured. She answered by leaning back in to him and turning her head to kiss him gently on the lips. She could feel him smile beneath her mouth, and she increased the pressure. But instead of deepening the kiss, he broke away and pressed his cheek to hers, so they could both look at the water.

"Your house, this place, it's a dream," Livvy said.

"It is. But most of all because it's completely mine. No family legacy to uphold, no portraits of ghastly dead relatives to display. Just the sea and the things that matter to me." He squeezed her a bit tighter as he said the last words, and she realized then that she was one of those things. Or at least she hoped she was becoming one.

But if that was to be true, she had to know more about him. "Why do you hate your family so much?"

He sighed and let go of her, turning around and leaning his elbows against the railing, so he could look her in the eyes. "I don't hate my family. Just my father. And by extension, the title. He's a bastard. Always has been."

"I'm sorry you lived with that. My parents were…difficult. But there was no question they loved me. Losing them was the hardest thing I've ever been through."

He shrugged. "S'all right. I hardly saw him. But it was hardest on my mum. By all accounts, she was a bright light. The life of every party. But when her parents arranged for her to marry my father, they condemned her to an unhappy life. She was rich, a viscountess, yes. But she was not loved. She withered under his casual cruelty. She was always loving to me. But as I grew older, I could tell when they'd been fighting. I'd hear her crying behind closed doors. Or find her in the library with a book, looking utterly exhausted, her eyes bloodshot. My brother never noticed and never even seemed to care. Just came to heel when my father called. The perfect heir."

Flynn turned and stared out at the horizon. But there was still something that bothered Livvy from her conversation with Flynn in the library. His mother had abandoned him. Surely, that had left its mark. She'd been angry when her parents died. With herself, for her role in it. But with them too. For leaving her and Judy all alone. For making her the head of the family and all that entailed.

"Did you resent your mother when she left?"

Flynn threw his head back and huffed out a breath. "At first, yes. I was only a boy. But it didn't take me long to realize that she didn't have a choice." Something dark passed through his eyes at that, and Livvy knew there was something more he wasn't saying. But she let him continue. "A choice between death and a life without one's children is no choice at all. But she did the only thing she could. She saved her life."

Livvy was realizing that was what Flynn did too. Made choices that made him feel alive. It was intoxicating. She hadn't done that since she was a girl. And her parents had taken every opportunity to remind her how selfish it was. She'd never believed them. Until it had cost them their lives.

But it was this vigor that meant Flynn wasn't built for anything but brief, torrid love affairs. She simply had to decide if she could survive that. Playing with fire meant she'd risk getting burned. Could she walk through the flames with only a few singes to show for it? Or would she have nothing left of her heart but a pile of ash?

"What about you?" He interrupted her anxious spiral of thoughts.

"Me?"

"Yes, your parents, where you grew up, what was it like?"

"Oh, well. Strict. Very strict. My mother was deeply religious.

Roman Catholic. She stressed piety above all, and she was always going on about how my love of books and fairy stories and piratical adventures would get me into trouble. My father was a military man, a naval captain. That's how I learned to fence. He always said even girls should know how to defend themselves. My mother disapproved, of course. Didn't think it was ladylike. But my father ruled the roost and claimed it was more feminine than learning to shoot or fistfight. She wouldn't have dared contradict him. He ran the house like one of his battleships."

Flynn turned and looked at her, and she admired the way the warm orange light of the afternoon bathed his face so that it looked like burnished gold. The gold strands in his blond hair glinted in the sun, and he looked rather like a Greek god. With a bruised nose.

"Did he have a whistle?" Flynn asked, the edges of his lips curling up in amusement.

"You think that's funny, but he did, in fact." The memory of it made her smile.

Flynn barked out a surprised laugh. "My God, two little girls being treated like naval cadets. What a way to grow up. Frankly, I think I prefer my father calling my mother a whore any chance he got."

She winced. "How terrible."

"Now it's my reminder of why I refuse to live life on anything but my own terms. In some ways, I suppose I was lucky. As the younger son, I had fewer expectations. Though my father still expected me to become a soldier or a man of the cloth, like the generations of second sons before me." When Livvy giggled, he added, "What's so funny?"

"I'm sorry, just imagining you as a vicar. It's ridiculous."

His eyes flashed with something wicked. "I'd wager I've

made more women call on God than I would have behind the pulpit."

Livvy bit her lip and blushed deeply. She had never done more than kissed a man. Last night with Flynn had been...intimate. His hands under her shirt had been exhilarating. His touch had ignited the most intense desire she had ever experienced. And when he said things like that, it made her flush with want. "I think I'd like to know what that's like," she whispered.

He studied her, seeming to assess whether she really meant it. But then he grinned. "Lucky for us, we have the whole night."

She blushed and looked down at her toes, painted a delicate pink in the peep-toe wedges that she'd borrowed from Judy. Her sister had insisted she wear them, wanting Livvy to feel pretty for her date. She'd had second thoughts about dinner with Flynn once she'd come home to the bungalow, remembering what had happened the last time she had insisted on doing what she wanted rather than what she was supposed to do. But Judy wouldn't hear it and had practically shoved her out the door.

Her neck flushed as Flynn wrapped his hand around her waist. "Still okay?" he whispered, his breath hot against her collar.

She nodded and tilted her head back so she could look into his blue eyes. They were as blue and fathomless as the ocean that crashed against the shore below them. She could get lost in them. She wanted to. But she was afraid. She extended her fingers and gently cupped his face, marveling as he nuzzled her hand. He closed his eyes and hummed in approval. He then turned his head ever so slightly and grazed her palm with his lips.

"Mmmm, I like that," she murmured.

He opened his eyes and met her gaze, searching for some kind of approval. "What do you want, Livvy?"

Desire flared between her legs. "For you to kiss me." She'd

barely gotten the words out when he brought his mouth down to hers. It was gentle at first, his tongue exploring her, the brush of his lips against her own. She sipped from him as if he were a sacred cup and his kiss was the manna of the gods. He slowly increased the pressure, wrapping her more tightly in his arms, and her knees began to buckle as she leaned into his embrace. Kissing him was overwhelming in the best way.

It made her heart race as she clawed at his back, pressing herself so tightly against him that there was not even a sliver of sunlight between them. He chuckled and lifted her up, letting her wrap her legs around his waist. He deposited her onto the railing of his deck, kissing her all the while, his hands roaming her back as if it were a treasure map. Sitting on the balustrade, she was the perfect height to fling her arms around his neck and dot his face with kisses.

He broke out into an infectious laugh, and she'd never seen such pure joy on his face before. Not even when they'd won the Catalina Regatta. She unclasped her hands from behind his head and gently ran them along the edge of his sweater.

He raised an eyebrow. "You never need to be shy with me, love."

Encouraged by his bravado, she dipped her hands beneath the hem of his shirt, feeling the ripples and contours of his abs and reaching higher until she had her hands on the hard angles of his chest. He planted a series of soft kisses along her jawline that made her shiver, before nipping at her earlobe. Taking it ever so gently between his teeth, he tugged, and she hummed in delight. She could feel him grin against her as he kissed her neck, trailing his kisses up and down. She gasped as he moved past a particularly sensitive spot, and he responded instantly, sucking and swirling his tongue over it.

His hands wandered to the dainty fabric-covered buttons of

her dress, and he nuzzled at her as his hands stilled, seeming to ask her permission. In answer, she took her hand out from under his shirt and undid her top button, pressing her forehead to his while they both caught their breath.

He locked eyes with her, and the deep blue of his irises pitched almost black as she led his fingers to the next button. He didn't need any more explicit instruction than that, and he expertly undid the top five buttons, opening enough room in her bodice to slip his hands beneath the flimsy fabric. He ran the rough pad of his thumb over her nipple through her bra, and she arched her back to press into his touch.

His signature devilish smirk emerged, and she briefly had the thought that she was finally living the daydream she'd had since she was seventeen years old. But thoughts quickly became impossible as he dipped his fingers beneath the taut band of her bra and his skin made contact with hers. His hands were rough and callused, not those of an aristocrat, but rather hands marked by years spent sailing and fencing.

Livvy's eyes fluttered with pleasure and she pushed further in to him. Each callus bore the shadow of the grip of a sword or the coil of a rope, and the notion drove her mad. He was as wild and rugged as the characters he played, the evidence there in the touch of his hands.

"Flynn, please," she murmured as he pinched her nipple between his thumb and forefinger.

"Please, what?" he growled.

"Please..." She searched her fevered mind. She didn't even know what to ask for. Anything to bring her a release. To push her over the crest he was driving her toward.

He kissed her fiercely and chuckled against her mouth. "It's all right, love, I know what you need."

He removed his hands from her bra, but she didn't have time

to mourn the loss of them before he gently lowered his head until his mouth was against the white cotton material. He sucked at her breast through the fabric. He looked up at her, and she watched as he laved her nipple, his tongue making the bra so wet that she could see the pink tip through the damp material. His eyes sparked as she grabbed the railing with her hands, holding on for dear life as he pleasured her with his mouth.

He held her gaze as he peeled the fabric down, taking her unadulterated nipple into his mouth. She gasped as he swirled his tongue in a way that made a jolt of molten desire surge through her. She couldn't help herself. He made her…wanton. Like one of the hothouse flowers turned pirate queens in his films. She ground her sex down into the railing, increasing the pressure on her most sensitive spot.

He grinned. "That's right, love, take your pleasure. It's what you deserve." Under normal circumstances, such words would've made her blush down to her toes. But she was too far gone. She held herself on the railing, rocking and grinding while he continued to kiss and suck at her breasts. It was all too much.

The feeling that she was at the top of a very tall peak increased and suddenly exploded. The golden tones of the afternoon became a panoply of orange and yellow stars clouding her vision as waves of pleasure crashed through her.

When they finally slowed, she realized that he was holding her in place as she slumped against him. Her forehead, glistening with sweat, was pressed against his shoulder and he was stroking a soothing pattern against her back.

She giggled against him, realizing how ridiculous she looked but not really caring. She pulled back and swiped at her brow, tugging at the blouse of her dress to attempt to generate some air.

"Hot?" he asked.

She nodded, still unable to form a coherent sentence.

Flynn had restored her damp bra to its rightful position at some point. Her neck was the color of the cotton-candy clouds in the sky, suffused with the heat of her pleasure.

She ran her hand along her sweaty nape. "I guess you weren't kidding when you said it's an unseasonably warm day for November."

She jumped down from the railing, straightening her skirt and buttoning up her blouse, suddenly self-conscious at how exposed she was. But that only made her hotter and she cast a longing glance at the sea.

He followed her gaze. "Do you want to swim?"

Her head snapped back to him. "Oh, heavens, no. I–I couldn't."

"Your father was a naval captain and he didn't teach you to swim?"

"No, no, of course I can swim. I just meant I didn't bring a bathing suit or anything." She clasped a bit more tightly at the neckline of her dress and peered back into the house, trying to see if any of the servants were watching.

"I'm sure we could find you one in the house. Someone's probably left one here at some point."

The idea that some other girl had stood on this deck like this, had taken her pleasure at Flynn's ministrations, made jealousy twist in Livvy's gut. She thought of that stupid black book and wondered how many of those girls had stood in this same spot. She knew it was foolish to be envious, and that he had never pretended to be anything but what he was. But the notion still made her queasy.

He grabbed her hand and tangled his fingers with hers, pulling her close and wrapping her in an embrace. "Hey, what's wrong?" He rested his chin on top of her head.

She tried to find the words. "I'm sorry for the way I acted.

How wild I was," she murmured into his chest. God, she must have seemed like a total innocent to him, coming undone so easily. "I promise it won't happen again."

"I sincerely hope that's not true." He chucked her chin with the tips of his fingers and lifted her head so he could look into her eyes. "Don't ever apologize for taking your pleasure with me. Watching you, the way you responded so readily to my touch, my...tongue, the way you rubbed yourself against the railing, that was—"

"But your staff... They could have seen us. I didn't think."

He reached out and smoothed down the wispy tendrils of her hair that had sprung up in the heat of their passion before gently planting a kiss on her forehead. "Is that what's worrying you? I gave them all the night off. Figured we could use some privacy. That's why I ordered in from Perino's...so I wouldn't need to waste any time cooking."

She blinked up at him, unable to put into words how thoughtful that was.

His smile fell before she could respond. "I hope that wasn't presumptuous of me."

Now it was her turn to comfort him, cupping his cheek with her hand. "No, not at all. Not after the way I drove you to distraction on set today."

He shrugged. "Occupational hazard."

She still felt inadequate, knowing the types of starlets and glamour girls he'd paraded through this house. She was a complete novice, not a practiced seductress. "Still, it was clumsy of me." She gripped his biceps, enjoying the solid feeling of strength beneath her hands. She let that ground her so she could say what she needed. "I...am... I didn't..." She swallowed, embarrassed. "I didn't give you the same satisfaction. I lost control."

He gave her a very serious look, and she braced herself for

what was coming. "Livvy, I want you to know...I have slept with some of the biggest movie stars in the world. At least one duchess. And even a traveling acrobat. But what happened between us just now was the single most erotic experience of my life."

She couldn't believe what he was telling her. "You're being kind."

He gripped her more tightly and forced her to look at him. "I promise you, I am not. Are you more inexperienced than some of my partners? Of course. But you are...so beautiful. So unexpected. So present. I never thought I would say this, but I'll take your unbridled enthusiasm over rote seduction any day. You are the most invigorating person I have ever met. And that, what we did, was just the beginning. I promise you that was immensely pleasurable for me, Livvy. You became a wild creature, and unleashing that in you was...staggering. As for my satisfaction, I told you before, we have the whole night ahead of us." He pulled her in to his chest once more and whispered in her ear. "You can have as little or as much of me as you want. You have pillaged and plundered my heart, and I am entirely at your mercy."

Her jaw dropped at his pronouncement, and her heart threatened to pound out of her chest. Flynn Banks thought she—demure homebody Olivia Blount—was sexy. It was the kind of thing that only happened in the movies. The type of thing her mother had warned would lead to her ruin. To the desecration of her entire family. Yet here it was, happening to her, and no one had come to smite her.

She looked up at him, the late afternoon sun giving him a golden halo, and a new wave of heat washed over her. She could practically feel her freckles emerging as the light licked at her face.

Suddenly, she felt brave. Reckless. "You're sure the staff is gone? They won't come back to check on you?"

He barked out a laugh. "No. They're not going to cut short a night off. That's certain."

She bit her lip, pondering the idea. Why not? Flynn Banks was out of his comfort zone here. Shouldn't she be willing to push the envelope a little too? To indulge her desires instead of taking care of everyone else's? "I'd like to go for that swim now. But we don't need to find me a bathing suit."

CHAPTER 21

JESUS CHRIST, THIS WOMAN WAS GOING TO KILL HIM, AND she had no idea of her own power.

Flynn tried to calm the unbearable stiffness in his nether regions that had arisen at her suggestion that they swim naked. Livvy leaned down and pulled her shoes off, unbuckling the straps on her little wedges that wound their way around her ankles in a tantalizing fashion. He resisted the urge to kneel and lick at the indentation beneath her ankle bone.

She set the shoes aside on his deck, and he locked on to the pale-pink polish on her toes that sparkled in the sunlight. She really was the most adorable woman he'd ever encountered.

Nervously, she reached for the buttons of her dress, and he coughed, turning around and using the moment as an excuse to adjust himself in his pants.

"You can look," she told him, quickly undoing any attempt he'd made at returning himself to a state of decency. "I don't mind."

He bit his lip so hard he tasted blood. "No, um, you should have your privacy."

"Oh, but I thought—"

He clocked the disappointment in her voice and cursed himself. She had bared her insecurities and sense of inadequacy to him, and now, he was rejecting the opportunity to watch her undress.

"Not because I don't want to, mind. Just that, erm... Well, you're making my body respond in ways that I would rather it didn't right now. For both our sakes."

He cast a glance over his shoulder and noticed that two rosy-pink circles had bloomed on her cheeks. "Oh. I see."

"So it might be best if I go down to the shore and get in the water first."

"Yes, I hear that cold water can be helpful." She was teasing him. And it was the cutest bloody thing he had ever experienced. He was suddenly possessed with the urge to take her and ravish her on the glass patio table right then and there. But he had a sneaking suspicion she had never been with a man in that way before. And he'd be damned if her first time was anything but the gentlest, most tender experience of her life.

Jesus, she really was making him soft, wasn't she? But only when it came to matters of the heart. Little Flynn was not getting the memo.

"So, if you'll excuse me..." This was getting painful now, the throb of his cock pressing through his shorts into the cold, hard metal teeth of his zipper. He sprinted down the ramp that led from his outdoor patio to the sand, whipping his shirt over his head as he went. Once he was safely in the shadow of the deck, he removed his pants, and the inconvenient sign of his desire immediately diminished as the air hit it. It might have been unseasonably warm, but it was still November. He folded his trousers and laid them on the sand before sprinting into the waves and diving beneath one that was breaking.

The water was brisk and bracing, but refreshing. He didn't remember the last time he'd swum naked. Probably in the

Cherwell at Oxford with some of his mates. Here, it might have been his home and private little patch of sand, but that didn't mean his valet needed to be confronted with the family jewels on a daily basis. His father had needed a servant to dress him top to bottom every day, but Flynn had a shred more dignity and self-possession.

He flipped onto his back and did a few strokes, paddling out through the foamy waves to a calmer, deeper spot. Now safely shrouded by the ocean, he called back to the shore. "Come on in. The water's fine."

She ran to the edge of the deck, completely naked now, and he plunged beneath the water before the sight of her curves and valleys could rattle his brain any further.

Before he knew it, she had swum out to him and was treading water, luxuriating in the sea.

"You look like a selkie," he told her.

She giggled and dove beneath the surface, wiggling her exposed toes in the air. When she emerged, she stuck only her head up from the waves. "I love swimming. The sea. It makes me feel part of nature, like I'm a creature that's part of a greater whole."

He thought his heart might explode. God, she became more wonderful with every moment he spent with her. "I swim every morning."

"You do? That must be wonderful. I always wished we had a pool, but we couldn't afford one. Even if we had, Mother thought swimming was indecent. All that ankle, you know."

Flynn chuckled. He was beginning to understand Livvy's emotional flagellation, her instinct to cut herself off from anything that made her happy. He wanted to be part of ending that tendency. "Well, you can stay and swim any morning you like." *Good going, Flynn, invite the lady to move in tonight, why don't you?*

He had been a rogue for so long that even the prospect of something more serious was turning him into a schoolboy.

But Livvy didn't balk at the offer, merely taking it as the generous suggestion it was. "That's very kind of you. Our bungalow at the Garden of Allah has pool access, but that thing looks like it hasn't been cleaned since Alla Nazimova lived there."

Flynn guffawed. "They like to advertise it as a resort playground for the rich and famous."

Livvy wrinkled her nose in disdain. "Maybe it was when it first opened, but it could use a fresh coat of paint and a new landscaping team."

"I hear Scott Fitzgerald lives there."

"I heard the same thing." She grimaced. "It's actually why I took a room there, sight unseen. That, and it was cheap and close to the studio."

He smiled a close-lipped smile, and she splashed gently at him.

"What?"

"Oh, nothing, it's just so very you to choose where you were going to live based on the residence of a famous author." He splashed a little back at her.

"Fat lotta good it's done me. I haven't seen him even once. I once saw a man discarding an empty bottle of gin in the dumpster behind our bungalow, and I rushed out with my copy of *The Great Gatsby* to ask him to sign it. But it turned out to be the night watchman."

Flynn burst out laughing. "Ohhh, I can just see it. You probably had your curlers in already, right?"

She harrumphed and sent a large splash of water careening toward him. It caught him by surprise and filled his mouth with salty liquid. Still laughing, now spluttering, he splashed back, raising his arms like a whale cresting the surface to help generate a larger wave. But Livvy was too quick for him. She dunked under, holding her nose, and the ocean settled back into itself before she popped up again.

"Not fair," Flynn protested. But he was smiling at her.

"You never remember to expect the unexpected with me. You always think you can win."

"Maybe when we first met. I'm a cocky bastard. I won't deny it. But now, I guess it's just fun to try." He shrugged, and she gave him a queer look before placing her face in the water and blowing bubbles in his direction. Then she tossed her head back and let her body float to the surface.

Until that moment, Flynn had nearly forgotten they were naked. But the tantalizing pink tips of her nipples poked out of the water, and he was thrown headlong back under the wave of desire that had sent him running into the water. He resisted the urge to catalog the details of her body, shimmering in the magical dance of the ocean water and the golden rays of the sun.

"This is so gorgeous," she murmured. He was unsure if she was talking to him or not, but she was right. It was. She was.

He wrested his eyes from the temptation of her naked flesh and turned his gaze to the horizon. The sun was even lower in the sky now, approaching the line of the water. It had begun to turn the wispy pockets of clouds in the sky pink and orange.

He lay back and floated, mimicking her pose. The gentle lull of the ocean held him aloft, and the white noise of the waves crashing on the shore, muffled by the cold water around his ears, instilled a peace in him. He looked up, taking in the full glory of the sky blanketed above him. It was one of those impossible Southern California sunsets, where the unseasonable warmth and the dry air combined to paint the sky with a watercolor brush, swirling together soft lavenders, fuchsia bursts, and burnt orange reveries.

Flynn had taken it for granted—how lucky he was to have this house, to live on the water, to be leading a life solely on his own terms. But he was starting to realize that everything was sharper with Livvy in his life. The beauty that had once been merely a backdrop was brought to startling clarity in her presence.

He sat back up and found her doing the same, treading water as she watched the sun accelerate toward the horizon, its circular blaze melting into the shape of a ridged seashell as it hit the waterline. He had floated nearer to her while on his back, and he reached out and took her hand under the water.

She looked at him and tugged him closer, so that her naked back was flush against his chest. He could feel the round shape of her ass pressing against him, and he fought back a rush of heady want as he wrapped his arms around the soft curve of her belly and held her close. She was slick and wet, like a mermaid in his arms.

It hit him then—as if she were a siren and he the poor sailor lured to his doom. A doom he welcomed with open arms. He was falling in love with her. The thought should terrify him, but instead, he was struck by how much he wanted to live in this moment. For once, he wasn't thinking of the next conquest, his next drink, or what regatta or horse race or fast car or dame in his black book he would use as a distraction. He thought only of her—the way the undulating shape of her body fit perfectly against his, the slick sensation of their skin under the water, the breathtaking beauty they were witnessing together.

She arched her neck, leaning her head against his shoulder, and they watched the sun finish sinking beneath the horizon.

They both gasped as an electric green flash blipped in the

sun's place. It was a blink-and-you'd-miss-it moment, one Flynn had only seen a handful of times in all his years living in Malibu. The conditions had to be just right to generate the phenomenon.

She twisted and wrapped her hands around his neck, bestowing a light kiss on his lips. She tasted of salt water and brine, and he groaned, relishing the moment before deepening the kiss. It was more timid than the earlier kiss they had shared on his deck. As if they had realized how fragile this thing between them was.

She shocked him when she wrapped her legs around his waist, pressing her entire naked body to his. The dappled tips of her breasts poked into his chest, cold from the water. He slipped one hand under her ass, cupping it gently to help keep her afloat, but the other he wound between them, tweaking her nipple and enjoying the gasp she emitted against his mouth. He clung to her, his tongue tangling with hers, as if they were both searching for something within the other.

The apex of her legs pulsed against his belly button, and he shivered. From desire or the cold of the water, he couldn't say.

He clutched her tightly to him, kissing the top of her head. The clouds had faded from periwinkle, pink, and orange to dark purple and gray. Within ten minutes, it would be dark.

"We should go in," he murmured against her ear. Her chin was nestled into his shoulder, resting in the hollow above his collarbone. She nodded gently, and he floated them backwards toward the shoreline, dragging their combined bodies against the tug of the current. When he got to where the water barely met his hips, he gently set her down and they walked to the sand holding hands. When they reached the shore, she pulled him back toward her, stood on tiptoe, and gave him a kiss that he felt all the way down to his toes.

Every part of him wanted to scoop and carry her up the ramp

to his deck, and then bring her straight to his four-poster bed. But he wanted to wine and dine her first, to make his intentions clear before making love to her. He couldn't let her think that she was another notch in his bedpost.

Because for the first time in his life, he wanted so much more.

CHAPTER 22

LIVVY RUFFLED A TOWEL THROUGH HER DAMP HAIR, TRYING to soak up the excess moisture. She looked at herself in the mirror of Flynn's impeccably tiled bathroom. Her lips were cherry-red, bee-stung from his kisses, and they contrasted with the pale white of her skin, made even paler by the cold of the water. Her hair was a mess, a curly, black mop zigzagging about her head. The soft press she had so perfectly coiffed with Judy's help had shrunk back to her natural springy curls.

She looked around the bathroom, but there wasn't a hairbrush in sight. Just an enormous mermaid mosaic spanning the entire back wall of the shower, no doubt made from the same tile that decorated the rest of the house.

The mermaid was sitting on top of a rock, her back to the viewer, and Livvy marveled at how much longing she could see in merely the angle of the mermaid's head. This entire house was a work of art curated meticulously by Flynn.

"Need any help up there?" Flynn called from downstairs.

"No, coming!" She gave herself one last glance in the mirror and sighed. Her hair was going to be messy, that was all there was to it. She double knotted the tie on the white terry-cloth robe Flynn had lent her. It was so oversized that it dragged along the floor, and she had to pull and drape it over her arm like a train.

She emerged to find Flynn waiting for her at the bottom of the stairs. He was wearing a pair of striped pajama pants, no shirt, and an apron. It made her giggle.

He took one look at her getup and swung himself into a deep bow. "My liege," he said with mock seriousness.

She played along, lifting her chin high and descending the tiled steps slowly, holding on to the wrought-iron railing. She came to the bottom step, and he reached out and grabbed her, swirling her around before he set her down and proffered his arm. "My lady, your banquet awaits."

He led her through the kitchen and back out to the deck that was now swathed in darkness. He'd lit the candle on the table, and the little flame flickered like a miniature lighthouse guiding them along the shore to their romantic rendezvous. He pulled out her chair and let her sit. Then, he poured her a glass of red wine before filling his. It was not, she noted, the one she had brought. The label was written entirely in French.

She took a sip, letting its rich, oaky flavor coat the inside of her mouth. It was heady and rich, with an aftertaste of something peppery. It was the best wine she'd ever tasted. "Flynn, this is… poetry in a bottle."

"It's a 1928 Châteaux Haut-Brion Bordeaux," he announced as he took a seat across from her.

She almost spit back into her glass in shock. She didn't know anything about wine, but she knew that name. And that anything under that label was expensive. She cringed. "Please don't open my bottle of wine."

He chuckled. "Wouldn't dream of it."

"I feel like an idiot."

He grabbed her hand and raised it to his mouth, grazing her

knuckles with a kiss. "You were being thoughtful; that means more than an expensive bottle of wine ever could."

She smiled and leaned back in her chair so she could take in the scene before her. She sipped another mouthful of wine, savoring the velvety sensation of it against the inside of her mouth. While she had been drying off, the sky had turned from a dusky purple to a deep royal blue, the stars just beginning to wink out. It was still quite warm, but a chill was in the air, and she drew the robe a bit tighter around her, curling her legs beneath her to sit cross-legged in the chair.

"God, how is that possible?" Flynn asked.

She cocked her head. "What?"

"That you look even more irresistible like that, sitting there with your feet tucked beneath you and your hair a mess."

She self-consciously raised a hand to the mass of her black curls.

"Don't you dare touch it. You should wear it like that more often. It's the most intoxicating thing I've ever seen."

She bit her lip, reaching for her fork, and took a bite while he watched her expectantly. "Good?"

Her eyes fluttered with pleasure. "Delicious." Never had a plate of pasta tasted so wonderful. It was warm and rich in flavor, bursting with the acid rush of fresh tomatoes, delectable fresh herbs, and a curious blend of spices. She twisted her fork around a mound of spaghetti and shoved more into her mouth, hardly caring what she looked like.

Flynn chuckled. "You know, before tonight, I never knew you had such an enormous appetite."

She blushed. "My parents taught me and Judy that a lady never admitted how much she wanted something. That an ascetic approach to life was the only moral option."

Flynn wrinkled his nose. "They sound dreary."

She laughed. "I suppose they were. But they loved us in their own detached way. They're both gone now. Judy and I have been on our own the last four years." She stopped, her voice catching. The memory of all that they'd lost and the challenges they'd faced almost overwhelmed her. But she had to go on. That had always been the only way to get through. "She was only fourteen when they got into the car accident. She was with them that night they passed away. She broke her leg in six places and was told she'd never dance again. That she'd probably have to use a cane to walk. But, well, you've met Judy."

He gave her a wan smile. "I have. That kid's braver than most men I know."

Livvy choked back a knot of emotion in her throat and nodded. "She is. She's kept me going." She steeled herself to tell Flynn the worst of it—the part that made guilt gnaw at her, day in and out, that made her feel like she had no right to mourn her parents. Because it was her fault they were gone. "It was supposed to be me in the car. My parents had three tickets for the opera that night. But I was being a brat. I wanted to see your new movie, *Seas the Day*. It was opening at the local theater that night. My mother told me I was being selfish like I always was. But Judy wouldn't hear it. She volunteered to go to the opera in my place. She knew how much your films meant to me."

"I'm beginning to understand why you were so wary of me when we first met," he said grimly.

"Flynn, no, it—" She struggled to find the words. "I did blame you, I'll admit. But not as much as I blamed myself. My mother and father were upset. Judy told me later that Mother was screaming at Father the entire drive, telling him that he shouldn't have allowed me to have my way. He was distracted. He missed the stop sign. Never even saw the truck coming." A single tear trailed down her face, and she swiped at it with the sleeve of her robe. "So, you see. It was my fault."

"How old were you?"

"Eighteen. Old enough to know better."

He scoffed. "Hardly. When I was eighteen, I was in my first year at Oxford, and the chaplain of my college tried to have me expelled for replacing all the holy water in the chapel with gin." The story broke the pall that had settled over them. Livvy laughed, gurgling and wet with the emotion that had overtaken her. Flynn knew how to lighten the mood without minimizing her story. It was an underappreciated skill.

"Livvy," he continued, more serious now. "It wasn't your fault. It was an accident. We can't control terrible things happening to us. There could've been a million reasons your father missed that stop sign."

"Maybe, but if I hadn't been so stubborn, my parents might still be alive. And I could've prevented Judy from getting hurt. At the very least, it would've been me with the broken leg.

When I learned what happened, I was flattened with grief and with guilt. I threw myself into taking care of Judy. It was the only thing keeping me going. I was supposed to go to college and study English that fall. Prepare to be the author I'd always hoped to be. But I used my college savings to send Judy to a rehabilitation clinic."

"Did she ask you to?"

"No, but—what else was I supposed to do? We're all each other has in the world. Because of me."

He took a bite of pasta, seeming to consider how to respond. "Far be it from me to tell you how to live your life, but did it ever occur to you that Judy never would have wanted you to sacrifice all that?"

"It wasn't her choice to make." Livvy struggled to keep a note of defensiveness out of her voice. "It was what I owed her. To give her back the life I nearly robbed her of."

Flynn popped a tomato from the salad into his mouth and gave Livvy a stern look. "Does she know? What you gave up for her?"

Livvy shook her head. "No, but—"

"No buts. Unless we're talking about your absolutely delectable one." Her mouth fell open at his bawdy remark, and he laughed. "I've warned you plenty of times, my dear, I'm a rogue through and through."

"I couldn't tell her. She never would've allowed it. I told her the funds all came from our parents' inheritance. When the fall came around and I didn't go off to college, I told her I'd changed my mind and didn't want to go, that I didn't need to go to college to be an author. I could write from home, the same as Jane Austen or Charlotte Brontë. She accepted it. Though I'm sure she knew it was a lie. But I had to make her better. I couldn't live with myself otherwise. And ever since, I've done everything I could to keep her safe. To make sure she never gets hurt again. That's all my parents wanted for either of us—to be well taken care of."

He poured himself a bit more wine and raised the bottle in question above her glass. She nodded, and he topped her off. "And where does Hollywood enter into this?"

"I took Judy to an audition for *Macbeth* at the Bowl, and they cast me instead. I felt so guilty. But she insisted I take the part. I was only meant to be an understudy, until the actress playing Lady Macbeth got offered a big movie role. Harry Evets saw the play, and well, here I am."

"I'm surprised you agreed to make the picture."

"Judy was vehement that I take the opportunity. She won me over when she insisted that it would get her closer to her own dreams. I realized she was right. There was no way we could afford to move to Los Angeles otherwise. And I did enjoy playing Lady Macbeth. It was the first time I'd spent that much time luxuriating in language and words since I stopped writing. Plus, it meant I didn't have to send her off on a Greyhound bus hoping for the best. I could go with her and keep an eye on her."

Flynn bit his lip, seeming to debate if he should say something. "Judy is eighteen years old now. The same age you were when you said you should have known better. Maybe it's time you let her make some of her own mistakes."

Livvy took another sip of her wine and pondered Flynn's words. "I'm not sure if I know how to do that."

"Well, the good news is you're dating the most irresponsible man in Hollywood." He winked at her. "People tell me I'm a bad influence."

Livvy rolled her eyes. "And you love that they do. Besides, I'm here tonight, aren't I? Instead of at home, pacing the living room floor and waiting for Judy to get home from set."

"See?" He shrugged. "It's already working."

She laughed again. "It's not that I want to be the mother hen, but I don't know how to be any other way. Even when she was little, I took care of her. I took her to her first dance classes when our mother refused. It's always been the two of us. She needs me." Livvy didn't say the other part—that she had never taken the time to mourn her parents. To sit with the grief of the loss. She needed Judy too. Because if she wasn't taking care of Judy, she might finally have to face her pain.

"She needs you to be her sister. Nothing less, nothing more. You've paid your penance. Forgive yourself, Livvy. I promise it's worth it. If nothing else, let me be a testament to the power of a life lived without looking back."

Livvy considered what he was saying. She knew that some part of him was right. Perhaps it was time to let go a little bit when it came to Judy. She had abnegated her own life, her own dreams to make sure that Judy was well.

It had been the right decision. And Judy was fine now. Thriving, even. She had been trying to get Livvy to live her own life for over a year. So maybe Judy had done more caretaking than she had realized. Maybe they both had. And maybe it was time for a change. But even the thought sent a shimmer of anxiety down her spine.

"I just worry about her. She's all I have."

Flynn took a meaningful sip of his wine and looked deeply into Livvy's eyes. "You have me now too."

The words pierced her heart. He had said this was real. Brought her here tonight for a romantic dinner. And yet—some part of her still didn't trust it. "For how long, Flynn? Until you get bored? This is temporary. Harry designed it that way."

His eyes flashed with something she couldn't identify. "Harry never intended our relationship to be real in the first place, and yet here we are." He reached across the table and took her hand, knitting his fingers with hers. She leaned forward, placing her chin on her hand and leaning on her elbow with her other arm. She didn't want to miss a word of this.

"I've been running for a long time," he continued. "For any number of reasons. To make my father angry. To live the life my mother wanted for me, not one trapped in the gilded cage my father had built. And frankly, because I liked it. It's been a hell of a good time. Even if I can't remember at least a third of it. But you, Livvy, you remind me to take a breath. To stop and smell the ocean. Watch the sunset. The way you savor every moment—the joy you had winning that regatta, the curve of your neck as you swayed listening to the orchestra, the expression of pure bliss on your face when you tasted that enchilada. You've made me realize that while being a libertine was fun for a time, it isn't anymore. I've been indulging myself for years, but it's been some time since I've truly enjoyed it. You changed that."

Her heart caught in her throat and she squeezed his hand more tightly. "I don't want you to change yourself for me. That only leads to unhappiness."

"But that's just it. You're not changing me. You're bringing me back to myself. You've made acting fun again, something more than a means of funding my extravagant lifestyle. I only wish I could do the same for you. Because it may not have been your dream, but you're a damn good actress."

Livvy sat up a little straighter, fully admitting something to herself for the first time. "You're right. Acting was never my dream. But I think maybe it could be. I didn't understand that I could still be a storyteller, even if I wasn't the one writing the stories."

Flynn got a faraway look in his eyes, and Livvy was surprised to hear his voice choked with emotion when he spoke. "That's it, isn't it? You've put into words something I've always known to be true but never understood. The stories we loved as children? We're a part of making them now. Of giving others that same escape they offered us."

"I didn't know it was possible," she confessed. "To find joy in my work again. To find a purpose beyond taking care of Judy. But Flynn, you've helped me turn acting from an obligation, a means to help Judy, into something that makes me excited to get out of bed every day."

"Your very existence makes me eager to get up every day. The night I met you, I was so damnably bored. There's only so much liquor and so many dames one can enjoy before they start to lose their novelty. But when I'm with you, I get the feeling I'll never be bored again."

Livvy's head was spinning, the combination of the wine and Flynn's confessions sending her reeling. Once, she had imagined hearing these things from a man. But she'd long since realized she would only find such romantic fantasies in her precious books. But now he was here, flesh and blood, holding her hand, and telling her...what, exactly?

"What do you mean?"

He ran a hand down his face. "Hell, I'm making a hash of this. I don't even know exactly what I mean. I only know that my days are richer with you in them. And I don't want our time together to end when this film is done or when Harry decides that we've sufficiently fooled everyone and my reputation has been successfully mended. Somewhere along the way, this became real to me. Maybe it always was. Because from the moment I saw you, I knew my life would never be the same. I want you, Livvy. More than I've ever wanted anything."

She huffed out a little gasp of air, trying to process everything he'd said. And the things he hadn't—the three little words she was starting to feel in her own heart but feared he might never be able to say.

Yet he had told her things tonight she had never expected to come out of his mouth. Maybe miracles did happen. After all, somehow her life had brought her here—to Hollywood, on the verge of making her screen debut, with her sister hale and happy, and Flynn Banks telling her that he wanted her. None of this was what she had expected. What she had even dreamed could be possible.

She had tried to remind herself it wasn't real, that it was all part of an act. But it was far past time she admitted to herself—and to Flynn—that she'd been having trouble pretending all along. It was time to be bold. Like the man she was falling for.

She reached for her wineglass and downed the last of it in a single gulp. Then, she stood and undid the tie of her robe, letting it fall to the deck. "I want you too."

CHAPTER 23

FLYNN GASPED AS LIVVY EXPOSED HERSELF TO HIM, AND he hardened immediately at the revelation that she wasn't wearing anything beneath the robe he'd lent her. The moonlight and the shadows of the evening sky bathed her body in an inky swirl of light and dark—from the curve of her waist into her hip, to the bright white of her rounded breasts and the rosy tint of her nipples.

He had never before known what it was to be speechless before a woman. All he could do was marvel at the spectacular beauty that stood before him. He'd only stolen glances earlier in the swirling morass of the sea. But now she was showing him everything, letting him drink it in.

He'd called her a selkie earlier, but he realized now that she was not some mere fantastical creature. She was a goddess, the moon and the stars in human form.

He swallowed, his throat suddenly dry. He stood, but then he changed his mind, not wanting to spook her, and forced himself to sit back down.

She giggled at his clear indecision, but then she caught herself and forced a serious look back onto her face. It only made him laugh in return.

"We're absurd, aren't we?" she muttered.

"Yes, but I'm rather enjoying it."

Her eyes sparkled and she bent over toward him, pressing her lips to his. He groaned and his hands went up to cup her naked bottom as she licked and teased at his mouth.

She broke apart from him and looked at him, a guileless expression on her face. "Take me to bed, Flynn."

He didn't need to be asked twice. He stood, picking her up and cradling her carefully before pushing the patio door open with his foot. It took all his self-control not to race up the stairs or deposit her on the living room couch and take her right there. But as he'd told her, they had all night. There was no need to rush.

His heart swelled as she sighed and leaned her head against his chest. He bent over and pressed a kiss to the top of her head. She released something between a hum and a giggle. "What is it?" he asked.

"You're so gentle," she mused. "I expected it to be like—"

"Like what?"

She blushed, and he realized what she was thinking of.

"Like one of my movies where the pirate ravishes the lady fair?"

She nodded, the pink color in her cheeks spreading down her neck and across the mounds of her breasts.

"Is that what you want?"

She bit her lip and the pink color continued to suffuse her body. Good God, she was not what he'd expected. Every time he thought he'd figured her out, she surprised him again. He'd imagined making gentle love to her, taking care. But she wanted to be plundered like a pirate's treasure. And far be it from him to deny her.

"Livvy," he growled. They had arrived at the foot of the stairs. "Do you want me to ravish you?"

She answered him with a bruising kiss, and he gave her ass a loving slap before throwing her over his shoulder and running up the stairs. She squeaked at the sudden movement, but then she laughed, a purehearted sound that shot straight to his cock, and he raced to his bedroom.

He threw her into the center of his four-poster bed, the down comforter puffing up around her. She leaned back and sat up on her elbows, and he had never seen anything so irresistible. He groaned as he realized she was staring at the obvious line of his erection in his pajama pants.

And then she licked her lips. Oh, she would be the end of him. He had seduced more women than he could count, but he had never had a siren in his bed.

She outstretched her hand and pointed at his pants before imperiously declaring, "Off."

"I thought *I* was supposed to ravish *you*," he quipped. She smirked and swirled her finger in the air, reiterating her request.

Flynn fumbled with the tie on his pants before letting them fall to the floor, his cock jutting out as he freed it. He had not worn undergarments either. Not because he'd expected them to end up here, but because he felt comfortable around her. Like he could be as free and unfettered as he wanted in her presence, and she wouldn't care. He hadn't been wearing a shirt to begin with, so now he stood entirely naked before her.

She sat up a little higher and took him in, and he resisted the urge to preen under her gaze. But he didn't move, standing still while she looked her fill.

"I didn't know," she murmured. He raised an eyebrow, not knowing what she meant until she finished, "That men could be so beautiful."

She pulled herself to her knees, crawling toward him. He stood at the edge of the bed as she placed her hands on his bare chest and explored the lines and ridges of his body while she stared into his eyes. He didn't dare blink. He was caught in a trance, powerless beneath her touch.

"Is this okay?" she asked.

He nodded, and then her hands dipped lower, tracing his abdomen before wandering to the sharp V that acted as a treasure map to his cock. She stroked gently in the space beneath his obliques, the touch of her hands leaving a heated pulse of desire in their wake. At last, she reached his dick, and he groaned as she took it in her hand, wrapping her palm around the shaft.

She let go, suddenly afraid of his reaction.

"Don't stop, please."

Emboldened, she grasped him harder this time, gliding her hand up and down. He bit his lip in an effort to maintain control while she played with him. As she quickened her pace, her hand responding to his increasingly jagged breaths, he bit down so hard he feared he might draw blood. She found the bead of moisture at the head, and without instruction, she flicked at it with her thumb, slicking his entire cock with it until it was glistening.

He hadn't said a word this entire time, grunting and breathing at her ministrations—and she had watched him, reveling in the effect of her touch. But as she bent down to put her mouth to him, he stilled her with his hand. "No."

She looked up at him, confused, and the perplexed little wrinkle of her nose nearly did him in. "But I thought—"

He chuckled, a sound low in his throat. "I can imagine few things as spectacular as your pretty little mouth on my cock, my dear, but not yet. Tonight is about you. And your pleasure."

Her confusion transformed into delighted shock, her mouth

popping into a perfect O. He pushed gently at her shoulder and she fell back on the bed, scrambling backwards on her elbows as he kneeled on the mattress before her.

She reached his headboard and leaned back, her dark, messy curls making a halo around her head on his pillows. If he had been a less experienced lover, he would've spent right then and there. She wanted to be ravished, but God, she was the one stealing his breath and his heart in one fell swoop.

"You are my pirate queen," he growled before launching himself onto his hands and knees above her. He bent his head down and plundered her mouth, tangling his tongue with hers and nipping at her bottom lip.

She met him hungrily, wrapping her arms around his neck and pulling him down toward her. He dotted her jawline with kisses before sucking at a spot on her neck that made her inhale sharply. He swirled his tongue over the spot, and she arched her body in response, her lower back coming up off the mattress. He nipped at her ear and she huffed out, "More."

"So impatient," he chided. He loved teasing her. Loved watching the physical effect of his touch and his words playing across her body. He nipped again at her neck but sucked more lightly this time. "I don't want to make too much of a mess for the makeup department."

She smiled brightly, a look of near-deranged delight. "It would shock them, wouldn't it? I think we should see how many marks you can make."

He laughed and nudged at her nose with his own. "You are far naughtier than I could ever have imagined."

She turned her head and met his eyes, and his heart skipped a beat at the look of pure adoration there. "I like the idea of being marked by you. Of there being some proof that you claimed me."

His cock twitched at her words, and he silently urged it to behave itself. It wasn't time yet. Hell, it might not be on the menu for the evening at all. Not unless she wanted it.

He leaned back and rested his head in his hand, letting his eyes roam up and down the terrain of her body. It was as if she was his personal treasure map, the valleys and mounds an island that only he could chart. He watched her suck in her breath and felt her pulse quicken as he dragged his fingers across her collarbone and the hollow between her breasts.

He held her gaze as he dipped lower until he cupped the mound of her sex. Her eyes widened, blown out by desire, and then he teased her, slowly dragging his finger up the length of her seam before pressing down on her clit. She gasped.

He kissed the tip of her nose. "X marks the spot?"

She giggled. "I think we've officially taken the metaphor too far."

He answered her by plunging a finger into her and making a circle on her clit with his thumb.

"Flynn," she gasped as he curved his finger up and worked it in and out of her, fucking her with his hand. Her eyes fluttered in pleasure, and he watched her carefully as he brought her to the brink.

"Is it too much?" he teased.

She shook her head furiously. "More."

He slid a second finger into her and she moaned at the added pressure, arching her back off the bed so that both fingers slid deeper inside her.

"Holy mother of God," she proclaimed as he hit a spot inside of her that drove her wild. He quickened his pace and put his mouth to hers, kissing her with a bruising passion as he drove his fingers harder and harder into her. He grinned against her mouth as he felt her tighten around his hand and then release, her pleasure leaving her dripping wet.

He slowly pulled his fingers from her sex, then locked eyes with her as he put them in his mouth, one at a time, licking the taste of her off of him while she watched. It tasted salty and clean, a mix of her fresh soapy scent with the brine of the sea.

He would die for another taste of it.

Livvy hadn't known it could be like that. That a man could make her feel that way with only his hand. Her fumbled kisses with high school boys had hardly prepared her for the tsunami of pleasure Flynn had sent crashing into her. Watching him lick her release from his fingers, she clenched her legs together and was shocked to discover that she already wanted him again. And this time, she wanted more than his fingers.

He pressed a kiss to her lips and started moving his way down her chest, taking one of her nipples between his teeth and flicking at it with his tongue. She moaned, breathless, and said, "Flynn, please."

He stopped, and she regretted saying anything.

"Too much?" he asked.

A warm feeling pooled in her belly at his kindness, his consideration. "No, no, it's just—" Her eyes involuntarily darted toward his dick, which was jutting fiercely up toward his belly.

He followed her gaze and chuckled. But then he grew serious. "Livvy, god knows I want to.. But have you—" He bit his lip, and she could tell it had been ages since he'd been with someone he had to ask.

"No." She shook her head. "Never. But Flynn, I want you. So much."

His brow furrowed and it took everything in her not to lean forward and kiss him right there. "If you're sure?"

"I've never wanted anything more in my life."

He wasted no time reaching across her to the nightstand and tugging open the drawer, removing a thin aluminum packet. She had never seen one before, but she knew what it was. Something to make sure she didn't have a baby. He tore it open with his teeth, rolling it down the length of his shaft. She swallowed, growing wet with need as she watched him.

"Almost ready." He winked at her.

He straddled her and used his hand to position the tip at her opening. He gave her a look, seeming to ask for final permission, and she answered by arching her back, drawing the tip of him into her. He plunged his hips forward, filling her to the brim.

"Oh," she squeaked.

He held himself very still, a bead of sweat dripping down his forehead, and she kissed him.

"It's okay."

"Did I hurt you?"

She lay still, adjusting to the feeling of him inside her. "No, it's not painful, just…different."

He smiled and kissed her fiercely, tugging her bottom lip between his teeth as he slid gently out, all the way to the tip, then plunged back into her. She gasped at the movement, enjoying the way she stretched to hold him, the sensation of him filling her up. He repeated the move a few more times, and she threw her head back, reveling in it. With each thrust, it felt better and better, the sense of discomfort giving way to waves of pleasure.

She tentatively moved her hips beneath him, rising up to meet him, and they both groaned as he hit a spot deep inside of her. Through gritted teeth, he muttered, "Fuck, Livvy, that is so good. You're such a good girl—"

But she robbed him of the breath to finish his thought, following his encouragement and thrusting more boldly. He swore loudly and bit his lip, clearly trying to maintain some semblance of control, but she ground against him, telling him with her body that it was okay to let go.

He buried himself in her until she could not see where he ended and she began. He wrapped his arms around her shoulders, kissing her with ferocity before rolling them over so that he could stand up.

Livvy wrapped her legs around him as he carried her from the bed, pushing her against the wall. She groaned as he held her there, capturing her mouth in a punishing kiss and driving himself into her over and over.

The new position was maddeningly good. When she felt as if she were near the precipice, he would stop and hold himself still, letting her pleasure ebb ever so slightly.

She wrapped her arms more tightly around his neck and nipped at his earlobe, and she felt him smile against her cheek.

"I want to take my time with you, for your first time," he said.

"And yet, you've taken me up against the wall."

"You did say you wanted me to ravish you." He smirked and her heart skipped a beat. Had any man ever been so infernally attractive? He slid his hands further beneath her bottom and pushed her up so that he was hitting a new angle inside of her.

"Mother of God," she hissed. "I've never felt anything so good in my entire life."

"Careful." He winked. "I might get cocky."

She looked pointedly down at where they were joined. "I thought you already were."

He guffawed and captured her mouth in a kiss. He rutted against her and she clawed at his back, desperate for purchase as everything from her waist down turned to jelly. She tangled her hands in his hair and pulled his mouth to hers, gasping in between kisses, "My. Handsome. Pirate."

He thrust again and carried her back to the bed, falling backwards so that she was on top. It was as if some part of her had been missing until now, and he had made her whole with their lovemaking. She felt deliciously full and tight and stretched to her breaking point.

She braced her arms on either side of his chest, swirling her hips in a circular motion without lifting off of him. Then she leaned forward and took his nipple between her teeth, copying what he had done to her. He hissed. With pain or pleasure, she wasn't sure, and she pulled back to ask, but she got her answer when he gently guided her head back to his chest.

"Don't stop."

She licked and flicked at him, all the while keeping her circular motions going, and when she had thoroughly ministered to both sides of his chest, he gasped, "Ride me, Livvy."

"What?" She sat back on her haunches.

"Ride me, until you finish. Until we both do."

The Livvy she had been would have blushed at such a sentiment. Perhaps even been shocked by it. But the Livvy she was tonight—the Livvy who went after her desires with a wicked abandon—wanted to chase that elusive tidal wave until pleasure crashed into her and left her seeing stars.

She did as he asked, bucking back and forth on top of him, experimenting with angles until he touched the spot inside of her that made her gasp.

He reached up and tweaked her nipples, tangling his hands

in her hair while she rode him harder. "Yes, my darling, just like that."

His words of approval made her wild with desire, and she adjusted so she could lift herself higher and drop more boldly onto him. My God, was this what she had been missing? No wonder her mother had warned her against it. She would like to do this and nothing else for at least a week. Perhaps a month. Hell, with Flynn, she might want to spend the rest of her days in his bed.

The wave of pressure inside her began to build, and she took his mouth with hers, tangling their tongues together. He answered her with a deeper thrust, one that made her groan, and she whispered in his ear, "Faster."

He obliged and moved his mouth to suck at her neck, and the pleasure was overwhelming. She had never dreamt it could be like this. No wonder Flynn was a rogue. She said a silent thank-you for all the practice he'd had before this moment, her jealousy entirely forgotten with the reward of such knowledge.

Without warning, her orgasm crashed into her as if she were a volcano erupting. She clenched hard, feeling the warm pressure of his dick inside of her, and the sensation made her pleasure even more intense, as if she had reached the top of one peak only to climb to another.

She moaned his name as she came undone in his arms, and he followed quickly behind her, a few quick thrusts and a grunt before his face scrunched up and a look of utter bliss washed over him.

She collapsed on top of him, enjoying the sensation of his sweat mingling with hers. After a moment, he kissed the top of her shoulder and rolled her gently to the side so his arm was cradling her and her head was lying atop his torso. She was still light-headed, and she lazily traced her hand up and down his chest, reveling in the light blond dusting of hair. He pressed a kiss to the top of her head and lay back.

She made a hum of contentment and snuggled as close to him as she could get, the afterglow of her pleasure still suffusing her body like some ethereal being had possessed her. He yawned, and she marveled at how safe she felt here, protected by his embrace.

Being intimate with a man had seemed this frightening, unknowable thing, and yet, she felt more cared for than she ever had in her life. Flynn had awakened something in her—not just something carnal, though she realized now how much richer her life could be with that in it. No, something untethered and wild. Something that made her feel like she could soar through the skies, free as bird, and always have a place to land. It was unusual, knowing she didn't have to be the one always looking out, always being cautious, always worrying. Because Flynn would do that for her.

She nuzzled his collarbone, throwing an arm across his chest to tangle them fully together. Flynn Banks was so much more than what she'd imagined—vulnerable and sexy and kind and funny. But not in the way he was on-screen. Rather, in a way that was altogether more real, and rougher around the edges. Those jagged edges were what made him who he was: a celluloid swashbuckler made flesh and blood.

She sighed with happiness and, without thinking, murmured against his chest, "I think I'm falling in love with you." But all that answered her was a soft snore, and a strange mix of relief and disappointment surged in her gut.

She wondered if she'd have the courage to tell him again.

CHAPTER 24

LIVVY AWOKE TO THE SOFT PRESSURE OF FLYNN'S HAND on her hip, absentmindedly stroking her belly. She smiled without opening her eyes, soaking in the moment and remembering the previous evening. Her legs were tangled with his and her hair was strewn across his chest. She wished she could capture this moment in a bottle, like the sand outside his house, and keep it with her always. She listened to the soft rising and falling of Flynn's breath and let it calm her, reveling in the sensation of being wrapped in each other in the vulnerability of sleep.

When she opened her eyes, she noted that the room was bathed in a gray early-morning light. But then suddenly, a cloud shifted and a ray of sun struck the opposite wall. She lifted her head to look at the clock on Flynn's nightstand and jolted straight up, realizing it was nearly 10:00 a.m. God, she hadn't left a note for Judy or called to tell her she wasn't coming home. Her sister had probably sent out a search party by now.

Livvy gently extricated herself from Flynn's arms, rolled over, and got out of bed. She hunted around the floor, desperate to find her clothes before she remembered that she had removed them to swim in the ocean. Was her dress still on the deck?

She noticed a plaid dressing gown hanging on the back of Flynn's door and pulled it on. Wrapping it tightly around her, she tried to dull the edge of panic. It was fine. Everything was fine. Judy probably assumed… Livvy blushed at what her sister probably assumed.

Flynn opened his eyes and stretched languidly, and the sight of him naked and laid out before her was almost enough to make her forget her need to check on Judy. He noted her blush and nodded at the way she'd covered herself in his robe. "Surely you're not shy, not after everything we did?"

He waggled his eyebrows, and she giggled in spite of herself. "No, it's just… I didn't realize we'd slept so late, and I never told Judy I wasn't coming home last night."

Flynn patted the bed next to him, urging Livvy to return. "We can give her a ring in a minute. Don't you want some breakfast first?" The look on his face said that breakfast had absolutely nothing to do with food. The offer was sorely tempting, but she needed to get home.

"Flynn, I need her to know I'm all right. What if she's imagining the worst?"

His wolfish smile fell, as if he had just remembered why Judy might jump to the direst possible conclusion. He sat up, ran a hand down his face, and yawned, before finding his striped pajama pants and pulling them on. "There's a phone in the kitchen. Come with me."

Livvy followed him downstairs. She wound her finger through the rotary dial on the phone hanging on the wall while he attempted to make coffee on the stove. Despite his cooking skills, she had to laugh at how inept he was here. He clearly was used to waking up to a fresh pot.

But any sense of humor evaporated when Judy didn't pick up. "That's not like her."

"Maybe she's in the ladies' room." Flynn still looked exhausted.

She took the small metal coffeepot from him and packed the grounds tightly into the base; it gave her something to do with her hands besides wringing them.

"Maybe...I'll try her again in a few minutes."

Once the coffee pot was bubbling away on the stove, Livvy returned to the phone and tried ringing their bungalow again. No one picked up. Livvy's stomach threatened to divulge its contents.

Flynn wrapped his arms around her waist and rested his chin on her shoulder. "It'll be all right."

But panic was swirling in her gut. Her alarm bells were going off. Any number of things could have happened. Judy could be out searching for her, worried she was dead in a ditch somewhere. Or Judy herself, God forbid, could be the one who was in trouble.

She grabbed at Flynn's hands and extricated herself from his embrace. "Something's wrong," she muttered.

"I think you're overreacting."

Livvy gave him a look.

"Go get your clothes off the deck and I'll drive you home."

She wasted no time doing as he said, not caring that her dress was lightly damp from the morning sea mist. Flynn had scarcely wrestled himself into a pair of khaki pants and a striped shirt before she was at the front door, bouncing on her toes like a child waiting to leave.

They drove in silence the entire way, and she turned over increasingly worsening scenarios in her mind. Flynn didn't try to reassure her again, just drove with a single-minded purpose. She wondered how things had gone so wrong, how she'd managed to turn the easy comfort of last night into this tense silence. But she couldn't rest until she knew Judy was okay.

After what seemed an interminable drive, creeping away from the foggy banks of the Malibu beach to the sunnier climes of Hollywood, they arrived at the Garden of Allah. Livvy didn't even wait for Flynn to come to a complete stop before opening the door of his roadster and running out.

"Judy, I'm home," she called out.

Her sense of foreboding grew, and she unlocked the front door to find the living room silent and still. She raced to the back to see if maybe Judy was asleep. But Judy's nightgown was still laid out on her twin bed, her slippers neatly arranged on the floor—the way Livvy had left it for her last night so that she could easily slip into bed after a late night on set dancing.

Judy had never come home. Livvy choked back a sob.

It's fine, she tried to tell herself. *Maybe Judy went to stay with a friend.* But the memories of the policeman coming to her door, telling her that her parents were dead and Judy was seriously injured, flashed before her eyes.

She bent over, holding onto the cheap cotton bedspread, and retched. Nothing came up but watery bile, and Livvy dabbed furiously at her eyes, trying to recover herself.

She would go to the Rolodex in the living room and see if there was any name there that would offer a clue to Judy's whereabouts. But when she emerged from the bedroom, she was startled to see that Flynn was standing on the stoop…talking to a police officer.

Her knees buckled and she braced herself against the wall.

Flynn looked over his shoulder and saw her, rushing to her aid. "Livvy, Livvy, it's all right. She's okay. She spent the night in jail, that's all. But she's alive. She's unharmed."

Flynn rubbed a gentle pattern on the small of her back and led Livvy to the sofa, before disappearing into the kitchen, running the sink, and returning with a glass of water.

Livvy gulped at it, trying to catch her breath. "Jail?" she whispered. "Did you say jail?"

Flynn stuck his head out the door. "Officer, will you please come in and explain to Miss Blount what you told me?"

Flynn took her hand and sat next to her on the couch. The officer stepped through the door, blocking out the sun with his hulking frame, and Livvy held back a gasp of fear.

He's not here to tell you the worst. Pull yourself together.

The officer removed his hand and worried the brim in his hands. "Sorry to drop in on you like this, miss, but your sister has been trying to reach you all night."

Livvy closed her eyes in shame. Judy had needed her. And she hadn't been here. She'd been too busy frolicking in the waves and Flynn Banks's bed. Once again, she had chosen Flynn over family, and Judy had gotten hurt. Rationally, she knew that it wasn't Flynn's fault her parents had died while she was watching one of his films. But the universe had a sick sense of humor. After four years of tamping herself down, denying herself her dreams, she'd finally felt free for one night. And it had coincided with her sister meeting some misadventure. She pushed the thought down, realizing all it would do was make her feel like she was the worst sister that had ever lived. "What, what happened?"

Flynn squeezed her hand a bit tighter, but it didn't cut through the numbness she'd come to rely on to survive.

"We arrested her last night for aggravated assault."

Livvy's mouth fell open. "My sister wouldn't assault someone. She's gentle and kind."

Flynn cleared his throat, cutting Livvy's excuses off. "Let the man finish, Olivia."

He was back to calling her Olivia, and only the strange gravitas of that got her to stop talking.

The officer scratched the back of his head, looking profoundly uncomfortable. "I'm not entirely sure of the details, miss.

I'm just a patrol officer sent out to see if I could find you. But it's my understanding that she attacked a guest at a studio party last night. The gentleman in question called the authorities, and she was taken in. She's being held for a ten-thousand-dollar bail."

If Livvy's jaw could reach to the floor, it would have hit it after hearing that sum. "Ten thousand dollars? That's, that's more money than I've ever seen in my life." It was the entirety of her year's contract with Evets's Studios.

Flynn waved his hand. "I'll pay it."

Livvy tried to protest. "No, Flynn, you can't do that. I won't let you."

"That's nothing to me. You've been helping me make sure I keep my career and, therefore, my money. Might as well put it to good use."

"But—"

"We'll discuss terms later. Let's just get Judy out for now."

She nodded, unsure if she was more grateful or ashamed that Flynn had come to her rescue. Particularly when her desire for him had kept her from knowing her sister needed help until now.

"But tell me, Officer," Flynn continued. "That seems an awful high price for a harmless little hoofer."

The officer scrunched up his face, clearly reluctant to share the next bit. "The gentleman she attacked insisted. He's got a lot of sway, so the captain had no choice."

"Who is it?"

"I'm not at liberty to disclose his identity."

Livvy wanted to shake the officer and curse Flynn. What were they doing still sitting here? She needed to go find Judy, to get her out of that terrible place.

She stood up, swaying a little unevenly on her feet. "You two can keep discussing the terms of my sister's arrest, but I need to bring her home."

The officer nodded. "I can drive you in the patrol car if you'd like, miss."

"There's no need," Flynn said. "I'll drive her. I need to come to write a check for the bond anyway."

Livvy wanted to object, to tell Flynn to keep out of it. He had already caused enough trouble. Last night, he told her she needed to let Judy make her own mistakes. Well, she certainly had now, hadn't she? The mother of all mistakes. Though something kept telling her she was missing part of the story. Judy would never attack someone. At least not without good reason.

She let Flynn lead her out the door and to the passenger side of his roadster. Right now, she needed to get Judy out. The rest of the details could wait.

CHAPTER 25

THE HOLLYWOOD PRECINCT STATION WAS HOUSED IN A gray stone building with a terra-cotta roof, a facility that looked more like a bank or an insurance agency than a center of law and order. Flynn had spent a few nights at this Wilcox Avenue station in his time, mostly drying out in the drunk tank after particularly louche evenings. Harry had always bailed him out the next morning, taking the cost out of Flynn's salary and scrubbing the incident from Flynn's criminal record. The studio had a half-dozen fixers on payroll, ready to clean up after their stars. But there was no erasing it from the papers, considering Flynn's caddish reputation.

Approaching the station, he was brought back to one particularly memorable evening at the Cocoanut Grove. The club had decided it would be a brilliant idea to have live animals for the evening, perching parrots and cockatoos around all the booths and the bandstand. He'd brought Rallo along as a joke, figuring that a real monkey would liven things up. But at one point during the night, a parrot had pooped in Flynn's drink, and Flynn, already three sheets to the wind, had tried to throttle it. The parrot had flown up to the top of a papier-mâché palm tree, and he'd sent Rallo climbing up after it.

By the time they'd gotten the monkey and the bird down,

the parrot had lost several feathers. How was Flynn to know the exotic bird trainer responsible for the creature was the guest of honor that night? Flynn had been arrested for destruction of private property, while Rallo, the little devil, had gotten off scot-free.

He opened his mouth to tell Livvy the story to try to lighten the mood, but one look at her ashen face told him this wasn't the time. Her lips, so plump and inviting last night, were twisted into a wrinkled little line. Her arms were crossed tightly over her chest as if she were holding herself together.

He pulled into the parking lot and put the car in park. "Let's get your sister."

Livvy nodded sternly, and Flynn didn't push her. He came around to open her door and played it off when Livvy didn't reach for his proffered arm, marching under the stone archway and through the glass side door alone.

He sighed and followed her, not knowing the right thing to do or say. He wanted to be there for her, to tell her that she didn't have to shoulder this by herself. But she was shutting him out.

Livvy marched into the precinct and told the officer at the front desk in an icy tone, "I'm here to see my sister."

The officer raised an eyebrow, stunned at Livvy's haughty demeanor. Flynn hadn't seen her like this since their first days together, donning the mask she wore to protect herself, to make people think she was above their reproach. But right now, all this was going to do was make things worse.

He interjected over her shoulder, "Her sister is Judy Blount. She was brought in last night on charges of assault. I'm waiting for my valet to bring me my checkbook, but then I will pay her bail." Flynn had called before they'd left the bungalow to see if Hugh could come to the station. He'd had to promise Hugh another day off next month to make up for it.

The officer met Flynn's gaze, and his eyes lit up. "Mr. Banks! Good to have you back here."

Livvy gave him a shocked look, reassuring him that it had been best to skip the story about the parrot.

He rubbed the back of his neck sheepishly. "Erm, yes. Well, can't say I feel the same."

The officer chuckled and opened the heavy wooden door to the right of his desk. "Miss Blount can receive one visitor at a time."

Flynn moved aside to let Livvy through. She looked back at him, but he couldn't tell if her expression was one of gratitude or irritation.

He looked at an uncomfortable wooden chair, stained and lonesome in the cramped reception area, and sighed, then took a seat to wait for Hugh.

As the officer led her back through a padlocked steel door, Livvy tried to hold herself extremely upright, projecting a courage she did not feel.

Down the hallway, he gestured to a cell. "She's in there."

As soon as he walked away, Livvy dropped all pretense. "Judy!"

Her sister jolted up on the squalid cot she was lying on, and a look of intense relief washed over her when she made eye contact with Livvy. Judy ran to the bars separating them and stuck her hands through, grabbing for Livvy. "Livvy, thank God. They said I had one phone call, and I called the bungalow. They even let me try a few times, but you never picked up."

"I know, I know, they told me. I'm so sorry." How could she

ever forgive herself for not going home last night, for choosing Flynn and herself over Judy. How many times would she fail her sister?

Livvy pressed a kiss to her sister's hand, noticing that Judy's nails had what looked like a layer of dried blood beneath them. She stepped back and took Judy in. She was still in her skimpy black showgirl costume from the night before. It was little more than a corset, a bustle full of feathers, and some fishnet tights. Livvy saw with horror that there was a rip in her sister's tights, a stain on her bodice, and a scratch on her cheek. A strong smell of vomit emanated from Judy's rat's nest of hair.

Livvy tried not to gag. "What happened? I thought you were filming a scene as background dancers."

Judy jutted out her chin, trying to look brave. But her lip quickly followed as she burst into tears. "I–I–I thought so tooo," she sobbed, drawing out the last word.

Livvy pulled Judy toward her and tried to hug her through the prison bars. Judy sobbed and sobbed, until she hiccupped and abruptly stopped, seemingly cried out.

"Billy Wilkes said we were supposed to be dancers in a scene."

Billy Wilkes—how Livvy hated that name. She'd known he was bad news from the day Judy had accepted the job at the Sphinx Club. She should've trusted her gut and made her sister turn down the offer. Even if Judy would've been mad at her. But they'd needed the money for rent, and that had clouded her judgment.

"But when we got to the studio, it was a big party. Celebrating their successful year at the box office, honoring the executives and salesmen. There were guys there that'd flown in from around the country. They said we were the night's entertainment, and they gave us these outfits." She gestured at her ensemble. "Told us to put them on. I thought well, what the heck? A gig is a gig. I can dance for a party as well as I can dance for a camera. But when they said we were the entertainment, they didn't just mean dancing. They meant we were there to entertain the men."

Livvy's stomach plunged. She knew what that meant. Every girl with a dream of Hollywood stardom did. The stories of studio bigwigs who liked to take their liberties had circulated backstage at the Hollywood Bowl. She was lucky that Harry's biggest imposition was insisting she pretend to date Flynn. How lucky, she hadn't realized.

"Did someone... Did they—" She couldn't even say the words. If Judy had been violated, she would find the man responsible and murder him with her bare hands.

Judy shook her head. "But they tried." She gulped, and Livvy could tell she was searching for the strength to finish her story. "We did our little performance, and then we were each assigned a table. Mr. Devlin seemed so nice at first."

The name sent alarm bells ringing in Livvy's head, but she couldn't remember why it was familiar to her.

Judy kept going. "He asked me to sit next to him, and he kept refilling my champagne glass. After a while, I started to get a headache and feel sick. I said I needed to run to the ladies' room, and he said he would help me. I said that wouldn't be necessary, but he insisted. He took my arm."

Judy held up her wrist, and Livvy gasped at the line of fingerprints visible in a ring of bruises. "What a brute."

"He brought me to the ladies' room, and I went in and was sick to my stomach. I've never had that much champagne before. I'm sorry, Livvy. I should have stopped after two glasses, but he kept pouring, and Billy told us our job was to be agreeable and make sure the men had a good time."

Livvy squeezed her sister's hand. "Don't apologize, Judy. No part of this is your fault."

"Anyway, I thought after I went to the bathroom, that was the end of it. I would tell Mr. Devlin I needed to go home because I wasn't feeling well. But when I came out into the little waiting room area, he was sitting in there on the little pouf in the center of the room, and he had—" Judy swallowed.

"You don't have to tell me the rest if you don't want to."

"No, I need to say it. He had unzipped his trousers, and he reached out for me and pulled my hand into his pants." Livvy felt like she might vomit now too. "I protested and backed up, and he tried to cajole me. He stood and he pressed his body weight against me, pushing me up against the wall. I hoped and prayed that someone else would come in and use the restroom, and it would end. But nobody did, so I slipped out from under his arms and tried to leave. He caught me around the waist, called me a tease, and flung me onto the lounge.

"I screamed and tried to get away, but he wouldn't stop. He started to climb on top of me, and I snapped. I slapped him, and with my other hand, I scratched at his face." She held up her hand again, showing off the dried blood under her fingernails. "He scratched me back, bit my lip until it bled. Called me an alley cat who needed to be tamed. I scratched him again, digging my nails harder into his face, and that's when he called for security and told them that I had attacked him unprovoked. That he had to fight me off because I was drunk and crazed."

"But that's a lie! Did you tell them he was lying?"

Judy's shoulders collapsed, and she shook with sobs. Livvy couldn't bear to have these bars between them. She needed to hold her sister, to make her understand that she would do anything to protect her. That she would never fail her again. To hell with Flynn. To hell with the picture. Judy was her top priority now. She should always have been.

"I couldn't. I was in shock. They put me in handcuffs and threw me in the back of a police wagon and drove me away."

Livvy pressed another kiss to her sister's forehead through the opening in the bars. "It's okay, it's okay. It would've been worse if you'd resisted the police. We will tell them the truth in court."

Judy looked up at her, a stark look of fear on her face. "No, Livvy, no trial. I want to forget this ever happened."

"But this man needs to pay for what he did to you—"

Judy shook her head sadly. "Do you think I was the only girl treated that way last night? They brought us there to be party favors. I fought back, and look where that got me."

Livvy wanted to scream, to tear down the walls of this station brick by brick. To march across the city, find Mr. Devlin's house, and burn it to the ground with him inside it. But most of all, she wanted Judy to be okay. To feel safe. To not have to think about this ever again.

So she simply nodded, and their conversation was interrupted by the arrival of the officer who had brought her back here. "Her bail is paid, she's free to go." He unlocked the door to Judy's cell, and her sister practically collapsed into her arms as Livvy led her out.

Flynn was still waiting, and he gave Judy such a look of concern it almost broke Livvy. "I'll drive you both home."

She didn't have the energy to argue and followed him out the door.

CHAPTER 26

THE RIDE BACK TO THE GARDEN OF ALLAH WAS THE TENSEST ten minutes of Flynn Banks's life. They were all squished together on the bench seat with Livvy in the middle, acting as a buffer between Flynn and Judy. She held Judy tight. The poor kid was in shock. She was shivering and hollow-eyed as if she'd seen a ghost.

When they finally pulled up to the bungalow, he hopped out and opened the door for them. Judy stumbled and he ran to catch her, but Livvy held her up instead.

"I've got her. I've always got her." The look she gave him was so cold that his heart got frostbite. Livvy blamed him for this. Somehow.

"Wait here," she muttered, before helping Judy into the house.

Flynn paced nervously by his car, grinding his foot into a piece of gravel that had come loose. God, this place had really deteriorated. Not for the first time, he wished he could help Livvy and Judy find better lodgings. But it was clear Livvy had only accepted his help today because she'd had no other choice.

She returned out the front door, looking like the weight of the world was on her shoulders. "I put her in bed. Hopefully, she can get some sleep."

He opened his arms to her, and to his surprise, she fell into them, crying into his chest. He held her and rubbed a soothing pattern on her back, hoping to calm her. "Did she tell you what happened?"

Through her tears, Livvy managed to choke out, "A man tried to, to, to have his way with Judy." Flynn swallowed, a wave of disgust mounting in his gut. "She fought him off."

He kissed the top of Livvy's head. "Did she say who it was? Did she know him? I'll tear him limb from limb."

She shook her head against his chest. "Judy doesn't want me to tell anyone. She wants to pretend it never happened."

"But—"

Livvy broke away from him, and there was something wild and angry in her eyes. "Stop, just stop."

He took a step back, her words landing like a physical blow. The fight fell out of her, and she looked more tired than she ever had.

"This"—she gestured between the two of them—"this is over. Real, pretend, whatever it was. I'll do what Harry asks. I'll go on studio-orchestrated dates. Be photographed together. The bare minimum to make sure I keep my contract so that I have enough money to move us back home when this is done. But that's all. I let myself get distracted. To believe that acting could be a job that would make me happy. But my only job is to take care of Judy. Nothing else can get in the way of that. Not a movie. Not a studio. And certainly not a man."

She delivered her speech with steely resolve, as if she'd been practicing it in her head on the drive home. But all Flynn wanted was to help. "You don't seriously think that if you had come home last night, this would have gone any differently?"

She lifted her chin and glared at him, her eyes swimming with tears. "I do. I would've been here to answer her call. To make sure she didn't spend a night in a jail cell."

"How would you have bailed her out?"

"I would have found a way," she snapped.

He cupped her cheek with his hand. "Livvy, why won't you let me help you?"

She twisted her face away, repelling his touch. "Because none of this would have happened if I'd been paying attention. I should have made Judy turn the job down that first day when she came home with an injured wrist. But I kept ignoring the signs. The twisted ankle. The black eye."

Flynn involuntarily winced at the mention of the black eye, and he realized a moment too late what he'd done. Livvy grabbed onto it like a dog with a bone. "You knew, didn't you?"

"Livvy, no, it's—"

"You told me to let it go. That she could take care of herself. That accidents happen. That I was overreacting."

"That is all still true. If you'll let me explain."

Livvy's eyebrows disappeared into her hairline. "Explain? Explain what? That you knew my sister was in danger? That you were aware she was being abused in her workplace, and you convinced me to ignore it?" She was practically shrieking now.

He tried to quiet her. "Hey, hey, calm down. You'll wake Judy up."

"As if you care," she spat out. "All you care about is yourself. That's all you've ever cared about. What was last night? Was my acting not good enough for you? Did you decide this whole charade would be more believable if you seduced me?"

He reeled back as if he'd been slapped. "That's not what happened last night and you know it."

Tears were streaming down her face now, and her breathing was ragged. It physically pained him that he couldn't say anything to make this right. To make her feel even slightly better.

He had kept the truth from her. Because Judy had asked him to. But more because he knew that if Livvy had known the truth, she would have shut herself up like a nun. And he couldn't allow that. Because it would have ruined their charade, yes. At first, that had been why. But then, something had changed along the way, and it had become about showing Livvy that she didn't have to deny herself happiness. That she could go after the things she wanted. Live wickedly. Whether or not that included him. But none of that mattered now, it seemed.

She shuddered and drew a shaky breath. "You're right. That's not what happened. What happened is that I believed you. When you told me she would be okay, I trusted you. Because I wanted you. I wanted you even though I knew I shouldn't. I turned my back on my sister to spend time with you, and she got hurt. Because of me."

"I don't think Judy would see it that way."

She ran her fingers through her hair, turning the already-tangled mess of her curls into a morass that made her look like a madwoman. "Only because she's too young to know better. I am supposed to protect her. To look out for her. Not to, to, to—"

"Not to what, Livvy? Not to free yourself from something that was never your fault? To live your own life? To fall in love?" The words were out of his mouth before he knew what he was saying.

A look of abject despair crossed her face before it was replaced with a wild fury. "I was going to say, 'Not to fuck Hollywood's favorite playboy,'" she snarled.

He reeled back as if she had slugged him. He'd never heard her be so crude. So cruel. As if he didn't know what he was. As if he hadn't chosen it. "I've never promised a girl more than a good time."

"All the better for them. If you ever do get married, I pity the poor girl who gets stuck with you."

"I think it's safe to say you needn't worry about that."

"No, I don't. Because all I am, all I ever was going to be, was another name in that little black book of yours. Do me a favor and draw a line through mine when you pencil it in."

God damn that black book. He wished he'd thrown into the ocean the morning Harry had first concocted this deranged PR stunt. "If you think I'm ashamed of my reputation, you've got another think coming."

"No, why would you be? You don't have any responsibilities. You've made sure of it. Flynn Banks, the poor little rich boy whose only job is to spend his father's money on booze and women because he can't bear doing something he doesn't want to do for even a moment."

"It's not that simple. It never was. You don't know what I endured. What my mother faced. What she almost—" His voice cracked. But he plowed ahead. "She told me to 'choose joy' because she was nearly deprived of the right to do the same. She wanted more for me. So yes, I enjoy myself. I don't deprive myself of a life out of some misplaced sense of martyrdom. Refusing to live because you believe you should've been the one to die won't bring your parents back, Livvy."

Her eyes flashed in anger, and she ran at him, pounding her fists into his chest. "You bastard! How dare you say such a thing? As if you know me. As if you know what it was like for me. For Judy. For the both of us. We were finally starting to get out from the under the weight of that loss. And now the worst possible thing that could happen to a woman happened to my sister. She'll have to live with that now too. Not just the memory of the accident. Of my parents' lifeless bodies lying there in the moments before she too lost consciousness. I thought that was the worst thing Judy would ever see, that she'd ever have to endure. But I was wrong." Her words descended into babble, and she began to sob, the pounding of her fists turning into a desperate clutching of his shirt. "I failed her," Livvy wailed.

He picked her up, and she didn't protest as he carried her into the small bungalow and laid her on the careworn sofa. He listened to her continued sobs as he went into the kitchen and filled her a glass of water, setting it gently on a coaster on the coffee table. Not that the table deserved any such care. It was stained and scratched in at least six different places.

He sighed. Livvy was right. He didn't know what it was like. To have nothing. To be constantly terrified of what would happen if you let your guard down even for a second. Because he'd never had to.

He'd designed a life where he could always choose joy and freedom. It hadn't been all that hard. He was a man, after all. But he'd seen the alternative every day as a child, watching his mother endure a life under his father's thumb. She had almost paid the ultimate price—but she found a way to remake her fate. He'd come to realize that his mother's selfishness was brave, because it became the only way for her to be happy. To live. From the time he'd gone to university, he knew he couldn't bear to go through life any other way. But that was a luxury Livvy had never had.

The irony was that, for the first time in his life, he wanted to choose to be responsible for someone else. To put someone else's happiness before his own. And that person would not let him. He bent down and smoothed her hair, running his fingers through it, as her sobs turned to sniffles, and she finally stopped altogether.

"Please go," she begged in a small voice.

And he did as she asked, because what else was there to do?

CHAPTER 27

FLYNN WAS IN HIS DRESSING ROOM, TOWELING OFF AFTER a particularly vigorous day of filming the climactic sword fight between his character and the dastardly governor of the Caribbean colony, who was actually a notorious pirate in disguise. He mopped the sweat from his brow and was leaning against the makeup banquette next to the mirror when there was a soft rap at the door.

"Come in," he called. "Harry! It's not often I see you out of your office these days. What's the trouble?"

Harry had a grim look on his face and was holding a stack of papers in his arms. "What are those?" asked Flynn.

"Advance copies of tomorrow's *Daily Variety*." He handed them over to Flynn. "Thought you'd want to see them. We're going to have end this little charade with the De Lesseps girl. Seems her sister is a real hellcat. This could ruin our efforts to repair your image entirely. We'll have to get ahead of this. Can you have Dash call Walter at the *Reporter* and ask him to run an item about how you and the girl have called it quits?"

Flynn only half listened as he scanned the headline on the front of the paper, and a trickle of dread ran down his spine. *Legion of Decency Brass Attacked by Showgirl.* He scanned the story below, fury replacing his fear. *Stanley Devlin was at the annual sales* dinner celebration for Shasta Peak Pictures when a drunken showgirl attacked him. Devlin. That bastard. His whole family was a bunch of bad apples. Flynn read on. *"I was minding my own business enjoying my after-dinner digestif when the girl came at me with no warning. She dug her nails into my face and left quite a mark."*

A bizarre pride surged in him. Judy had held her own. But Devlin was twice her size. It was a miracle she hadn't been hurt worse.

Thankfully, our boys in blue were only too happy to assist, and they arrested the girl. She has been identified as Judy Blount, sister to starlet Liv de Lesseps. She was held at $10,000 bail, but Blount's bond was met by none other than Flynn Banks, who is reportedly making whoopee with her movie-star sister. "The girl might have a flush protector," Devlin told Variety. *"But I intend to prosecute to the full extent of the law. And I'd suggest Evets's Studios think twice about offering Miss De Lesseps a contract. If she's anything like her little sister, she could prove to be a liability."*

Flynn's blood was boiling now. The nerve of this man. To attack an innocent girl and then frame her as the aggressor when she didn't welcome his advances! And Devlin was on a board that had deemed *Flynn's* reputation a detriment to the moral health of American audiences. He was sick.

"This is a lie," Flynn hissed. "All of it."

Harry gave him a queer look. "I thought there might be more to the story, considering you bailed the girl out. Not exactly part of our agreement to clean up your act."

"Judy did nothing wrong. It was Devlin who attacked her. He's a pig. And I'm not turning my back on Livvy now. She helped me and you by agreeing to the whole publicity stunt. I'm not going to drop her like a hot potato because you've decided she's morally inconvenient."

Harry chuckled. "If I didn't know better, I'd say that this little faux romance has gotten to you."

Flynn didn't bother to answer that. Instead, he said, "We have to stop this. It can't go to print. It will ruin Livvy. It will ruin both of them. And it's a pack of lies." A dozen scenarios raced through Flynn's head. Livvy couldn't lose her job at the studio. Without Judy's income, it would be the only thing keeping the sisters afloat. But it was more than that. He thought back to their conversation on the deck only a few nights ago. How Livvy had said that acting was her new dream. Because of him. Livvy had said she was going to move back north after the picture finished, but he hoped he could convince her otherwise before they wrapped. For her own sake. She'd deprived herself of so much. He'd be damned if he was going to let anyone take this from her too. "I'm going to stand by her. We have to do everything we can to protect her."

"While I'd rather not have the name of the studio's new leading lady dragged through the mud," interjected Harry, "I'm curious how you think we can head this off. I can get *Variety* to hold it. But not for more than a few days. Stanley Devlin holds a lot of sway in this town. I might have power, but he has more."

Flynn grimaced. "Yes, you had no trouble kowtowing to him when he threatened to not give my pictures a seal of approval."

"You didn't exactly make it easy to present a counterargument." Harry huffed. "And no one will take your word over a man whose entire reputation is built on being one of the moral arbiters of motion pictures."

Flynn crumpled the paper in his hand in frustration. There had to be some way to stop Devlin. "And if this does go to print? What will that mean for Livvy?"

Harry shrugged. "We'll see if your picture with the girl is a success. If it is, I'll sign her and tell her she has to cut ties with her sister. If it isn't, we'll cut her loose."

Flynn saw red. Harry was going to make Livvy choose between Judy and her dreams. Again. Not on his watch. "You can't do that. I thought when you and Joan muzzled Leda Price, we were done with this sort of thing."

Harry chuckled. "Oh, Flynn, as long as there are eyes to read the gossip, there will be people to print it. Besides, this is more than hearsay. This is a powerful man making a very serious accusation."

Flynn slammed his fist into his dressing room mirror and Harry jumped. A hairline crack spread beneath Flynn's hand, and he braced himself against the makeup ledge. "I don't know how yet, but I'm going to protect Livvy. If it costs me my career, so be it. But she and Judy are going to keep their dignity if I've got anything to say about it."

With that, he reached for his sweater and stormed out, leaving Harry standing alone in the dressing room. It was a shame, really. If he'd stayed even a moment later, Flynn would've seen the studio boss start to laugh as Harry muttered under his breath, so no one could hear, "I'd always hoped you'd surprise me one of these days, Banks."

Flynn peeled into his driveway, having raced home from the studio far above the speed limit, determined to get back to the peace of the sea and his library where he could think straight. But as he pushed through his front door and turned to descend the steps to the library, a voice he had not heard in years echoed from the foyer. "Is that any way to greet your mother after twenty-five years?"

Flynn stepped dead in his tracks. His mother in Malibu? It couldn't be. She hadn't left Paris since the night she had escaped. There, she had been safe from his father and his minions. The only way to get to America was via a ship from Southampton, which would've meant returning to England. So, he and his mother had corresponded only by letters. But his father was dead now. And she was here.

He turned to face her. Ready to deliver a witty quip about her long absence. But with one look at her face—timeworn and beautiful, radiant with happiness—something inside him broke. He released a guttural sob and flung himself into her arms, leaving her nonplussed and awkwardly patting his back. But soon it was as if he was a boy again. She held him tight and led him toward the library, where he'd been heading before he'd even known of her presence.

Half an hour later, his mother was installed in his favorite burnt-orange chair and he was sitting across from her on a stool as they sipped their tea in the library. He had recovered himself enough to try to get to the bottom of why his mother had turned up in his house with no warning after twenty-five years.

"So, let me get this straight. You came because you thought I was getting married?" He blew at the mug in his hand, trying to get his cup of Assam to cool down.

"Yes." She gave him a knowing, close-lipped smile. "I must admit I was surprised, given your reputation. But then once I saw the girl in photographs in those fan magazines, I understood."

Flynn shook his head, trying to clear the fog of confusion. "But, Mother, I'm not getting married. I was never even engaged."

"That's not what Miss Powers said in her letter inviting me to your nuptials."

Flynn dragged a hand down his face. Of course. Rhonda. She

had brought his mother here? To what end? But he had to admit he was happy for it. Even if she'd traveled thousands of miles to attend a wedding that had never been anything more than a figment of Rhonda Powers's imagination.

"I am not, nor have I ever been engaged to Miss Powers."

His mother frowned. "But then, why—"

"Rhonda is... Well, she's convinced herself that we're meant to be, but we never even dated, Mother. She claims I jilted her at the altar and has made my life a living hell ever since, but I assure you there isn't the slightest chance of our marrying. I can't imagine a lifetime stuck with that redheaded harpy."

Violet's brow wrinkled in confusion. "But your fiancée is raven-haired."

He stood up in frustration. "Mother, I have no fiancée!"

"You seemed so close to that girl in the pictures," she murmured. "You looked genuinely happy. In all the years of seeing your photograph in the papers, I'd never seen you look that way. Content. At ease. The way you'd looked as a small boy."

It hit him then. The photos his mother had seen. They weren't of him and Rhonda. They were of Livvy—the ones Harry had sent out to every movie magazine and Hollywood rag that would publish them. The staged pictures intended to sell their relationship and the idea that Flynn Banks had cleaned up his act. He swallowed down a fresh wave of tears.

"I was...close to that girl. But she was never my fiancée. Never anything but a way to show the world I'd changed. It was a setup. The studio wanted everyone to think we were falling for each other, but none of it was real." If he said it enough times, maybe he would accept it as the truth.

Violet gave him a knowing look. The same one she used to give him as a child when he'd insist he hadn't had any sweets while a ring of sugar coated his lips. "I know what I saw in those photographs, and it was very real."

"It doesn't matter what you thought you saw. My relationship with Livvy is fake." It was exhausting, trying to explain this. To deny the feelings he knew they both had for each other. He sat back down, suddenly weary to his bones. He was resigned to the fact that Livvy would never share his bed again. He'd told Harry he wouldn't abandon her, and that was true. But he wouldn't force himself on her against her will either. She would set the terms—when and where they'd be seen. One day, the magical night they'd shared here together would fade to a warm memory, one he could think of fondly and without the piercing ache in his chest it currently caused.

He sipped at his tea as his mother perused the items on the side table next to the chair. Her eyes lit on the copy of *Treasure Island* still sitting there, untouched since the night of the Halloween party. "You still have it," she murmured.

His heart twinged. "Of course I do. It's my most prized possession."

She gave him a watery smile. "I wish I could have given you more. Left some better advice in my absence. But it all happened so quickly."

He thought of the letter he had tucked away in the globe, sitting just out of arm's reach from his mother. The one that had made clear to him why his mother had left their family the way she did. "You don't need to apologize or explain. You did what you had to do. Besides, you couldn't have offered me better advice. You told me to 'choose joy,' and I have lived every day by those words."

Violet flipped open the cover of the dog-eared book and traced over the words she had inscribed so many years ago. The ones that Flynn had set his life to, like the steady pace of a metronome or the winding of a watch. "You've tried, anyway. And that is all that a mother can hope for."

Flynn ran his hands through his hair in irritation. "What do you mean, *I've tried*? I have lived my life entirely on my own terms, answering only to my whims. The only factor I've ever used to make a decision is whether or not the choice will bring me pleasure. I've drank what I want, slept with who I want—" His mother's eyebrows lifted, and he realized he probably should've omitted that bit. She might lead a bohemian life in Paris, but there were certain things a mother preferred not to hear uttered by her son. "And despite what the misleading missive that has brought you here suggests, I have kept to my pledge to never, ever marry. To instead, choose joy."

She nodded, taking in his words and seeming to collect her thoughts. "Am I to understand that you took my urging to 'choose joy' to mean that you should avoid romantic entanglements, most particularly matrimony?"

He was well and truly exasperated now. "Of course. What else could you have meant? Marriage was a prison for you. It nearly proved your death sentence."

"Well, now, that's a tad dramatic."

He stood and crossed to the globe, rifling through the papers he kept tucked in the fixture's drawer. "It is not. I have the proof of it here." He found the letter containing his father's dark secret and thrust it at her. "You thought I didn't know. You were trying to protect me. But I found this the summer after you left, hidden away in Father's study. Incontrovertible proof that he planned to murder you."

She took the paper, brown and crinkled with age, and studied it, reading through the lines he'd committed to memory. It was a letter from his father to the local chemist.

> *Bertie, I require a tincture of henbane for the she-devil. Do not send it with our next delivery lest the servants see. Let me know when it is ready and I will send my man to retrieve it.*

Flynn remembered the rage he had felt the first time he had read those words. He'd leaned over and retched in his father's rubbish bin. His mother hadn't abandoned him. She had escaped before his father had murdered her with deadly henbane. But he was shocked now when his mother suddenly burst out laughing.

"I fail to see what is so funny about the fact that Father planned to kill you."

Violet scrubbed her face with her hands, trying to recover herself. "Oh, Flynn, I see why you might think that. But no."

"No? How can you say this is anything other than what it looks like?"

"Because I asked your father to buy me henbane. I told him I was having difficulty sleeping and that I required it so that I might rest."

"But he called you a she-devil. He hid it from the servants."

"Yes, well, he did have a lot of colorful names for me."

Flynn began to pace between the bookshelves. His whole life, he had believed that his father was a monster. One who had planned to kill his mother. That his mother had left to save herself from this terrible plot. "But why would you ask him for it?"

"Because I needed a powerful sleeping draught for *him*. To drug him and give myself time to escape with Pierre. I knew if I tried to sneak it in myself, he would catch me. And my plans would come to naught. But if I asked him for it, then he would never suspect my true use for it."

Flynn's head was spinning as he tried to recalibrate his

understanding of his father, his mother, and the night she fled, leaving him and Edgar alone. Flynn had always suspected that his father knew that he had found the letter about the henbane. Because for years after, Lord Banks had been unnecessarily cruel, favoring Edgar in all things. Flynn rubbed absentmindedly at his side, remembering the time his father had kicked him in the ribs like a dog. Flynn had always chalked it up to the cost of knowing the truth.

Violet rose and took his hands in hers. "My darling boy, your father was a monster. Make no mistake about that. He was a cruel man, rapacious and greedy. The only happy days I ever had in his home were the ones I spent with you. But he was not a murderer."

Flynn let his arms go limp in his mother's grasp. "Edgar said the old man had something to tell me. That he wanted to clear his conscience before he died. I had assumed it must be this."

His mother smiled again. "Oh, I suspect I know what he wanted to tell you."

Flynn pinched his nose between his fingers and scrunched up his nose. "I've already had one life-altering revelation today. I don't know if I can stand another."

Violet chuckled. "It's an awfully good thing you're an actor, because you're far too dramatic for any other profession."

He groaned in response, to which she replied, "Perhaps you should sit down."

She led him gently to the velvet chair and deposited him in it. She kneeled next to him, the way she had done beside his bed when she tucked him into sleep at night, and she rubbed a soothing pattern over his knee. "I should have told you this years ago, but I thought I was protecting you." He looked at her expectantly. He had no idea what she could possibly have to confess. "But the truth is, you are not your father's son. You are the product of my affair with Pierre. It's why your father was so cruel to you. He suspected you were not his. Though he could never prove it."

Flynn was stunned. He was not a Banks. Not a product of a hateful man. "So, he wanted to use his dying breath to disavow me?"

His mother shrugged. "It seems so. But it doesn't matter. He couldn't omit you from the will without admitting he was cuckolded. You would think the fact I ran away with Pierre and never returned would pretty demonstrably prove that. But he could not weather the shame of having a bastard born under his roof."

Flynn's mind was reeling. All these years he'd spent hating his father, and the man was not even his own flesh and blood. The Banks name, all of it, was not his problem. Even if Harry fired him, Edgar had no leverage to guilt him into returning to England or pouring his funds into that moldering estate. He was, at last, free of the yoke of the aristocracy. He sighed, relief flooding his senses, and he blinked back tears.

"I hope you are not too disappointed," his mother murmured. "But you are and always have been the product of my joy. That is why I wrote those words for you. To remind you what joy can bring, even amidst pain and great unhappiness."

He pulled his mother to her feet and into a tight hug. "I am so bloody grateful that I no longer have to think of that terrible man as my father."

He held her close, trying to convey all the love and respect he had for his mother and her courage through their embrace. He pulled apart, leaving the shoulder of her dress a bit damp with his tears of relief. She cupped his cheeks in her palms and looked up at him with the pure joy and love he remembered from his childhood. As she wiped away the tears still streaming down his face, she asked, "Now what's this about choosing joy meaning you should never marry?"

"I thought it was a warning. You never married Pierre."

She scoffed. "Because I was still legally married to your father, and he refused to grant me a divorce. Now that he's dead, I plan to marry Pierre as soon as I return to Paris." She released his face and flashed the enormous engagement ring on her left hand in front of his eyes.

He smiled and kissed his mother on the cheek. "I wish you two nothing but happiness." She patted him on the back in response, and he realized what an utter fool he had been. Denying himself a companion because he believed it would only spell misery. If only he had figured it out sooner. That joy and love were not mutually exclusive. That, in fact, they were possibly contingent upon each other. Perhaps then it would not have been too late for him and Livvy.

His mother grabbed his hands and squeezed. "When I told you to choose joy, I meant for you to choose love. To choose companionship. To choose a woman who makes you happy. Not a marriage you deemed advantageous to your rank and status."

"I see that now."

She looked at him expectantly. "And?"

"And what?"

"This raven-haired beauty. Why are you not banging down her door this minute? Confessing your undying love."

"I do not have undying love for her," he retorted, but even he couldn't finish the thought without realizing what a lie it was. His mother giggled at the look on his face. "Even if I did...love her terribly, she doesn't want me."

"So, fix it then."

Fix it. That was what he had promised Harry he would do, wasn't it? He didn't know how. But he did know that moping in his library was not the way to get answers. There was only one option. He needed to pay a visit to Stanley Devlin.

CHAPTER 28

FLYNN PULLED HIS ROADSTER INTO THE STEEP DRIVEWAY that led to Stanley Devlin's Hollywood Hills home.

"Good God, that's ugly." Dash whistled in disgust at the Gothic monstrosity that rose up between them. The stone house loomed at the top of a hill with gargoyles atop every pillar.

"All it needs is a drawbridge," Flynn quipped.

Dash chuckled. Flynn had called his best friend and asked him to come as moral support. And to prevent him from committing murder. Flynn had no idea how tonight was going to go, but he did know it was a terrible idea to face Devlin alone. In his rearview mirror, the sun was setting over the ocean in the distance, and it cast the gray stone of the house in a yellow light that made the entire structure look like it was emanating a strange illness.

He pulled in front of the garage, and he and Dash hopped out. Dash shivered and buttoned his coat as a brisk wind swept around them.

Flynn looked at his pal. "Thanks for coming, mate."

"Look, you dried me out when Joan broke my heart; it's the least I could do."

Flynn grinned. "Eh, nothing you wouldn't have done for me."

Dash shrugged, but Flynn noticed a slight upward crook at the edges of his mouth.

The house was quiet and seemed nearly deserted, so Flynn blew on his knuckles. "Here goes nothing," he huffed and rapped on the door. It swung open with an eerie creak almost instantly, and he exchanged a look with Dash. "You think Devlin's a vampire?"

Dash shuddered and made the sign of the cross as a butler emerged from the shadows.

"Mr. Devlin is expecting you." The man was stone-faced, and he immediately turned on his heel, disappearing back into the dark hallway.

Dash gestured to say, *After you*, and Flynn stepped over the threshold. His eyes slowly adjusted to the dim light, and he took in the long, narrow hallway lined with old masters' paintings. The butler had opened a door at the end of the hall, and Flynn cracked his knuckles, ready for a fight.

"Come in, Banks," Devlin called out. The man's slimy drawl made Flynn's skin crawl. His stomach turned, thinking of how terrified Judy must have been with this creature descending upon her.

He took a breath, tugged down the edges of his sport coat, and stepped in the room. Dash followed on his heels.

"Ah," drawled Devlin. "You brought your fellow miscreant."

"Yes, well, recent incidents suggest no one should be caught out alone with you."

Devlin smirked. "I see Judy Blount has gotten to you."

"She didn't tell me a damn thing," retorted Flynn. "I saw the headlines you've been planting, and I realized immediately what had happened. That girl never would have attacked you unprovoked."

"Take a seat, Banks. Mr. Howard."

Flynn looked at his friend and Dash nodded toward the

chair, signaling for him to sit first. Flynn preferred to stand, but he pulled out the stiff leather chair opposite Devlin's desk and sat on the very edge. Dash plunked down into the chair next to him.

"I assume Miss Blount asked you to visit me," Devlin said.

"She has no idea I'm here. I came because I won't stand idly by while you try to ruin Judy and Livvy."

Devlin turned so the low light in the room caught the side of his face, and Flynn choked back a gag at what he saw. Four thin lines ran from Devlin's temple down his cheek to the edge of his mouth. The wounds were still bright red around the edges, and Flynn thought one of them was oozing pus.

"Miss Blount's handiwork," Devlin spat out.

"Too bad she didn't get both sides," Flynn retorted.

Dash quietly put his hand out and grabbed Flynn's knee, reminding him to keep hold of himself.

"I'm not going to let you run that story."

Devlin grinned, showing off all his teeth like a lion licking its chops. "And just how do you plan to stop me?"

This was the part where Flynn had to bluff. "Name your price."

"Hah. You English aristocrats think your money is worth more because it comes with a title. Look around you, Mr. Banks. I don't need your cash."

"Come now, Devlin, be reasonable," interrupted Dash. "At least hear out Flynn's offer."

"What is there to hear? He doesn't have anything I want. Unless he can get me the girl."

Flynn gripped the arm of the chair, digging his nails into the dark wood. It was that or belt Devlin across the face. "You will never touch her again."

Devlin laughed, a cold, high, unnatural sound. "You seem to have confused yourself with the heroes you play on screen. I'd like to see you try and stop me."

Flynn jumped out of his chair, but Dash grabbed the back of his jacket. "Easy, Flynn, easy."

"*Tsk, tsk,* Banks. Short temper, have we?"

Flynn sat down and crossed his arms over his chest. "When someone talks about a dame like that, yeah."

"You're telling me you're a Boy Scout?" Devlin sneered.

"No. But I've never ignored a lady when she said no. That's a line I don't cross. No decent man would."

Devlin rolled his eyes. "So noble. The girl was asking for it, wearing that skimpy little outfit, cavorting around on the stage like that. That's the cost of a Hollywood career, and she knew that."

"No, she didn't," Flynn growled. "She was terrified and just trying to do her job."

"Her job was to entertain the guests." Devlin picked a bit of dirt from under his nails and flicked it in Flynn's direction. "So I'd say refusing me was dereliction of her duties."

Flynn grabbed the chair so fiercely, he felt it crack under his hand. Dash gave him a look and hissed, "Flynn, pull it together."

"Fine. You don't want my money. What do you want then? I'll give you anything if you promise to kill the story and leave Judy and Livvy alone. Print anything you want about me, but those girls are blameless and they're gonna stay that way."

Devlin scratched at his chin, making a show of it. "Interesting. What a strange position I find myself in—a carte blanche offer from Flynn Banks. I'm sure there are many in town who would kill for such a bargain." He smirked, and Flynn grimaced. The man truly was despicable. "I don't need money, true. But I'm tired of presiding over the studios indirectly, helping Hays and Breen keep morally objectionable content off-screen."

"Considering *your* morally objectionable behavior off-screen, I can see why that wouldn't satisfy you," Flynn quipped.

Devlin sneered at him. "The swashbuckler is trying his hand at becoming the comic, I see. Terrible jokes aside, you're right. Pulling strings from the Hays office isn't enough. But it just so happens my sister-in-law has a controlling stake in Shasta Peak Pictures. And if I were to do something to make her happy, well, she might be tempted to sign it over to me."

Flynn grit his teeth. "Get on with it then."

Devlin smiled at him, a shark circling its prey. "There are few things that would please her more than to see her daughter happily married."

"Rhonda," Flynn huffed out, realizing where Devlin was going.

"Rhonda," Devlin agreed.

Dash looked back and forth between the two men, seemingly not understanding what they were talking about. Funny, Flynn thought, when he never would have met the woman if she hadn't turned up at Dash and Joan's house party.

Flynn had vowed to never marry. And he'd never met a woman who had tempted him to change his mind. Until Livvy. But now Livvy wanted nothing to do with him, and all he could offer her was protection. He could sacrifice himself to keep her and Judy safe from the lies of Stanley Devlin. It wasn't exactly what his mother meant by choosing joy. In fact, it was the complete opposite. But it was the only card he had left to play. It was that simple, really. "Fine."

Devlin's eyes widened. "You're serious?"

"If you promise to leave Judy and Livvy alone. To kill the story. And never so much as blink in their direction again."

Devlin extended his hand, and Flynn reluctantly took it, grimacing as the man's sweaty palm clenched his. Under different circumstances, he would've laughed at Devlin's aggressive show of manliness. It was pathetic, really.

Devlin chuckled darkly. "I never thought I'd live to see the day."

"Would someone mind telling me just what the hell is going on?" Dash interjected.

"I'm going to marry Rhonda Powers," Flynn gritted out.

"Flynn, no!"

Flynn put his hand up. "Don't try to talk me out of it, Dash. I told Mr. Devlin I'd give him anything he wanted—and marrying his niece is what he wants. I have no choice."

"Surely there's something else. He could...produce your next film? Buy your house for a song?"

Devlin stood up, placing his hands flat on the desk. "He let me set the terms, and these are my terms. Now, if you gentleman would excuse me, I have to call my sister-in-law and let her know the happy news."

Flynn knew when he'd been dismissed, and he stood, practically dragging Dash out of the room with him as Devlin called after him, "May you never know a moment's peace with the girl, Banks."

Dash was still gaping at Flynn, his head swiveling between Flynn and Devlin. "But, but—"

"Let's go, Dash."

Flynn managed to get them out the front door, narrowly avoiding hitting his head on the molding in the process. The fresh air seemed to awaken something in Dash, who took off the second he was outside and sprinted to the roadster to block Flynn from the driver door. "I don't think you should drive. You must be off your nut. It's the only explanation."

Flynn tugged at his friend. "Ha-ha, very funny. Move."

Dash leaned forward and sniffed Flynn. "I'm serious. What have you had to drink today?"

Flynn shoved Dash a little, now genuinely annoyed. "Come off it. I've never been more sober in my life."

Dash looked at him, searching his face, before Dash's body curled in disappointment and he moved aside. "How could you agree to that?"

"Because it was the only way to keep her safe. To make sure Devlin doesn't launch a vendetta against two innocent young women."

"But the studio... Surely Harry could call one of his fixers, and they could—" Flynn opened his door and gestured for Dash to slide across the bench seat and get in before him. Dash did, burying his face in his hands. "There has to be another way."

"No one could get that story killed. Harry stalled them for a few days, but that was the best he could do. I'm the only one who can stop it."

"But—" Dash threw his head back against the seat and looked up at the sky. Flynn hoped he wasn't asking God for an answer, because he was fairly certain he'd worn out any goodwill he had with the man upstairs a long time ago. "Flynn, you don't love Rhonda. Hell, you don't even like her."

Flynn turned the key in the ignition, desperate to return to the familiar confines of his Malibu home, the relaxing splash of the waves on the sand, and his well-stocked bar cart. Though there was the small problem of having to admit to his mother what he'd just done. "No, I don't like Rhonda." He turned his head behind him as he backed out of the driveway. "But I'm doing this because I love Livvy."

He hadn't said it before. Hadn't even dared to think it really. But sitting in that office while Devlin stared him down and relished the way Flynn wriggled like a fish caught on his hook, he had known. He'd known it before too, when his mother had shown him what an idiot he'd been all these years. But he hadn't realized the depths to which he would go for her until he was cornered. He would do anything for Livvy.

He wished he'd told her when he still had the chance. Wished he'd realized sooner. But that was his misfortune. For once, he was choosing to be responsible, choosing to take care of someone else over his own happiness. It was simple—he loved Olivia Blount, so he had to marry Rhonda Powers.

CHAPTER 29

FLYNN BANKS TO MARRY SOCIALITE RHONDA POWERS IN SURPRISE CHANGE OF HEART!

Call it a silver-screen scenario. It seems Hollywood's favorite swashbuckler is finally tying the knot. After jilting socialite Rhonda Powers, daughter of the late founder of Shasta Peak Pictures, Flynn Banks has had a change of heart.

Of late, he's been spotted on the town in the company of his new costar, Liv de Lesseps. But the short-lived romance appears to have ended, sending Banks back into the arms of his former fiancée. This time, it seems, it's for keeps.

Banks and Powers will exchange vows early next month at Blessed Sacrament in Hollywood. The bride's uncle, a member of the Production Code Administration's board, will give the girl away. "When Flynnie came back to me and told

> me he wanted to make an honest woman out of me, I simply couldn't wait to marry him," the blushing bride tells *Screenland*. "I couldn't bear a long engagement, and Uncle Stan was able to use his pull at Blessed Sacrament to squeeze us into the schedule." Barely a month after their engagement, Banks and Powers will become man and wife. Ladies, get out your hankies, the day we thought would never come has arrived—Hollywood's most eligible bachelor and notorious rogue is officially off the market!

Judy had left the magazine on Livvy's pillow, open to the page about Flynn's impending nuptials. Livvy had dumped it in the wastebasket next to her bed without even bothering to read it. Who cared what Flynn Banks did? Hadn't she known from the beginning that anything real with him was an absurd proposition? She'd known better—and she'd let herself believe in the fantasy for a few hours anyway. But Judy's assault and arrest had been the wake-up call she needed. Flynn Banks was nothing but an unhealthy distraction.

The two had barely spoken since she'd dismissed him that morning. Oh, they'd delivered their dialogue on the soundstage, of course. She wasn't going to muck up her job. Not when it was the only thing keeping her and Judy from the street. But there had been no more studio-arranged dates. Not when the news had broken only a few days later that Flynn planned to marry Rhonda. So beyond their on-screen interactions and a terse "hello" and "good night," she had nothing to say to him. She couldn't allow herself more. He had charmed her once, convinced her to let her guard down, to taste what it was to be wicked, with no regard for anyone else—and it had ended in disaster.

She could never open the door to that possibility again. Judy was her only priority.

Though her sister was being a pest at the moment. The first few days, she had been practically catatonic, lying in bed and crying. Livvy had been distraught seeing Judy that way, but she had let her be, leaving food on her nightstand and taking it away hours later when Judy barely touched it. Just when Livvy was on the verge of calling a doctor she probably couldn't afford, she had come home from the studio one day to find Judy up and about, freshly showered after a week of wearing the same pair of pajamas. The entire bungalow had been cleaned within an inch of its life—and that damn magazine was on Livvy's pillow.

The next day, Judy had fished the magazine out of the wastebasket and was now making a habit of leaving it places for Livvy to find. First, it had been slid in between the pages of her script for Livvy to find when she was reviewing lines. A few days after that, Livvy found it in her underwear drawer. The following week, Judy had placed it in the linen closet on top of freshly laundered bath towels.

But today, today was the final straw. Flynn was getting married tomorrow, and Livvy had hoped she'd seen the last of Judy's ridiculous antics. But when Livvy had gone into the icebox to fish out leftovers for dinner, she discovered that Judy had left the magazine under a piece of aluminum foil on top of the hamburger casserole they had made.

"Judy," Livvy called. Her sister immediately walked into the kitchen, which made Livvy suspect that Judy had been spying on her to see her reaction.

Livvy held up the offending article, now lightly stained with tomato sauce. "This has to stop."

If she expected Judy to look sheepish and apologize, she was mistaken. Instead, her sister jutted out her chin in a gesture of defiance. "I won't stop until we talk about it."

Livvy sighed. "What is there to talk about? He's marrying Rhonda Powers. Our relationship was a publicity stunt. Why should I care?"

Judy crossed her arms and harrumphed. "But you do care. I know you do."

"No, Judy, I don't. You're the only person I care about."

"Damn it, Livvy, that's my point. I was so happy for you when it seemed like things with Flynn were going well. I know you told me over and over it was all for show, but I could tell you genuinely liked him. Maybe more. Can you honestly say you didn't have feelings for him?"

Livvy bit her lip. She wanted to vehemently protest, but she couldn't lie to Judy. "Maybe I did. A little. But I got carried away by the charade. That's all." She threw the magazine on the counter and went to take Judy in her arms. "I promise it will never happen again."

Her sister strained against her embrace. "That's exactly what I was afraid you'd say." Livvy was horrified to see tears welling in her sister's eyes. "Haven't you denied your happiness for my sake long enough?"

Livvy dodged the question, pretending that she'd never done any such thing. "I've never—"

Judy swiped furiously at her eyes. "Ever since the accident, you've put me first. You've been there for every appointment, every rehab session. You made sure nothing would stop me from dancing again."

"If you don't want to dance anymore, you don't have to. We can leave Hollywood tomorrow. Or next week, after I wrap the picture. We don't have to stay here. My career doesn't matter."

Judy held up her hand. "Stop! Do you even hear yourself? 'My career doesn't matter.' How could you possibly think that's what I want for you? You've already given up so much for me—college, your dreams of being a writer." Livvy tried to protest, but Judy wouldn't let her. "No, don't pretend like you don't know what I'm talking about. You haven't picked up a pen since I came home from the hospital. And the worst part is, I let you give it all up. Because I was too weak then to argue with you about it. That's something I'll regret for the rest of my life. But when that actress left and they bumped you up from an understudy at the Hollywood Bowl, I hoped that this was the universe's way of giving you a second chance. Of helping you find a new way to tell the stories that you so loved. Acting might not have been your dream, but these last few months, I thought that maybe you'd changed your mind. That you'd found something in it that made you come alive again. Made you happy."

Livvy scrunched up her face in some twisted mix of guilt and pain. Judy was right. She had been happy. Somehow, becoming Liv de Lesseps had changed her life for the better. She was still a storyteller, just like she'd always dreamed she would be. And she loved it. To give it up now, after she'd already lost Flynn, would be crushing. But not as devastating as what Judy had been through. Still, she couldn't lie to her sister. "Fine. I've fallen in love with acting. Is that what you want me to say? That becoming someone else on-screen, putting myself in the service of someone else's story, is more rewarding than I ever dreamed it could be. That I should be thanking you every day for making me take that understudy job."

"I knew it!" Judy interrupted. "You can't just give that up, Livvy. To do what? Move back to Saratoga? There's nothing there for us. We didn't just come here for me. You're a talented actress, and I can see how fulfilled your work makes you. If you decide you truly don't want to act anymore, you don't have to. You can still be a writer, Livvy! Like you told me when you gave up your spot at college, to be a writer all you have to do is write. So, pick up your pen and do it. I'll work to support us both. But we're not leaving with our tails between our legs. The last thing I would want is for you to give it up for me, out of some misguided belief that it will keep me safe. How much have you already sacrificed for me? I'm grateful, Livvy. Don't think I'm not. But it's been four years. You get to live your own life."

Livvy frowned and walked to the doorway that divided their tiny kitchenette from their so-called living room. She leaned against the wall, her back to Judy. "No, I don't. I tried, Judy. I really did. But I flew too close to the sun. I decided to do what I wanted for once, not what I knew I was supposed to do. And it brought disaster to our door. You got hurt. Maybe I couldn't have prevented it, but I could've been there for you when it happened. That made me realize that I should've stuck to the deal I made with God the night of the accident. Sitting at your bedside, praying you'd pull through, I promised him a life for a life. But I broke that promise, and you're the one who paid the price. I won't break it again."

Judy startled her by coming up behind her, wrapping her arms around her stomach, and resting her head on her shoulder. "Don't you see that's the opposite of what I want? We both survived. There's no trade to be made here. You fought for me when I didn't think I had the strength to fight for myself. But that's done now. Our reward is that we both get to live."

Livvy leaned back into her sister's embrace, pondering her words and how much they sounded like what Flynn had tried to tell her that horrible day they'd bailed Judy out. Now, she was holding back tears. "But if I'd been here at the bungalow that night—"

"Nothing would have happened differently. They still would have hauled me off to jail at Devlin's orders. Except you would have panicked and possibly done something hasty you'd come to regret. This way, you had Flynn to help you think straight. If he hadn't been with you, hadn't jumped in to pay my bail, what would you have done?"

Livvy balled her hands into a fist. "I would have made them let you out."

Judy scoffed. "You see? That's exactly what I mean. Then we both would've ended up in a jail cell, and what good would that have done?"

Judy let go of her and grabbed her hand, leading Livvy to the couch and wrapping her arm around her shoulder. Livvy couldn't remember the last time she'd felt cared for like this. Like someone else was willing to shoulder the burden with her. She was beginning to realize it was because she hadn't let anyone.

She gripped Judy's hand so hard that her knuckles turned white. "You know that all I've ever wanted is to make sure nothing horrible ever happened to you again."

Judy nodded, and her throat was choked with emotion as she began to speak. "Of course I know that. But you can't keep me safe forever. Neither of us would truly be living. Bad things happen, and there's nothing either of us can do to prevent them. Can't it be enough to know that you've taught me to protect myself as best as I can?"

Livvy closed her eyes and inhaled deeply. "I want it to be. But it's hard."

Judy hugged her tight. "I know. Things that night could've been so much worse. But I protected myself. I fought back. Because that's what you taught me to do."

Livvy snorted through her tears, pride flaring in her chest. "You did take a chunk out of that man's face, didn't you?"

Judy grabbed her shoulders and pushed Livvy back, studying her closely. Tears swam in her eyes. "I did." She released a watery giggle. "You should've seen the look on his face. He was shocked that a girl would do such a thing."

Livvy barked out a laugh. "I'll bet he was. Last time he'll mess with a Blount sister. Serves him right." Her tears turned into an uncontrollable fit of snot-filled giggles, and she struggled to regain composure. Judy laughed along with her until they both collapsed on the couch.

"What a fine mess I've made for us both." Livvy gasped, clutching her stomach with one hand and swiping at her eyes with the other.

Judy got serious then. "No, Livvy. No mess. You've done the best you could, and it's more than I could ever have asked for. Everyone should be so lucky to have a sister as wonderful as you. But what I want more than anything is just that—for you to be my sister. Not my caretaker, not my mother, not my protector—my sister."

Livvy swallowed and gave Judy a weak smile. "You know, Flynn said the same thing."

"He did?"

Livvy nodded. "Yes, he told me that I should let you make your own mistakes. That you needed a sister, not a mother hen."

Judy grinned. "That Flynn Banks, he's a smart man."

Livvy bit her lip, holding back a fresh wave of tears. "He is. He really is. Even if he works hard to make the papers think otherwise."

Judy grabbed Livvy's upper leg and squeezed. "I knew it! You do still have feelings for him."

"What? No, it's just—"

"Olivia Jane Blount, don't lie to me." Judy put her hands on her hips and gave her a stern look, but she couldn't hold it for long. Her frown melted into a beatific smile. "Livvy, just admit that you like him."

Livvy closed her eyes and exhaled. "Fine." She scrunched up her face, not wanting to admit the truth. What she'd never allowed herself to tell him—while he was awake, at least. "I more than like him, okay? I, Olivia Blount, am hopelessly, wretchedly in love with Flynn Banks."

Judy kicked her feet and squealed in delight. "I knew it. I knew it. I knew it."

"I don't know what you're so happy about," Livvy grumbled. "He's marrying Rhonda Powers. Tomorrow."

"Oh, Livvy, you don't think he actually wants to marry her, do you?"

Livvy thought back to the night at the symphony fundraiser. The way Flynn had looked at Rhonda like she was a hungry crocodile. He'd clung to Livvy as if she were a life raft. But that could have been an act, another part of following Harry's orders. Because it was good for the picture and both their careers. "Flynn always insisted he wasn't the marrying kind, but—"

Judy didn't answer, just stood up and ran into the kitchen, returning with the movie magazine that was now permanently stained with tomato sauce. "Did you actually read the article?" She shoved it under Livvy's nose, and Livvy snatched it away.

"No, the headline was enough." She studied the text and gasped when she got to the relevant bit of information. "Uncle Stan... Why, he's—"

Judy crossed her arms and nodded, entirely satisfied with herself. "Yes, he is. When I read that Rhonda's Uncle Stan was a member of the PCA board, I immediately realized something fishy was happening. That's why I kept leaving the article out for you. I hoped you would notice too."

"I had decided to forget about Flynn Banks and anything that ever passed between us."

Judy rolled her eyes. "Well, you refused to take the bait, so I called up Dash Howard."

"You what?"

"Hush. I called up Dash Howard because I thought if anyone would know what was happening, he would. He confirmed my fears. Rhonda Powers's Uncle Stan is none other than Stanley Devlin, the man who attacked me at the party."

Livvy remembered then why the name Stanley Devlin had been so familiar. She had met him that night at the fundraiser. Rhonda had introduced him to her and Flynn.

"But if Stanley Devlin is her uncle, then that means...that means, what?"

"It means, dear sister, that Flynn Banks doesn't want to marry Rhonda Powers any more than you'd like to marry Benito Mussolini. Dash told me as much. He was there when Flynn agreed to it. Turns out, Flynn is more like you than we thought."

"What do you mean?"

"He's a self-sacrificing, well-intentioned idiot."

"I am not a—"

Judy stuck her tongue out at her, and Livvy couldn't help but laugh. "You are, but that's not the point. The point is that Flynn agreed to marry Rhonda because it was the only way to stop Stanley Devlin from trying to ruin both of us in the papers."

Livvy clutched the movie magazine to her chest. She didn't

know what she'd expected Judy to say, but it wasn't that. Flynn Banks, a man with so many notches in his bedpost he needed multiple beds for them all, was getting married—to protect her and Judy. It was insane. How could he do such a thing?

She had to stop him. Had to tell him that whatever happened, she and Judy could face it. That he didn't need to marry Rhonda Powers if he didn't want to.

But how could she? The wedding was tomorrow.

A knock at the door made Livvy jump. "Are you expecting visitors?"

Judy gave Livvy a sheepish look. "Don't get mad, but I thought we might need reinforcements."

Judy opened the door to reveal Dash Howard and Joan Davis on the front step of their shabby bungalow.

Dash gave Judy a quick hug and stepped inside. He surveyed the tiny room, nodding in acknowledgment at Livvy. "Jeez, Flynn wasn't kidding when he said your living quarters left a lot to be desired."

Joan followed behind Dash, rolling her eyes. "Forgive my husband. We're still working on teaching him basic tact."

"What are you doing here?" Livvy gaped, still not processing the fact that two of the biggest movie stars in the world were standing in her entryway.

Dash gave her a wicked, megawatt smile. "We're here to help you break up a wedding."

CHAPTER 30

FLYNN LOOKED IN THE MIRROR AND STRAIGHTENED HIS bow tie. The damn thing felt more like a noose. He studied his reflection—from the gray morning coat he wore (complete with tails) to the matching top hat perched on his head. He looked ridiculous in this monkey suit. He'd much rather be wearing one of his pirate costumes, if he was being honest. At least those were meant to look over-the-top.

But Rhonda had insisted she get the white-tie wedding of her dreams, and who was he to deny her? Every time he'd opened his mouth to protest one of her more absurd suggestions—be it the live peacocks that would surround them at the altar or the twenty individually carved ice sculptures she'd designed for the reception—Stanley Devlin's maniacal face and Judy Blount's split lip flashed in his memory. And he'd think, *Well if the dame wants peacocks, she can bloody well have peacocks then. As long as Judy and Livvy are safe.*

From the hall, Flynn heard someone whistling the "Wedding March." Or wait, was it a funeral dirge? When Dash opened the door, his gaze twinkling with mischief, Flynn rolled his eyes. "What were you whistling?"

"Here comes the corpse, heading for his demise," Dash sang.

"Oh, shut it." Flynn was already dreading this. Did Dash have to make it worse?

Dash laughed, clearly very amused by his own antics. At least that made one of them. "You've only got yourself to blame, pal."

"Don't remind me," Flynn grumbled.

"Because I know today is going to be hard for you—"

"I'd rather have a root canal," Flynn muttered.

Dash ignored him. "I've brought you a surprise."

Flynn wasn't sure he was ready for whatever Dash had for him. On the night before Dash's wedding, Flynn had tried to get him to strip naked and perform with an exotic dancer in a Reno nightclub. So he didn't really trust that Dash had noble intentions. Turnabout was fair play, after all.

But when Dash opened the door a little wider, Flynn was delighted to see Lionel Berry, and following close behind the animal trainer, Rallo, wearing a miniature top hat and bow tie of his own. "Rallo!" Flynn exclaimed.

"You've already got a monkey of a best man," Dash teased, pulling a face. "So I figured what was one more?"

Flynn kneeled as the little monkey ran to him, leaping onto the arm that Flynn extended. "Come to join the wedding party, have you?" Perched on his outstretched hand, the monkey tilted its head from side to side and bared its teeth in what Flynn hoped was a grin. "Yes, well, I feel the same. But what can we do?"

He stood and Rallo scampered up and took his perch on Flynn's shoulder. The steady weight of his cinematic sidekick unraveled something in Flynn, and the tension in his spine released ever so slightly. No matter what happened, no matter how miserable his marriage to Rhonda, he still had his friends.

He studied himself in the mirror as Rallo reached up and tilted Flynn's top hat at a rakish angle, lending his finery more of a piratical air.

"That's more like it." Flynn grinned. The monkey made a

little bow, and he laughed for what felt like the first time in weeks. "Oh, thank you, Dash. Truly."

His best friend clapped him on the shoulder. "Of course. I thought you could use your best primate."

The two men and the monkey studied themselves in the mirror. Flynn had to admit they looked good. Even if he felt more like he was going to meet a firing squad than walk down the aisle to his future spouse. At least he'd look dapper doing it.

His stomach fell when someone from the hall called out. "Five minutes until the procession begins."

But Dash's smile didn't waver. He gripped Flynn's shoulder a little tighter and said, "It's going to be fun. I promise."

And then he winked.

Livvy took a deep breath and choked on the sudden whiff of incense that overwhelmed her senses. She tried not to cough as she receded into the shadows of the archway above the small private chapel at the side of the church. She felt ridiculous. Joan had nicked her a nun costume from wardrobe after Livvy realized it was the only way to get herself into the church without being recognized. Had she stolen the idea directly from Flynn's film *The Prince and the Pirate*? Yes. But thus far she'd had good luck borrowing ideas from his movies.

As the guests had begun to file in, Livvy had filtered in with them, kneeling by a display of candles and pretending to pray anytime someone looked in her direction. The fuller the church got, the fewer people noticed her. And she was able to survey the Church of the Blessed Sacrament more keenly. The aisle was lined with a cloying overabundance of flowers—shocks of white freesia and hot-pink daisies that didn't go together even a little bit. Her eyes nearly bugged out of her skull when a man in a brown jumpsuit led three peacocks down the aisle and tied them to little ropes surrounding the altar.

Well, there was no accounting for taste, she supposed. Though the presence of large birds with beaks and talons might significantly complicate things.

She recited the plan to herself in her head, making sure she wasn't forgetting anything. If they pulled this off, it would be a miracle. Especially now that she had peacocks to contend with. Maybe she should try actually praying while kneeling here. It couldn't hurt.

But any thought of prayer evaporated as a hush fell over the crowded pews and a woman at the front began warbling a rather off-key version of "I Love You Truly." Livvy crept forward in her best imitation of a solemn nun, concealing herself behind a marble pillar as she watched the procession begin.

Flynn led the way, with a woman she thought might be his mother on his arm. Livvy's heart fluttered at the sight of him in his top hat and tails. Rallo sat on his shoulder, and she had to laugh at the monkey's matching hat and bow tie. She and Rallo locked eyes for a brief moment, and the monkey chittered at the sight of her.

Flynn's head snapped in her direction, and she pulled herself more tightly behind the pillar in the nick of time. She hoped Flynn hadn't seen her yet. It would ruin everything.

"Rallo, no!" she heard Flynn gasp. But she didn't allow herself to look at what transpired. This wasn't a good hiding place. It was too exposed.

She looked at the high marble pulpit to the side of the altar. There was a rope across it, so they wouldn't be using it today. Maybe she could sneak up there when the crowd was distracted.

Another voice interjected, "Keep going. Lionel will find him." That was Dash, calling out to Flynn from the back of the church. She reminded herself to breathe. They'd gone over the plan at least ten times. Dash knew what was supposed to happen. He would keep them on course. Rallo was meant to distract Flynn, not give them away. But she had to trust that Dash was ready to improvise.

Livvy leaned back against the pillar and closed her eyes, trying to calm herself, when she felt something tug at the hem of her habit. She looked down and saw the mischievous little monkey standing at her feet.

"Nuts," she muttered under her breath. She knelt and scooped him up as the monkey wrapped its soft, furry arm around her neck in an embrace. "I'm happy to see you too, Rallo, but you have to go back to Flynn."

Rallo stuck out his tongue and burrowed his head into her chest. That was a no, then.

She turned her head and peered over her shoulder. Flynn was finishing his march to the altar with the reluctant posture of a man headed for the gallows. The loss of Rallo seemed to have robbed him of his willpower. *Just hang on, Flynn.*

Shortly behind Flynn followed Dash and Joan, arm in arm. Dash was Flynn's best man, and Joan was a bridesmaid at Flynn's request. When they passed by her pillar, Dash nodded in Livvy's direction, so subtly that only someone looking for it would notice.

Rallo peeked his head out from the folds of her black habit and looked between her and Dash. Did the little rascal know what they were up to? No, he was a monkey. He couldn't possibly.

A flurry of other bridesmaids and groomsmen processed in,

and then it was time for the bride to make her grand entrance. The woman singing wrapped up her song, and the organist began to play Handel's "Processional."

The guests in the crowded pews stood and turned to face the back of the church, where Rhonda Powers was dressed in a gown that looked more like an ornately decorated petit four than a wedding dress. Livvy couldn't help but roll her eyes.

Her mouth went dry as she spied Stanley Devlin on his niece's arm. The bastard was walking Rhonda down the aisle to marry a man he'd blackmailed into it. His sickeningly smug smile made her want to claw his eyes out.

But this was Livvy's moment to act. While the rest of the church was distracted, she seized the opportunity to scamper from her place in the shadows to the stone stairs that led to the pulpit. She clung tightly to Rallo, snuggled in her robes, as she sprinted toward them and fell to her knees once she was tucked behind the marble wall that surrounded the stairs.

She held her breath and listened. The "Processional" continued, and everything appeared to be going off without a hitch. No one had seen her.

She continued to crawl up the steps until she reached the flat landing of the pulpit. She was now above and to the side of the altar where Flynn and the wedding party stood. She snuck a peek as Devlin deposited Rhonda at the altar, making a show of kissing her hand.

Livvy concealed a scoff of disgust at his attempt to play the chivalrous gentleman. She wished that they could expose him. But for now, the plan was to disgrace his family. The only way to get Flynn out of this was to create a scandal—and the only way to do that was for Livvy to make a scene.

Livvy ducked back down and listened as the priest began the

ceremony. "'Dearly beloved, we are gathered here today to celebrate the union of these two individuals in holy matrimony.'"

Not if I have anything to say about it.

She settled back against the inside of the pulpit and waited for the ceremony to go on. It would be quite some time before they reached her cue, so she might as well get comfortable. She half listened, waiting for the words, "Speak now or forever hold your peace."

She would then interrupt the ceremony and claim that she was working at the convent the night that Rhonda abandoned her baby on their front steps. That Flynn could not marry this woman who had conceived a child out of wedlock and then concealed it from him. It wasn't true, and it was going to require the best acting she'd ever done in her life. But, as Judy had helped her realize, she was excited to tackle the challenge. Part of her did genuinely feel bad about besmirching Rhonda Powers's reputation with such a gargantuan lie. But it was the only thing she could come up with on such short notice that would stop the wedding and leave Flynn's own reputation intact.

After only a few minutes, Livvy had a crick in her back from crouching in the pulpit. She tried to adjust and Rallo squirmed. He crawled out of her habit and began bouncing around the small area where they were hiding.

"Stop," she hissed through clenched teeth, praying no one could hear her above the priest's droning below.

She reached for him, springing forward, and he jumped away, eluding her grasp. She climbed to her knees, hoping it would be easier to catch him if she wasn't sitting down, but Rallo gave her a look of disdain and jumped up onto the ledge of the pulpit.

Stanley Devlin was in the middle of a reading about love being patient and kind. Livvy slowly pushed herself up, trying to only expose the top of her head as she crept up behind Rallo, hoping if she snatched him down, no one would notice. But the monkey was too quick for her.

The next part seemed to happen in slow motion as Rallo leapt from his perch on the pulpit.

"Rallo, no!" Livvy cried, unable to stop herself. She sprang up and reached after him, but all her hand grasped was air. The monkey seemed to have a singular purpose, landing atop the tulle pastry of a veil piled on Rhonda's head and beginning to tear it to shreds.

Flynn's look of shock shifted as he burst into laughter, doubling over while Rallo continued to terrorize his bride-to-be.

Rhonda screamed and clawed at her head, causing Rallo to tug on her veil and push it backwards before hopping back to Flynn's shoulder. Flynn, still laughing, reached for Rhonda, trying to prevent her from falling back as the weight of her veil pulled her down. Instead, he fell with her and landed on top of her, tangling in the layers and layers of her gown and veil. Rallo crouched atop them, grabbing snatches of tulle and lace and throwing them into the air.

In horror, Livvy watched this all unfold. This was so far from the plan, she had no idea what to do.

The entire church was in an uproar. Except for Flynn's mother, who was standing to the side laughing hysterically. Stanley Devlin had picked up the golden crucifix from the altar and was now swinging it wildly at Rallo. He missed and instead, as the monkey ducked, Devlin collided with Dash, who was also trying to intervene.

"Bannkkkkksss," Devlin bellowed as Dash fell to his knees, clutching his gut in pain. Joan rushed to help her husband.

Flynn looked apoplectic as Devlin raised the crucifix again, apparently trying to brain the monkey. "Don't you fucking dare," he cried, struggling to extricate himself from the dress and tangling himself further.

But he needn't have worried. With one look at the crucifix being held as a weapon, Rallo bared his teeth and jumped onto Devlin's face. The monkey held on to the man's ears and dug his legs into the barely healed wound on his face. Livvy would have felt bad for Devlin if he didn't deserve it so much.

Livvy looked around desperately. The guests were screaming in confusion. Some of them had stood and made a run for the exit. She had to stop this, but if she tried to go back down the stairs, she could end up crushed in the crowd. Dash was still out of commission, with Joan trying to get him to sip from the chalice of communion wine as he lay crumpled on the floor.

Her eye caught on the green fabric hanging next to the pulpit. She looked up, noting that it hung from some type of metal rod at the top of the church and reached nearly to the floor. It was better than nothing. She grabbed it and pulled it back, creating as much momentum as she could in the tiny area she had to work with.

Climbing onto the edge of the pulpit, she quickly made the sign of the cross with her right hand. The only time she'd ever prayed and meant it was the night of the car accident. So, she wasn't exactly devoutly religious. But, hey, it couldn't hurt.

Livvy swung forward in the air, clinging to the material, and her stomach plunged as she heard the fabric tear. She looked up and watched as one edge of the banner unraveled from where it was clasped to the rod. She clung to the ripping fabric, descending to the ground at an angle. Miraculously, she landed on her feet. Maybe she should consider going to church more often.

She grabbed Flynn and tried to drag him backwards, away from Rhonda, who was crying and flailing on the ground. "Sister, please!" he bellowed, before he snapped his head back and made eye contact. "Livvy? What are you doing here? And why are you dressed like a nun?"

"I'll explain later." She tugged on him again, heading back in the direction of Dash and Joan, who were now leaning against the altar.

"I thought we had a backup plan," Livvy muttered to Joan.

"Not for this."

The crowd was now climbing over one another, racing to get to the back doors of the church. There was no way they could escape that way. If it wasn't such a disaster, Livvy would have laughed. All of this over a little monkey?

"What is the meaning of this?" Devlin blustered as he gripped Rhonda under her arms and tried to heave her to her feet. But Rhonda did nothing to help him, continuing to blubber on the floor incoherently.

Rallo had jumped off Devlin's face and was playing in Rhonda's skirts, upending the fabric, making it hard for her to see what was happening. Each time Devlin tried to shoo the monkey away, Rallo hissed at him and snapped his teeth.

"Someone get rid of that thing," he yelled. He raised his foot, trying to stomp on Rallo, but the monkey sprang away to the top of the altar. Instead, Devlin came down on Rhonda's leg buried under her skirts.

She shrieked in pain. "You idiot!"

"Like you're helping!" he yelped.

Rhonda slugged her uncle, making contact with his groin, and he doubled over in pain.

"Stupid bitch," he growled. "I should never have forced Banks to marry you."

The comment only made Rhonda cry harder. He hauled back

to slap her, and this time, Rallo did bite him, grabbing his hand and chomping down on his finger until Devlin howled in pain. The priest was cowering under his chair in the corner.

Devlin shrieked and started spinning in a circle, trying to propel Rallo to let go, but the monkey only bit down harder. Flynn's mother was now doubled over, tears of laughter streaming down her face. At least someone was enjoying themselves.

Suddenly, emerging from behind them in the nave, Judy ran out, slightly breathless.

"Where did you come from?" Livvy and Flynn burst out in unison. Judy was supposed to be waiting in the getaway car, far from any potential run-in with Devlin.

"Never mind, I've got the car out back. Let's go."

The three of them turned to leave, but Livvy stopped, kneeling to help Dash. "Dash, can you stand long enough to reach the car?"

He nodded and started to stand, but then doubled over to his knees. "Go without me," he croaked.

Livvy looked up, seeing Flynn and Judy had already made it to the side door.

"Livvy, come on." Judy frantically waved her arms, beckoning.

Livvy froze, looking back and forth between Dash and Flynn. She'd come to rescue Flynn, but Dash had been essential to their success. They needed him.

Joan squeezed her arm and gave her a look of permission. "Go on, get out of here. He'll be all right once he can breathe again."

Livvy nodded and sprinted after her sister, trying not to slip as she took the marble steps down from the altar's platform two at a time.

But just as she reached the door, her habit snagged. She turned and her eyes widened as she locked eyes with Devlin, who was holding tight to her gown. "Not so fast, Miss De Lesseps."

She wrenched the fabric from his hands, hearing it tear, and stumbled slightly out the open door as Devlin advanced on her, something menacing in his eyes. "You couldn't just let Banks save you and your sister. Couldn't let him marry my idiot niece. You had to play the hero."

She took one step gingerly down the stone steps, trying to back away. Flynn was already in the car. Judy laid on the horn, trying to get Livvy to run. But she couldn't. She was paralyzed with fear as Devlin approached.

He raised his left hand and held it out to Livvy like the ghost of Banquo pointing his bloody hand at Macbeth. In the place of his pointer finger was a bloody stump.

She let out a gasp of shock. Oh God. Rallo had bit his finger clean off.

As if on cue, the monkey came scampering out of the church, Devlin's finger in his mouth. He dropped it at Livvy's feet like it was a prize he had won for her. She gagged, trying to swallow down her impulse to vomit.

"You're going to regret this," Devlin sputtered. "You and your harlot sister."

A firm hand wrested itself on Livvy's back, reassuring her. "Before you start pointing fingers, Devlin, I'd make sure you have all of your own," Judy growled.

No. This wasn't supposed to happen. Judy wasn't supposed to face him again. She should have stayed in the car.

But her sister grabbed Livvy's shoulder and pulled her back. "Go get in the car, I'll handle him."

Livvy struggled against every impulse she had to protect her sister. Judy wasn't even supposed to be here. Livvy studied her sister, her breath catching at the fire in Judy's eyes. Pride flared in Livvy's chest. Judy didn't need her protection. Right now, she was braver than Livvy had ever dared to be. Flynn had been right. If Judy said she could handle it, Livvy believed her.

Rallo followed right behind Livvy and jumped into the car, crawling over the front seat and into Flynn's lap, then tucking in his tail and snuggling calmly into a ball. The monkey closed his eyes, unmoved by the fact that he had just dismembered one of the more powerful men in Hollywood.

Livvy rolled the window down so she could hear what was happening between her sister and Devlin.

"You're a despicable man," Judy spat out.

Devlin grinned, the maniacal look on his face chilling Livvy to the bone. "If you think I'm despicable now, wait until I get going. When I'm finished with you and your sister, the pearl-clutchers will be chasing you from Hollywood with tar and feathers."

"You're the one who should be run out of town on a rail."

Voices at the end of the alley interrupted Judy and Devlin's volley of threats. "I think I see them," someone called.

Before Livvy knew what was happening, Walter Pince of *The Hollywood Reporter* was barreling toward the car, with a photographer in tow. She recognized him from his photo next to his column, his fresh-faced youth a standout among the dour older men that dominated the staff. He couldn't have been more than twenty-three years old. She was vaguely aware that Flynn and Walter were friendly, and she sent up a silent thanks that he had been the member of the press to find them first.

Walter ran up, nearly out of breath, and leaned against the back end of the car, holding his side like he had a cramp. The press pass in his lapel pocket was torn and his hat looked rather squashed. "It's a madhouse out there." He gestured to the front of the church, gasping for air. Walter peered into the back seat, addressing Flynn. "What happened in there? A woman claiming to be your mother found me and told me something about a nun and a monkey. I could barely understand her, she was laughing so hard."

Flynn grinned. "Good to know her sense of humor is as strong as ever."

"I'll tell you what happened," Devlin snarled. Coming down the steps and pushing his way past Judy, he puffed up his chest and got in Walter's face. Walter turned a light shade of puce as Devlin jabbed at his chest with his bloody hand. "That monkey attacked me on their orders."

Livvy scoffed. "That's absurd. He's a trained monkey, but he's not that good."

Rallo lifted his head from Flynn's lap to chitter in protest.

Livvy reached her arm back to pat Rallo on the head. "Not that we didn't appreciate it," she whispered under her breath.

Judy stormed down the steps behind Devlin and stood before Walter with her hands on her hips. "You want to know what happened? I'll tell you. This man"—she thumbed in Devlin's direction—"attacked me at Shasta Peak Pictures' annual sales celebration last month. He tried to, to, to—" Judy's voice became choked with emotion.

"Lies," Devlin sputtered.

Livvy opened the door to hop out of the car and grab her sister's hand. "Judy, it's okay. You don't have to share this."

Judy squeezed Livvy's hand in return and squared her shoulders. She swallowed, and a note of tremulous courage returned to her voice. "No, I want to. I have to. To make sure he never hurts anyone else. I was wrong before, when I said I wanted to forget it. I can't—for the sake of the next girl."

Walter scribbled frantically in his notebook. "What did he try to do, miss?"

"To molest me. To have his way with me. He informed me that the girls at this party were the studio's 'entertainment' for the night. Said that since we'd been paid for, we'd better deliver. He followed me into the powder room—"

"Disgusting. Lies, all lies. Now I'll add slander to your charges as well. I intend to prosecute. Write that in your notebook! For this brat's attack last month and for everything that happened today."

By this time, Flynn had hopped back out of the car as well. He cleared his throat. "Walter, I can corroborate the girl's story. I bailed her out of jail the morning after. She had scratches and bruises all over her body. Though as you can see from Devlin's face, she put up a hell of a fight."

For the first time, Walter noticed the wound on Devlin's cheek, and he whistled. "Boy, she did at that! Nice work, miss." He tipped his hat at Judy.

Judy preened a little. "Thank you."

"So"—Walter licked his finger and turned the page of his steno pad, poised to write down whatever she said next—"Shasta Peak Pictures paid you and other women that night to perform?"

"As dancers, yes. We were all Billy Wilkes's girls. From the Sphinx Club. We were told we were there to be background dancers in a movie. But when we got there, it turned out we were the entertainment at this party. I wasn't aware there were additional...duties expected of us."

"But Devlin here assumed you were his for the taking? That you were aware these other 'services' were part of your job responsibilities?"

Judy nodded and swallowed. "He told me that if I didn't do as he said, he'd blackball me. That I'd better lie back and get comfortable on the casting couch if I wanted to make it in Hollywood."

"Preposterous!" Devlin was getting increasingly angry, his face turning a dangerous shade of purple and his slicked-back, thinning hair sticking out at odd angles.

"Quiet, Devlin," Flynn roared. "Unless you want me to tell the monkey to take off something more significant than your finger." Flynn looked pointedly at Devlin's crotch and the man flinched, involuntarily shielding his nether region with his hands.

"You wouldn't dare," Devlin snarled. But then, Rallo pressed his face against the glass and let out a terrifying shriek. Livvy didn't even know a monkey could produce a sound like that.

Without warning, all the color drained from Devlin's face and he crumbled to the ground.

"Shit," Flynn muttered. He kneeled down and checked Devlin's neck for a pulse. "He's fine. Just unconscious. Walter, you'd better call the paramedics." He eyed Devlin's injured hand. "I think he's lost a fair bit of blood."

"Or he's terrified of Rallo." Livvy laughed.

Flynn grinned and looked at the monkey, who still had his face pressed against the glass of the back passenger window. "Fine work, my friend."

In response, Rallo stuck out his tongue and distorted his face into a grotesque contortion. The entire group laughed in relief, and the tension that had been fizzing throughout Livvy's body since the ceremony dissipated slightly.

Flynn pushed the unconscious Devlin up, got his hands under the man's arms, and dragged him away from the car, laying him out near the steps. Noticing Devlin's finger still sitting where Rallo had dropped it, he picked it up, grimacing, and set it on top of Devlin's chest. Then he stood, brushing off the knees of his morning suit. "Walter, if you don't mind, these girls have so kindly arranged a getaway car for me, and I'd like to make use of it."

The reporter chuckled. "Of course, Banks. There's just one thing I don't understand."

"What's that?"

"Why were you gonna marry that louse's niece? If all of this is true?"

Flynn sighed and ran his hand down his face. "I suppose because...I wanted to take responsibility for someone other than myself. For once."

He gave Livvy a somber look, and her heart sank. She had hurled accusations at him, accused him of building a life that meant he didn't have to care about anyone but himself. About anything but his own pleasure. She couldn't read his expression now. Did he intend his words about responsibility to be a rebuke of her own? Or as an apology?

Walter stuck his pencil behind his ear and tipped his fedora forward on his head. "What does that mean?"

Flynn gave the reporter a sad little smile. "It means for the first time in my life, I was trying to do a good turn. Devlin was threatening to ruin the girl and her sister. I made a deal with him to keep their names out of the papers. Simple as that. Doesn't mean I would've been a good husband. I made no such promise in that regard. I've been told I would make a lousy one, in fact."

He gave Livvy a pointed look. She closed her eyes, furious with herself. How wrong she'd been. But she couldn't simply take back her words. After how she'd treated him, did she expect him to embrace her and say all was forgiven? To take her in his arms and tell her that he was so relieved she'd come, because in truth the only person he wanted was her?

No. Her only intention had been to stop the wedding. To make sure Flynn didn't have to sacrifice himself for her. She hadn't wanted that on her conscience. It shouldn't be so crushing that her rescue hadn't ended with some great love scene. That instead it was concluding with a harried escape and his invoking her words as the reason he had almost destroyed his life.

Suddenly, someone from the front of the church cried, "I think they went that way." Their heads all snapped to see if they were about to be rushed by a crowd, but instead, there was only an older woman, her hat in disarray atop her head, barreling down the alley and gasping for breath. As she got closer, Livvy realized it was the woman she had guessed was Flynn's mother.

"Mother?" Flynn asked, confirming Livvy's assumption. "What are you doing?"

"Buying you time," she huffed.

The woman clutched at her side as Flynn turned to their group. "Er, everyone this is my mother, Violet." They all nodded and smiled their hellos.

She smiled back. "It's nice to meet you. Especially you." She beamed at Livvy. "But the meet and greet will have to wait. You'd all better get out of here. I told them the crowd you'd gone out on the opposite side of the church, but they'll realize soon enough it was a lie."

They sprang into action at her words, moving back to the car. But Flynn stopped before any of them could get in. "Aren't you coming with us?"

"No," she insisted. "I'll keep trying to throw them off the scent." A mass of people, what seemed to be at least half the population of the church, started to turn into the alley. Violet straightened her hat, steeled herself, and turned to head back toward the crowd.

"Mother," Flynn called after her. Violet turned around, still jogging backwards in the direction of the wedding-goers. "Thank you."

A bright smile broke out on Violet's face then. "My pleasure. And, son?"

"Yes?"

"Remember to always choose joy."

Flynn smiled for the first time that day, before nodding at Livvy and Judy, who ducked into the car at his signal. "Walter," he added. "I'll give you the full story anytime you like. But right now, it's high time I make like a runaway groom."

"I'll hold to you that." The two men both looked at Devlin, who was starting to stir. "You better go. I'll take care of him."

Judy had already started the engine when Flynn slid into the back seat. He'd barely pulled the door closed when Judy peeled away, the car bouncing up and over a curb. Livvy's thoughts were so scrambled that she wasn't even sure where they were. But Judy drove confidently as Flynn ducked down, making sure no reporters or wedding guests spotted them as they made their getaway.

Once they were a few blocks away from the church, Flynn popped back up and stared out the back window, checking to see if anyone had tailed them. But the coast was clear. It was a beautiful December day in Hollywood, bright and brisk. The streets were relatively quiet, as if the city had yet to really wake up.

All too soon, the car approached the familiar entrance to the Garden of Allah apartments. "We thought no one would know to look for you here," Judy told Flynn by way of explanation for their destination. "You can lay low here for a bit, and then one of us can drive you home."

He made a gruff assent of thanks, and Livvy mourned the end

of this little bubble of peace and quiet in his company. It hadn't been enough. To just be with him. It would never be enough. But she'd held tightly to Judy for so long. She couldn't do the same to Flynn. It wasn't fair to him.

She had to learn to let go of the things she loved. Even if it broke her heart.

CHAPTER 31

WHEN THEY PULLED UP TO THE SHABBY LITTLE APARTMENT, Judy idled in the driveway. "Go ahead," the kid said. "I just need to find something."

Livvy opened her door and climbed out, and Flynn followed swiftly behind her, Rallo springing out after him. They'd have to call Lionel to come pick up the rascally primate. But no sooner was Flynn standing in the gravel driveway than Judy started to back up.

"Where are you going?" Livvy called.

"Need something at the store. I forgot!" Judy smiled and whipped the car around, peeling off with the urgency of someone who had intentions other than merely running an errand.

"Subtle," Flynn chortled.

Livvy removed her wimple, loosing her raven-black curls, and Flynn was momentarily breathless at the way the sunlight caught her hair. "I'm sorry about her. She has a silly idea that this was going to have a romantic conclusion."

Flynn tilted his head but didn't speak. Livvy seemed so unsure of herself. It was cute, really. Would've been cuter if his heart wasn't beating out of his chest.

"Want to go inside?" "Shall we take a walk?" they asked at the same time.

"We can go inside if you'd like," Flynn told her. He didn't know how to play this. He'd never done it before. Except onscreen. And that usually involved a cutlass.

Livvy gave him a warm but timid smile. "No, some fresh air would be nice. Let me just get out of this thing." She gestured at her habit.

"I don't know, I think it's sexy," he teased.

She blushed deeply. "I wasn't aware you had a thing for convent girls."

Flynn took a mock stern pose, his hands on his hips, and stuck out his hand, pretending to admonish her. "'Get thee to a nunnery!'"

She stuck her tongue out at him. "I'd stick to swashbuckling. Shakespeare's not for you." She opened her front door and Rallo scampered in ahead of her. "I'll be right back."

Flynn waited for her to return for what seemed like an eternity, running through a litany of speeches in his head. Trying to find the words to tell her how he felt. They all sounded trite and silly. He had hoped that agreeing to marry Rhonda Powers would have given some indication of the depth of his love for Livvy. But she seemed frightened, embarrassed almost.

She appeared back in the doorway, wearing a long-sleeved, two-toned knit sweater and a gray pencil skirt. "Okay, all set."

"You're right." He smiled. "You do look better without the habit."

She smiled. "Do you think Rallo will be okay alone in there? He curled up on a throw pillow and went right to sleep."

Flynn chuckled. "He's had a busy morning. Let him rest. Shall we?" When he proffered his arm, she shut the door behind her and skipped down the steps to take it, though she kept a comfortable bit of distance between their bodies. Why was she being so skittish?

"The pool and the gardens are that way," she said. "They're not much. But it's better than walking through the rows of houses."

He set off in the direction she had pointed out, and they walked companionably in silence for a moment. But soon he couldn't bear the quiet. "You caused quite the stir today."

She blushed. Damn it, this was a terrible start. "I'm sorry. I didn't intend to. I was simply supposed to object and accuse Rhonda of abandoning her baby at the convent. So you wouldn't have to marry her. I didn't mean to turn the whole thing into a circus."

He grinned. "Oh, I quite enjoyed it."

She stopped cold. "Really? It was a madhouse. Rallo bit off a man's finger!"

"Yes, I shall have to buy him plenty of bananas to thank him for that."

Her face bloomed into an even wider smile, and she shook her head. "Oh, you're terrible."

"What? Devlin deserved it. They should give Rallo the medal of honor."

"He'd probably try to eat it."

"Probably. Maybe they should give you a reward instead."

"Pfft, for what? Causing a scene at the wedding of one of Hollywood's most famous bachelors?" She dropped his arm and walked away from him then, wrapping her arms around herself as if she was cold, even though it was comfortably warm in the sunshine. "At least you're free now. I couldn't let you marry that woman. Not once Dash told me why you'd agreed to do it."

He didn't understand. He thought she'd come today to win him back. To tell him she loved him and wanted to ride off into the sunset. But she was closing herself off, withdrawing. He went up behind her and placed his hands on her shoulders.

"Don't beat yourself up, Livvy. So things went a little haywire. The important thing is I'm not married to Rhonda Powers, and we exposed Stanley Devlin for the hypocritical bastard he is."

She whirled to face him. "Don't you think he'll make it worse for us now?"

Flynn shrugged. "He'll try. But Walter's a good man. He'll print the truth. And I'll tell him as much or as little of it as Judy and you are comfortable with me sharing."

Livvy ran her fingers through her hair in nervous exasperation. "Why would you agree to such a thing in the first place? I would have handled it."

He took her hand and tangled his fingers with hers. At first, she seemed reticent. Surprised, even. But then she clasped his hand tightly and a burst of affection swirled in his chest.

He lifted their hands to his mouth and kissed the top of hers. "That's exactly why. You've been handling things for you and Judy for so long, I thought it was high time someone took the burden off of you."

"Even if it would make you miserable?"

He nodded and met her gaze, her eyes searching his for something. What, he didn't know. "You were right when you said I'd built myself a pleasure palace, determined not to let anything unpleasant or messy into my life."

She broke away from him and buried her face in her hands. "No, I wasn't. I'm sorry. I should never have said those things. It was cruel and uncalled for. It was you who was right. This whole time, Judy's been yearning for me to stop holding on so tight, to be her sister, not her mother."

He approached Livvy once more and wrapped his hands around her waist. She tensed at the feel of it, but as he lay his head on her shoulder, she sighed gently and relaxed back in to him. "So, we were both right then. Maybe we weren't the nicest in how we told each other. But we weren't wrong."

She nodded and slid her hand back down to his, pulling him along to continue their walk.

He took a breath. "Until I met you, Livvy, I was still a scared little boy. Rebelling against my father, missing my mother. Wanting to live a life with no stakes, so that no one could ever hurt me. But you taught me that's not possible. You fenced your way into my heart when I wasn't looking—and you're the one who got hurt. All I did in agreeing to marry Rhonda was try to balance the scales. To take on some of that weight you've carried alone for so long."

She shot him a pained look of surprise, and he worried he'd somehow said the wrong thing. They had come to the pool area now. The tile around the edges was chipped and the water was murky, a sickening green color. But the area was peaceful and quiet, surrounded by a ring of palm trees that stood silent sentry over the watery playground.

He opened the wrought-iron gate and pulled her through with him, taking her in his arms. She made a little *oomph* sound as he caught her and held her close, kissing the top of her head.

"Flynn, you don't have to—"

"Hush." He reached up and tucked a stray curl behind her ear. "None of this is because I have to. It's because I want to. You taught me there's joy in responsibility, in taking on the burdens of others."

She pressed her face into his chest, and he squeezed her tightly. He could feel his shirt turning damp from her tears. He realized he was still wearing his tux and felt utterly ridiculous. But Livvy didn't seem to mind as she practically blew her nose into the ruffles of his crisp white shirt.

It should have been disgusting, but he found it adorable. God, he really was gone for her.

He rubbed her back and let her finish crying. When she had, Livvy leaned back and looked up at him. "And you taught me that I don't always have to take on that burden. That I should share it with others. That I should allow myself a full life, with joy and sorrow. Whatever comes. That taking on the weight of the world for the ones I love is not living, it's burying myself alive."

He kissed the tip of her nose. "It seems we've both learned valuable lessons from each other. Well, and my mother turned up to knock some sense into me."

The mention of his mother made her suddenly seem to remember herself, and she broke away. "We have learned a lot from each other." She nervously smoothed the twill of her skirt. "And I want you to know that I don't expect more from you than that." She turned away and studied the pool, its water rippling in the winter wind. "Whatever Judy was trying to set up here, I didn't... I don't expect—"

He came around in front of her and set his hands on her shoulders, looking her hard in the face. Enough of this hinting at it, of this cataloging the ways she'd made his life better.

"Livvy, are you telling me you don't love me?" He stared at her, refusing to break away. "That you did everything today out of some sense of duty?"

She bit her lip. "All I knew was you couldn't marry her. Not for my sake. I—"

"You swashbuckled for me." He smiled at that, remembering the glorious sight of her swinging down from that pulpit to the ground while he attempted to free himself from the morass of Rhonda's skirts. He hadn't known then it was Livvy. But he had thought to himself that the nun, whoever she was, was quite spectacular.

She looked down, a shy smile on her face. "I hadn't intended to."

He gently nudged her chin up to look at him. "But you did. And it was the most impressive thing I've ever witnessed." Her eyebrows went up in disbelief. "So, I ask you again, Olivia Blount, do you love me or not?"

She nodded, one timid little tilt of her head, as if she were scared to admit it. It was all he needed, and he pressed his face to hers, kissing her more forcefully than he ever had. He broke away and pressed his cheek to hers.

"That's good. Because I love you Olivia Blount, Liv de Lesseps, my Livvy. Whatever you choose for me to call you, I love you." He pulled back so he could look at her. "I think I've loved you from the moment you pretended to have no idea who I was. Certainly since I watched you eat an enchilada like you'd discovered nirvana. When I realized that it was you swinging from that pulpit like a Valkyrie ready to ride into Valhalla, I knew any future without you would be a half-life."

Livvy's eyes were watery with tears. She reached out and drew his head down to her mouth, pressing a gentle kiss to the corner of his lips before offering a fuller embrace. He returned her kiss, pulling her more tightly to him, and she knit her hands together behind his neck to run her fingers through his hair. She bit his lip and tugged at it, and he groaned with pleasure.

"I love you, Flynn," she murmured as she dotted his face with kisses. "You are so much more than what I'd dreamed you'd be."

"You're everything I'd told myself I couldn't want, yet somehow better. I want to dedicate my life to your happiness, Livvy. Because without you, without your joy, there is no purpose to my own."

She gently undid the white bow tie that was somehow still

pristine around his neck and used the edges of it to pull his face back to hers. After another kiss, she pressed her forehead to his and whispered, "You are my favorite rogue, for as long as you want me."

"I think I can safely say that's forever. But there's something I have to do first." He pulled his notorious little black book out of his inner breast pocket.

"You brought that with you to your wedding?" Livvy eyed him skeptically.

"It comforted me in my hour of need." She rolled her eyes. "Besides, I thought maybe if I pulled it out when the priest asked for objections, Rhonda would change her mind." He produced a small pencil from the same coat pocket, licked his finger, and flipped to a blank page. *Olivia Blount,* he wrote, as she watched him. Then, he tore the page from the book, folded it in half, and tucked it back in the pocket right above his heart.

"That should be the only page I need from this from now on." He looked around for a rubbish bin and not finding one, he chucked the book into the moldering pool. She gasped, her mouth forming a perfect O, and he laughed.

"Flynn, you shouldn't have done that."

He shrugged. "I'll leave it for F. Scott to find." She giggled, and he stopped her laugh with a kiss.

Without ending the kiss, he picked her up, holding her like a groom carrying his bride across the threshold, and she pulled back, yelping in delighted surprise. "What? I'm dressed for it," he quipped.

She threw her head back and laughed before kissing him once more. She caressed his face and toyed with his hair as he carried her in the direction of her bungalow. "My pirate," she murmured.

"My treasure," he returned. He nipped at her earlobe and

then swirled his tongue around the spot behind her ear that he knew drove her wild. He was rewarded with the feel of her arching against him while he held her. "Do you think Judy will come back anytime soon?" he huffed out, growing breathless from their kisses. He squeezed her bottom with his hand, making the intentions behind his question clear.

Her eyes danced merrily in response. "I have a feeling she won't be back for hours."

"Good." He grinned. "Then I can ravish you in every room." He held her even more tightly and broke into a light run, with Livvy laughing all the way back to the apartment. Her laugh was his favorite sound in the world, and he would do everything in his power to ensure he could hear it multiple times a day, every day for the rest of his life. A pirate and his mate.

CHAPTER 32

| ONE MONTH LATER |

LIVVY STEPPED OUT OF THE DINGHY AND ONTO THE DOCK, careful not to get the heel of her champagne-colored shoe caught between the wooden planks. She dropped the skirt of her shimmering dress, and it swirled like liquid gold around her knees and ankles as she reached for Flynn's hand.

Behind them, in the purple light of dusk, loomed the Catalina Casino, the gem of Avalon Bay with its rounded structure. Its tall, scalloped archways were illuminated in shades of silver and gold for the New Year's dance.

Flynn tucked her arm beneath his and straightened the fox fur stole she wore, leading her up the pier toward the walkway. In a few moments, they were at the front of the casino, and Livvy gasped at the beautiful mosaic tile that lined the entrance. A mermaid with blond hair, floating in a sea of teal tile, stretched high above them, surrounded by two panels that featured the curls of ocean waves, brightly colored fish, and adorable seahorses. It was even more impressive than the tile at Flynn's home.

"It's stunning," she gasped in wonder.

"No, you are," Flynn whispered into her ear, nuzzling her bare neck. She swatted at him and warmed. It was a terrible line, but it still made her go all squishy inside every time he told her she was beautiful. "But if you think this is good, wait until we're inside."

Flynn wasn't exaggerating. Every room held more wonders than the last. The art deco building was extraordinary, from the designs in its tiled entryway to its lush red ceilings and walnut-paneled hallways. She oohed and aahed as they made the climb to the twelfth floor and entered the enormous ballroom. An outdoor circular balcony granted them a three-hundred-sixty-degree view of the harbor and the ocean that separated them from the mainland in the distance. Around the edge of the ballroom were beautifully decorated tables and chairs, each with a spray of red roses at their center. The stage at the front of the room held a forty-piece band, currently playing "Stompin' at the Savoy" while couples Lindy Hopped their way around the magnificent dance floor.

Livvy couldn't help but swing her hips lightly in time to the music as she swiveled her head, trying to take it all in. The chestnut wood paneling continued across the back of the room, where a large bar was built into the wall. But the best feature was the room's fan-vaulted ceiling with a gold metal chandelier and a large globe light at its center.

"Is it what you imagined?" Flynn leaned over and asked her.

She nodded. "So much more."

The band concluded their song, and the couples on the floor broke out into a smattering of applause. It was early still, and she knew the floor would only get more crowded as the night went on. The band nodded on beat as the band leader counted off a quicker syncopation and they broke out into "Sing, Sing, Sing."

Livvy couldn't suppress a trill of excitement, and Flynn chuckled. "Would you like to dance?"

"God yes," she answered, and he showed her over to a table

next to the window where she could deposit her stole and the small clutch she was using as a handbag. He took her hand and they headed down three steps and out onto the floor, Flynn twirling her into his arms.

The music twinkled along, and he led her through a sequence of basic swing steps before turning her into a series of spins. By the time the song ended, she was gasping for air and smiling so wide her face hurt.

"Having fun?" Flynn asked, pulling her toward him.

All she could do was nod vigorously as she tried to catch her breath. That day when they'd won the regatta and stared at the casino in the distance, Flynn had promised to bring her here. She had thought it was a hollow pledge at the time, something he'd tossed off in the moment. But the reality of it now was so much more than she had dreamed. "I didn't know you could dance like that," she huffed out.

"When you're a member of the British aristocracy, it comes with the territory." He shrugged.

"A former member," she corrected. Just after Christmas, Flynn had sent his brother a letter, renouncing any claim he had to the family title and fortune. As his mother's bastard, he technically had no right to it anyway, but Edgar didn't need to know that. He'd spare him that indignity at least. Better his brother just believe he'd forsaken his duty once and for all. Flynn had enough money here, and he had never wanted the strings his family legacy came with. So, he'd freed himself to enjoy his life with Livvy on his own terms. Just as his mother had done before him. "Besides, I doubt they teach the Lindy Hop to future dukes."

He chuckled. "No, you're right. That I learned how to do from a cigarette girl at the Palomar Ballroom. She was a rather, uh, vigorous girl."

Livvy rolled her eyes. "Remind me to write her a thank-you note."

Flynn laughed more loudly now. "I love it when you get a little jealous."

"I'm not jealous," Livvy teased. "I would've hated to teach you to dance. After all, I already had to teach you to fence." She winked at him as his jaw dropped in mock outrage.

The band struck up another fast-paced song, and he proffered his hand to continue dancing, but she shook her head. "I need a break."

Flynn led her off the floor and directed them to the highly polished bar at the back of the room. It wasn't crowded. It was so long, taking up the entire back half of the space, that Livvy suspected there wouldn't be a line all night, no matter how many people were thirsty. Flynn ordered a whiskey soda for himself and a gimlet for her before leading them to the outdoor balcony.

Flynn raised his glass and clinked it to Livvy's. "To us."

"To us," she agreed, giving him a quick kiss and leaning in to him. He wrapped his arms around her and rested his head gently atop hers as she looked out across the ocean. The stars were beginning to twinkle and the moon was a bright orb reflected in the water's surface.

He hummed along to the music pouring out of the doors, and they stood together in utter contentment.

"What's Judy up to tonight?" Flynn asked eventually.

"Oh, Walter is taking her to dinner at Perino's, then dancing at the Biltmore." Judy had started dating the newspaper man shortly after the aborted Powers wedding. The day after their escapades, Judy had gone to his desk at the *Hollywood Reporter* to tell her side of the story. Walter Pince got the editor to put it on the front page, and it had led to Stanley Devlin being summarily fired from his position with the Production Code Administration. Every studio in town had blacklisted the man, barring him from their lots and their parties. Not that Hollywood didn't have plenty like Devlin still in their ranks. He made a convenient scapegoat for other powerful men's abuses. But at least there was one less wolf in sheep's clothing prowling the studio streets.

The day after the story ran, Walter—who Livvy had confirmed was, in fact, twenty-three—had called to ask Judy to dinner, and they'd been inseparable ever since. It made Livvy happy to know her sister was being cared for in her absence. She was still working to stop mothering her. Old habits die hard, after all.

With Stanley Devlin fired from the PCA and his blackmailing exposed, Rhonda Powers had retreated from the public eye. Flynn's reputation issues had vanished seemingly overnight. Not that it mattered, since he was dating his extremely respectable leading lady. For real, this time. Harry had stopped arranging dates and photo ops for them, but the press was none the wiser that their relationship had ever been anything but genuine. The papers still followed their romance with a breathless fervor, and Flynn and Livvy didn't even mind. It was good publicity for the picture, which would come out in February.

"Remember our meal from Perino's?" Flynn whispered into her ear, nipping lightly at her earlobe as they continued admiring the ocean view.

"I do." A pulse of want rushed through her from her earlobe to the tips of her toes.

She turned her head up to graze his jaw with a fierce kiss before replying. "And I look forward to having more of that dessert later tonight."

Flynn's eyes widened, and his irises blew out with want. "Careful," he growled. "You wouldn't want to give me a bad reputation."

She raised her eyebrows. "Wouldn't I though? I think I've done enough to bolster it. It's time the rogue I was promised makes a return."

He bent over to kiss her, flinging his arms wide so that he didn't splash any of his drink onto her, and she stumbled backwards slightly, bowled over by the force of his enthusiasm.

She giggled and broke away from him. "I think I'm a bad influence on you."

"It's one of my favorite things about you," he retorted.

The band finished their up-tempo number and started playing "Night and Day." Livvy closed her eyes, leaned her head back, and soaked in the sound of the music. "God, I love this song."

"Want to dance?" Flynn reached for her glass and set both of their nearly finished drinks on a high-top table a few feet from them.

"I want to stay out here a while longer."

"We can still dance." Flynn took her in his arms and pressed his cheek to hers, rocking them gently back and forth in the moonlight. It was one of those impossibly warm California winter nights. A precursor to that mysterious but inevitable week of January weather that reminded her why people moved here in droves, before things went back to months of gloomy days and spitting rain.

Livvy hummed along, and Flynn began to croon, "'Night and day, you are the one…'"

He was dreadfully off-key, but Livvy loved it anyway. "I think you'll have to leave the musicals to Don Lamont," she teased.

He chuckled, the breath from his laugh tickling the side of her face. "It's a good thing that Harry's already set my next picture with you then."

She made a sigh of contentment in reply, thinking about the

contract she'd signed right before Christmas. Harry had offered her three years on the Evets's Studios payroll at triple the pay of her measly starting salary. Plus an option for another three years when it was up. It was the ticket to a future she'd never known she wanted. The promise of a new dream. One that fit nicely with the novel she'd secretly started writing during breaks in her dressing room. She hadn't even told Flynn yet. It was still too new. But it turned out that when you weren't spending every waking hour fretting about other people in your life, there was more time to write.

They kept dancing, and Livvy soaked it all in. The beautiful ballroom behind them, decorated with such care. The warm feel of Flynn's arms around her as he held her and rocked her gently in time to the music. The smell of the brine from the ocean far below them.

She and Judy had been through so much these last years. But now she was at peace. More than at peace—she was happier than she'd ever thought possible. About to ring in the New Year with the man she loved. Secure in her career and content in the knowledge that her sister was as well cared for as she could possibly be.

"'Till you let me spend my life making love to you,'" Flynn talked-sang into her ear.

She nuzzled his neck. "Mmm, that sounds nice."

"Does it?" he asked, taking a step back from her and pulling a small, black velvet box out of his pocket. He didn't get down on one knee, but simply popped the lid open with his thumb. A single emerald-cut diamond in a bezel setting winked back at her, twinkling in the moonlight.

She covered her mouth with her hands, truly in shock. Flynn Banks, resolute bachelor and rapscallion, was proposing to her. "Flynn, I told you already that being with you is enough. If you don't ever want to get married, we don't have to." She didn't want him to feel marriage was an obligation.

He frowned. "Is that a no?"

"No!" she shrieked, and he laughed in response. "I mean, yes. It's a yes. Of course, it's a yes."

"Good." He smiled, relief washing over his face. "But I did practice a speech, if you'd humor me."

She extended her trembling hand, ready for the ring, and answered breathlessly, "I want to hear every word."

He took the ring from the box and slid it onto her finger. As he did, he told her, "Livvy, for many years, I swore I'd never marry. Because of my parents, I believed that marriage was a prison doomed to make its victims miserable. I watched as wiser men than me fell victim to its allure. I called them fools. But that was before I knew you. Before I understood the joy that could come from choosing to spend my life with someone. From making a promise and a pledge to love someone at their best and their worst. Marriage isn't a trap. Not when it's with you. It's simply the next chapter in our love story." He gave her a gentle kiss as he clasped her now beringed hand to his chest. "It would be the honor of my life if you'd let me write it with you."

"Yes," she whispered. "A thousand times yes."

He bent his head and pressed a thousand yeses to her lips in return, before whispering against her mouth, "There's just one thing you have to remember."

"What's that?" she asked, tangling her hand in the curls at the nape of his neck and pulling him down for another kiss.

"You're marrying a scoundrel."

She grinned against his mouth and kissed him as he lifted her gently and spun her in a circle with her feet off the ground. With her arms around his neck, she studied the face of the man she loved, the rogue she would marry. It would be the adventure of a lifetime. And with Flynn at her side, she knew that she was ready to face anything. Because he'd helped her see that truly living meant going after the things you wanted. Even the ones that were a little wicked. Because of Flynn, she knew that you had to choose joy for yourself instead of merely making choices that ensured it for others.

She gazed at him adoringly as he returned her to the ground. A firework boomed behind them, apparently launched from one of the sailboats docked in the harbor below. They jumped in unison, falling closer together, and laughed.

She gave him a sly look. "Thank you for the reminder, but you're forgetting something."

"What?"

"I happen to like scoundrels." She sealed her proclamation with a kiss.

FILMS TO PAIR WITH *A STAR IS SCORNED*

Captain Blood (1935)—The blueprint for nearly every Errol Flynn swashbuckler that came after and the film that made Flynn a star (and heir apparent to Douglas Fairbanks). Flynn stars as the titular Peter Blood, a physician wrongfully accused of treason and enslaved. Eventually, Blood and his fellow captives plot an escape and become the most fearsome pirates of the West Indies. Blood also woos the niece of the local military commander, Arabella Bishop. This marked Flynn's first pairing with Olivia de Havilland, launching one of the most indelible screen duos in history.

The Adventures of Robin Hood (1938)—The most famous team-up of Errol Flynn and Olivia de Havilland, this Technicolor adventure film casts the duo as Robin Hood and his Maid Marian. The balcony scene in this film is mirrored in the one that Flynn and Livvy perform—and it was rumored that De Havilland botched multiple takes of the love scene to get an (ahem) rise out of Flynn.

The Sea Hawk (1940)—Another classic swashbuckler for Errol Flynn, this time sans Olivia de Havilland. Here, Flynn portrays an English privateer in the employ of Queen Elizabeth I (Flora Robson) as she works to defeat the Spanish Armada. Flynn famously is paired with a capuchin monkey in the film, key in his relationship with the queen, which inspired Rallo. (The actor also owned a gibbon named Chico that he kept in his dressing room).

Against All Flags **(1952)**—This swashbuckler pairs Errol Flynn with Maureen O'Hara, who plays a female pirate, Prudence "Spitfire" Stevens. O'Hara was famous for often doing her own stunts and her own sword fighting, most notably here and in *At Sword's Point*. She trained with real-life studio fencing master, Fred Cavens, who features in *A Star Is Scorned*.

White Christmas **(1954)**—You're likely wondering what a classic Christmas movie is doing here alongside all these pirate movies. But the sister dynamic between entertainers Judy (Vera-Ellen) and Betty (Rosemary Clooney) was highly influential in the relationship between Livvy and Judy here. This charming tale of a quartet of performers who try to bring a Christmas surprise to their former Army general is a perennial favorite.

AUTHOR'S NOTE

Thank you for once again journeying back to Hollywood's Golden Age with me (and if this is your first time, welcome)! Even though this book was the hardest of the three for me, it was also the most fun—Flynn Banks is an utter delight to write, and I'm honestly sad I'll be spending significantly less time with him bouncing around in my head.

As you likely guessed, Flynn is inspired quite heavily by his namesakes, Errol Flynn and Douglas Fairbanks. I've always thought Errol Flynn, particularly in his swashbuckler mode, to be devilishly handsome and intriguing. But in real life, he was also an alcoholic and a predator. In short, not someone to romanticize. He had a close friendship with on-screen lover, Olivia de Havilland, who admitted to having a crush on Flynn but never taking their relationship beyond that. She seemed a somewhat steadying influence on him, and I always wondered what would've happened if they had gotten together and he'd truly reformed his wilder ways. Thus, *A Star Is Scorned* was born.

I highly recommend learning more about De Havilland if you haven't. She wrote her own memoir, *Every Frenchman Has One* (a wife, get your mind out of the gutter). *Olivia De Havilland: Lady Triumphant* by Victoria Amador is an excellent portrait of the star, who had a far more complex relationship with her sister, Joan

Fontaine. Most notably, De Havilland sued Warner Bros. over the terms of her unfair contract and won, changing Hollywood and contract law forever. I tried to inject some of De Havilland's fierce sense of justice into my own Livvy.

As for the real Errol Flynn, beyond the sexual assault charges, some of his more colorful biographical details made it into my Flynn. He did share a beach cottage in Malibu with David Niven, which was dubbed "Cirrhosis By the Sea." Though I based my Flynn's home on the historic Adamson House in Malibu, which features all of the tile described in the book. He was an avid sailor, owning a boat he named the *Sirocco*. And he did, sadly, later in life, inject vodka in oranges to hide his drinking habits on set.

Beyond that, my tale of the Production Code Administration and Hollywood hypocrisy is very much based in reality. Will Hays, his PCA, and the Legion of Decency held an undue amount of power in Hollywood from around 1934 until the mid-1960s, reviewing scripts, the moral rectitude of movie stars, and films for anything they deemed to be objectionable.

But while these men (they were always men) spent their time defining morality for the rest of America, they omitted themselves from the equation. It's well-documented that studio executives regularly abused their talent, the ubiquitous "casting couch" ever-present in the lives of so many women in Hollywood. Nowhere was this more evident than at Hollywood "stag parties" and studio sales conventions where women were lured into appearing as dancers, only to discover their job as the night's entertainment entailed far more than they knew.

Stanley Devlin's attempted rape of Judy Blount is based on the story of Patricia Douglas, the subject of David Stenn's documentary *Girl 27*. In 1937, Douglas, like Judy, was hoodwinked into attending a studio sales convention as a dancer, told she was going to a location shoot for a film. At the party, MGM salesman David Ross forced Douglas to drink until she was sick and then raped her. There are countless stories of people in Hollywood in the 1930s warning women not to attend any parties period, and accounts of men considering women to be "party favors" at these events.

Douglas stands apart as one of the first women to go public about sexual assault in Hollywood. She filed a criminal complaint against Ross and the studio with the Los Angeles D.A.'s office and took her story to the press. In response, MGM orchestrated a massive smear campaign against Douglas, ruining her career and reputation. Douglas never got the justice she so deserved in her own lifetime, but I'm indebted to her bravery for sharing her story in a time when women who dared to speak out were not merely silenced, but destroyed.

I hope I restored some dignity to her name and her experiences with Judy's story and happier ending. Ostensibly, our world has improved somewhat since the 1930s—and there are so many incredible survivors who have shared their more recent stories. I think, though, of all the women who saw what happened to Patricia Douglas and never were able to share theirs. May they have found their peace when they were not able to find their voice.

ACKNOWLEDGMENTS

Somehow we're here again, and to be honest, this time I wasn't sure I'd make it. Writing this book was far harder than anything else I've ever written—it took time and considerable patience to ferret out the right story for Flynn and Livvy. But I have to thank my incredible agent, Taylor Haggerty; her assistant, Jasmine Brown; my editor, Christa Desir; and her assistant editor, Letty Mundt, for their amazing support, the grace they gave me in continuously pushing back deadlines while I waited for the pieces to fit together in my head, and the spectacular insight and suggestions they provided when I needed a sounding board.

Thank you to all my readers for journeying back to Hollywood's Golden Age with me. It's one of my favorite places to spend time, be it on screen or on the page, and it fills me with such joy that readers have embraced my happy place in this way. Thank you to the torchbearers of cinema history for guiding me and my fellow cinephiles—Turner Classic Movies, the incredible programmers and staffs of the American Cinematheque and the New Beverly, and the team at the Academy Museum. You've filled my cup over and over in so many ways.

And to the best film professors there ever were—Drew Casper and Rick Jewell. You fed my insatiable curiosity for film history and watered it with encouragement, affection, and support. I wouldn't be here without you.

To the rest of the Root Literary team, you're the best agency in the world and I don't even think that's hyperbole. To the Sourcebooks team, thanks for shepherding three of my Old Hollywood books into the world—I can never fully express my gratitude for taking a chance on me and these stories. Brittany Pearlman, boy am I lucky to have you on my team. Thank you for all you do. Thanks also to Pam Jaffee, Katie Stutz, Alyssa Garcia, Heather Hall, and Shannon Barr. And to Stephanie Gafron for designing my deliriously beautiful covers.

Kristin Dwyer and Molly Mitchell, you are the romance superheroes we all need. I'm so grateful for Leo PR and all you've done to support my work. You go above and beyond to make your authors feel seen and appreciated, and I'm so grateful to have you in my corner.

Liz Locke and Jenny Nordbak were once again the best beta readers a girl could ask for—thank you for always reading and championing my work when it's not even fully formed. You make it possible for me to keep going.

Oddly, I want to thank the staff and team of New York City's Drama Bookshop. Though I live in California, I have somehow found myself editing all three of my Hollywood novels while in the city—and the Drama Bookshop has proved an endless source of inspiration and respite.

To my friends—there are so many of you, and I'm so blessed to have you all in my life. Laura, Lauren, Jessica, Olivia, Kimberly, Kyle, Keith, Ash, Marken, Ethan, Vince, Oriana, Kerrington, Kristin, Eliz, Kate, Evelyn, Brandon, Mikko, Set, the Schwenes, the Hivelys, and so so many more—thanks for always showing up for me in big ways and small. You make me feel so loved. Kate, thank you also for showing me around the Adamson House. It brought Flynn's house to life for me in vivid, beautiful glory.

Thank you so much to my colleagues at EW for your unwavering support of my writing (and all those cover reveals!). I know a lot of romance writers have to keep their books secret from their employer, so it's no small thing that you all show such love for me and my work.

John, my person. I love you so. Thanks for feeding me when I'm busy typing away, talking up my books like it's your job, and just generally being a supportive cuddly human whom I adore. Ordering off menu was the best choice I ever made.

Last but not least, to my family, who are truly unparalleled in their love and support of me. Grandma, Dad, Mary, Lee, Jenn, Liza, Robert, and Micah, I love you all so much and am so grateful to always have you in my cheering section.

Margaret, I dedicated this book to you because while it is a love story, it is also a story about the love between two sisters and the unshakable bond that they share. You inspired that—I would go to the same lengths as Livvy to protect you and help you reach your dreams. And I know you would do the same. You are one of my favorite people on the planet and getting to call you my sister is both a privilege and a joy. *Sisters, sisters, never were there such devoted sisters...*

And to my mom, who treats each book as a rare and special achievement worthy of unfettered praise. You are one of a kind and the definition of what an incredible mother is supposed to be. Thank you for Rally and Halo and the joy you bring via all the friends. Rallo is my homage to them, but also to you, and the delight you bring through them. Rally, may this bring you the fame you long for. Mom, thank you for making me a bookworm and feeding my creative fire (and for letting me hoard so many books). Being your daughter is still my favorite story to tell.

ABOUT THE AUTHOR

Maureen Lee Lenker is the author of *It Happened One Fight* and *His Girl Hollywood*. She is an award-winning journalist who has written for *Turner Classic Movies, The Hollywood Reporter, Ms. Magazine*, and more. A senior writer for *Entertainment Weekly*, she maintains a quarterly romance review column, "Hot Stuff," in addition to covering film, TV, and theater. She is a proud graduate of the University of Southern California and the University of Oxford. Maureen calls Los Angeles home, where you'll either find her at the beach or in a repertory movie house, if she's not writing.